D0191396

NORA ROBERTS

FOREVER MacGREGOR

Includes *For Now, Forever* & *The Winning Hand*

Silhouette Books

SILHOUETTE™

Recycling programs for this product may not exist in your area.

Forever MacGregor

ISBN-13: 978-1-335-14755-4

Copyright © 2021 by Harlequin Books S.A.

For Now, Forever
First published in 1987. This edition published in 2021.
Copyright © 1987 by Nora Roberts

The Winning Hand
First published in 1998. This edition published in 2021.
Copyright © 1998 by Nora Roberts

This edition published by arrangement with Harlequin Books S.A.

For questions and comments about the quality of this book, please contact us at CustomerService@Harlequin.com.

Silhouette
22 Adelaide St. West, 40th Floor
Toronto, Ontario M5H 4E3, Canada
www.Harlequin.com

Printed in Lithuania

MIX
Paper from responsible sources
FSC® C021394

CONTENTS

FOR NOW, FOREVER

Prologue

"Mother."

Anna MacGregor clasped hands with her son as he crouched at her feet. Panic, fear, grief surged through her and met a solid wall of will. She wouldn't lose control now. She couldn't. Her children were coming.

"Caine." Her fingers were icy as they tightened on his, but they were steady. Her face was almost colorless from the strain of the past few hours, and her eyes were dark. Dark, young and frightened. It flashed through Caine that he'd never seen his mother frightened before. Not ever.

"Are you all right?"

"Of course." She knew what he needed and brushed her lips over his cheek. "Better now that you're here." With her free hand she gripped Diana's as her daughter-in-law sat beside her. Wet snow clung to Diana's long dark hair and was already melting on the shoulders of her coat. Anna took a long breath before she looked back at Caine. "You got here quickly."

"We chartered a plane." There was a little boy inside the grown man, the attorney, the new father, who wanted to scream out a denial. His father was invulnerable. His father was the MacGregor. He couldn't be lying broken in a hospital. "How bad is he?"

She was a doctor and could tell him precisely—the broken ribs, the collapsed lung, the concussion and the internal bleeding, which her colleagues were even now struggling to stop. She was also a mother. "He's in surgery." She kept her hand tight on his and nearly managed to smile. "He's strong, Caine. And Dr. Feinstein is the best in the state." She had to hold on to that and to her family. "Laura?"

"Laura's with Lucy Robinson," Diana said quietly. She knew well what it was like to hold emotions in. Slowly she massaged Anna's fingers. "Don't worry."

"No, I'm not." This time Anna managed the smile. "But you know Daniel. Laura's his first granddaughter. He'll be full of questions when he wakes up." And he would wake up, she promised herself. By God, he would.

"Anna." Diana slipped an arm around her mother-in-law's shoulders. She looked so small, so frail. "Have you eaten?"

"What?" Anna gave a tiny shake of her head then rose. Three hours. He'd been in surgery for three hours. How many times had she been in the operating room, fighting to save a life while a loved one agonized in these plastic waiting rooms, these cold corridors? She'd struggled and studied to be a doctor to ease pain, to heal—to somehow in some way make a difference. Now, when her husband was hurt, she could do no more than wait. Like any other woman. No, not like any woman, she corrected herself, because she knew what the operating room looked like, what it sounded and smelled like. She knew the instruments, the machines and the sweat too well. She wanted to scream. She folded her hands and walked to the window.

There was a will of iron behind her dark, quiet eyes. She'd use it now for herself, for her children, but mostly for Daniel. If it were possible to bring him back with sheer desire, she would do so. There was more to doctoring, much more to healing, she knew, than skill.

The snow had nearly stopped. The snow, she thought as she watched it fall thinly, had caused the roads to be slick and treacherous. The snow had blinded some young man, caused his car to spin out of control, and crash into her husband's foolish little two-seater. Her hands balled into fists.

Why weren't you in the limo, old man? What were you trying to prove with that flashy red toy? Always showing off, always... Her thoughts trailed away, going back in time. Her hands unclenched. Wasn't that one of the reasons she'd fallen in love with him? Wasn't that one of the reasons she'd loved and lived with him for nearly forty years? *Damn you, Daniel MacGregor, no one can tell you anything.* Anna pressed her fingers to her eyes and nearly laughed. She couldn't count the number of times she'd said that to him over their lifetime together. And adored him for it.

The sound of footsteps had her whirling, bracing. Then she saw Alan, her oldest son. Daniel had sworn before he had ever had a child that one of his offspring would be in the White House. Though Alan was close to making the oath reality, he was the only one of her children who took more after herself than their father. The MacGregor genes were strong. The MacGregors were strong. She let herself be folded in Alan's arms.

"He'll be glad you're here." Her voice was steady, but there was a woman inside her who wanted to weep and weep. "But he's bound to scold you for bringing your wife out in her condition." Anna smiled at Shelby and held out a hand. Her daughter-in-law with the fiery hair and soft eyes was big with child. "You should sit down."

"I will if you will." Without waiting for an answer, Shelby led Anna to a chair. The moment Anna sat, Caine put a cup of coffee in her hands.

"Thank you," she murmured and sipped for his sake. She could smell it, strong and hot, feel it scald her tongue, but she couldn't taste it. Anna listened to the ding of the electronic pages, the quick slap of rubber-soled shoes on tiled floor. Hospitals. They were as much her home as the fortress Daniel had built for the two of them. She'd always felt comfortable in them, confident in their antiseptic halls. Now she felt helpless.

Caine paced. It was his nature to do so—to prowl, to stalk. How proud she and Daniel had been of him when he'd won his first case. Alan sat beside her, quiet, intense, just as he'd always been. He was suffering. She watched Shelby slip a hand into his and was content. Her sons had chosen well. *Our sons,* she thought, trying to communicate with Daniel. Caine with his quietly strong-willed Diana, Alan with his free-spirited Shelby. Balance was needed in a relationship almost as much as love, as much as passion. She'd found that. Her sons had found that. And her daughter…

"Rena!" Caine was across the room, holding his sister.

How alike they look, Anna thought vaguely. So slim, so bold. Of all her children, Serena came closest to matching Daniel's temper and stubbornness. Now her daughter was a mother herself. Anna could feel Alan's quiet strength beside her. *They're all grown. When did it happen? We've done so well, Daniel.* She closed her eyes for only a moment. She could allow herself only a moment. *You wouldn't dare leave me to enjoy it all alone.*

"Dad?" With one hand Serena held on to her brother; with the other, she gripped her husband.

"Still in surgery." Caine's voice was rough with ciga-rettes and fear as he turned to Justin. "I'm glad you could come. Mom needs all of us."

"Momma." Serena went to kneel at her mother's feet, as she always had when she needed comfort or conversa-tion. "He's going to be fine. He's stubborn and he's strong."

But Anna saw the plea in her daughter's eyes. *Tell me he's going to be all right. If you say so I'll believe it.*

"Of course he's going to be fine." She glanced up at her daughter's husband. Justin was a gambler, like her Daniel. Anna touched Serena's cheek. "Do you think he'd miss a reunion like this?"

Serena let out a shaky laugh. "That's just what Justin said." She smiled, seeing that Justin already had an arm around his sister's shoulder. "Diana." Serena rose to ex-change an embrace. "How's Laura?"

"She's wonderful. She just got her second tooth. And Robert?"

"A terror." Serena thought of her son, who already wor-shiped Grandpa. "Shelby, how are you feeling?"

"Fat." She flashed a smile and managed to conceal the fact that she'd been in labor for more than an hour. "I called my brother." She turned to Anna. "Grant and Gennie are coming. I hope it's all right."

"Of course." Anna patted her hand. "They're family, too."

"Dad's going to be thrilled." Serena swallowed over the fear that had lodged in her throat. "All this attention. And then there's the little announcement Justin and I have to make." She looked at him, willing her courage to return. "Justin and I are going to have another baby. Have to in-sure the line. Momma—" her voice broke as she knelt down again "—Daniel will be so smug about it, won't he?"

"Yes." She kissed both of Serena's cheeks. She thought

of the grandchildren she had, of those she would have. Family, continuity, immortality. Daniel. Always Daniel. "He'll consider it all his doing."

"Wasn't it?" Alan murmured.

Anna fought the tears back. How well they knew their father. "Yes. Yes, it was."

There was more pacing, murmuring, hand-holding as the minutes dragged by. Anna set her half-finished cup of coffee aside, cold and unwanted. Four hours and twenty minutes. It was taking too long. Beside her, Shelby tensed and deliberately began to breathe deeply. Automatically Anna placed a hand on the mound that was her grandchild.

"How close?"

"Just under five minutes now."

"How long?"

"Couple of hours." She gave Anna a look that was a little excited, a little terrified. "A bit more than three, actually. I wish I could've timed it better."

"You've timed it perfectly. Do you want me to go with you?"

"No." For a moment, Shelby nuzzled into Anna's neck. "I'll be fine. We're all going to be fine. Alan—" she held out both hands wanting to be hauled to her feet "—I'm not going to have the baby at Georgetown Hospital."

He drew her up gently. "What?"

"I'm going to have it here. Very soon." She laughed a bit when he narrowed his eyes. "Don't try logic on a baby, Alan. It's ready."

The entire clan clustered around her, offering help, advice, support. In her calm, efficient way, Anna summoned a nurse and a wheelchair. With little fuss she had Shelby settled. "I'll be down to check on you."

"We're going to be fine." Shelby reached over her shoulder for Alan's hand. "All of us. Tell Daniel it's going to be a boy. I'm going to see to it."

She watched as Shelby and Alan disappeared behind elevator doors just before Dr. Feinstein walked into the hall. "Sam," Anna exclaimed and was on him in seconds.

At the doorway of the waiting room, Justin held Caine back. "Give her a minute," he murmured.

"Anna." Feinstein put his hands on her shoulders. She wasn't just a colleague now or a surgeon he respected. She was the wife of a patient. "He's a strong man."

She felt hope surge and willed herself to be calm. "Strong enough?"

"He lost a lot of blood, Anna, and he's not young anymore. But we've stopped the hemorrhaging." He hesitated, then realized he respected her too much to evade. "We lost him once on the table. In seconds, he was fighting his way back. If will to live counts, Anna, he's got a hell of an edge."

She folded her arms around her chest. Cold. Why were the hallways so cold? "When can I see him?"

"They'll be bringing him up to ICU." His hands were cramping after hours of delicate work. He kept them firm on her shoulders. "Anna, I don't have to tell you what the next twenty-four hours mean."

Life or death. "No, you don't. Thank you, Sam. I'm going to talk to my children. Then I'll come up."

She turned to walk back down the hall, a small, lovely woman with gray threading through her deep sable hair. Her face was finely lined, her skin as soft as it had been in her youth. She'd raised three children, worked her way to the top of her profession and had spent over half of her life loving one man.

"He's out of surgery," she said calmly, calling on the

control she'd been born with. "They're taking him to Intensive Care. They've controlled the bleeding."

"When can we see him?" The question came from several of them at once.

"When he wakes up." Her tone was firm. She was in charge again, and being in charge was what she did best. "I'm going to stay here tonight." She glanced at her watch. "He may float in and out a bit, and he'll be better knowing I'm there. But he won't be able to talk until tomorrow." It was all the hope she could give them. "I want you to go down to Maternity and check on Shelby. Stay as long as you like. Then go back to the house and wait. I'll call as soon as anything changes."

"Mother—"

She cut Caine off with a look. "Do as you're told. I want you rested and well when your father's ready to see you." She lifted a hand to Caine's cheek. "For me."

She left her children and comfort to go to her husband.

He was dreaming. Even through the drugs, Daniel knew he was dreaming. It was a soft world full of visions, tapestried with memories. Still, he fought it, wanting, needing to orient himself. When he opened his eyes, he saw Anna. He needed nothing else. She was beautiful. Always beautiful. The strong, stubborn, coolheaded woman he'd first admired, then loved, then respected. He tried to reach out but couldn't lift his hand. Infuriated at his weakness, he tried again, only to have Anna's voice float smoothly over him.

"Lie still, darling. I'm not going anywhere. I'm staying right here and waiting." He thought he felt her lips on the back of his hand. "I love you, Daniel MacGregor. Damn you."

His lips curved. His eyes closed.

Chapter 1

An empire. At the time he'd turned fifteen, Daniel Mac-Gregor had promised himself he'd have one, build one, rule one. He always kept his word.

He was thirty years old and working on his second million with the same drive that had earned him his first. As he always had, he used his back, his brains and pure guile in whatever order worked best. When he'd come to America five years before, Daniel had had the money he'd saved by working his way up from miner to head bookkeeper for Hamus McGuire. He'd also brought a shrewd brain and towering ambition.

He could have passed for a king. He topped six-four with a build bold enough to suit his height. His size alone had kept him out of a number of fights, just as his size had seduced some men into challenging him. Either way was fine with Daniel. He was reputed to have a temper, but he considered himself a mild sort of person. Daniel didn't think he'd broken more than his share of noses in his day. He didn't consider himself handsome, either. His jaw was long and square, and running along its right edge was a scar that he'd gotten when a loose beam had toppled down on him in the mines. As a sop to his vanity, he'd grown a beard in his teens. A dozen years later it remained, deep red and well trimmed around his face, blending with a mane of hair that was too long for fashion. The combination made him look both fierce and royal, which pleased him. His cheekbones rose high and wide, and his mouth appeared surprisingly soft in its cushion of wild red hair. His eyes were a deep brilliant blue that lit with humor and goodwill when he smiled and meant it, just as they cooled to frost when he smiled and didn't.

Imposing. That was one adjective used to describe him. Ruthless was another. Daniel didn't care how he was described as long as he didn't go unnoticed. He was a gambler who played the odds boldly. Real estate was his wheel, and the stock market was his game table. When Daniel gambled, he played to win. The chances he'd taken had paid off. And when they had, he'd taken more. He never intended to play it too safe, because with safety came boredom.

Though he'd been born poor, Daniel MacGregor didn't worship money. He used it, wielded it, played with it. Money equaled power, and power was a weapon.

In America he found himself in a vast arena of wheeling and dealing. There was New York with its fast pace and hungry streets. A man with brains and nerve could build a fortune there. There was Los Angeles with its glamour and high stakes. A man with imagination could fashion an empire. Daniel had spent time in both, dabbled in business on either coast, but he chose Boston as his base and as his home. It wasn't simply money or power he sought, but style. Boston with its old-world charm, its stubborn dignity and its unapologetic snobbishness suited Daniel perfectly.

He'd come from a long line of warriors who had lived as much by wit as by the sword. His pride in his line was fierce, as fierce as his ambition. Daniel intended to see his line continue with strong sons and daughters. As a man of vision, he had no trouble seeing his grandchildren taking what he'd molded and building on it. There could be no empire without family to share it. To begin one, he needed the proper wife. Acquiring one, to Daniel, was as challenging and as logical as acquiring a prime piece of real estate. He'd come to the Donahues' summer ball to speculate on both.

He hated the tight collar and strangulating tie. When a man was built like a bull, he liked his neck free. His clothes were made in Boston by a tailor on Newbury Street. Daniel used him as much because his size demanded it as for the prestige. Ambition had put him in a suit, but he didn't have to like it. Another man dressed in the elegant black dinner suit and pleated silk shirt would have looked distinguished. Daniel, in either tartan or dress blacks, looked flamboyant. He preferred it that way.

Cathleen Donahue, Maxwell Donahue's eldest daughter, preferred it, as well.

"Mr. MacGregor." Fresh out of finishing school in Switzerland, Cathleen knew how to serve tea, embroider silk and flirt elegantly. "I hope you're enjoying our little party."

She had a face like porcelain and hair like flax. Daniel thought it a pity her shoulders were so thin, but he, too, knew how to flirt. "I'm enjoying it more now, Miss Donahue."

Knowing most men were put off by giggles, Cathleen kept her laugh low and smooth. Her taffeta skirts whispered as she positioned herself beside him at the end of the long buffet table. Now, whoever stopped for a taste of truffles or salmon mousse would see them together. If she turned her head just a fraction, she could catch a glimpse of their reflection in one of the long narrow mirrors that lined the wall. She decided she liked what she saw.

"My father tells me you're interested in buying a little piece of cliff he owns in Hyannis Port." She fluttered her lashes twice. "I hope you didn't come here tonight to discuss business."

Daniel slipped two glasses from the tray of a passing waiter. He'd have preferred Scotch in a sturdy glass to champagne in crystal, but a man who didn't adjust in certain areas broke in others. As he drank, he studied Cathleen's face. He knew Maxwell Donahue would no more have discussed business with his daughter than he would have discussed fashion with her, but Daniel didn't fault her for lying. Rather he gave her credit for knowing how to dig out information. But while he admired her for it, it was precisely the reason he didn't consider her proper wife material. His wife would be too busy raising babies to worry about business.

"Business comes second to a lovely woman. Have you been to the cliffs?"

"Of course." She tilted her head so that the diamond flowers in her ears caught the light. "I do prefer the city. Are you attending the Ditmeyers' dinner party next week?"

"If I'm in town."

"So much traveling." Cathleen smiled before she sipped her champagne. She'd be very comfortable with a husband who traveled. "It must be exciting."

"It's business," he said. Then he added, "But you've just returned from Paris yourself."

Flattered that he'd been aware of her absence, Cathleen

almost beamed. "Three weeks wasn't enough. Shopping alone took nearly every moment I had. You can't imagine how many tedious hours I spent in fittings for this gown."

He swept his gaze down and up as she'd expected. "I can only say it was well worth it."

"Why, thank you." As she stood, posing, his mind began to drift. He knew women were supposed to be interested mainly in dresses and hairstyles, but he'd have preferred a more stimulating conversation. Sensing she was losing his attention, Cathleen touched his arm. "You've been to Paris, Mr. MacGregor?"

He'd been to Paris and had seen what war could do to beauty. The pretty blonde smiling up at him would never be touched by war. Why should she be? Still, vaguely dissatisfied, Daniel sipped the dry bubbling wine. "Some years ago." He glanced around at the glitter of jewels, the sparkle of crystal. There was a scent in the air that could only be described as wealth. In five years he'd become accustomed to it, but he hadn't forgotten the smell of coal dust. He never intended to forget it. "I've come to prefer America to Europe. Your father knows how to throw a party."

"I'm glad you approve. You're enjoying the music?"

He still missed the wail of bagpipes. The twelve-piece orchestra in white tie was a bit stiff for his taste, but he smiled. "Very much."

"I thought perhaps you weren't." She sent him a slow, melting look from under her lashes. "You aren't dancing."

In a courtly gesture, Daniel took the champagne from Cathleen and set both their glasses down. "Oh, but I am, Miss Donahue," he corrected, and swept her onto the dance floor.

"Cathleen Donahue continues to be obvious." Myra Lornbridge nibbled pâté and sniffed.

"Keep your claws sheathed, Myra." The voice was low and smooth, by nature rather than design.

"I don't mind when a person's rude or calculating or even a bit stupid—" with a sigh, Myra finished off the cracker "—but I do detest it when one is obvious."

"Myra."

"All right, all right." Myra poked at the salmon mousse. "By the way, Anna, I love your dress."

Anna glanced down at the rose-colored silk. "You picked it out."

"I told you I loved it." Myra gave a self-satisfied smile at the way the folds draped over Anna's hips. Very chic. "If you'd pay half the attention to your wardrobe as you do your books, you'd put Cathleen Donahue's nose out of joint."

Anna only smiled and watched the dancers. "I'm not interested in Cathleen's nose."

"Well, it isn't very interesting. How about the man she's dancing with?"

"The red-haired giant?"

"So you noticed."

"I'm not blind." She wondered how soon she could make a dignified exit. She really wanted to go home and read the medical journal Dr. Hewitt had sent her.

"Know who he is?"

"Who?"

"Anna." Patience was a virtue Myra extended only to her closest friends. "Fe fi fo fum."

With a laugh, Anna sipped her wine. "All right, who is he?"

"Daniel Duncan MacGregor." Myra paused a bit, hoping to pique Anna's interest. At twenty-four, Myra was rich and attractive. Beautiful, no. Even at her best, Myra knew she'd never be beautiful. She understood beauty was one route to power. Brains were another. Myra used her brains. "He's Boston's current boy wonder. If you'd pay more attention to who's who in our cozy little society, you'd recognize the name."

Society, with its games and restrictions, didn't interest Anna in the least. "Why should I? You'll tell me."

"Serve you right if I didn't."

But Anna only smiled and drank again.

"All right, I'll tell you." Gossip was one temptation Myra found impossible to resist. "He's a Scot, which is obvious I suppose from his looks and his name. You should hear him talk, it's like cutting through fog."

At that moment, Daniel let out a big, booming laugh that raised Anna's eyebrows. "That sounds as though it would cut through anything."

"He's a bit rough around the edges, but some people—" she cast a meaningful look at Cathleen Donahue "—believe that a million dollars or so smooths out anything."

Realizing that the man was being weighed and judged by the size of his bank balance, Anna felt a twinge of sympathy. "I hope he knows he's dancing with a viper," Anna murmured.

"He doesn't look stupid. He bought Old Line Savings and Loan six months ago."

"Really." She shrugged. Business only interested Anna when it involved a hospital budget. Sensing the movement to her left, she turned to smile at Herbert Ditmeyer standing with an unfamiliar gentleman. "How are you?"

"Glad to see you." He was only a few inches taller than Anna and had the lean, ascetic face of a scholar, with dark hair that promised to thin in a matter of years. But there was a strength around his mouth that Anna respected, and he had a sense of humor it took a sharp wit to understand.

"You're looking lovely." He gestured to the man beside him. "My cousin, Mark. Anna Whitfield and Myra Lornbridge." Herbert's gaze lingered just a moment longer on Myra, but as the orchestra began a new waltz, he lost his nerve and took Anna's arm. "You should be dancing."

Anna matched her steps to his naturally. She loved to dance, but preferred to do so with someone she knew. Herbert was comfortable. "I heard congratulations are in order—" she smiled up into his dependable face "—Mr. District Attorney."

He grinned. He was young for the position but had no intention of stopping there. If he hadn't considered it bad form, he might have told Anna of his ambitions. "I wasn't sure Boston news traveled as far as Connecticut." He glanced to where Myra was dancing with his cousin. "I suppose I should have known better."

Anna laughed as they twirled around another couple. "Just because I've been out of town doesn't mean I don't want to keep up with what's happening here in Boston. You must be very proud."

"It's a beginning," Herbert said lightly. "And you—one more year and we'll have to call you Dr. Whitfield."

"One more year," Anna murmured. "Sometimes it seems like forever."

"Impatient, Anna? That's not like you."

Yes, it was, but she'd always managed to conceal it so successfully. "I want it to be official. It's no secret that my parents disapprove."

"They might disapprove," Herbert added, "but your mother doesn't have any trouble mentioning you're in the top ten percent of your class for the third year running."

"Really?" Surprised, Anna thought it over. Her mother had always been more apt to praise her hairstyle than her grades. "I'll have to be grateful for that then, though she still harbors the hope that some man will come along and make me forget about operating rooms and bedpans."

As she spoke, Herbert turned her. Anna found herself looking directly into Daniel MacGregor's eyes. She felt her stomach muscles tighten. Nerves? Ridiculous. She felt the quick chill that raced down her spine and up again. Fear? Absurd.

Though he still danced with Cathleen, he stared at Anna. Stared at her in a way that was designed to make a young woman's cheeks flush. Anna stared back coolly while her heart raced. Perhaps it was a mistake. He seemed to take it as a challenge and smiled very slowly.

With a detached admiration, she watched him maneuver. Catching the eye of another man on the edge of the dance floor, Daniel gave a quick, almost imperceptible signal. Within moments, Cathleen found herself dancing in the arms of another man. Anna braced herself for the next step.

With the ease of experience, Daniel weaved through the dancers. He'd noticed Anna the moment she'd begun to dance. Noticed, then watched, then calculated. As soon as she'd glanced over and had given him that coolly appraising stare, he'd been hooked. She didn't have the stature of Cathleen, but seemed small and delicate. Her hair was dark and looked as warm and soft as sable. Her eyes matched it. The rose hue of her dress set off her creamy skin and smooth shoulders. She looked like a woman who would fit easily into a man's arms.

With the confidence he carried everywhere, Daniel tapped Herbert's shoulder. "May I cut in?"

Daniel waited only until Herbert had relinquished his hold before he clasped Anna and swirled her back into the dance. "That was very clever, Mr. MacGregor."

It pleased him that she knew his name. It pleased him as well that he'd been right about the way she'd fit into his arms. She smelled like moonbeams, soft and quiet. "Thank you, Miss...?"

"Whitfield. Anna Whitfield. It was also very rude."

He stared a moment because the stern voice didn't fit the quietly lovely face. Always one to appreciate a surprise, Daniel laughed until heads turned. "Aye, but I go with what works. I don't believe I've seen you before, Miss Anna Whitfield, but I know your parents."

"That's very possible." The hand holding hers was huge, hard as rock and incredibly gentle. Her palm began to itch. "Are you new to Boston, Mr. MacGregor?"

"I'll have to say yes because I've lived here only two years, not two generations."

She tilted her head a bit farther so that she could keep her eyes on his. "You have to go back at least three not to be new."

"Or you have to be clever." He twirled her in three quick circles.

Pleasantly surprised that for his size he was light on his feet, Anna relaxed just a little. It would be a shame to waste the music. "I've been told you are."

"You'll be told so again." He didn't bother to keep his voice low, though the dance floor was crowded. Power, not propriety, was his forte.

"Will I?" Anna cocked a brow. "How odd."

"Only if you don't understand the system," he corrected her, unsinged. "If you can't have the generations behind you, you need money in front."

Though she knew it was true, Anna disliked both forms of snobbery. "How fortunate for you society has such flexible standards."

Her dry, disinterested voice made him smile. She wasn't a fool this Anna Whitfield, nor was she a silk-coated barracuda like Cathleen Donahue. "You've a face like the cameo my grandmother wore around her neck."

Anna lifted a brow and nearly smiled at him. The look made him realize he'd said no more than the truth. "Thank you, Mr. MacGregor, but you'd be better off saving your flattery for Cathleen. She's more susceptible."

A frown clouded his eyes, and he looked fierce and formidable, but it cleared quickly, before Anna could gauge her reaction. "You've a cool tongue in your head, lassie. I admire a woman who speaks her mind…to a point."

Feeling aggressive for no reason she could name, Anna kept her gaze directly on his. "What point is that, Mr. MacGregor?"

"To the point where it becomes unfeminine."

Before she'd anticipated his move, Daniel swung her through the terrace doors. Until that moment she hadn't realized just how hot and stuffy the ballroom had become. Regardless of that, Anna's normal reaction with a man she didn't know would have been to excuse herself firmly and finally and walk back inside. Instead, she found herself stopping just where she was, with Daniel's arms still around her, the moonlight pouring over the flagstones and warm roses scenting the air.

"I'm sure you have your own definition of femininity, Mr. MacGregor, but I wonder if you keep it in tune with the fact that we're in the twentieth century."

He enjoyed the way she stood in his arms and subtly insulted him. "I've always considered femininity a constant thing, Miss Whitfield, not something that changes with years or fashion."

"I see." His arms seemed to fit around her a bit too easily. She drew herself away to stroll to the edge of the terrace nearest the gardens. The air was sweeter there, the moonlight dimmer. The music became more romantic with distance.

It occurred to her that she was having a private conversation, one that might have been approaching an argument, with a man she'd only just met. Yet she didn't feel any urge to cut it short. She'd taught herself to be comfortable around men. She'd had to. As the only woman in her graduating class, Anna had learned how to deal with men on their own level and how to do so without constantly rubbing against their egos. She'd gotten through the first year of criticism and innuendos by staying calm and concentrating on her studies. Now she was about to enter her last year of medical school, and for the most part, Anna was accepted by her colleagues. She was perfectly aware, however, of what she would face when she began her internship. The stigma of being labeled unfeminine still stung a bit, but she was long resigned to it.

"I'm sure your views on femininity are fascinating, Mr. MacGregor." The hem of her dress skimmed the flagstone as she turned. "But I don't think it's something I care to discuss. Tell me, what is it exactly that you do in Boston?"

He hadn't heard her. He hadn't heard anything from the moment she'd turned back to face him. Her hair swung softly just at her white, smooth shoulders. In the thin rose-colored silk, her body looked as delicate as fine china. The moonlight filtered over her face so that her skin was like marble and her eyes as dark as midnight. A man hears nothing but the thunder when he's struck by lightning.

"Mr. MacGregor?" For the first time since they'd stepped outside, Anna's nerves began to hum. He was huge, a stranger, and he was looking at her as though he'd lost his senses. She straightened her shoulders and reminded herself she could handle any situation that came along. "Mr. MacGregor?"

"Aye." Daniel pulled himself out of his fantasy and stepped closer. Oddly Anna relaxed. He didn't seem as dangerous when he stood beside her. And his eyes were beautiful. True, there was a very simple genetic reason for their shade. She could have written a paper on it. But they were beautiful.

"You do work in Boston, don't you?"

"I do." Perhaps it had been a trick of the light that had made her look so perfect, so ethereal and seductive. "I buy." He took her hand because personal contact was vital to him. He took it because part of him wanted to be assured she was real. "I sell."

His hand was warm and as gentle as it had been when they'd danced. Anna drew hers away. "How interesting. What do you buy?"

"Whatever I want." Smiling, he stepped a bit closer. "Whatever."

Her pulse accelerated, her skin heated. Anna knew there were emotional as well as physical causes for such things. Though she couldn't think of them at the moment, she didn't back away. "I'm sure that's very satisfying. That leads me to believe you sell whatever you no longer want."

"In a nutshell, Miss Whitfield. And at a profit."

Conceited ox, she thought mildly and tilted her head. "Some might consider that arrogance, Mr. MacGregor."

She made him laugh with the cool, calm way she spoke, the cool, calm way she looked even when he could see traces of passion in her eyes. She was a woman, he thought, who could make a man wait on the doorstep with bouquets and heart-shaped boxes of candy. "When a poor man's arrogant it's crude, Miss Whitfield. When a man of means is arrogant, it's called style. I've been both."

She felt there was some truth in his words but wasn't willing to give an inch. "Strange, I've never felt arrogance changes with years or with fashion."

He took out a cigar as he watched her. "Your point." His lighter flared, highlighting his eyes for one brief instant. In that moment, Anna realized he was dangerous after all.

"Then perhaps we should call it a draw." Pride prevented her from stepping back. Dignity prevented her from continuing what was, despite logic, becoming interesting. "Now, if you'll excuse me, Mr. MacGregor, I really must get back inside."

He took her arm in a way that was both abrupt and proprietary. Anna didn't jerk away, and she didn't freeze; she merely looked at him as a duchess might look at a dust-covered commoner. Faced with that serene disapproval, most men would have dropped their hand and mumbled apologies. Daniel grinned at her. *Now here's a lass,* he thought, *who'd make a man's knees tremble.* "I'll see you again, Miss Anna Whitfield."

"Perhaps."

"I'll see you again." He lifted her hand to his lips. She felt the soft, surprising brush of his beard across her knuckles, and for a moment, the trace of passion he'd seen in her eyes flared full blown. "And again."

"I doubt we'll have much occasion to socialize, as I'll only be in Boston for a couple of months. Now, if you'll excuse me—"

"Why?"

He didn't release her hand, which troubled her more than she could permit to show. "Why what, Mr. MacGregor?"

"Why will you only be in Boston for a couple of

months?" If she were running off to get married it might change things. Daniel looked at her again and decided he wouldn't allow it to change anything.

"I go back to Connecticut at the end of August for my last year in medical school."

"Medical school?" His brows drew together. "You're not going to be a nurse?" His voice carried the vague puzzlement of a man who had no understanding of, and little tolerance for, professional women.

"No." She waited until she felt him relax. "A surgeon. Thank you for the dance."

But he had her arm again before she could reach the door. "You're going to cut people open?" For the second time she heard his laughter boom out. "You're joking."

Though she bristled, she managed to make it appear she was simply bored. "I promise you I'm much more amusing when I joke. Good night, Mr. MacGregor."

"Being a doctor's a man's job."

"I appreciate your opinion. I happen to believe there is no such thing as a man's job if a woman is capable of doing it."

He snorted, puffed on his cigar and muttered, "Pack of nonsense."

"Succinctly put, Mr. MacGregor, and again, rude. You are consistent." She walked through the terrace doors without looking back. But she did think of him. Brash, crude, flamboyant and foolish.

He thought of her as he watched her slip into the crowd. Cool, opinionated, blunt and ridiculous.

They were both fascinated.

Chapter 2

"Tell me everything."

Anna set her purse on the white linen cloth and smiled at the hovering waiter. "I'll have a champagne cocktail."

"Two," Myra decided, then leaned forward. "Well?"

Taking her time, Anna glanced around the quiet, pastel restaurant. There were half a dozen people she knew by name, several others she knew by sight. She found it cozy, safe and serene. There were times in the rush and fury of classes and studies when she longed for moments like this. There would be a way somehow, someday to have both in her life. "You know, the one thing I miss about living in Connecticut is having lunch here. I'm glad you suggested it."

"Anna." Myra saw no reason to waste time on polite chatter when there was news ready to break. "Tell me."

"Tell you what?" Anna countered, and enjoyed the flash of frustration in her friend's eyes.

Myra took a cigarette out of a thin gold case, tapped it

twice, then lit it. "Tell me what happened between you and Daniel MacGregor."

"We had a waltz." Anna picked up her menu and began to scan it. But she caught herself tapping her foot as the music crept back into her head.

"And?"

She shifted her gaze over the top of the menu. "And?"

"Anna!" Myra cut herself off as their drinks were served. Impatient, she pushed her cocktail aside. "You were out on the terrace with him, alone, for quite some time."

"Really?" Anna sipped her champagne, decided on a salad and closed the menu.

"Yes, really." With calculated flamboyance, Myra blew smoke at the ceiling. "Apparently you must have found something to talk about."

"I believe we did." The waiter returned, so Anna ordered her salad. Seething in frustration, Myra ordered lobster Newburg and told herself she'd fast through dinner.

"Well, what did you talk about?"

"I seem to remember one of the topics was femininity." Anna took another casual sip but wasn't quite able to conceal the anger that leaped into her eyes. Seeing it, Myra put out her cigarette and perked up.

"I assume that Mr. MacGregor has some definite opinions on the subject."

Anna sipped again, savoring the taste of the champagne before she set her glass down. "Mr. MacGregor is an opinionated boor."

Thoroughly pleased, Myra cupped her chin in her hand. The little veil attached to her hat fell just below her eyes but didn't conceal their enthusiasm. "I was nearly certain about the opinionated, but I would have bet heavily against the boor. Tell me."

"He admires a woman who speaks her mind," Anna continued, firing up, "to a point. To a point," she repeated with a quick unladylike snort. "That point stops wherever it conflicts with his outlook."

A little disappointed, Myra shrugged. "He sounds like any other man."

"It's men like him who see women as subsidiary to their manhood." Sitting back, Anna began to tap her fingers in a slow, steady rhythm on the white cloth. "We're fine as long as we're baking cookies, diapering babies and warming the sheets."

After choking on a sip of champagne, Myra swallowed. "My goodness, he did get under your skin in a very short time."

Deliberately Anna drew herself back. She detested losing her temper and reserved the privilege for something of real importance. She reminded herself that Daniel MacGregor didn't fit the bill. "He's rude and arrogant," she said more calmly.

Myra gave it a moment's thought. "That may be," she agreed. "But it's not necessarily a mark against him. I'd rather be around an arrogant man than a stuffy one."

"Stuffy he's not. Didn't you see that maneuver he pulled on Cathleen?"

Her eyes lit up. "No."

"He signaled to some man to cut in while they were dancing so he could cut in on Herbert and dance with me."

"How clever." Myra beamed approval, then laughed at Anna's expression. "Come on, darling, you have to admit it was. And Cathleen's much too involved with her own charms to have noticed." Myra gave a sigh of pleasure as her lobster was served. "You know, Anna, you should be flattered."

"Flattered?" She stabbed at her salad. "I don't see why

I should be flattered that some enormous, self-important dolt of a man preferred to dance with me."

Myra paused to appreciate the scent of the lobster. "He's certainly enormous, and he may be a dolt, but he is important. And in a rough sort of way, he's attractive. Obviously, from the way you've brushed others off, you aren't interested in the smooth, sophisticated type."

"I have my career to think of, Myra. I don't have time for men."

"Darling, there's always time for men." With a laugh, she took another forkful of lobster. "I don't mean that you have to take him seriously."

"I'm glad to hear that."

"But I don't see why you should just toss him back."

"I have no intention of reeling him in."

"You're being stubborn."

Anna laughed. One of the reasons she was so fond of Myra was that her friend saw things clearly—her way. "I'm being myself."

"Anna, I know what becoming a doctor means to you, and you know how much I admire what you're doing. But," she continued before Anna could comment, "you're going to be in Boston for the summer, anyway. What's the harm in having an attractive escort who's obviously going places?"

"I don't need an escort."

"Needing and having are two different things." Myra broke off the corner of a roll and swore to herself she'd only eat half of it. "Tell me, Anna, are your parents still pressuring you about your decision to go into medicine? Are they still lining up eligible men to change your mind?"

"They've already lined up three potential candidates for my hand this summer." She had to convince herself to be amused and nearly managed it. "At the top of the list is the grandson of my mother's doctor. She thinks his connection to medicine might influence me."

"Is he attractive?" Myra waved away the question at Anna's scowl. "Never mind, then. My point is that your parents are going to continue to toss all of these men your way, hoping something sticks. But—" she added a bit of butter to her roll "—if you were seeing someone…"

"As in Daniel MacGregor."

"Why not? He certainly seemed interested last night."

Anna took the roll Myra had buttered and bit into it. "Because it's dishonest. I'm not interested."

"It might keep your mother from inviting every single man between twenty-five and forty over to your house for tea."

Anna let out a long breath. Myra had a point there. If just once her parents would understand what it was she needed, what she was striving for… *For your own good.* How many times had she heard that particular phrase? *If* she ever married and *if* she ever had children, those four words would never come out of her mouth.

Anna was well aware her parents had stopped arguing about her going to medical school only because they'd been certain she'd be out again before the end of the first semester. If it hadn't been for Aunt Elsie, Anna was aware she'd probably never have managed medical school at all. Elsie Whitfield had been her father's eccentric older sister—a spinster, who had made her money, some said, bootlegging whiskey during prohibition. Anna could hardly fault her however the money had been earned, since Aunt Elsie had left her a legacy large enough for tuition and independence, with no strings attached.

Don't marry a man unless you're damn sure of him, Anna remembered Elsie advising. *If you've got a dream, go*

after it. Life's too short for cowards. Use the money, Anna,
and make something out of yourself, for yourself.

Now she was only months away from the dream—
graduation, her internship. It wasn't going to be easy for
her parents to accept. It would be harder still when they
learned she intended to begin her internship at Boston
General—and that she didn't intend to live at home while
she was doing it.

"Myra, I've been thinking about getting my own place."

With the fork halfway to her mouth, Myra stopped.
"Have you told your parents?"

"No." Anna pushed away her salad and wondered why
life was so complicated when so many things seemed clear
to her. "I don't want to upset them, but it's time. I'm a grown
woman, but they're never going to see me as one while I'm
living in their home. Also, if I don't make the break now,
they're going to expect me to go on living with them after
I graduate."

Myra sat back and finished what was left of her champagne. "I think you're right. I also think you'd be wise to
tell them after it's a fait accompli."

"So do I. How would you like to spend the afternoon
apartment hunting?"

"I'd love it. Right after some chocolate mousse." She signaled the waiter. "Still, Anna, that doesn't solve the problem with Daniel MacGregor."

"There isn't any problem."

"Oh, I think you can depend on one. Chocolate mousse,"
she told the waiter. "Don't spare the whipped cream."

In his newly decorated office, Daniel sat behind an enormous oak desk and lit a cigar. He'd just completed a deal in
which he'd bought the lion's share of a company that would

manufacture televisions. Daniel calculated that what was now a novelty would become a staple in the American home in a matter of years. Besides, he enjoyed watching the little box himself. It gave him a great deal of satisfaction to buy something that entertained him. Still, his biggest project at the moment was revamping the teetering Old Line Savings and Loan to make it the biggest lending institution in Boston. He'd already started by extending two major loans and refinancing several others. He believed in putting money into circulation where it could grow. The bank manager was horrified, but Daniel figured the man would bend or find other employment. In the meantime, Daniel had some research to do.

Anna Whitfield. He knew her family background because her father was one of the top attorneys in the state. Daniel had nearly retained him before he'd decided to go with the younger, more flexible Herbert Ditmeyer. Now that Herbert had been elected district attorney, he might have to do some rethinking there. Maybe Anna Whitfield's father was the answer. He'd just about decided that Anna was.

Her family home on Beacon Hill had been built in the eighteenth century. Her ancestors had been patriots who'd started a new life in the New World and had prospered. The Whitfields were, and had been for generations, a solid part of Boston society.

Daniel respected nothing more than a strong lineage. Prince or pauper didn't matter, just strength and endurance. Anna Whitfield came from good stock. That was Daniel's prime prerequisite for a proper wife. She had a head on her shoulders. It hadn't taken him long to learn that, though she was studying something as odd as medicine, she was at the top of her class. He didn't intend to pass along soft brains to his children. She was lovely. A man looking for a wife and a mother for his children had to appreciate beauty. Especially that soft, creamy sort.

She also wasn't a pushover. Daniel didn't want a simpering, blindly obedient wife—though he did expect a woman to respect the fact that he called the shots.

There were a dozen women he could woo and win, but none of them had presented him with that little bit extra. A challenge. After one meeting with Anna, Daniel was certain she would give him that. Being pursued by a woman flattered the ego, but a challenge—a challenge fired the blood. There was enough warrior in him to look forward to the fight.

If he knew one thing, it was how to lay the groundwork for a takeover. First, he found out his opponent's strengths and weaknesses. Then, he played on both. Picking up the phone, Daniel kicked back in his chair and began.

A few hours later, Daniel was struggling with the knot in his black, silk tie. The only problem with being wealthy, as far as he could see, was having to dress the part. There was no question that he presented an imposing figure in dress black, but he never stopped straining against the restrictions. Still, if a man was out to sweep a woman off her feet, he was ahead of the game if he did it in his Sunday best.

According to his information, Anna Whitfield would be spending the evening at the ballet with friends. Daniel figured he had his accountant to thank for talking him into renting a box at the theater. He might not have put it to much use thus far, but tonight would make up for all that.

He was whistling as he walked down the stairs to the first floor. Most people would have considered his twenty-room house a bit overindulgent for one man, but to Daniel, the house, with its tall windows and gleaming floors, was a statement. As long as he had it, he'd never have to go back to the three-room cottage he'd grown up in. The house said what Daniel needed it to say—that the man who owned it had success, had presence, had style. Without those things, Daniel Duncan MacGregor was back in the mines with coal dust ground into his skin and reddening his eyes.

At the foot of the stairs, Daniel paused to bellow, "McGee!" He got a foolish surge of pleasure at the way his voice bounced off the walls.

"Sir." McGee walked down the long hall, erect and unbending. He'd served other gentlemen in his time, but never one as unconventional or as generous as MacGregor. Besides, it pleased him to work for a fellow Scot.

"I'll need the car brought around."

"It's waiting for you outside."

"The champagne?"

"Chilled, of course, sir."

"The flowers?"

"White roses, sir. Two dozen as you requested."

"Good, good." Daniel was halfway to the door before he stopped and turned around. "Help yourself to the Scotch, McGee. You've got the evening off."

With no change of expression, McGee inclined his head. "Thank you, sir."

Whistling again, Daniel went outside to the waiting car. He'd bought the silver Rolls on a whim but had had no cause to regret it. He'd given the gardener the extra job of chauffeur and had pleased them both by outfitting him in a pearl-gray uniform and cap. Steven's grammar might be faulty, but once he was behind the wheel, he was the soul of dignity.

"Evening, Mr. MacGregor." Steven opened the door, then polished the handle with a soft cloth after he'd closed it again. Daniel might have bought the Rolls, but Steven considered it his baby.

After settling himself in the quiet luxury of the back seat, Daniel opened the briefcase that was waiting for him. If it took fifteen minutes to drive to the theater, it meant he had fifteen minutes to work. Idle time was for his old age.

If things went according to plan, he'd have that piece of property in Hyannis Port by the following week. The cliffs, the tough gray rock, the tall green grass reminded him of Scotland. He'd make his home there, a home he already imagined in his mind's eye. There'd be nothing to compare with it. Once he had it, he'd fill it with a wife and children. So he thought of Anna.

The white roses were spread on the seat beside him. The champagne was cased in ice. He only had to sit through the ballet before he began his courting. He picked up a rose and sniffed. The scent was quiet and sweet. White roses were her favorite. It hadn't taken him long to find that out. It would take a hard woman to resist two dozen of them, a hard woman to resist the luxury he'd offer her. Daniel dropped the rose back with the others. He'd made up his mind. It would only be a short time before he made up hers, as well. Satisfied, he sat back and closed the briefcase as Steven pulled up in front of the theater.

"Two hours," he told his driver, then on impulse picked up one of the roses again. It wouldn't hurt to start his campaign a bit early.

The scene in the lobby of the theater was one of glitter and silk. Long sweeping dresses in pastels contrasted with dark evening suits. There was a glow of pearls, a sparkle of diamonds and everywhere the feminine scent of perfume. Daniel wandered through the crowd, not so much aloof as preoccupied. His size and presence coupled with his casual manner had fascinated more than one woman. Daniel took this with a smile and a grain of salt. A woman who was easily fascinated would be easily bored. Wide mood swings weren't what a wise man looked for in a mate. Especially when the man was prone to them himself.

As he strolled through the crowd, he was distracted now and again and stopped with a friendly word or greeting. He liked people, so it was an easy matter for him to socialize, whether in the lobby of the theater or in the pits at one of his construction sites. Since he was first and last a businessman, he was comfortable talking about one thing while thinking of something entirely different. He didn't consider it dishonest, merely practical. So while he stopped here, paused there, he kept a sharp lookout for Anna.

When he saw her, he was struck just as hard and just as fast as he'd been at the summer ball. She wore blue—pale, pale blue that made her skin glow as white as new milk. Her hair was swept up and back with combs so that her face was unframed and more like his grandmother's cameo than ever. He felt a pang of desire, then something deeper and stronger than he'd expected. Still, he waited patiently until she turned her head and their eyes met. She didn't, as another woman might have, blush or flirt but simply met his stare with a calm, appraising look. Daniel felt the excitement and challenge of the game as he moved to her.

In a move that was too smooth to be considered rude, he homed in on her and ignored the group around them. "Miss Whitfield, for the waltz."

When he offered her the rose, Anna hesitated, then saw there was no polite way to refuse. Even as she took the rose, its scent drifted to her. "Mr. MacGregor, I don't believe you've met my friend, Myra. Myra Lornbridge, Daniel MacGregor."

"How do you do?" Myra offered her hand, carefully sizing him up. He looked her directly in the eye, his own eyes cool and cautious. Myra discovered that, though she wasn't certain she liked him, she respected him. "I've heard a great deal about you."

"I've had some business with your brother." She was smaller than Anna, though rounder. One look told Daniel she'd be formidable but interesting.

"That's not who I heard it from. Jasper never gossips, I'm afraid."

Daniel sent her a quick grin. "Which is why I like doing business with him. You enjoy the ballet, Miss Whitfield?"

"Yes, very much." She sniffed the rose involuntarily, then annoyed with herself, lowered her hands.

"I'm afraid I haven't seen many and don't seem to get the full impact." He added a rueful smile to the charm of the rose. "I'm told it helps if you know the story or watch with someone who truly appreciates ballet."

"I'm sure that's true."

"I wonder if I could ask you a great favor."

Warning signals flashed and made her narrow her eyes. "You can ask, of course."

"I've a box. If you'd sit with me, maybe you could show me how to enjoy the dancing."

Anna only smiled. She wasn't so easily taken in. "Under different circumstances I'd be glad to help you out. But I'm here with friends, so—"

"Don't mind us," Myra cut in. Whatever devil prompted her to interfere urged her further. "It's a shame for Mr. Mac-Gregor to sit through *Giselle* without really appreciating it, don't you think?" Eyes wicked, she smiled at Anna. "You two run right along."

"I'm grateful." Daniel looked at Myra, and his eyes, which had been cool, warmed with humor. "Very grateful. Miss Whitfield?"

Daniel offered his arm. For one quick, satisfying instant,

Anna considered tossing his rose on the floor and grinding it underfoot before stomping away. Then she smiled and tucked her arm through his. There were better ways of winning a match than tantrums. Daniel led her away, tossing a wink at Myra without breaking stride. Myra caught it and Anna's scowl with the same aplomb.

"Isn't it odd to hold a box at the ballet without being able to appreciate it?"

"It's business," Daniel told her briefly as they walked up the stairs. "But tonight I'm sure I'll get more than my money's worth."

"Oh, you can count on it." Anna swept through the doors and took her seat. Carefully she set the rose across her lap and allowed Daniel to remove the ivory lace wrap she'd tossed on as an afterthought. Beneath it, her shoulders were bare. Both of them became aware of how stunning the lightest touch of flesh against flesh could be. Anna folded her hands and decided to pay him back by giving him exactly what he'd asked for.

"Now, to give you the background." In the tone of a kindergarten teacher reciting *Little Red Riding Hood*, Anna told him the story of *Giselle*. Without giving him a chance to comment throughout the lecture, she went on with everything she knew about ballet in general. Enough, she thought, to put a strong man to sleep. "Ah, here's the curtain. Now pay attention."

Satisfied with her tactics, Anna settled back and prepared to enjoy herself. She couldn't concentrate. Within the first ten minutes her mind wandered a dozen times. Daniel sat quietly beside her, but he wasn't cowed. Of that she was certain. She thought that, if she turned her head only a few inches, she'd see him grinning at her. She looked straight ahead. She'd deal with Myra, she thought grimly, for boxing her in with a red-bearded barbarian. And she wouldn't look at him. She wouldn't, she promised herself, even think about him. Instead, she'd absorb the music, the color, the dancing of a ballet she loved. It was romantic, exciting, poignant. If she could only relax, she'd forget he was there. Deliberately she took five deep breaths. Then he touched her hand, making her pulse jolt.

"It's all about love and luck, isn't it?" Daniel murmured.

She realized that, barbarian or not, he understood and, from the quiet tone of his voice, that he appreciated. Unable to resist, she turned her head. Their faces were close, the lights were dim. The music swelled and crested over them. A little piece of her heart weakened and was lost to him. "Most things are."

He smiled, and in the shadowed light seemed incredibly virile, incredibly gentle. "A wise thing to remember, Anna."

Before she could think to resist, he linked his fingers with hers. Hands joined, they watched the dance together.

He kept close during intermission, catering to her before she could prevent him. Somehow he maneuvered her until it was too late to make excuses and rejoin her friends for the last half. As she took her seat after the intermission, Anna told herself she was simply being polite by remaining in his box until the final curtain. It wasn't a matter of wanting to be there, or of enjoying herself, but of good manners. She managed to sit primly for five minutes before she was again caught up in the romance of the story.

She felt the tears come as Giselle faced tragedy. Though she kept her face turned and blinked furiously, Daniel gauged her mood. Without a word, he passed her his handkerchief. She took it with a little sigh of acceptance.

"It's so sad," she murmured. "It doesn't matter how many times I see it."

"Some beautiful things are meant to be sad so we can appreciate the beautiful things that aren't."

Surprised, she turned to him again with tears still clinging to her lashes. He didn't sound like a barbarian when he spoke that way. Somehow, she wished he had. Disturbed, Anna turned back for the final dance.

When the applause died and the lights came up, she was composed. Inside, her emotions were still churning, but she blamed that on the story. Without a sign that she'd been moved, she accepted Daniel's hand as he drew her to her feet.

"I can honestly say I've never enjoyed a ballet more." In the courtly manner he could draw out without warning, he brushed his lips over her knuckles. "Thank you, Anna."

Cautious, she cleared her throat. "You are welcome. If you'll excuse me, I have to get back to the others."

He kept her hand in his as they walked from the box. "I took the liberty of telling your friend Myra that I'd see you home."

"You—"

"It's the least I can do," he interrupted smoothly, "after you were nice enough to educate me. It made me wonder why you hadn't thought of going into teaching."

Her voice cooled as they walked down the stairs to the lobby. He was laughing at her, but she'd been laughed at before. "It isn't wise to take on responsibility for someone else without asking first. I might have had plans."

"I'm at your disposal."

She didn't lose her patience often, but she was close. "Mr. MacGregor—"

"Daniel."

Anna opened her mouth, then closed it again until she was certain she could be calm. "I appreciate the offer, but I can see myself home."

"Now, Anna, you've already accused me of being rude once." He spoke cheerfully as he maneuvered her to his car. "What kind of man would I be if I didn't at least drive you home?"

"I think we both know the kind of man you are."

"True." He stopped just outside the door, where a few people still loitered. "Of course, if you're afraid, I'll get you a cab."

"Afraid?" The light came into her eyes. Passion, fire, temper, it didn't matter, Daniel was learning to love it. "You flatter yourself."

"Constantly." With a gesture, he indicated the door Steven was holding open. Too angry to think, Anna stepped inside and was struck by the warm, sultry scent of roses. Gritting her teeth, she swept them into her arms so that she could sit as close as possible to the far door. It only took an instant for her to realize Daniel was too overwhelming to make the distance viable.

"Do you always keep roses in your car?"

"Only when I'm escorting a beautiful woman."

She wished she had the heart to toss them out the window. "You planned this carefully, didn't you?"

Daniel drew the cork out of the chilled champagne. "No use planning if you're not careful."

"Myra tells me I should be flattered."

"My impression of Myra is that she's a smart woman. Where would you like to go?"

"Home." She accepted the wine and sipped to steady her nerves. "I have to get up early in the morning. I'm working at the hospital."

"Working?" He turned to frown at her as he settled the bottle back in its bed of ice. "Didn't you say you had another year before you'd finished your training?"

"Another year before I have my degree and start my internship. Right now, my training also includes emptying bedpans."

"That's nothing a young woman like you should be doing." Daniel tossed back the first glass of champagne and poured another.

"I assure you, I'll take your opinion for what it's worth."

"You can't tell me you enjoy it."

"I can tell you I enjoy knowing I've done something to help someone else." She drank again and held out her glass. "That may be difficult for you to understand, since it is not business. It's humanity."

He could have corrected her then. He could have pointed out that he'd donated enormous funds toward setting up medical services for the miners in his region of Scotland. It wasn't something his accountant had advised, but something he'd had to do. Instead, Daniel focused on the one thing designed to make her furious.

"You should be thinking about marriage and a family."

"Because a woman isn't able to handle anything more than a toddler tugging on her apron while another's growing under it?"

His brow lifted. He supposed he should be used to the blunt way American women phrased things. "Because a woman's meant to make a home and a family. A man has it easy, Anna. He only has to go out and make money. A woman holds the world in her hands."

The way he said it made it difficult for her to spit back at him. Struggling for calm, she sat back. "Did it ever occur to you that a man doesn't have to make a choice between having a family or having a career?"

"No."

She nearly laughed as she turned to look at him. "Of

course, it didn't. Why should it? Take my advice, Daniel, look for a woman who doesn't have any doubts about what she was meant to do. Find one who doesn't have windmills to battle."

"I can't do that."

She had a half smile on her face, but it faded quickly. What she saw in his eyes sent both panic and excitement rushing through her. "Oh, no." She said it quickly and drained her glass. "That's ridiculous."

"Maybe." He cupped her face in his hand and watched her eyes widen. "Maybe not. But either way, I've picked you, Anna Whitfield, and I mean to have you."

"You don't pick a woman the way you pick a tie." She tried to summon up both dignity and indignation, but her heart was beating much too fast.

"No, you don't." He found the sudden breathlessness in her voice arousing and skimmed a thumb along her jaw to feel the warmth. "And a man doesn't treasure a piece of cloth the way he'll treasure a woman."

"I think you've lost your mind." She put her hand to his wrist, but his hand didn't budge. "You don't even know me."

"I'm going to know you better."

"I don't have time for this." She looked around, frantic, and saw they were still several blocks from her home. He was a madman, she decided. What was she doing in the back of a Rolls with a madman?

Her unexpected jolt of panic pleased him. "For what?" he murmured, and stroked a thumb down her cheek.

"For any of this." Perhaps she should humor him. No, she had to be firm. "Flowers, champagne, moonlight. It's obvious you're trying to be romantic, and I—"

"Should be quiet for just a minute," he told her, and decided the point by closing his mouth over hers.

Anna gripped the roses in her lap until a thorn pierced her skin. She never noticed. How could she have guessed his mouth would be so soft or so quietly clever? A man of his size should have been awkward or overbearing when he wrapped his arms around a woman. Daniel gathered her to him as if he'd done so countless times. His beard brushed her face and sensitized her skin while she struggled to remain unmoved. Her fingers itched to comb through his beard, and she reached for him before common sense could prevent it.

Something hot and fierce leaped inside her. Passion she'd kept firmly controlled, strictly in bounds, strained free to make a mockery out of everything she had once believed of herself. If he were mad, then so was she. With a moan that was part protest, part confusion, she gripped his shoulders and hung on.

He'd expected a fight, indignation at the least. He'd thought she might pull herself away and level one of those cool looks to put him in his place. Instead, she pressed against him and made his impulsive demand flare like a torch in high wind. He hadn't known she could peel away his control with such delicate fingers and leave him stripped and vulnerable. He hadn't known she would make him want with such gut-wrenching desire. She was just a woman, one he'd chosen to complete his plans for success and power. She wasn't supposed to make him forget everything but the feel and taste of her.

He knew what it was to want—a woman, wealth, power. Now, with Anna pressed to him, with the scent of roses filling his head and the taste of her filling his soul, she was all those things in one. To want her was to want everything.

She was breathless when they drew apart, breathless, aroused and frightened. To combat her weakness, Anna fell back on dignity. "Your manners continue to be crude, Daniel."

He could still see the dregs of passion in her eyes, still feel it vibrating from her, or himself. "You'll have to accept me as I am, Anna."

"I don't have to accept you at all." Dignity, she told herself. At all costs, she needed to preserve some semblance of dignity. "A kiss in the back seat of a car means nothing more than the time it takes to accomplish it." It wasn't until that moment that she realized they were parked in front of her house. How long? she wondered. If color surged into her cheeks, she told herself it was anger. She fumbled with the door handle before the driver could come around and open it for her.

"Take the roses, Anna. They suit you."

She only looked over her shoulder and glared. "Goodbye, Daniel."

"Good night," he corrected, and watched her run up the walk with the pale blue dress swirling around her legs. The roses lay on the seat beside him. Picking one up, he tapped it against his lips. The bloom wasn't as soft as she was or as sweet. He let it fall again. She'd left them behind, but he'd just send them to her in the morning, perhaps with another dozen added. He'd only begun.

His hand wasn't quite steady when he picked up the bottle of champagne. Daniel filled his glass to the rim and downed it in one long swallow.

Chapter 3

The next morning Anna was at work at the hospital. The time she spent there brought her part pleasure, part frustration. She'd never been able to explain to anyone, neither her parents nor her friends, the excitement she felt when she walked into a hospital. There was no one who would understand the satisfaction she gained from knowing she was part of it—the learning and the healing.

Most people thought of hospitals with dread. To them, the white walls, glaring lights and smell of antiseptics meant sickness, even death. To Anna, they meant life and hope. The hours she spent there each week only made her more determined to be a part of the medical community, just as the hours she spent each week poring over medical books and journals made her more determined to learn everything there was to learn.

She had a dream that she'd never been able to share with anyone. To Anna, it was both simple and pretentious: she wanted to make a difference. To accomplish her dream, she had to devote years of her life to learning.

Working as a layman, sorting linen, dispensing magazines, she still learned. Anna watched interns drag themselves through rounds after snatches of sleep. A great many of them wouldn't make it to a residency no matter how high their marks had been in medical school. But she would. Anna watched, listened and made up her mind.

She learned something else, something she was determined never to forget. The backbone of the hospital wasn't the surgeons or the interns. It wasn't the administrators, though they dispensed the budget and made the policies. It was the nursing staff. The doctors examined and diagnosed, but the nurses, Anna thought, the nurses healed. They spent hours on their feet, walked miles of corridor each day. Whatever hat they were wearing—clerk, maid, cleaning woman or comforter—Anna saw the same thing: dedication, often laced with fatigue. The interns were run ragged to weed out the weak. The nursing staff was just run ragged.

It was then, the summer before her last year of medical school, that Anna made herself a promise. She would be a doctor, a surgeon, but she would be one with a nurse's compassion.

"Oh, Miss Whitfield." Mrs. Kellerman, the senior nurse, stopped Anna with a brisk hand signal, then finished filling out a chart. She'd been a nurse as long as she'd been a widow, twenty years. At fifty she was as tough as iron and as tireless as an adolescent. Kellerman was as gentle with her patients as she was hard on her nurses. "Mrs. Higgs in 521 was asking about you."

Anna shifted the stack of magazines she carried. Five twenty-one would be her first stop. "How is she today?"

"Stable," Kellerman answered without looking up. She

was in the middle of a ten-hour shift and hadn't time for chitchat. "She spent a restful night."

Anna bit back a sigh. She knew Kellerman would have checked Mrs. Higgs's chart personally and could have given her exact information. She also knew Kellerman's opinion of the system. Women were meant to function in certain areas, men in others. There was no crossover. Rather than question Kellerman, Anna walked down the hall. She'd see for herself.

The blinds were open in Mrs. Higgs's room. Sunlight poured through and slashed brilliantly over white walls, white sheets. The radio was on low. Mrs. Higgs lay quietly in the bed. Her thin face was lined more deeply than it should have been on a woman not yet sixty. Her hair was thinning, the gray dull and yellowing. The spots of rouge she'd applied that morning stood out like fire on her pale cheeks. Though her color made Anna apprehensive, she knew everything was being done that could be done. At the end of each of her frail hands, Mrs. Higgs's nails were tinted deep red. It made Anna smile. Mrs. Higgs had told her once that she could lose her looks, but never her vanity.

Because the woman's eyes were closed, Anna shut the door quietly. After setting down her magazines, she walked to the chart at the foot of the bed.

As Kellerman had said, Mrs. Higgs was stable—no better, no worse than she had been for more than a week. Her blood pressure was a bit low and she was still unable to hold solid food, but she'd passed the night comfortably. Satisfied, Anna moved to the window to draw the shades.

"No, dear, I like the sun."

Anna turned and found Mrs. Higgs smiling at her. "I'm sorry. Did I wake you?"

"No, I was dreaming a bit." The pain was always there,

but Mrs. Higgs continued to smile as she held out a hand. "I was hoping you'd come by today."

"Oh, I had to." Anna took a seat beside the bed. "I borrowed one of my mother's fashion magazines. Wait until you see what Paris has in store for us for the fall."

With a laugh, Mrs. Higgs turned off the radio. "They'll never top the twenties. That was fashion with daring. Of course, you had to have good legs and nerve." She managed a wink. "I did."

"You still do."

"The nerve, not the legs." Sighing, Mrs. Higgs shifted. Anna was up immediately to rearrange her pillows. "I miss being young, Anna."

"I wish I were older."

Mrs. Higgs sat back, weak, and let Anna arrange her covers. "Don't wish the years away."

"Not years." Anna sat on the edge of the bed. "Just this next one."

"You'll have your degree in the blink of an eye. Then there will be times you'll miss all the work and confusion you went through to get it."

"I'll have to take your word for it." Efficient and unobtrusive, Anna took her pulse. "Right now, all I can think about is getting through the summer and starting again."

"Being young is like having a wonderful gift and not being quite sure what to do with it. Do you know the pretty nurse, the tall one with the red hair?"

Reedy, Anna thought as she moved her fingers from the woman's wrist. She recalled from the chart that Mrs. Higgs wasn't due to have medication for an hour. "I've seen her."

"She was helping me this morning. Such a sweet thing. She's getting married soon. I liked hearing her talk about her sweetheart. You never do."

"I never do what?"

"Talk about your sweetheart."

There were a few tired-looking flowers in a glass next to the bed. Anna knew one of the nurses must have brought them in, because Mrs. Higgs had no family. Leaning over, she tried to perk them up. "I don't have one."

"Oh, I don't believe that. A lovely young woman like you must have a handful of sweethearts."

"They distract me when they line up at my door," Anna told her, then grinned when the older woman chuckled.

"Not far from the truth, I imagine. I was only twenty-five when I lost my husband. I thought, I'll never marry again. Of course, I had sweethearts." A little dreamy, a little sad, Mrs. Higgs stared up at the ceiling. "I could tell you stories that would shock you."

With a laugh, Anna tossed back her hair. The sunlight slanted across her eyes, making them deeper, warmer. "You couldn't shock me, Mrs. Higgs."

"I was a dreadful tease, I'm afraid, but I had so much fun. Now, I wish…"

"What do you wish, Mrs. Higgs?"

"I wish I'd married one of them. I wish I married one and had children. Then there'd be someone who'd care and remember me."

"You have people who care, Mrs. Higgs." Anna reached for her hand again. "I care."

She wouldn't give in to the pain, or worse, the self-pity. Mrs. Higgs gave Anna's hand a quick squeeze. "But there must be a man in your life. Someone special."

"No one special. There is a man," Anna continued in a cooler tone. "He's just a nuisance."

"What man isn't? Tell me about him."

Because the tired eyes had brightened, Anna decided to humor her. "His name is Daniel MacGregor."

"Is he handsome?"

"No—yes." Anna shrugged her shoulders then dropped her chin on her hand. "He's not the kind of man you'd see in a magazine, but he's certainly not ordinary. He's more than six foot, about six-three, I'd say."

"Big shoulders?" Mrs. Higgs asked, perking up.

"Definitely." She had decided to make him sound larger than life for Mrs. Higgs's sake, then realized she didn't have to exaggerate. "He looks like he could heft two grown men on each one."

Delighted, Mrs. Higgs settled back. "I always liked big men."

Anna started to scowl, then admitted to herself that her description of Daniel was better for Mrs. Higgs than the Paris fashions. "He has red hair," she continued, then waited a beat, "and a beard."

"A beard!" Mrs. Higgs's eyes brightened. "How dashing."

"No…" The image of Daniel came to her mind much too easily. "It's more ferocious. But he does have lovely eyes. They're very blue." She frowned again, remembering. "He tends to stare."

"A bold one." Mrs. Higgs nodded approval. "I could never abide a wishy-washy man. What does he do?"

"He's a businessman. A successful one. Arrogant."

"Better and better. Now, tell me why he's a nuisance."

"He won't take a simple no for an answer." Restless, Anna rose and walked to the window. "I made it very clear to him that I wasn't interested."

"Which has made him determined to change your mind."

"Something like that." *I've picked you, Anna Whitfield.*

I mean to have you. "He's sent me flowers every day this week."

"What kind?"

Amused, Anna turned back. "Roses, white roses."

"Oh." Mrs. Higgs gave a sigh that was young and yearning. "It's been too many years to count since someone sent me roses."

Touched, Anna studied her face. Mrs. Higgs was tiring. "I'll be glad to bring you some of mine. They do smell wonderful."

"You're a sweet child, but it's not the same, is it? There was a time…" Her words trailed off, and she shook her head. "Well, that's passed now. Perhaps you should take a closer look at this Daniel. It's never wise to toss away affection."

"I'll have more time for affection after I finish my internship."

"We always think we'll have more time." With another sigh, Mrs. Higgs let her eyes close. "I'm betting on Daniel," she murmured, and drifted off to sleep.

Anna watched her a moment. Leaving Mrs. Higgs with the sunlight and the magazine from Paris, Anna left, closing the door behind her.

Hours later, Anna walked out into the afternoon light. Her feet were tired, but her spirits were high. She'd spent the last part of her shift in Maternity, listening to new mothers and holding babies. She wondered how long it would be before she'd be in on a delivery and share in bringing in new life.

"You're even lovelier when you smile."

Startled, Anna spun around. Daniel was leaning against the hood of a dark blue convertible. He was dressed more casually than she'd seen him before, in slacks and a shirt open at the collar. As the light breeze ruffled his hair, he grinned at her. He looked, though she hated to admit it, wonderful. While she hesitated, trying to gauge the best way to handle him, Daniel straightened and walked to her.

"Your father told me you'd be here." She looked so... competent, he decided, in the dark skirt and white blouse. Not as delicate as she'd looked in the rose or blue gowns, but every bit as lovely.

In a casual gesture, she tucked her hair behind her ear. "Oh. I didn't realize you were well acquainted with my father."

"Now that Ditmeyer's district attorney, I needed another lawyer."

"My father." Anna struggled with a surge of temper. "I certainly hope you haven't retained him because of me."

Daniel's smile was slow and easy. Yes, every bit as lovely. "I don't mix business with personal matters, Anna. You haven't answered any of my calls."

This time she smiled. "No."

"Your manners surprise me."

"They shouldn't, considering your own, but in any case, I did send you a note."

"I don't consider a formal request for me to stop sending you flowers communication."

"You haven't stopped sending them, either."

"No. You've been working all day?"

"Yes. So now, if you'll excuse me—"

"I'll drive you home."

She inclined her head in the cool manner he'd come to wait for. "That's very kind of you, but it isn't necessary. It's a lovely day and I don't live far."

"All right, I'll walk with you."

She discovered she was gritting her teeth. Deliberately Anna relaxed. "Daniel, I'm sure I've made myself clear."

"Aye, that you have. And I've made myself clear. So—"

he took both of her hands in his "—it's just a matter of seeing which one of us holds out the longest. I intend for it to be me. There isn't any harm in our getting to know each other better, is there?"

"I'm sure there is." She began to see one of the reasons he was so successful in business. When he chose, the charm just oozed out of him. It wasn't every man who could lay down a challenge with a friendly smile. "You have to let go of my hands."

"Of course…if you'll take a drive with me."

The light came into her eyes. "I don't respond to bribes."

"Fair enough." Because he was coming to respect her and because he still intended to win, he released her hands. "Anna, it's a lovely afternoon. Take a drive with me. Fresh air and sunshine are good for you, aren't they?"

"They are." Where was the harm? Maybe if she humored him a bit, she'd be able to convince him to put his considerable energy elsewhere. "All right, a short drive then. You have a beautiful car."

"I like it, though Steven pouts whenever I go out without him and the Rolls. Pitiful thing for a grown man to pout." He started to open the door for her then stopped. "Do you drive?"

"Of course."

"Fine." Daniel drew the keys out of his pocket and handed them to her.

"I don't understand. You want me to drive?"

"Unless you'd rather not."

Her fingers curled around the keys. "I'd love to, but how do you know I'm not reckless?"

He stared at her a moment then burst into delighted laughter. Before she realized it, he swung her up and in two dizzying circles. "Anna Whitfield, I'm crazy about you."

"Crazy," she muttered, trying to straighten her skirt and her dignity when her feet touched the ground again.

"Come along, Anna." He plopped into the passenger seat with a wicked grin. "My life and my car are in your hands."

With a toss of her head, she rounded the hood and took her own seat. Unable to resist, she sent him a coolly wicked smile. "A gambler, are you, Daniel?"

"Aye." He settled back as the engine sprang to life. "Why don't you head out of town a bit? The air's fresher."

A mile, she told herself as she pulled away from the curb. Two at the most.

Soon, they had somehow gotten ten miles out of town and laughing.

"It's wonderful," she called over the wind. "I've never driven a convertible before."

"Suits you."

"I'll remember that when I decide to buy one of my own." She caught her bottom lip between her teeth as she negotiated a curve. "I just might look into it soon. I'll be moving into an apartment closer to the hospital, but a car is handy."

"You're moving out of your parents' home?"

"Next month." She nodded. "They didn't object as much as I'd anticipated. I suppose the best thing I ever did was to go to college out of state. All I have to do is convince them they don't have to furnish it for me."

"I don't like the idea of you living alone."

She turned her head briefly. "That isn't an issue, of course, but in any case, I'm a grown woman. You live alone, don't you?"

"That's different."

"Why?"

He opened his mouth, then shut it again. Why? Because, although he didn't worry about himself, he'd worry about her. However, that wasn't a reason she'd accept. He'd learned that much about Anna. "I don't live alone," he corrected her. "I have servants." Smug, he waited for her argument.

"I don't think I'll have room for any. Look how green the grass is."

"You're changing the subject."

"Yes, I am. Do you often take afternoons off?"

"No." He grumbled a bit, then decided to let it drop. He could always check out her apartment for himself and make certain it was safe. If it wasn't he could damn well buy it. "But I decided catching you at the hospital was the only way to see you alone again."

"I could have said no."

"Aye. I was betting you wouldn't. What do you do in there? You can't stick needles and knives in people yet."

She laughed again. The wind smelled delicious. "For the most part I visit patients, talk to them, pass out magazines. I may help sort or change linen if they need me."

"That's not what you're going to school for."

"No, but I'm learning nonetheless. Doctors or even the nurses can't give patients a lot of personal attention, simply because of lack of time and too much volume. I'm free to do that now, if only for a short while. And it helps me understand what it's like to lie there hour after hour, sick, uncomfortable or just bored. I'm going to remember that when I start my practice."

He'd never thought of it just that way before, but he did remember the lingering illness that had taken his mother when he'd been ten. He remembered, too, how difficult it had been for her to be confined to bed. The sickroom smell was just as clear to him now as the scent of the mines.

"Doesn't it bother you to be around sick people all the time?"

"If it didn't bother me, I wouldn't feel the need to be a doctor."

Daniel watched the way the wind tossed her hair back away from her face. He'd loved his mother, had sat with her every day, but he'd dreaded facing her illness and watching her fade. Anna, young, vital, was choosing to spend her life facing illness. "I don't understand you."

"I don't always understand myself."

"Tell me why you go into that hospital every day."

She thought of her dream. Why would he understand when no one else did? Then she thought of Mrs. Higgs. Perhaps he could understand that. "There's a woman in the hospital now. A couple of weeks ago they operated, removed a tumor and part of her liver. I know she's in pain, but she hardly ever complains. She needs to talk, and I can give her that. It's all the doctoring I can do now."

"But it's important."

She turned to him again, and her eyes were dark and intense. "Yes, to both of us. Today she was telling me that she wished she'd married again after her husband died. She wants someone to remember her. Her body's giving up, but her mind's so sharp. Today I was telling her about you—"

"You talked about me."

She could've bitten her tongue. Instead, Anna carefully explained. "Mrs. Higgs got on the subject of men, and I told her I knew one who was a nuisance."

He took her hand and kissed it. "Thank you."

Fighting amusement, she increased her speed. "Anyway, I described you. She was impressed."

"How did you describe me?"

"Are you vain as well, Daniel?"

"Absolutely."

"Arrogant, ferocious. I don't know if I remembered to include rude. The point is, if I can sit and talk to her for a few minutes every day, bring a little of the outside world into her room, it makes it easier. A doctor has to remember that diagnosis and treatment aren't enough. Maybe they're nothing at all without compassion."

"I don't think you'll forget that."

She felt a tug at her heart. "You're trying to flatter me again."

"No. I'm trying to understand you."

"Daniel…" How did she deal with him now? She could handle the arrogance, the flamboyance, even the demands. But how did she deal with the kindness? "If you really want to understand me, you'll listen to me. Earning my degree, starting my practice aren't just the most important things in my life. For now, they're the only things. I've wanted this too long, worked too hard to be distracted from it by anything or anyone."

He trailed a finger down her shoulder. "Are you finding me a distraction, Anna?"

"It isn't a joke."

"No, none of it is. I want you to be my wife."

The car swerved as her hands went limp on the wheel. Hitting the brakes, Anna came to a screeching halt in the middle of the road.

"Does this mean yes?" Because he enjoyed the blatant shock on her face, he grinned.

It took her another ten seconds to find her voice. No, he wasn't joking. He was insane. "You're out of your mind. We've known each other a week, seen each other a hand-ful of times and you're proposing marriage. If you go into business deals with this kind of abandon I can't understand why you're not bankrupt."

"Because I know which deal to make and which to toss out. Anna—" he reached out and took her shoulders "—I could have waited to ask you, but I don't see the point when I'm sure."

"You're sure?" With a long breath she tried to control the chaos of emotions inside her. "It may interest you to know that it takes two people to make a marriage. Two willing, dedicated people who love each other."

He dismissed that. "There are two of us."

"I don't want to get married, not to you, not to anyone. I have another year of school, my internship, my residency."

"I may not like the idea of you becoming a doctor—" nor was he convinced she'd pull it off "—but I'm willing to make some concessions."

"Concessions?" Her eyes went nearly opaque with temper. "My career is not a concession." Her voice was entirely too calm, too quiet. "I've tried to be reasonable with you, Daniel, but you simply don't listen. Try to get this through your head. You're wasting your time."

He drew her closer, aroused by her temper, infuriated by her rejection. "It's mine to waste."

Not as gently as he had before, nor as patiently, he crushed his mouth to hers. She might have resisted; he didn't know. In that moment Daniel was too absorbed in the needs churning inside of him, the emotions swirling through him, to be aware of compliance or objection.

Her lips were warmed from the strong sun, her skin soft from whatever female magic she performed on it. He wanted her. It was no longer a matter of his choosing or his planning. Desire overwhelmed, enclosed and ruled him.

This was how she'd thought he would be: strong, demanding, dangerous, exciting. She couldn't make herself object, though she knew it should have been simple. Cold. How could she be cold when her body had so suddenly turned to fire? Unfeeling. How could she not feel the sensations racing through her? Despite all logic, despite all will, she melted against him. In melting, she gave more than she'd known she had. She took more than she'd known she wanted.

She'd want again. While her blood thudded frantically in her head, she knew it. As long as he was near, as long as she could remember his touch, she'd want again. How could she stop it? Why did she want to? There were answers. She was sure there were answers if only she could find them. It was logic she needed, but the weakness took over until she was lost in the power they made together.

When strength returned, it was entwined with passion. But passion, she could control. Fighting regrets, Anna pulled away. She straightened in the seat and stared directly ahead until she was certain she could speak.

"I'm not going to see you again."

The first prick of fear surprised him. Daniel shoved it away and turned her face toward his. "We both know that's not true."

"I mean what I say."

"I'm sure of it. But it's not true."

"Damn you, Daniel, no one can tell you anything."

It was the first time he'd heard her lash out in anger, and though she quickly controlled herself, he saw that her temper was something to respect.

"Even if I were in love with you, which I'm not," she continued, "nothing could come of it."

He twisted a lock of her hair around his finger and released it. "We'll just wait and see."

"We won't—" She broke off and jumped as a horn blared. A car bumped along beside them. The elderly man driving paused long enough to glare at them and shout something that was lost under the sound of his motor as he went around them and continued down the road. When Daniel started to laugh, Anna laid her forehead on the steering wheel and joined him. She'd never known anyone who could make her so furious, make her so weak and still make her laugh.

"Daniel, this is the most ridiculous situation I've ever been in." Still chuckling, she lifted her head. "I'd almost believe we could be friends if you'd stop the rest of this business."

"We will be friends." He leaned over and kissed her lightly before she could move away. "I want a wife, a family. There comes a time when a man needs those things, or nothing else is worthwhile."

She folded her arms on the wheel and rested her chin on them. Calm again, she stared off into the tall grass along the road. "I believe that—for you. I also believe that you made up your mind to marry and set out looking for the most suitable woman to fit the bill."

He shifted, uncomfortable. It wouldn't be easy to have a wife who could read you that well. But he'd picked Anna. "Why do you think that?"

"Because it's all business to you." She gave him a steady look. "One way or the other."

He wouldn't evade—couldn't with her. "Maybe so. The thing is, you fit. Only you."

Sighing, she leaned back. "Marriage isn't a business transaction, or it shouldn't be. I can't help you, Daniel." Anna started the car again. "It's time we went back."

He laid a hand lightly on her shoulder before she began the turn. "It's too late to go back, Anna. For both of us."

Chapter 4

Lightning snaked across the sky and thunder rumbled, but the rain held off. The night, though summer had barely begun, was almost sultry. Now and again the wind moved through the trees with no sound and no power to cool the air. Enjoying the heat and the threat of a storm, Myra stopped in front of the Ditmeyers' with a high-pitched squeal of brakes.

"What a dreadful noise." She flipped down the mirror on her visor to check her face. "I really must get that fixed."

"Your face?" Anna's bland smile was answered with easy good humor.

"Before it's over, certainly, but immediately, that nasty noise."

"You might try driving with a bit more…discretion," Anna suggested.

"Now what fun would that be?"

Laughing, Anna stepped from the car. "Remind me not to let you drive my new car."

"New car?" Myra let the door slam, then fussed with the strap of her dress. "When did you get a new car?"

It must be the air, she thought, that made her feel so restless, so reckless. "I was thinking perhaps tomorrow."

"Great. I'll go with you. A new apartment, a new car." Myra linked arms with Anna as they strolled up the walk. The scent of their perfumes, one subtle, one flamboyant, merged. "What's come over our quiet little Anna?"

"A taste of freedom." Tossing her head back, she looked at the sky. It boiled with clouds. Excitement. "One taste and I've discovered I'm insatiable."

It wasn't a word Myra associated with Anna, except when it came to her studies. Unless she missed her guess, her friend's thoughts had strayed from her medical journals. Speculating, she touched her tongue to her top lip. "I wonder just how much Daniel MacGregor has to do with it."

Anna paused to lift a brow before she rang the bell. She recognized the look in Myra's eye and knew just how to handle it. "What would he have to do with my buying a new car?"

"I was thinking about the insatiable."

It was difficult to keep her face sober, but Anna managed to ignore the wicked smile Myra tossed her. "You're looking around the wrong corner, Myra. I've just decided I want to drive back to Connecticut in style."

"Something red," Myra decided. "And flashy."

"No, something white, I think. And classy."

"It'll suit you, won't it?" With a sigh, Myra stepped back to study Anna. Her dress was the color of the inside of a peach, very pale, very warm, with the sleeves thin and cuffed at the wrists. "If I tried to wear a dress that color,

I'd fade into the wallpaper. You look like something in a bakery window."

With another laugh, Anna took her arm again. "I didn't come here to be nibbled on. In any case, flashy suits you, Myra, the way it suits no one else."

Pleased, Myra pursed her lips. "Yes, it does, doesn't it?"

When the Ditmeyers' butler opened the door, Anna swept inside. She couldn't explain why she felt so good. Maybe it was because her routine at the hospital was becoming more and more rewarding. Maybe it was the letter from Dr. Hewitt and the fascinating new surgical technique he'd told her of. It certainly had nothing to do with the white roses that continued to arrive every day.

"Mrs. Ditmeyer."

Stout and formidable in lavender voile, Louise Ditmeyer came to greet both of her guests. "Anna, how lovely you look." She stopped to study Anna's pale peach dress. "Just lovely," she continued. "Pastels are so suitable for a young girl. And, Myra…" She swept a glance down Myra's vivid emerald-green silk. The disapproval was evident in her gaze. "How are you?"

"Very well, thank you," Myra said sweetly. *Silly old fish.*

"You're looking wonderful, Mrs. Ditmeyer." Anna spoke up quickly, well able to read Myra's thoughts. To keep her friend in line, she gave her the tiniest of nudges in the ribs. "I hope we're not too early."

"Not at all. There are several people in the salon. Come along." She swept along ahead of them.

"Looks like a battleship," Myra muttered.

"Then watch your mouth or you'll get torpedoed."

"I do hope your parents are coming." Mrs. Ditmeyer paused in the doorway and took a pleased survey of her guests.

"They wouldn't miss it," Anna assured her, and wondered if anyone would dare tell Louise Ditmeyer that lavender made her look jaundiced.

Mrs. Ditmeyer signaled to a servant. "Charles, some sherry for the young ladies. I'm sure you two can mingle on your own. So much to do." With that, she was bustling off.

Feeling aggressive, Myra sauntered up to the bar. "Make it bourbon, Charles."

"And a martini," Anna put in. "Dry. Behave yourself, Myra. I know she's annoying, but she's Herbert's mother."

"Easy for you to say." With a mumble, Myra took her drink. "As far as she's concerned, you've got halo and wings."

Anna winced at the description. "You're exaggerating."

"All right, just the halo then."

"Would it help if I spilled my drink on the carpet?" Anna plucked out the olive.

"You wouldn't," Myra began, then gasped as Anna tilted her glass. "No!" Myra righted it with a giggle. "I'd forgotten how easily you take a dare." She took the olive from Anna and ate it herself. "I wouldn't mind so much if you spilled it on the dragon, but the carpet's too lovely. Poor Herbert." She turned to study the other guests. "There he is now, cornered by that didactic, man-hunting Mary O'Brian. You know, he is attractive in an intellectual sort of way. It's a pity he's so…"

"So what?"

"Good," Myra concluded. "Now then." She lifted her glass to hide her grin. "There's someone I don't think anyone would call good."

She didn't even have to turn. The room seemed smaller all at once, and warmer. Warmer and charged. She felt the excitement, remembered the thrill. For a moment, she panicked. The terrace doors were to her right. She could be through them and away in an instant. She'd make an excuse later, any excuse.

"My, my." Myra laid a hand on Anna's arm and felt her tremble. "You've got it bad."

Furious with herself, Anna set her glass down then picked it up again. "Don't be ridiculous."

Amusement mixed with concern. "Anna, it's me. The one who loves you best."

"He's persistent, that's all. Outrageously persistent. It makes me nervous."

"All right." Myra knew better than to try to budge Anna off course. "We'll leave it at that for now. But since it seems to me that you need a minute to pull yourself together, let's go rescue Herbert."

Anna didn't argue. She did need a minute. An hour. Maybe years. It didn't matter that she'd considered and weighed her reaction to Daniel and had judged it to be purely physical. The reaction remained, and it grew each time she saw him. She didn't care for the edgy excitement he could bring to her just by being in the same room, so she would ignore him and relax. It had always been possible for her to control the reactions of her body. *Breathe slowly,* she told herself. *Concentrate on individual muscles.* The strain in her shoulders eased. They were, after all, at a very proper dinner party surrounded by other people. It wasn't as if they were sitting in a parked car on a lonely road. Her stomach tightened.

"Hello, Herbert." Myra eased her way to his side. "Mary."

"Myra." Obviously annoyed with the interruption, Mary turned to Anna. As she did, Herbert rolled his eyes. Amused and sympathetic, Myra tucked her arm through his. "Put any good criminals in jail lately?"

Before he could comment, Mary sent Myra a withering

look. "Really, you make it sound like a game. Herbert is a very important part of our judicial system."

"Really?" Myra arched a brow as only she could. "And I thought he just tossed crooks in the slammer."

"Regularly," Herbert quipped, his voice dry, his look solemn. He nodded at Myra. "I do my best to make sure the streets are safe. You should see the notches on my brief-case."

Delighted he could play the game, Myra leaned closer and batted her lashes. "Oh, Herbert, I simply *adore* tough guys."

It was, unfortunately, a fiendishly clever mimicry of Cathleen Donahue, Mary's closest friend. She sniffed and stiffened. "If you'll excuse me."

"I think her nose is out of joint." Myra looked wide-eyed and innocent. "Anna, what's your medical opinion?"

"Terminal cattiness." Anna patted Myra's cheek. "Careful, love, it's catching."

"Quite a performance."

Anna froze, then forced herself to relax. How could she have guessed that such a big man could move so quietly?

"Good evening, Mr. MacGregor." Myra held out a friendly hand. The dinner party wouldn't be boring after all. "Did you enjoy the ballet?"

"Very much, but I liked your act every bit as much."

Herbert greeted Daniel with a quick handshake. "You'll find that Myra's never dull."

Flattered and surprised, Myra turned to him. "Why, thank you." Going with impulse, she made up her mind on the spot. She loved Anna like a sister. She decided to do what she thought best for her. "I think I could use another drink before dinner. You, too, Herbert." Without giving him a chance to agree, she pulled him along.

With a shake of his head, Daniel watched her maneuver Herbert through the crowd. "She's something."

Anna watched her steam toward the bar. "Oh, she's definitely something."

"I like your hair."

She nearly reached a hand up to it before she stopped herself. Because she hadn't had the time to fuss with it after her day at the hospital, she'd simply pulled it straight back. She'd hoped to look sophisticated at best, competent at the least. Her face was unframed and vulnerable. "Have you been to the Ditmeyers' before?"

"You're changing the subject again."

"Yes. Have you?"

A smile hovered around his mouth. "No."

"There's a wonderful collection of Waterford in the dining room. You should take a look at it when we go in to dinner."

"You like crystal?"

"Yes. It seems cold until the light hits it and then, there are so many surprises."

"If you agreed to have dinner with me at my home, I could show you mine."

She dismissed the first part of the statement as nonsense, but honed in on the second. "You collect?"

"I like pretty things."

The tone was clear. Her look was as direct and as calm as ever. "If that's a compliment, I'll take it for what it's worth. But I have no intention of being collected."

"I don't want you on a shelf or in a glass case. I just want you." He took her hand, tightening his fingers on hers when she would have drawn away. "You're skittish," he commented, and found that fact pleased him.

"Cautious." Without moving her head, Anna shifted her gaze to their joined hands. "You have my hand."

He intended to keep it. "Have you noticed how well yours fits into it?"

She brought her eyes back to his. "You have very large hands. Anyone's would fit into it."

"I think not." But he released her hand, only to take her arm.

"Daniel—"

"It looks like we're going in to dinner."

She couldn't eat. Anna's appetite was never large, which constantly made Myra grumble, but tonight it was nonexistent. At first, she'd thought it a trick of fate that Daniel was seated next to her at the long banquet table. But one look at his face and she was certain he'd arranged it. He made his way without problem through the seafood appetizer and the soup course while she nibbled for form's sake.

He was attentive, infuriatingly so, while all but ignoring the woman on his right. He leaned close and murmured to her, encouraged her to try a bit more of this, taste a bit of that. Forced by upbringing to keep her manners in place, Anna struggled for composure. Her parents were seated closer to the head of the table. From that direction she saw both speculation and approval. She set her teeth and tried to choke down beef Wellington. It didn't take her long to realize there was speculation going on at other points of the table as well. She caught the smiles, the nods, the whispers behind lifted hands. Daniel was making it clear, publicly, that he considered them a couple.

Her temper, always so well controlled, began to heat. Very deliberately Anna cut a piece of meat. "If you don't stop playing the lovesick suitor," she murmured, sending him a smile, "I'm going to knock my wineglass in your lap. You'll be very uncomfortable."

Daniel patted her hand. "No, you won't."

Anna took a deep breath and bided her time. As dessert was served, she scooted her hand along the table and nudged. If he hadn't glanced down just at that instant, he'd have missed it and would have had a lapful of burgundy. He made a quick grab. The glass tilted the other way. Before he could right it, half the contents had splatted over the tablecloth. He heard Anna swear under her breath and nearly roared with laughter.

"Clumsy." He sent an apologetic look toward his hostess. "I've such big hands." Unrepentant, he used one of them to pat Anna's leg under the table. He thought, but couldn't be sure, that he heard her grind her teeth.

"Think nothing of it." Mrs. Ditmeyer surveyed the damage and decided it could have been worse. "That's what tablecloths are for. You haven't spilled any on yourself, have you?"

Daniel beamed at her, then at Anna. "Not a drop." As the buzz of conversation picked up again, Daniel leaned toward Anna. "Admirable and very quick. I find you more and more exciting."

"You'd have been more excited if my aim had been better."

He lifted his glass and touched it to hers. "What do you think our hostess would do if I were to kiss you right here, right now?"

Anna picked up her knife and examined it as though admiring the pattern. The look she sent Daniel was as tough as nails. "I know what I'd do."

This time he did laugh, loud and long. "I'll be damned, Anna, you're the only woman for me." His announcement carried easily down both ends of the table. "But I won't kiss you now. I don't want you trying your first surgery on me."

After dinner there was bridge in the parlor. Though she detested the game, Anna considered volunteering to keep herself occupied and in a group. Before she could manage it, she was urged along outside by a half-dozen younger people.

The storm still threatened and the moon was covered with clouds, but the air was freshened by the building breeze. As the rain crept closer, the wind began to dance around her skirt. There were lights placed strategically here and there so that the trees and the garden were bathed in a muted glow. Someone had turned on the radio inside so that music flowed through the windows. The group started out wandering aimlessly, then slowly paired off.

"I wonder if you know much about gardens," Daniel asked her.

She hadn't expected to be rid of him easily. With a shrug, Anna kept several of her friends in view. "A bit."

"Steven's a better driver than a gardener." Daniel leaned over to sniff at a fat white peony. "He's neat enough, but he lacks imagination. I was hoping for something more…"

"Showy?" Anna suggested.

He liked the word. "Aye. Showy. Colorful. In Scotland we had the heather, and the brambles were full of wild roses. Not the pretty tame sort you buy at the flower shop, tough ones, with stems as thick as your thumbs and thorns that could rip a hole through you." Ignoring Anna's murmur of disapproval, he plucked off a bloom and tucked it behind her ear. "Delicate flowers are nice for looking at, for seeing in a woman's hair, but a wild rose—they last."

She'd forgotten she didn't want to be alone with him, forgotten to keep within a cautious distance of her friends. She wondered what a wild rose would smell like and if a man like Daniel would rip it out or leave it in the brambles to grow as it chose. "Do you miss Scotland?"

He looked down at her, for a moment lost in his own memories. "Sometimes. When I'm not too busy to think about it. I miss the cliffs and the sea and the grass that's greener than it has a right to be."

It was in his voice, she realized. Mourning. She'd never thought it possible to mourn for land, only for people. "Are you going to go back?" She found herself needing to know and afraid of his answer.

He looked away a moment and the lightning flashed, reflecting fast and sharp on his face. Her heart thudded wildly. He looked the way she'd always imagined Thor would look—bold, ruthless, invulnerable. When he spoke, his voice was quiet and should have soothed her. She felt only more excitement. "No. A man makes his own home in his own time."

She ran a finger down a fragile vine of wisteria. Just a trick of the light, she told herself. It was silly to be moved by a trick of the light. "Don't you have family there?"

"No." She thought she heard pain in his voice, pain that went deeper than mourning, but his face was impassive when she looked up. "I'm the last of my line. I need sons, Anna." He didn't touch her. He didn't need to. "I need sons and daughters. I want you to give them to me."

Why, when he still spoke the outrageous, did it no longer seem so outrageous? Uneasy, Anna continued along the path. "I don't want to argue with you, Daniel."

"Good." He caught her around the waist and spun her again. The solemn look that had been in his eyes was replaced by a grin. "We'll drive to Maryland and be married in the morning."

"No!" Though it wounded her dignity, she tried to wiggle away.

"All right. If you want a big wedding, I'll wait a week."

"No, no, no!" Why it struck her as funny, she didn't know, but she began to laugh as she pushed at his chest.

"Daniel MacGregor, under all that red hair, you have the hardest head known to man. I will *not* marry you tomorrow. I will not marry you in a week. I will not marry you ever."

He lifted her off her feet so that their faces were level. When she got over her shock, Anna found it an odd and not entirely unpleasant sensation. "Bet?" he said simply.

Her brow lifted and her voice was cool as a mountain stream. "I beg your pardon?"

"God, what a woman," he said, and kissed her hard. The visions that came and went in her head swirled so quickly that she couldn't separate them. "If I didn't want to do the honorable thing, I swear I'd toss you over my shoulder and be done with it." Then he laughed and kissed her again. "Instead I'll make you a wager."

If he kissed her just once more, she'd be too giddy to remember her name. Clinging to dignity, she braced her hands on his shoulders and looked stern. "Daniel, put me down."

"Damned if I will," he said, and grinned at her.

"You'll be lame if you don't."

He remembered her threat with the wineglass. A compromise, Daniel decided, and set her down, but he kept his hands around her waist. "A wager," he repeated.

"I don't know what you're talking about."

"You said I was a gambler, and right you were. What about you?"

She discovered her hands were resting against his chest and dropped them. "Certainly not."

"Ha!" There was a dare in his eyes she found hard to resist. "Now you lie. Any woman who takes herself off to be a doctor, thumbing her nose at the system, has gambling in her blood."

And right he was. She tilted her head. "What's the wager?"

"There's a lass." He would have lifted her off her feet

again if she hadn't narrowed her eyes at him. "I say you'll have my ring on your finger within the year."

"And I say I won't."

"If I win, you spend the first week as my wife in bed. We'll do nothing but eat, sleep and make love."

If he'd meant to shock her, he'd fallen short of the mark. Anna merely nodded. "And if you lose?"

His eyes were alive with the challenge, with the taste of victory. "Name it."

Her lips curved. She believed in making the stakes high. "You give a grant to the hospital, enough for a new wing."

He didn't hesitate. "Done."

If she was sure of anything, it was that he would keep his word, no matter how absurd the circumstances. Solemnly she extended her hand. Daniel took it for the official shake, then brought it to his lips. "I've never gambled for higher stakes, nor will I again. Now let me kiss you, Anna." When she backed away, he caught her again. "We've set the wager and named the stakes, but what are the odds?" He brushed his lips against her temple and felt her shiver. "Aye, Anna, my love, what are the odds?"

Slowly he skimmed his mouth over her skin, teasing, promising, but never quite meeting her mouth. His hands, at once gentle and confident, roamed up her back to toy with the sensitive skin of her neck, then retreat again to her waist. He could feel the instant when her body gave in to its own needs and to his. He could feel his own climb higher. But he continued slowly, effortlessly to seduce.

The thunder rumbled again, but she thought it was her own heartbeat. When lightning flashed, it was like the fire in her own blood. What was passion? What was need? What was emotion? How could she tell when no man had ever brought her any of those things with such intensity before?

She knew it was vital to separate them, but they flowed together into one incandescent sensation.

This was beauty. As her body went fluid, she recognized it. This was danger. When her muscles went lax, she accepted it.

His mouth brushed over hers again but didn't linger. Frustrated, edgy, she moaned and strained closer. Did he laugh, or was it the thunder again?

Then the skies opened and rain poured over them. With a curse, Daniel swooped her off her feet. "You owe me a kiss, Anna Whitfield," he shouted. He stood a moment while the rain poured down his wild mane of hair. The lightning was in his eyes. "Don't think I'll forget." With that he bundled her close and ran for the terrace.

Was it any wonder she was distracted in the hospital the next day? Anna found herself walking down corridors, then having to stop and sort out where she was going and what she was doing. It worried her. It infuriated her. What if she had her degree, if she had patients and became so easily rattled? She simply couldn't permit herself to think of anything but her duties as long as she was in the hospital.

But she remembered the wild thrill of being carried in Daniel's arms through the pounding summer storm. She remembered, too, the way he'd burst through the terrace doors and sent the quiet bridge game into chaos by demanding towels and a brandy for her. It should have been humiliating. Anna had found it sweet. That was something else that worried her. Thinking of how Louise Ditmeyer's eyes had widened like saucers, Anna smothered a laugh. He'd certainly added spice to a sedate dinner party.

She spent the majority of her day in the wards, bringing books and magazines to the patients and talking to them as they lay in beds set side by side. Lack of privacy, Anna thought, could be as debilitating as the illnesses that had brought them there. But there was only so much room, so many doctors. She smiled a bit, thinking that the impulsive bet she'd made with Daniel would do some good.

With a glance at her watch, she realized she had less than an hour to meet Myra. Today, she'd pick out her new car. Something practical certainly, she reminded herself. But not dull. Maybe it was foolish to be excited over the purchase of four wheels and an engine, but she kept thinking of the long, solitary drives she'd take. She'd been speaking no less than the truth when she'd told Myra that she wanted freedom. She thought of it now and longed for it. Still, she couldn't leave for the day without stopping in on Mrs. Higgs.

Planning the rest of her day as she went, Anna made her way to the fifth floor. She'd take Myra out to dinner and splurge. There was nothing Myra would like better. Then maybe they'd drive out of town and give the new car a test. Some weekend soon they'd drive out to the beach and spend the day in the sun. Pleased with the idea, Anna swung through the door of 521. Her mouth fell open.

"Oh, Anna, we were afraid you wouldn't come by."

Sitting up in bed, eyes bright, Mrs. Higgs fussed with the edge of her sheet. On the table beside her was a vase of red roses, fresh, flamboyant and fragrant. Sitting beside the bed like a suitor was Daniel.

"I told you Anna wouldn't leave without coming in to see how you were." Daniel rose and offered her a chair.

"No, no, of course I wouldn't." Confused, Anna approached the bed. "You're looking well today."

Mrs. Higgs reached for her hair. The young redheaded nurse had helped her brush it that morning, but she hadn't been able to use a rinse for weeks. "I'd have fixed myself up a bit if I'd known I was having a caller." She looked at Daniel with nothing less than an adoring smile.

"You look lovely." He took one of her thin hands between both of his.

He sounded as though he meant it. What impressed Anna most was the fact that his voice carried none of the patronizing tone that so many people used when speaking with the ill or the old. Something flashed in Mrs. Higgs's eyes. It was both gratitude and pride.

"It's important to look your best when you have a gentleman caller. Isn't that right, Anna?"

"Yes, of course." Anna wandered to the foot of the bed and tried unobtrusively to read the chart. "The flowers are beautiful. You didn't mention you were coming to the hospital, Daniel."

He winked at Mrs. Higgs. "I like surprises."

"Wasn't it nice of your young man to come by and visit me?"

"He's not—" Anna caught herself and softened her voice. "Yes, yes, it was."

"Now I know you two want to run along, and I won't keep you." Mrs. Higgs spoke briskly, but her energy was flagging. "You'll come again?" She reached up for Daniel's hand. "I so enjoyed talking with you."

He heard the plea she tried so desperately to hide. "I'll come again." Leaning over, he kissed her cheek.

When he stepped back, Anna adjusted Mrs. Higgs's pillows and made her more comfortable with a few efficient moves. He saw then that Anna's hands weren't just soft, delicate things made to be kissed, but that they were competent, strong and sure. It brought him a moment's discomfort. "Now you try to rest. You mustn't tire yourself."

"Don't worry about me." Mrs. Higgs sighed. "Go have fun."

She was already dozing when they walked from the room.

"Are you done here for today?" Daniel asked as they started down the hall.

"Yes."

"I'll drive you home."

"No, I'm meeting Myra." As always the elevator was slow and temperamental. Anna pushed the button and waited.

"Then I'll drop you." He wanted her to himself, away from the hospital where she'd looked so efficient and at home.

"No, really. I'm meeting her a couple of blocks away." Anna stepped into the elevator with him.

"Have dinner with me tonight."

"I can't. I have plans." Her hands were locked tightly together as the doors opened again.

"Tomorrow?"

"I don't know, I…" Emotions churning, she walked out into sunshine and fresh air. "Daniel, why did you come here today?"

"To see you, of course."

"You went to see Mrs. Higgs." She continued to walk. She'd only mentioned the name once. How was it he'd remembered? Why should he have cared?

"Shouldn't I have? It seemed to me she looked only the better for a bit of company."

She shook her head, struggling to find the right words. She hadn't known he could be kind, not really kind when the gesture brought no gain. He was in business, after all, where there was profit and loss and accounts to be forever balanced. The price of the roses would have meant nothing to him, but the gift of them everything to Mrs. Higgs. She wondered if he knew.

"What you did means more at this point than any of the medicine they can give her." She stopped then and turned. He could see the swirl of emotion in her eyes, the steady intensity of feeling that locked on him, and demanded. Anna asked, "Why did you do it? To impress me?"

No one could lie to eyes like that. He had done it to impress her, and had been damn pleased with the idea until he'd begun to talk to Mrs. Higgs. He'd seen a mirror of his mother's fading beauty and tired dignity. And he'd go see her again, not for Anna, but for himself. He had no way of explaining it to her, and no intention of exposing feelings that had been private for so long.

"The main idea was to impress you. I also wanted to see what it was about that place that keeps bringing you back. I still don't understand it all, but maybe I see part of it now."

When she said nothing, he stuck his hands in his pockets as they walked. This woman worried him a good bit more than he'd anticipated. He wanted to please her—he was surprised how much. He wanted to see her smile again. He'd have even settled for one of her cool, regal stares. Frustrated, he scowled straight ahead. "Well, damn it, were you impressed or not?"

She stopped to look up at him. Her eyes were cool, but he couldn't read them. Then she took him totally by surprise. She put her hands on both sides on his face. In her strong, unhurried way, she drew his face down until she could touch her lips to his. It was hardly more than a hint of a kiss, but it exploded through him. She held him there a moment, her eyes locked on his. Then saying nothing, she released him and walked away.

For the first time in his life, Daniel found himself speechless.

Chapter 5

Daniel sat in his office in the Old Line Savings and Loan, puffing on his cigar and listening to the long-winded report from his bank manager. The man knew banking, Daniel conceded, and he was a whiz with figures. But he couldn't see more than two feet in front of his face.

"Therefore, in addition to my other recommendations, I further recommend that the bank foreclose on the Halloran property. Auctioning this property off would cover the outstanding principal, plus, in a conservative estimate, yield a five percent profit."

Daniel tapped his cigar in an ashtray. "Extend it."

"I beg your pardon?"

"I said extend the Halloran loan, Bombeck."

Bombeck pushed his glasses up on his nose and fluttered through his papers. "Perhaps you didn't understand that the Hallorans are six months behind on their mortgage payments. In the past two months, they've failed to keep current with the interest. Even if Halloran finds work as he claims he will, we can't expect the loan to be brought up to date within this quarter. I have all the figures here."

"I don't doubt it," Daniel muttered, bored. *Your work,* he thought, *should never bore you, or you lose your touch.*

Drawing the papers out, Bombeck placed them on Daniel's desk. They were, as Bombeck was, tidy and assiduously correct. "If you'll just look them over, I'm sure we can—"

"Give the Hallorans another six months to bring the interest up to date."

Bombeck blanched. "Six—" Clearing his throat, he shifted in his chair. His neat hands worked together. "Mr. MacGregor, I'm sure your sympathies toward the Hallorans are admirable, but you must understand that a bank can't be run on sentiment."

Daniel drew on his cigar, paused, then blew out a haze of smoke. There was the slightest of smiles on his mouth, but his eyes, if Bombeck had dared to look at them, were cold as ice. "Is that so, Bombeck? I appreciate you telling me."

Bombeck wet his lips. "As manager of Old Line—"

"Which was about to go belly up one month ago when I bought it."

"Yes." Bombeck cleared his throat again. "Yes, indeed, Mr. MacGregor, that's precisely the point. As manager, I feel it my duty to give you all the benefit of my experience. I've been in banking for fifteen years."

"Fifteen?" Daniel said as if impressed. Fourteen years, eight months and ten days. He had the employment records of everyone who worked for him, down to the cleaning woman. "That's just fine, Bombeck. Maybe if I give this to you in different terms, you'll understand my way of thinking." Daniel leaned back in his chair so that the sun shooting through the window behind him turned his hair to fire.

Though he hadn't planned it that way, he'd have been more than satisfied with the effect. "You estimate a five percent profit if we foreclose and auction the Halloran property. Have I got that right?"

Sarcasm skimmed over Bombeck's head. "Exactly so, Mr. MacGregor."

"Good. Good. However, over the remaining twelve years of the Halloran mortgage, we would see a long-term profit of, conservatively speaking, triple that."

"Over the long-term, of course. I could get you the exact figures, but—"

"Excellent. Then we understand each other. Extend it." Because he enjoyed doing so, Daniel waited a beat before dropping his bomb. "We'll be lowering the mortgage rates by a quarter percent starting next month."

"Lowering, but Mr. MacGregor—"

"And raising the interest on savings accounts to the highest allowable rate."

"Mr. MacGregor, that will throw Old Line deeply in the red."

"In the short-term," Daniel agreed briskly. "In the long-term—you were understanding the long-term, weren't you, Bombeck?—in the long-term we'll make up for it with volume. Old Line will have the lowest mortgage rates in the state."

Bombeck felt his stomach churn and swallowed. "Yes, sir."

"And the highest rates on savings accounts."

He could almost see dollar bills flying away on little wings. "It will cost the bank…" Bombeck couldn't even imagine. "I could work up the figures in a few days. I'm sure you'll see what I'm trying to say. With a policy like that, in six months—"

"Old Line will be the biggest lending institution in the

state," Daniel finished mildly. "I'm glad we agree. We're going to advertise in the papers."

"Advertise," Bombeck murmured as if in a dream.

"Something big—" Daniel measured with his hands, enjoying himself "—but distinguished. Why don't you see what you can come up with and get back to me? Say, by ten tomorrow."

It took Bombeck a few seconds to realize he'd been dismissed. Too dazed to argue, he tidied his papers and rose. As he walked out, Daniel ground his cigar in the ashtray.

Dim-witted, nearsighted dunderhead. What he needed was someone young, fresh out of college and eager. He could salvage Bombeck's pride by making up a new position for him. Daniel felt strongly about loyalty, and dunderhead or not, Bombeck had been with Old Line for nearly fifteen years. It was something he might just discuss with Ditmeyer. That was a man whose opinion Daniel trusted.

Bankers had to realize it was their business to gamble. It was certainly Daniel's. Rising, he walked to the window behind his desk and looked at Boston. At this point, his whole life was a gamble. The money he'd earned could be lost. He shrugged at that. He'd earn more again. The power he now wielded could fade. He'd build it back up again. But there was one thing he was coming to understand, that if lost, couldn't be replaced. Anna.

When had she stopped being part of his master plan and become his life? When had he lost track of the deal and fallen in love? He could pinpoint it to the instant—the instant she'd taken his face in her hands, looked so solemnly into his eyes and touched her mouth to his. He'd gone beyond attraction, beyond desire, beyond the challenge.

His systematic courtship had been blown to bits. The blueprint so carefully drawn was in tatters. From that moment, he'd become only a man totally bewitched by a woman. So now what? That was one question he had no answer for. He'd wanted a wife who would sit patiently at home while he took care of business. That wasn't Anna. He'd wanted a wife who wouldn't question his decisions, but go quietly about making them into fact. That wasn't Anna. There was a part of her life that would always remain separate from him. If she succeeded in her ambition, and he was coming to believe she would, she'd have *Doctor* in front of her name before a year was out. To Anna, it wouldn't simply be a title, but a way of life. Could a man whose business made such demands, took such long hours out of his day, have a wife whose profession did exactly the same?

Who would make the home? he wondered, pulling his fingers through his hair. Who would tend the children? Better if he turned his back on her now and found a woman who'd be content to do those things and nothing else. Better, if he followed the advice she'd given him and chose a woman who had no windmills to battle.

He needed a home. It was difficult for him to admit, even to himself, just how desperately he needed one. He needed family—the scent of bread baking in the kitchen, flowers sitting in bowls. Those were the things he'd grown up with; those were the things he'd done too long without. He couldn't be sure he would have them with Anna. And yet... If he found them without her, he didn't think they would matter.

Damn woman. He looked at his watch. She'd be nearly finished at the hospital now. He had a meeting across town in just under an hour. Determined not to let his life be run by someone else's schedule, he sat behind his desk again and picked up Bombeck's report. After one paragraph, he slammed it down again. Grumbling and swearing, he stalked out of his office.

* * *

She'd spent five hours on her feet. With a tired satisfaction, Anna thought about a long hot bath and a quiet evening with a book. Perhaps she'd just soak and plan how she'd decorate her apartment. In two weeks she'd have the keys in her hand and rooms to furnish. If her feet weren't certain to object, she'd poke around a few antique stores now. With pleasure, she thought of the shiny white convertible waiting for her in the lot next door. The car meant more than the fact that she didn't have to walk home. It meant independence.

Taking the keys out of her purse, she jiggled them in her hand and felt on top of the world. Anna had never considered her ego very large, but when her father had all but drooled on the upholstery, then demanded a ride, she'd felt her head swell. He'd approved finally. She'd used her own money, her own judgment, and there had been no criticism. She remembered the way he'd dragged her mother outside and pulled her into the back seat with him. Anna had tooled around Boston for nearly an hour with her parents as cozy as teenagers behind her.

She'd understood that they'd begun to think of her as something more than a little girl who needed guidance. Whether they'd realized it yet or not, they'd accepted her as an adult. Maybe, she thought, just maybe, there would be pride when she earned her diploma.

Giddy with success, Anna tossed her keys into the air and caught them again. She walked straight into Daniel.

"You weren't looking where you were going."

She'd been happy before, but was happier yet to have seen him. She could almost admit it. "No, I wasn't."

He'd already decided on the way to deal with her. His way. "You're having dinner with me tonight." When she opened her mouth, he took her by the shoulders. His voice was loud enough to turn heads, his eyes fierce enough to turn them forward again. "I won't have any arguments. I'm tired of them and don't have time at the moment, anyway. You're having dinner with me tonight. Be ready at seven."

There were a number of things she could do. In the space of seconds, Anna thought of them all. But she decided the best way was the least expected. "All right, Daniel," she said very demurely.

"I don't care what... What?"

"I said I'd be ready." She looked at him, her eyes calm, her smile serene. It threw him completely off balance, as she'd been certain it would.

"I— All right, then." He scowled and stuck his hands in his pockets. "See that you are." He'd gotten precisely what he'd wanted, but he stopped halfway to his car and looked back. Anna was standing just where she'd been, in a pool of sunlight. Her smile remained as quiet and sweet as an angel's kiss. "Damn women," Daniel mumbled as he yanked open the door of his car. You couldn't trust them.

Anna waited until he'd pulled off, then rocked with laughter. Seeing him stumble and stutter had been better than any argument. Still laughing, she went to her car. An evening with Daniel, she admitted, would certainly be more interesting than a book. Turning the key in the ignition, she felt the power. She had control. And she liked it.

He brought her flowers. Not the white roses he still insisted on sending her day after day, but some tiny, impudent violets from his own garden. It pleased him to watch her arrange them in a little glass vase as he spoke with her parents. He looked big and brash in her mother's dainty parlor. He felt as nervous as a scrawny boy on his first date.

Edgy, he sat on a chair he felt better suited to a dollhouse and shared a tepid cup of tea with Mrs. Whitfield.

"You must come to dinner soon," Mrs. Whitfield told him. The constant delivery of roses had made her quite hopeful. It had also given her something to brag about over bridge. The truth was she didn't understand her daughter and never had. Of course, she could tell herself that Anna had always been a sweet, lovely child, but she herself was simply out of her depth when doing something other than choosing material for a dress or a meal from a menu. Anna, with her calm stubbornness and unshakable ambitions, was completely beyond her scope.

Still, Mrs. Whitfield wasn't a fool. She saw the way Daniel looked at her daughter and understood very well. With a strange mixture of relief and regret, she pictured Anna married and raising her own family. If Daniel's manners were a bit rough, she knew her Anna would smooth them out quickly enough. Perhaps she'd be a grandmother in a year or two. It was another thought that brought mixed feelings. Sipping her tea, Mrs. Whitfield studied Daniel.

"I realize you and John are business associates now, but we'll have to keep that in the office. Of course, I know nothing about the business anyway." She reached over to pat Daniel's hand. "John won't tell me a thing, no matter how I badger him."

"And badger, she does," Mr. Whitfield put in.

"Now, John." With a light laugh, she aimed a killing look. If this man had serious intentions toward her daughter, and she was certain he did, she meant to find out everything there was to find out about him. "Everyone's curious about Mr. MacGregor's dealings. It's only natural. Why just the other day, Pat Donahue told me you'd bought some property of theirs in Hyannis Port. I hope you're not thinking of leaving Boston."

Daniel didn't have to scent the air to know which way the wind blew. "I'm fond of Boston."

Deciding she'd let him sweat long enough, Anna handed Daniel her wrap. Grateful, he was up like a shot and bundling her into it.

"You children have a lovely evening." Mrs. Whitfield would have risen to walk them to the door, but her husband put a hand on her shoulder.

"Good night, Mother." Anna kissed her mother's cheek, then smiled up at her father. She'd never realized he was so perceptive. With a smile, she kissed him, as well.

"Enjoy yourself." In an old habit, he patted her head.

Daniel felt he could finally breathe again when they stepped outside. "Your house is very—"

"Crowded," Anna finished, then laughed as she tucked her arm through his. "My mother likes to fill it up with whatever catches her eye. I didn't realize until a few years ago how tolerant my father is." Pleased that he'd brought the blue convertible, she gathered her skirts and slid into her seat. "Where are we going for dinner?"

He took his own seat and let the engine roar. "We're having dinner at home. My home."

Anna felt a quiver of nerves come and go. Using her best weapon, will, she eliminated the fluttering in her stomach. She hadn't forgotten the feeling of control. She'd handle him. "I see."

"I'm tired of restaurants, I'm tired of crowds." His voice was tense and tight. Why, *he's* nervous, she realized, and felt a jolt of pleasure. He towered over her even when sitting. His voice had a timbre that could make the windowpanes rattle, but he was nervous about spending an evening with her. It wasn't easy, but she tried hard not to be smug.

"Oh? I had the impression you enjoyed being around a lot of people," she said very calmly.

"I don't want a bunch of them staring at us while we eat."

"Amazing how rude some people can be, isn't it?"

"And if I want to talk to you, I don't need half of Boston listening to me."

"Naturally not."

He fumed and turned into his driveway. "And if you're worried about propriety, I have servants."

She sent him a bland look. "I'm not worried in the least."

Not sure how to take it, he narrowed his eyes. She was playing games with him, of that he was sure. He just wasn't sure of what kind, or of the rules. "You're mighty sure of yourself all at once, Anna."

"Daniel." She reached for the door handle and let herself out. "I've always been sure of myself."

She decided with one sweeping look that she liked his house. It was separated from the road by a line of hedges that came to her shoulder. The privacy they provided wasn't as cold or impersonal as a wall, but it was just as sturdy. As she looked at the tall windows, some of which were already softly lit behind curtains, she could smell the mixture of scents from the side garden.

Sweet peas she recognized, and smiled. She had a weakness for them. He'd chosen an imposing house, large enough for a family of ten, but he hadn't forgotten to make it a home with something as simple as flowers. She waited until he'd joined her on the edge of the walkway.

"Why did you choose it?"

He looked at the house with her. He saw the brick, attractively faded with age, the windows, with their shutters freshly painted. There was no sense of kinship, only of ownership. After all, someone else had built it. As he drew in the evening air, he didn't smell the sweet peas, but her.

"Because it was big."

She smiled at that and turned to watch a sparrow on a branch of a maple in the front yard. "I suppose that's reasonable. You looked uncomfortable in my mother's parlor, as if you thought if you turned around you might knock down a wall. This suits you better."

"For the moment," he murmured. He had other plans. "You can watch the sunset from those windows." He pointed, then took her arm to lead her up the walk. "You won't for very many more years."

"Why?"

"Progress. They're going to toss buildings up and block out the sky. Not everywhere, but enough. I'm breaking ground on one myself next month." Opening the door, he drew her into the hall and waited.

The swords crossed on the wall to her left drew her eyes first. They weren't the delicate, almost feminine foils used in duels by lace-cuffed swashbucklers. They were thick, heavy, deadly broadswords with undecorated hilts and dull, well-used blades. It would take two hands and a strong man to lift one. It would take skill and brute strength to use one to attack or defend. Unable to resist, Anna walked closer. She had no trouble imagining what one of them could do to flesh and bone. Still, though she could term them lethal, she couldn't term them ugly.

"The swords are from my clan. My ancestors used them." There was pride in his voice, and simplicity. "The MacGregors were warriors, always."

Was it a challenge she heard from him? It might have been. Anna stepped closer to the swords. The edges of the blades weren't dulled, but as treacherous as ever. "Most of us are, aren't we?"

Her response surprised him, but perhaps it shouldn't have. He knew she wasn't a woman to shudder and faint over a weapon or spilled blood. "The English king—" he nearly spat it and had Anna's full attention "—he took our name, our land, but he couldn't take our pride. We hacked off heads when we had to." His eyes were deep, blue and brilliant when he looked at her. She had no doubt he would wield the sword with a ferocity equal to that of his ancestors if he felt justified. "Mostly the heads of Campbells." He grinned at that and took her arm. "They thought to wipe us out of Scotland, but they couldn't."

She found herself wondering how he'd look in the clothes of his country, the kilt, the plaid, the dirk. Not ridiculous, but dramatic. Anna looked back up at the swords. "No, I'm sure they couldn't. You've good reason to be proud."

His hand moved up to her cheek and lingered. "Anna..."

"Mr. MacGregor." McGee stood still as a stone as Daniel whirled on him. There was a look in Daniel's eyes that would have made a strong man shudder.

"Aye?" In the one word, Daniel conveyed a thousand pungent curses.

"A call from New York, sir. A Mr. Liebowitz says it's quite important."

"Show Miss Whitfield into the parlor, McGee. I'm sorry, Anna, I have to take this. I'll be as quick as I can."

"It's all right." Relieved she'd have a few moments alone, Anna watched Daniel stride down the hall.

"This way, miss."

She noticed the brogue, which was heavier than Daniel's, and smiled. He'd keep his own around him when he could. With a last glance at the swords, she followed Mc-

Gee's ramrod back into the parlor. It made her mother's
look like a closet. If big was what Daniel wanted, big was
what he had.

"Would you care for a drink, Miss Whitfield?"

Distracted, Anna turned blankly. "I'm sorry?"

"Would you care for a drink?"

"Oh, no, thank you, I'm fine."

He gave her the smallest and staunchest of bows. "Please
ring if you require anything."

"Thank you," she said again, anxious to be rid of him. The
minute she was alone, she turned a slow circle. Big, yes—
much bigger than the average room. Unless she missed her
guess, he'd had walls removed and combined two into one.

The unusual size was complemented by unusual furnish-
ings. There was a Belker table twice the size of the wheel of a
car, carved so ornately that the edges looked like lace. A high-
backed chair done in rich red velvet sat beside it. He could
hold court in it, she thought, and smiled at the idea. Why not?

Rather than sit, Anna simply wandered. The colors were
flashy and bold, but somehow she felt perfectly comfortable with them. Maybe she'd lived with her mother's pastels
long enough. A sofa took up nearly an entire wall and would
have required four strong men to move it. With a laugh,
she decided Daniel had chosen it for exactly that reason.

Along the west window was a collection of crystal, Waterford, Baccarat. A vase, two feet high, caught the begin-
nings of the sunset and danced with it. Anna picked up a
bowl that fit into the palm of her hand and wondered what
it was doing there among the giants.

He found her like that, standing in the western light,
smiling at a small piece of glass. His mouth went dry.
Though he said nothing, could say nothing, she turned toward him.

"What a wonderful room." Enthusiasm added color to her cheeks, deepened her eyes. "I imagine in the winter, with a fire, it would be spectacular." When he didn't speak, her smile faded. She took a step closer. "The telephone. Was it bad news?"

"What?"

"Your call. Has it upset you?"

He'd forgotten it, just as he'd forgotten everything. It didn't sit well with him that a look from her could tie his tongue and his stomach up in knots. "No. I'll have to go into New York for a couple of days and straighten out a few things." Including himself, he thought ruefully. "I have something for you."

"I hope it's dinner," she said, smiling again.

"We'll have that, too." It occurred to him that he'd never felt awkward around a woman until now. Drawing a box out of his pocket, he handed it to her.

There was a moment of panic. He had no business offering her a ring. Then as common sense took over, panic faded. The box wasn't the small velvet sort that held engagement rings, but an old cardboard one. Curious, Anna opened the lid.

The cameo was nearly as long as her thumb and perhaps twice as wide. Old and lovely, it sat in a little bed of tissue paper. The profile was gentle and serene, but the head was tilted up with just a touch of pride as well.

"It favors you," Daniel murmured. "I told you once."

"Your grandmother's," she remembered. Touched, she lifted a finger to trace the outline. "It's beautiful, really beautiful." It was more difficult than it should have been to close the lid again. "Daniel, you know I can't take this."

"No, I don't." Taking the box from her, he opened it

again and drew out the cameo, which he'd attached to a velvet ribbon himself. "I'll put it on for you."

She could almost feel his fingers brush the nape of her neck. "I shouldn't take a gift from you."

He lifted a brow. "You can't tell me you worry about gossip, Anna. If you concerned yourself with what people said or thought, you wouldn't be going to your school in Connecticut."

He was right of course, but she tried to stand firm. "It's an heirloom, Daniel. It wouldn't be right."

"It's my heirloom and I'm tired of having it shut in a box. My grandmother would want it to be worn by someone who'd appreciate it." In a surprisingly smooth manner, he slid the ribbon around her neck and fastened it. It fit into the subtle hollow of her throat as if it had been destined to rest there. "There now, that's where it belongs."

Unable to resist, she reached up to touch it. Common sense slipped away. "Thank you. We'll say I'm keeping it for you. If you want it back—"

"Don't spoil it," he interrupted, and took her chin in his hand. "I've wanted to see you wear it."

She couldn't stop the smile. "And you always get what you want?"

"Exactly." Pleased with himself, he rubbed a thumb over her cheek before he dropped his hand. "Will you have a drink? There's some sherry."

"I'd rather not."

"Have a drink?"

"Drink sherry. Is there another choice?"

He felt his nervousness drop away. "I've some prime Scotch sent—smuggled if you want the truth—from a friend of mine in Edinburgh."

She wrinkled her nose. "It tastes like soap."

"Soap?" He looked so astonished that she laughed.

"Don't take it personally."

"You'll try it," he told her as he went to the bar. "Soap." While he poured, his voice dropped to a mutter. "This isn't the swill you get at one of your stiff-necked Boston parties."

Damn it, the longer she knew him, the more endearing he became. Anna found her hand had wandered to the cameo again. She took a deep breath and reminded herself of the feeling of being at the wheel. Control. When he handed her a glass, she studied it. It was very dark and, she thought, very likely to be as lethal as the swords on the wall. "Ice?"

"Don't be silly." He tossed back his glass and challenged her. Anna took a deep breath and gulped some down.

Warm, potent and smooth. Frowning a bit, she sipped again. "I stand corrected," she told him, but handed back the glass. "And if I drink all of it, I won't stand at all."

"Then we'll get some food into you."

With a shake of her head, she offered her hand. "If that's your way of saying it's time for dinner, I accept."

He took her hand and held it. "You won't get too many pretty words out of me, Anna. I'm not polished. I don't have any plans to be."

His hair flowed around his face, untamed and magnificent. The beard gave him the look of the warrior they both knew was in his blood. "No, I don't think you should."

No, he wasn't polished, but he surrounded himself with beauty. It wasn't the quiet sort Anna had become used to, but a bold, bracing beauty that could grab you by the throat. He had a shield and a pike on the wall of the dining room and below them was a Chippendale breakfront any collector of fine antiques would have envied. The table itself was massive, but set on it was the loveliest china Anna had ever seen. She sat in a chair that would have suited a medieval castle and found herself completely relaxed.

The sun came in red-gold slants through the windows. As they ate, the light softened and dimmed. With silent efficiency, McGee came to light candles, then left them again.

"If I told my mother about this meal, she'd try to steal your cook." Anna took a bite of chocolate torte and understood the phrase *sinfully rich*.

It gave him a quiet sort of pleasure to watch her enjoy his food, eat from the plates he'd chosen himself. "You can see why I prefer this to a restaurant."

"Absolutely." She took another bite, because some things weren't meant to be resisted. "I'm going to miss home cooking when I move into my apartment."

"What about your own?"

"My own what?"

"Cooking."

"It doesn't exist." Studying him, she took another bite. "Your eyebrows come straight together when you frown, Daniel, but don't worry, I intend to learn my way around a kitchen. Self-preservation." Linking her fingers, she rested her chin on them. "I don't suppose you cook."

He started to laugh, then thought better of it. "No."

She discovered she liked catching him off guard that way. "But, naturally, you find it odd that I, as a woman, don't know how."

It was difficult not to admire her logic even when he was on the wrong end of it. "You've a habit of boxing a man into a corner, Anna."

"I enjoy the way you fight your way out. I know this may be a dangerous boon to your ego, but you're an interesting man."

"I've a very big ego. It takes a lot to fill it. Why don't you tell me how I'm interesting?"

She smiled and rose. "Another time perhaps."

He caught her hand as he stood. "There will be another time."

She didn't believe in lies, and in evasions only when the truth didn't suit. "It seems there will. Mrs. Higgs talked of nothing but you today," she said as they walked back toward the parlor.

"Lovely woman."

She had to grin. He said it with such self-satisfaction. "She expects you to come back."

"I said I would." He saw the question in her eyes and stopped. "I keep my word."

"Yes." She smiled again. "You would. It's very good of you, Daniel. She has no one."

Uncomfortable, he frowned. "Don't put a halo on me, Anna. I intend to win the bet, but I'd as soon do it without false pretenses."

"I've no intention of putting a halo on you." She flicked the hair from her shoulder. "And I've no intention of losing the bet."

At the doorway to the parlor, she stopped again. There were candles, dozens of them, glowing throughout the room. Moonlight spilled in through the window to compete. There was music, quiet, bluesy. It seemed to come from the shadows. Anna felt her pulse race but continued into the room.

"Lovely," she commented, noting the silver coffee urn had been set up near the sofa.

As Daniel went to pour brandy, she stood, looking completely at ease. She wondered if her muscles could knot any tighter. "I like the way you look in candlelight," he told her as he handed her a snifter. "It reminds me of the first night I met you, when you stood on the terrace near the gardens. There were moonbeams on your face, shadows in your eyes." When he took her hand, he thought for a moment that it trembled. But her eyes were so steady. "I knew then when I looked at you that I had to have you. I've thought of you every day and every night since."

It would have been easy, too easy, to give in to the thoughts bursting in her head. If she did, she could feel his mouth on hers again and wait, tingle for the touch of those big, wide-palmed hands on her skin. It would have been easy. But the life that she'd already chosen, or that had chosen her, wasn't.

"A man in your position must know how dangerous it is to make a decision on impulse."

"No." He lifted her hand and kissed her fingers, slowly, one by one. The breath backed up in her lungs.

Through sheer will she spoke calmly, and she hoped, carelessly. "Daniel, are you trying to seduce me?"

When would he ever, how would he ever, get used to that quiet voice and frank tongue? After a half laugh, he drank some brandy. "A man doesn't seduce the woman he intends to marry."

"Of course, he does," Anna corrected and patted his back when he choked. "Just the same as a man seduces women he doesn't intend to marry. But I'm not going to marry you, Daniel." She turned away to walk to the coffeepot, then looked over her shoulder. "And I'm not going to be seduced. Coffee?"

He didn't just love her, he realized. He very nearly adored her. There were a great many things he found he wasn't certain of at that moment, but he knew without a doubt he couldn't live without her. "Aye." He walked to her and took the cup. Maybe he was better off with something in his hands. "You can't tell me you don't want me, Anna."

Her body was tingling. He had only to touch her to feel her need, her weakness. She made herself look at him. "No, I can't. That doesn't change anything."

He set the coffee down untasted. He'd have preferred throwing it. "The hell it doesn't. You came here tonight."

"For dinner," she reminded him calmly. "And because, for some odd reason, I enjoy your company. There are some things I have to accept. There are others I can't risk."

"I can." He reached out and cupped her neck gently, though it was difficult to be gentle when he wanted to drag her to him and plunder. He felt her quick move of resistance, ignored it and pulled her closer. "I will."

When his mouth was on hers, Anna accepted one more thing. Inevitability. She'd known they couldn't be together without passion rising up. Yet, she'd come to him freely and on equal terms. Between them there was a fire raging that she could only bank for so long. There would come a time, she knew, when nothing would stop it from consuming both of them. She slid her arms up his back and stepped closer to the heat.

When he lowered her to the sofa, she didn't protest but drew him closer. Just for a moment, she promised herself hazily, just for a moment she'd have a taste of what it could be like. His body was so firm against her. She could sense the desperation, sense it, and despite all good judgment, she reveled in it.

His mouth raced over her face. Her name was murmured again and again against her lips, her throat. She could taste the fire of brandy as his tongue met hers. The scent of candlewax surrounded her. With the music came a low, pulsing beat that urged, teased, enticed.

He had to touch her. He thought he'd go mad if he

couldn't have more. Then as he slid his hand over her, felt the softness, the race of her heart, he knew he'd never get enough. His hands, so wide, so large, passed over her with a tenderness that made her tremble. When he heard his name in her shaky whisper, he fought to keep himself from grabbing what he longed for. He brought his mouth back and found hers warm, willing and open.

Desperate, he fumbled with the buttons running down the front of her dress. His hands were so large, the buttons so small. The blood began to pound in his head. Then he discovered, to his delight, that his dignified Anna wore silk and lace next to her skin.

She arched when he found her, arched and shuddered, then strained for more. He was taking her beyond the expected, beyond the anticipated and into dreams. Large, wide-palmed hands continued to pass over her with incredible gentleness. They stroked, lingered, tested. Unable to resist, she let him guide her. Control no longer seemed essential. Ambitions became unimportant. Need. There was only one. For one mindless moment, she gave herself to it.

There was a desperation in him that grew sharper each time his heart beat. He knew what he wanted, what he would want until the grave. Anna. Only Anna. Her mouth was hot on his, her body cool and slim. The images that rushed through his mind were as dark and dangerous as any uncharted land. She clung to him and seemed to give everything. His head spun with it. Then she buried her face against his throat and went very still.

"Anna?" His voice was rough, his hands still gentle.

"I can't say this isn't what I want." The tug-of-war going on inside of her left her weak and frightened. "But I can't be sure it is." She shuddered once, then drew back. He could see her face in the candlelight, the skin pale, the eyes dark. Beneath his hand her heartbeat was fast and steady. "I never expected to feel this way, Daniel. I need to think."

Desire burned inside him. "I can think for both of us."

She lifted her hands to his face before he could kiss her again. "That's what I'm afraid of." Shifting, she sat up. Her dress was open nearly to her waist, with her soft white skin exposed for the first time to a man. But she felt no shame. Steadily she began to hook the buttons. "What is happening between us—what could happen between us—is the most important decision in my life. I have to make it myself."

He took her by the arms. "It's already been made."

Part of her thought he was right. Part of her was terrified he was. "You're sure of what you want. I'm not. Until I am, I can't promise you anything." The fingers that had been steady trembled before she could control them. "I may never be able to promise you anything."

"You know when I hold you that it's right. Can you tell me that when I touch you you don't feel that?"

"No, I can't." The more agitated he became, the calmer she forced herself to be. "I can't, and that's why I need time. I need time because whatever decision I make has to be made with a clear head."

"Clear head." Furious, aching with need, he rose to stalk the room. "My head hasn't been clear since the first time I laid eyes on you."

She rose, as well. "Then whether you like it or not, we both need time."

He picked up the brandy she'd left unfinished and downed it. "Time's what you need, Anna." He turned to her. She'd never seen him look fiercer, more formidable. A smart woman would guard her heart. Anna struggled to remember that. "I'll be in New York for three days. There's your time. When I come back, I'm coming for you. I want your decision then."

Her chin lifted, exposing a slender, elegant neck. Dignity covered her in a cool, silent wave. "Don't give me deadlines and ultimatums, Daniel."

"Three days," he repeated and set down the snifter before he snapped it in two. "I'll take you home."

Chapter 6

When three days turned into a week, Anna didn't know whether to be relieved or infuriated. Trying to be neither, to simply go about her life as she always had, wasn't possible. He'd given her a deadline, then didn't even bother to show up to hear her decision, which, she admitted, she hadn't made yet.

Invariably, whenever Anna set her mind to a problem, she solved it. It was a matter of thinking through all the levels and establishing priorities. There seemed to be too many levels in her relationship with Daniel for her to deal with each or any one of them rationally. On the one hand, he was a rude, boastful annoyance. On the other, he was fun. He could be unbearably arrogant—and unbearably sweet. His rough edges would never be completely smoothed off. His mind was admirably quick and clever. He schemed. He laughed at himself. He was overbearing. He was generous.

If she couldn't successfully analyze Daniel, how could

she hope to analyze her feelings for him? Desire. She'd had very little experience with that feeling, aside from her ambitions, but she recognized it. How would she recognize love? And if she did, what would she do about it?

The only thing Anna became certain of during Daniel's absence was that she missed him. She was certain of it because she'd been so sure she wouldn't even give him a second thought. She thought of little else. But if she gave in, if she threw caution to the winds and agreed to marry him, what would happen to her dream?

She could marry him, have his children, dedicate her life to him—and resent everything they built together because she would have divorced herself from her vocation. That meant living half a life, and Anna didn't think she could do it. If she refused him and went on with her plans, would that mean half a life, as well?

Those were the questions that tormented her at night, that nagged at her throughout the day. Those were the questions she found, then rejected answers for. So she made no decision, knowing once it was made, it would be final.

She forced herself to continue her routine. To tone down speculation and questions, she went to the theater with friends and attended parties. During the day, she threw herself into her work at the hospital with energy born of frustration.

Habitually she visited Mrs. Higgs first. Anna didn't need a degree to see that the woman was fading. Before seeing to all her other duties, Anna could spend as much time in 521 as needed.

A week after she'd last seen Daniel, making certain her smile was in place, Anna opened the door to Mrs. Higgs's room. This time the shades were drawn and there were more shadows than light. They seemed to be waiting. Anna saw

Mrs. Higgs was awake, staring listlessly at the faded flowers on her table. Her eyes brightened when she saw Anna.

"I'm so glad you came. I was just thinking of you."

"Of course I came." Anna set the magazines down. Instinct told her that pictures weren't what Mrs. Higgs needed today. "How else could I give you all the gossip about the party I went to last night?" On the pretext of tidying the sheets, Anna scanned the chart. Her heart sank. The deterioration of the past five days was increasing. But she was smiling as she took her seat beside the bed. "You know my friend Myra?" Anna was aware how much Mrs. Higgs enjoyed stories about Myra's escapades. "Last night she wore a strapless black dress cut two inches past discretion. I thought some of the older ladies would faint."

"And the men?"

"Well, let's just say Myra didn't miss a dance."

Mrs. Higgs laughed, then caught her breath as pain sliced through. Anna was on her feet instantly.

"Lie still. I'll get the doctor."

"No." Surprisingly strong, the thin hand gripped hers. "No, he'll just give me another shot."

Trying to soothe, Anna rubbed the frail hand as she took her pulse. "Just for the pain, Mrs. Higgs. You don't have to be in pain."

Calmer, Mrs. Higgs settled back again. "I'd rather feel pain than nothing. I'm all right now." She managed a smile. "Talking to you is much better than medicine. Did your Daniel come back yet?"

Still monitoring her pulse, Anna sat again. "No."

"It was so kind of him to visit me before he left for New York. Imagine his coming by here before he went to the airport."

The fact that he had was just one of the things that added to Anna's confusion. "He likes visiting you. He told me."

"He'd said he'd come again when he got back from New York." She looked at the week-old roses she refused to let the nurses take away. "It's so special to be young and in love."

Anna felt a stab of pain herself. Did he love her? He'd chosen her, he wanted her, but love was a different matter. She wished she had someone to talk to, but Myra had seemed so preoccupied lately and no one else would understand. She could hardly pour her problems out on Mrs. Higgs when she'd come to comfort. Instead, she grinned and patted her hand. "You must have been in love dozens of times."

"At least. Falling in love, that's the roller coaster, the ups and downs, the thrills. Being in love, that's the carousel—around and around with music playing. But staying in love…" She sighed, remembering. "That's the maze, Anna. There are all the twists and turns and dead ends. You have to keep going, keep trusting. I had such a short time with my husband, and never tried the maze again."

"What was he like, your husband?"

"Oh, he was young, and ambitious. Full of ideas. His father had a grocery store, and Thomas wanted to expand it. He was very clever. If he'd lived… But that wasn't meant. Do you believe some things are meant, Anna?"

She thought about her need to heal, her studies. She tried not to think of Daniel. "Yes. Yes, I do."

"Thomas was meant to die young, like a lovely flash fire. Still, he packed so much into the short years. I admire him more as I look back. Your Daniel reminds me of him."

"How?"

"That drive—the kind you can see on their faces. It tells you they're going to do amazing things." She smiled again, fighting back another surge of pain. "There's a ruthlessness that means they'll do whatever is necessary to accomplish it, and yet there's kindness, very basic kindness. The kind that made Thomas give a handful of candy to a child who didn't have the money. The kind that makes your Daniel visit an old woman he doesn't know. I've changed my will."

Alarmed, Anna straightened. "Mrs. Higgs—"

"Oh, don't fret." She closed her eyes a moment, willing her body to build back some strength. "I can see on your face you're worried I've tangled you up in it. Thomas left me a nest egg, and I invested. It's given me a comfortable life. I have no children, no grandchildren. It's too late for regrets. I need to give something back. I need to be remembered." She looked at Anna again. "I talked to Daniel about it."

"To Daniel?" Disturbed, Anna leaned closer.

"He's very smart, just like Thomas. I told him what I wanted to do, and he told me how it could be done. I've had my lawyer set up a scholarship. Daniel agreed to let me name him executor so he can handle the details."

Anna opened her mouth to brush the subject of death aside, then realized she would be doing so only for herself. "What kind of scholarship?"

"For young women going into medicine." Pleased with the stunned look on Anna's face, Mrs. Higgs smiled. "I knew you'd like it. I thought about what I could do, then I thought of you, and of all the nurses here who've been so kind to me."

"It's a wonderful thing, Mrs. Higgs."

"I could have died alone, without anyone to sit and talk to me. I was lucky." She reached out and curled her fingers around Anna's hand. Because it was difficult to feel, she tightened them. Anna felt barely any pressure. "Anna, don't make the same mistake I did by thinking you don't need anyone. Take love where it's offered. Let it live with you. Don't be afraid of the maze."

"No," Anna murmured. "I won't."

There was barely any pain now, barely anything at all. Mrs. Higgs stared at the outline of light around the shades. "Do you know what I'd do if I could start all over again, Anna?"

"What would you do?"

"I'd have it all." The light was blurring, but she managed to smile. "It's so foolish to think you have to settle for pieces. Thomas would have known better." Exhausted, she closed her eyes again. "Stay with me a little while."

"Of course I will."

So she sat in the shadowed room. Keeping the frail hand in hers, she listened to the sound of breathing. And waited. When it was over, she fought back the surge of anger, the wave of denial. Carefully, Anna rose and pressed a kiss to Mrs. Higgs's forehead. "I won't forget you."

Calm, controlled, she walked down the corridor to Mrs. Kellerman. Deluged by five new admissions, the nurse gave her a brief glance. "We're a bit rushed now, Miss Whitfield."

She stood very straight. When she spoke her voice held both authority and patience. "You'll need to call the doctor for Mrs. Higgs."

Instantly alert, Mrs. Kellerman rose. "She's having pain?"

"No." Anna folded her hands. "Not anymore."

Understanding flickered in her eyes, and, Anna thought for a moment, regret. "Thank you, Miss Whitfield. Nurse Bates, call Dr. Liederman immediately. Five twenty-one." Without waiting for an answer, she went down the corridor herself. Anna followed her as far as the door and again waited. Moments later, Kellerman looked back. "Miss Whitfield, you don't need to stay here now."

Determined, Anna kept her hands folded and her eyes direct. "Mrs. Higgs had no one."

Compassion came through, and for the first time, respect. Stepping back from the bed, Kellerman put a hand on her arm. "Please wait outside. I'll tell the doctor you want to speak to him."

"Thank you." Anna walked down the corridor to the little L that was the waiting room and sat. As the minutes passed, she grew calmer. This was what she would face, she reminded herself, day after day for the rest of her life. This was the first time—her stomach knotted and unknotted—but not the last. Death would become an intimate part of her life, something to be fought, something to be faced. Starting now, this minute, she would have to learn to defend herself against it.

On a deep breath she closed her eyes. When she opened them again, she saw Daniel walking toward her.

For a moment, her mind went blank. Then she saw the roses in his hand. Tears welled up, brimmed and were controlled. When she rose her legs were steady.

"I thought I'd find you here." Everything about him was aggressive—his walk, his face, his voice. She thought only briefly of the luxury of throwing herself into his arms and weeping.

"I'm here every day." That wouldn't change. Now, more than ever she knew she couldn't let it.

"It took longer than I thought to work things out in New York." And he'd spent his nights restless and wakeful thinking of her. He started to speak again in the same tough, no-nonsense tone, but something in her eyes stopped him. "What's wrong?" He only had to see her glance at the roses to know. "Damn." With a whispered oath he let them fall to his side. "Was she alone?" ·

That he would ask that first, that he would think of that first, made her reach out her hand to him. "No, I was with her."

"That's good then." Her hand was icy in his. "Let me take you home."

"No." If he were too kind, her composure would never hold up. "I want to speak with her doctor."

He started to object, then slipped an arm around her shoulders. "I'll wait with you."

In silence, they sat together. The scent of the roses flowed over her. They were young buds, very fresh, still moist. Part of a cycle, she reminded herself. It wasn't possible to appreciate life unless you understood, accepted, the cycle.

Anna rose very slowly when the doctor joined them. "Miss Whitfield. Mrs. Higgs spoke of you to me many times. You're a medical student."

"That's right."

He nodded, reserving judgment. "You're aware that we removed a tumor—a malignant one some weeks ago. There was another. If we had operated again, it would have killed her. Our only choice was to make her as comfortable as possible."

"I understand." She understood, too, that one day she'd have to make such decisions herself. "Mrs. Higgs had no family. I want to make the funeral arrangements."

Her composure surprised him as much as her statement. Studying her face, he decided if she made it through medical school, he'd be interested in having her intern under him. "I'm sure that can be easily done. We'll have Mrs. Higgs's attorney contact you."

"Thank you." She offered her hand. Liederman found it cool, but firm. Yes, he'd like to watch her train.

"We're leaving," Daniel told her when they were alone.

"I haven't finished my shift."

"And you won't today." Taking her by the arm, he led her to the elevator. "You're allowed to let yourself breathe. Don't argue," he said, anticipating her. "Let's just say you're humoring me. There's something I want to show you."

She could have argued. Just knowing she had the strength to do so made her relent. She'd go with him because she knew she'd come back tomorrow and do whatever needed to be done.

"I'll have my driver take us to my house," he told her as they stepped outside. "We'll want my car."

"I have mine." Daniel only lifted a brow and nodded. "Wait a minute." Walking to the Rolls, he dismissed Steven. "We'll use yours. Do you feel like driving?"

"Yes. Yes, I do." She walked to the little white convertible.

"Very nice, Anna, but then I've always admired your taste."

"Where are we going?"

"North. I'll direct you."

Content to drive, to feel the wind and know no destination, she headed out of town. For a time, he left her to her own thoughts.

"Shedding tears doesn't make you weak."

"No." She sighed and watched the sun slant across the road. "I can't yet. Not yet. Tell me about New York."

"A mad place. I like it." He grinned and threw his arm over the seat. "It's not a place to live, not for me, but the excitement can get into your blood. You know Dunripple Publishing?"

"Yes, of course."

"Now it's Dunripple and MacGregor." He'd been satisfied with the way the deal had swung, or more accurately, the way he'd pushed it.

"Prestigious."

"Prestigious be damned," he told her. "They needed new blood and cold cash."

"What did you need?"

"To diversify. I don't like bundling all my interests together."

She frowned a bit, thinking. "How do you know what to buy?"

"Old companies losing ground, new companies breaking it. The first gives me something to fix, the second something to—" he hesitated, unsure of what word would suit "—explore," he said finally.

"But you can't be sure all the companies you buy will make it."

"All of them won't. That's the game."

"Sounds like a vicious one."

"Maybe; it's life." He studied her. Her face was still a bit too pale, her eyes a bit too calm. "A doctor knows all his patients won't make it. It doesn't stop him from taking a new one."

He understood. She should have expected it. "No, it doesn't."

"We all take risks, Anna, if we're really alive."

She drove mostly in silence, following Daniel's directions. Thoughts rushed in and out of her head, feelings tossed freely inside of her. It was a long quiet drive and should have calmed her. By the time they drove along the coast, she was tight with nervous energy. Spotting a little store, Daniel gave a wave of his hand.

"Stop in here."

Agreeable, Anna pulled into the gravel lot beside it. "Is this what you wanted to show me?"

"No. But you're going to get hungry."

She pressed a hand on her stomach before she opened

the door. "I think I already am." Thinking they'd hardly do better than a box of crackers, Anna followed him inside.

It was a crowded little hodgepodge of a store, with canned goods lined on shelves, dry goods packed in doorless cupboards. A freshly waxed floor shone back at her. A fan creaked in slow circles swirling the heat.

"Mr. MacGregor!" With obvious pleasure, a round woman eased herself from a stool behind the counter.

"Ah, Mrs. Lowe. Pretty as ever."

She had a face like a horse and knew it. She greeted the flattery with a loud guffaw. "What can I do for you today?" She gave Anna an unconcealed survey, grinned and showed a missing incisor.

"The lady and I need the makings of a picnic." He leaned over the counter. "Tell me you have some of that mouth-watering roast beef you gave me last time."

"Not an ounce." She winked at him. "But I have some ham that'll make you roll your eyes and thank your Maker."

All charm, he took her pudgy hand and kissed it. "I'll roll my eyes and thank you, Mrs. Lowe."

"I'll make a sandwich for the lady. And two for you." The look she gave him was as shrewd as it was friendly. "I'll throw in a thermos of lemonade—if you buy the thermos."

"Done."

With a cackle, she made her way into a back room.

"You've been here before," Anna said dryly.

"Now and again. Quite a little place." He knew the Lowes ran it themselves and kept it stocked and spotless. "I'm thinking if they added themselves another room, put in a counter and a grill, Mrs. Lowe could make herself famous with her sandwiches."

She saw the look in his eyes and smiled. "Lowe and MacGregor."

With a laugh, he leaned on the counter. "No, sometimes it's best to be a silent partner."

When Mrs. Lowe came back, she carried a huge wicker basket. "Have your picnic and bring the basket back—it's not new." She winked again. "But the thermos is."

Daniel took out his wallet and pulled out bills. Enough to make Anna's eyebrow lift. "My best to your husband, Mrs. Lowe."

The bills disappeared into some handy pocket. "You and the lady have a good time."

"We will." Toting the basket, Daniel swung through the door. "Do you trust me to drive?"

Anna already had the keys in her hands. She hadn't allowed anyone behind the wheel but herself, though her father had hinted and Myra had nagged. Hesitating only a moment, she handed them to him.

Moments later, they were driving straight up. She'd never seen a road so narrow, so winding. The view over the side took her breath away with its sheer cliffs. There was color among the endless gray: touches of red, hints of green. In places it seemed as though the rock had been hewn away with a broadax, in others hacked at with a pick. Waves crashed free against rock, then washed back only to crash again. There was violence here, she thought. An endless war that was also a cycle. With the smell of the sea around her, she leaned back.

Mile after mile they climbed. Trees that dotted the sides of the road grew slanted, leaning away from the constant wind. Anna wondered what Daniel would do if another car came down the road toward them. It didn't worry her. She watched a sea bird skim over the surface of the water below, then soar up toward the sun.

When the road leveled again, she was almost disappointed. Then she saw the stretch of land ahead. Over-grown, rocky, desolate, it spread out to the very edge of the cliff. Something shot into her, sharp as an arrow, sweet as a kiss. Recognition.

Daniel stopped the car and stood, absorbing everything. As it always did, the wildness of it drew him. He could feel the sea, feel the wind. He was home.

Saying nothing, Anna stepped from the car. She was buffeted by the turbulence there, but she could also sense the peace. Whether it was in the air or the land itself, she knew this sense of constant movement and inner stillness would always remain.

"This is your land," she murmured when he stood beside her.

"Aye."

The wind blew her hair into her face, but she pushed it back, impatient. She wanted to see clearly. "It's beautiful."

She said it so simply that he couldn't speak. Until that moment he hadn't realized just how desperately he wanted her to accept it, to understand it. More, he hadn't known how important it was to him that she love it as he had from the first moment he'd seen it. The sun beat down on his face as he brought her hand to his lips.

"The house will go there." He pointed, and began to walk with her. "Near the cliff, so you'll hear the sea, al-most be part of it. It'll be made of stone, tons of it, so it'll rise up and hold its own. Some of the windows will come nearly to the ceiling and the front door will be as wide as three men. Here—" he stopped, gauging the position with his eyes "—there will be a tower."

"Towers?" Almost hypnotized, Anna looked up at him. "You make it sound like a castle."

"That's right. A castle. The MacGregor seal will stand above the door."

She tried to imagine it and shook her head. She found it both exciting and incomprehensible. "Why so much?"

"It'll last. My great-grandchildren will know it." Leaving her, he walked back to the car for the basket.

Unable to judge his mood or her own, Anna helped spread the blanket Mrs. Lowe had provided. Besides the sandwiches, there was a bowl of well-spiced potato salad and two thick slices of cake. With her skirt flowing over her knees, Anna sat cross-legged and ate while she watched the clouds.

So much was happening so fast, and yet it seemed her life was suspended in some kind of limbo. She no longer knew what she'd find if she turned right, if she turned left. The path that had once seemed so clear to her had taken on some odd curves. She couldn't see around them. Because Daniel was quiet, she kept her silence, aware he was no more comfortable than she.

"In Scotland," he began, as if talking to himself, "we lived in a little cottage no bigger than the garage on your house. I was five, maybe six, when my mother took sick. After she'd delivered my brother, she was never really well again. My grandmother would come every day to cook and help tend the baby. I'd sit with my mother, talk to her. I didn't realize then how young she was."

Anna sat with her hands in her lap and her eyes intense. A few weeks before, she would have listened politely if he had spoken of his past. Now, it seemed half her world hinged on what he would say. "Go on, please."

It wasn't easy for him, nor had he planned to speak of it. Now that he'd begun, he discovered he'd needed to tell her all along. "My father would come home from the mines, his skin black, his eyes red. God, how tired he must have been, but he sat with my mother, played with the baby, listened to me. She hung on, nearly five years, and when I was ten, she just slipped away. She was suffering the whole time, but she never complained."

Anna thought of Mrs. Higgs. This time she let the tears fall. Daniel said nothing for a moment but listened to the sea.

"My grandmother came to live with us. Tough old bird. She made me toe the line—study in books. When I was twelve I went to work in the mines, but I could read and write and work with figures better than the grown men. I was as big as some of them already." He laughed at that and flexed his hand into a fist. More than once he'd been grateful for it.

"The mines were hell. Dust in your lungs, in your eyes. Every time the earth shook, you waited to die and hoped it'd be quick. I was about fifteen when McBride, who owned the mine, took notice of me. He found out I was clever with numbers, so he used to have me come in and do a bit of figuring for him. In his way, he was a fair man, so I was paid for the extra work. Within a year, I was out of the mines and doing his books. My hands were clean. As soon as I'd started working, my father had me put half my earnings in a tin jar. We could have used the money day to day, but he wouldn't have it. Even when I was making more in the office, he made me put half the money aside in that jar. It was the same with my brother, Alan."

"He wanted you to get out," Anna murmured.

"Aye. He had a dream for me and Alan to get out of the mines, away from everything he'd had to live with." He turned to her, his eyes hot and angry. "I was twenty when the main shaft caved in. We dug for three days, three nights. Twenty men were gone, my father and my brother with them."

"Oh, Daniel." She reached out, resting her head against his shoulder. It was more than grief. She could feel the fury, the resentments, the guilt. "I'm sorry."

"When we buried them, I swore it wasn't the end. It was the beginning. I'd make enough to get out. By the time I did, it was too late to take my grandmother. She'd lived a long time and only asked me one thing before she died, that I see the line go on, that I not forget where we'd come from. I'm keeping that promise, Anna—" he turned her so she'd look at him "—for her, for me, with every stone that goes into this house."

She understood him now, perhaps too well for her own good. She understood that there on the windswept cliff in the middle of the barren land he'd chosen she'd finally, irreversibly fallen in love with him. But with understanding came only more questions.

Rising, she walked toward the plot of land where he envisioned his home. He'd build it, she knew. And it would be magnificent. "They'd be proud of you."

"I'll go back one day to see it all again, to remember it all. I'll want you with me."

She turned, and as she did, wondered if she'd been waiting to make that move all of her life. Perhaps it was the first step into the maze. "I'm afraid I'll never be able to give you everything you want, Daniel. I'm more afraid that I'll try."

He stood and walked toward her. There was still too much space between them when he stopped. "You told me you needed time. I asked you to make a decision. Now, I'm asking you what it is."

Anna stood, poised on the edge of everything.

Chapter 7

She wanted to give him everything he asked, to give him things he'd never even dreamed of. She wanted to take everything she could grab and hold on to. In that moment she understood what taking just one step forward could mean to both of them. She wondered if he did. One step forward would irrevocably change their lives even if a step back could somehow be taken later. One step and there would be no altering what was said, what was done or what was given. Anna believed in destiny, destiny met with eyes open and mind clear.

Though common sense fought to remain in charge, her heart slowly, willfully took command. What was love? In that moment she understood only that it was a force larger, stronger than the logic she had always lived by. Love had started wars, toppled empires, driven men mad and turned women into fools. She could reason for hours, but she would never diminish the power of that one all-encompassing force.

They stood on the cliffs, with the wind roaring against the rocks, moaning through the high grass, beating against the land he'd chosen to fulfill a dream and a promise. If Daniel was her destiny, she would meet him head-on.

He looked fiercer than ever, almost frightening, with his eyes burning into hers and the sun fiery at his back. Zeus, Thor, he might have been either. But he was flesh and blood, a man who understood destiny and would break mountains to achieve the one he had chosen. He'd chosen her.

She took her time, determined to make her decision with a clear head. But the emotions boiling inside her weren't calm. How could she look at him, read the need in his eyes and be calm? He'd spoken of family, of promises, of a future she wasn't sure she could share with him. But there was something she could share now, something she could give, and give only once. Leading with her heart, Anna stepped forward and into his arms.

They came together like thunder, urgent, tempestuous, strong. Her mouth met his with all the chaotic longing she'd held down. She felt the power soar, the fire spread fast and out of control. There was only here; there was only now.

His hands were in her hair, his fingers raking desperately through it so that the combs she wore fell unheeded to the ground. His mouth was restless and urgent, rushing over her face, meeting her lips, then moving on, as if it were vital that he taste everything at once. She heard her name come low and vibrant, then tasted it herself as he murmured against her mouth. Even as she pressed strongly against him, she felt the give of her own body, the incredible fluid yielding only a woman can experience. Her mind leaped forward with the pleasure of discovering the magic of submission when mixed with demand. Then her thoughts scattered, leaving only one. She was where she wanted to be.

Together they lowered themselves to the grass, wrapped so tightly that even the wind couldn't come between them. Like lovers separated for years, they rushed together with no holding back, no hesitation. Eager to feel the delight of flesh against flesh, she tugged on his shirt. Muscles he'd earned while still a boy corded his arms, rippled over his back. Aroused by the sheer strength of him, she allowed her hands free play, and learned the spiraling joy of having a man—her man—groan at her touch.

He wanted her—here, now, exclusively. She could feel it with every beat of her own pulse. Until that moment she hadn't realized just how important it had been to her to be sure of it. Whatever else he wanted from her, whatever plans he'd scrupulously made were tossed to oblivion by one overpowering force. Desire. It was pure; it was desperate; it was theirs.

He'd wanted to be careful, to be gentle, but she was driving him beyond anything he'd experienced. Fantasies, dreams paled foolishly beside reality. She was much more than a goal to be won or a woman to be wooed. Her hands were slim and strong and curious, her mouth warm and insistent. The need that pounded through him concentrated at the base of his neck so that the sound of it roared through his brain, leaving him deaf to the crash of the waves far below. He could smell the wild grass as he buried his lips at her throat, but her scent, subtle, quiet, was more pervasive. She was so small, so heart-breakingly soft that he fought to keep his work-toughened hands easy as he undressed her, but she arched against each touch, wantonly demanding more.

He couldn't resist her, nor could he resist any longer the pressure building inside him. Racing against passion, he yanked the rest of her clothes aside and gave himself to need. Her skin was pale as milk under the hot summer sun, her body as trim and efficient as her mind. No other woman, no dream had ever aroused him more. With a sound that rumbled deep in his throat, he met her gasp of astonished pleasure.

There was more? She had thought it impossible, but everywhere his lips tarried brought her fresh bursts of unspeakable delight. Should she have known a man and a woman could share something so dark, so sultry under a full sun? Could she have known that she, always so self-disciplined, so rational, would give herself to passion in a field of grass on a cliff top? All she understood was that it didn't matter when, it didn't matter where, it was and would always be Daniel.

Her emotions seemed to race just ahead of reason. She wanted to savor each new experience, but before she could absorb one, another tumbled down on her, layering all into a mass of sensations impossible to separate. With a breathless laugh she realized it wasn't necessary to understand each one, but simply to feel. There was no fear in her as desire began to peak, but a wild anticipation.

The blood pounded in his veins, swam in his head until he thought he'd explode from it. Her body burned with the same fire as his, she moved to the same throbbing music. But she was innocent. He knew, even as he ached to take her with fury and speed, that control was vital. Her arms clutched him, her hips thrust up in uninhibited offering. And the fear of harming something so precious snaked through him. He struggled to catch his breath when she reached for him.

"Anna—"

"I want you." Her murmur was like thunder in his ear. "I need you, Daniel." In hearing it, sweet pain spread through him. In saying it, she felt glorious.

"I won't hurt you." He lifted his head to see her lips curve, her eyes cloud.

"No, you won't hurt me."

He called on all his strength of will as he slipped into her. She was so warm, so moist that his head nearly burst with a new flood of emotion. He'd had women before. But not like this. He'd given himself to passion before. Never, never like this.

She felt him enter her, pierce her, fill her. Her innocence was gone in a heartbeat with a pleasure so vast that all pain was smothered. Power. It swept over her like the wind, like the thunder, eclipsing that first surge of wonder. Drunk with it, she gripped him tighter. She heard him call her name before his mouth fastened on hers. They hurled aside control and took each other.

He knew about the cat that swallowed the canary. As he lay on the wild grass with Anna at his side, Daniel felt like a cat who'd feasted on a baker's dozen. The contentment that had somehow always skidded just out of his reach settled through him with a sleepy sigh.

He'd chosen a lovely, intelligent woman to marry. It was a logical choice for a man who intended to build an empire that would last for generations. Wasn't it lucky he'd fallen in love and discovered she was also caring, sweet and passionate? His wife-to-be, the mother of his yet-to-be-born children, fit him like a glove. He decided it paid to be lucky as well as shrewd.

She was quiet beside him but he knew from the easy way she breathed, the content way her hand rested in his, that she was lost in thoughts, not in regrets. Her head was nestled in the crook of his shoulder so naturally that he could have sworn they'd lain just like this before, grass soft at their backs, the sky clear and blue above. Cloud watchers, he thought. Children would toss themselves on the ground to find images and dreams in the clouds. He'd never had much time for it as a boy. With Anna, he could make time, and he wouldn't have to look for dreams.

He could have lain there for hours, with the surf and the wind and the sun. He had his woman, his land, and it was only the beginning. But he knew, of course, that they had to leave for the city soon. What he wanted with her and for her couldn't be accomplished in an empty field. But he kept his arm around her and lingered while dozens of plans formed and shifted in his head.

"There's more than enough room for us in the house," he said, half to himself. With his eyes nearly closed and the quiet glow of loving still lingering, he could picture her there. She'd add the touches he too often forgot—bowls of flowers, music. "Of course, you might want to change some things. Flounce it up some."

She watched the way the sun played through leaves. She'd just taken the step forward. It was already time for the step back. "Your house is fine the way it is, Daniel."

"Aye, well it's only temporary." He stroked his fingers through her hair while he looked at the plot where he would build his dream. Their dream now. How much sweeter it was now that he had someone to share it with. "When this one's finished we'll sell the one in Boston. Or maybe we'll keep it for business. I'll be cutting down on my traveling once I have a wife."

Overhead clouds moved slowly, too lofty to be persuaded by the wind that rustled the grass. "Traveling's important to your business."

"For now." She felt his shoulder move under her head in a careless shrug. "Before long, they'll come to me. And they'll come here. I don't intend to marry, then spend my time away from my wife."

Her hand rested lightly on his chest. She wondered if he knew how smugly he used the phrase *my wife*. A man might use the same tone to describe his shiny new car. "I'm not going to marry you, Daniel."

"I'll still have to fly into New York now and again, but you can go with me."

"I said I'm not going to marry you."

With a laugh, he pulled her up until she lay half across him. Her skin was warm from sun and loving. "What do you mean you're not going to marry me? Of course, you are."

"No." She laid a hand on his face. Her touch was as soft as her eyes. "I'm not."

"How can you say that now?" He had her by the shoulders. Panic was his first reaction as he recognized the calm, patient look. Part of his success was the ability to turn panic to anger, and anger to determination. "It's not the time for games."

"No, it's not." Calm, she shifted away and began to dress.

Torn between puzzlement and fury, he grabbed her wrists before she could slip into her blouse. "We've just made love. You came to me."

"I came to you freely," she returned. "We needed each other."

"And we're going to go on needing each other. That's why you're going to marry me."

She tried to let out her breath slowly, soundlessly. "I can't."

"Why in hell not?"

Her stomach muscles were beginning to quiver. Her skin was chilled under the bright summer sun. She wanted him to release her but knew he'd ignore any resistance. Suddenly she wanted to run, to run faster than she ever had. Instead, she remained still. "You want me to marry you, start a family, pick up and go whenever and wherever your business or whims take you." She had to swallow because she knew she spoke the truth. "To do that I'd have to give up something I've wanted almost as long as I can remember. I won't do it, Daniel, not even for you."

"This is nonsense." To prove it he gave her a brisk shake. "If the damn degree is so important, go on and get it then. You can study just as easily married to me."

"No." Easing away, she busied her hands with her clothes. She wouldn't be bullied, and she wouldn't be charmed, though he seemed to be an expert on both. "If I went back to school as Mrs. Daniel MacGregor, I'd never finish. You'd stop me even if you didn't mean to."

"Damn it, that's ridiculous." He stood naked and glorious with the sun at his back. For a moment Anna wanted to open her arms and invite him back to her, to agree with anything he said. Purposefully she stood.

"It's not. And I'm going to earn my degree, Daniel. I have to."

"So you're choosing your doctoring over me." Hurt, angry, he didn't care if his words were unfair. He saw the one thing that would make his life whole, make it real, slipping away.

"I want you both." She swallowed. How could she judge his reaction when she still wasn't sure of her own? "I won't marry you," she repeated. "But I'll live with you."

His eyes narrowed into slits. "You'll what?"

"I'll live with you in your house in Boston until September. After that we could get an apartment off campus. And then…"

"And then what?" His words shot out like sand from under a tire.

She lifted her hands then let them fall. "Then I don't know."

Her head was thrown back in pride so that the wind tossed her hair. But her face was very pale, her eyes unsure. He loved her to the point of madness and his anger was nearly as great. "Damn you, Anna, I want you for a wife, not for a mistress."

The doubts cleared from her eyes to be replaced by a fury to match his own. No longer pale, her skin glowed with indignation. "And I'm not offering to be one." Turning on her heel, she started back to the car. He grabbed her by the arm and whirled her around so quickly that her feet nearly slid out from under her.

"What the hell are you offering then?"

"To live with you." It wasn't often she shouted, but when she did, she gave it everything. If he hadn't been so angry, there would have been room for respect. "Not be kept by you. I don't want your money or your big house or your dozen roses a day. It's you I want. God knows why."

"Then marry me." Still naked, still raging, he dragged her against him.

"Do you think you can have anything you want just by yelling louder, just by being stronger?" She shoved him away and stood, small and slim and stunning. "I'll give you only so much and no more."

He dragged both hands through his hair. How was a man to deal with such a woman? "If you won't think of your reputation, I have to."

She lifted a brow. "You have to do nothing but think of your own." In the regal manner she could assume so effortlessly, she let her gaze drift over him. "You don't seem very concerned about it now."

In one furious move, he swept up his pants. Another man might have looked foolish. Daniel looked magnificent. "A few minutes ago I seduced you," he began.

"Don't delude yourself." Cool and confident, she picked up his shirt. "A few minutes ago we made love. It had nothing to do with seduction."

He took the shirt from her and slipped it on. "You're tougher than you look, Anna Whitfield."

"That's right." Pleased with herself, she started to gather up the picnic things. "You told me once to take you as you are. Now I'm telling you the same. If you want me, Daniel, it has to be on my terms. Think about it." She left him half-dressed and walked to the car.

They barely spoke on the long drive back. Anna was no longer angry, but drained. So much had happened in a short span of time, and none of it had been in her carefully worked out plans. She needed time to think, to evaluate and to recharge. Daniel was electric. He didn't have to speak for her to read his temper.

The hell with his temper, she thought recklessly. Let him be angry. It was something he did well. Not everyone looked magnificent when he ranted and raged.

His mistress. Her own temper began to sizzle but she waited for it to subside. She'd be no man's mistress, Anna told herself as she settled back and folded her arms. And no man's wife until she was ready. She would, though the thought still made her pulse skittish, be one man's lover. In her own quiet fashion, she was as determined as Daniel to have her way.

Live with him. Daniel gripped the wheel tightly as he took a turn faster than a rational man would have dared. He was offering her half of everything he had, half of everything he was. Most importantly, he was offering her his name. And she was tossing it back in his face.

Did she think he would have taken her innocence if he

hadn't believed they were committed to each other? What kind of woman would refuse an honest proposal and opt to run off like a renegade child thumbing her nose at what was proper? He wanted a wife, damn it, a family. She wanted a piece of paper that said she could poke needles into people.

He should have taken her advice from the beginning. Anna Whitfield was the last woman in Boston who would make him a suitable wife. So he would forget about her. He'd drop her at her door, say a cool goodbye and drive away. But he could still taste her, still feel the way her skin had slid under his fingers, still smell the scent of her hair as it had floated around her body—and his.

"I won't have it."

With a squeal of brakes he stopped at the curb in front of her house. A few yards away, Anna's mother clipped roses. At the explosion, she looked up and nervously gripped her shears. The fact that a quick glance showed her none of her neighbors were about relieved her only a little as Daniel gunned the convertible's engine.

"That," Anna said with perfect calm, "is your privilege."

"Now you listen to me." Turning slightly, Daniel gripped her by both shoulders. He didn't want to argue, he didn't want to fight; the moment those patient brown eyes met his he wanted to drag her against him and make love with her until they were both too exhausted to speak.

Anna lifted a brow. "I'm listening."

He groped for what needed to be said. "What happened between us doesn't happen with everyone. I know."

She smiled a little. "I'll have to take your word for that."

Frustration boiled. "That's part of the problem," he mumbled and ordered himself to be as calm as she. "I want to marry you, Anna." In the rose bushes, Mrs. Whitfield dropped her shears with a quiet thump. "I've wanted to marry you from the first minute I saw you."

"That's part of the problem." Because most of her heart was already his, Anna lifted both hands to his face. "You wanted what was suitable and decided I was it. You want me to fit a slot in your life. Perhaps I could, but I won't."

"It's more than that now—much more." As he dragged her closer, she saw the flare of desire in his eyes then tasted it on his lips. Without hesitation, without artifice, Anna met his greed with her own. Yes, it was more than that now—perhaps more than either of them could deal with. When they were together like this, everything else faded into insignificance. That's what frightened her. That's what exhilarated her.

Desperately, he pushed her away again. "You see what we have together. What we could have."

"Yes." Her voice wasn't as steady now, but her determination hadn't wavered. "And I want it. I want you—but not marriage."

"I want you to share my name."

"And I want to share your heart first."

"You're not thinking clearly." Neither was he. Cautious, he dropped his hands from her shoulders. "You need a little time."

"No, I don't." Before he could stop her she slipped from the car. "But it's obvious you do. Goodbye, Daniel."

Mrs. Whitfield watched her daughter stride easily toward the house. Moments later she watched Daniel drive recklessly down the street. Then remembering whose car he was driving, he ground the gears into Reverse and backed up as recklessly as he'd gone forward. He slammed the door, shot a ferocious look at the house and stamped away in the opposite direction. Hand to her heart, she dashed up the walk and through the front door.

"Anna!" Fluttering her hands, she caught her daughter at the base of the staircase. "What's going on?"

Anna wanted to be alone. She wanted to go to her room, shut the door and lie on the bed. There was so much to absorb, so much to savor. She needed to weep and wasn't even sure why. Patient, she waited. "Going on?"

"I was clipping the roses." Flustered, Mrs. Whitfield shook her half-filled basket. "And I heard, well I couldn't help but hear..." She let her words trail off, unnerved by Anna's calm brown eyes, which suddenly seemed so mature. To give herself a minute, Mrs. Whitfield carefully pulled off her gardening gloves and laid them on a table.

"I understand you weren't eavesdropping, Mother."

"Of course not! I wouldn't dream—" She caught herself sliding away from the point and straightened her shoulders. "Anna, are you and Mr. MacGregor— Did you...?" The sentence wandered away as she shifted her hands on the basket.

"Yes." With a private smile, Anna stepped from the landing. "We made love this afternoon."

"Oh." It was a feeble response, but the only one she could come up with.

"Mother—" Anna took the basket from her hands "—I'm not a child any longer."

"Obviously." With a deep breath, Mrs. Whitfield faced her duty. "However, if Mr. MacGregor has seduced you, then—"

"He didn't."

Having revved herself up, Mrs. Whitfield could only blink at the interruption. "But you said—"

"I said we made love. He didn't have to seduce me."

Anna took her mother by the arm. "Maybe we should sit down."

"Yes." Shaky, she let herself be led. "Maybe we should."

In the parlor Anna sat beside her mother on the sofa. How should she begin? Never in her wildest dreams had she imagined sitting with her mother in this fussy parlor and discussing romance, love and sex. Taking a deep breath, she plunged. "Mother, I'd never been with a man before. I wanted to be with Daniel. It wasn't something I did impetuously, but something I gave a great deal of thought to."

"I've always said you think too much," Mrs. Whitfield responded automatically.

"I'm sorry." Used to parental criticism, Anna laid her hands quietly in her lap. "I know it's not something you want to hear, but I can't lie to you."

Love, propriety and confusion warred together. Love won. "Oh, Anna." In a rare gesture, Mrs. Whitfield gathered Anna close. "Are you all right?"

"Of course I am." Touched, Anna let her head rest against her mother's shoulder. "I feel wonderful. It's like— I don't know—being unlocked."

"Yes." She blinked back tears. "That's how it should be. I know we've never really talked of such things. We should have, but then you went off to that school and those books..." She remembered her shock when she had picked one up to give it a casual glance. "I suppose it all made me feel inadequate."

"It's nothing like books." Anna discovered she could savor it after all.

"No, it's not." She shifted to take both her daughter's hands. "Books can be closed. Anna, I don't want you to be hurt."

"Daniel won't hurt me." She was warmed even now, remembering how gentle he'd struggled to be. "In fact, he's much too concerned about not hurting me. He wants me to marry him."

Mrs. Whitfield breathed a sigh of relief. "I thought I heard him say so, but you sounded as though you were fighting."

"Not fighting, disagreeing. I'm not going to marry him."

"Anna." When her mother drew away, her face was stern. "What kind of nonsense is this? I admit I don't always understand you, but I know you well enough to be sure nothing would have happened between the two of you if you hadn't cared very deeply."

"I do." Losing some of her composure, Anna pressed her fingers to her eyes. "Maybe too much, it's frightening. He wants a wife, Mother, almost the way a man wants a shoe that fits well."

"That's just their way." On firmer ground, Mrs. Whitfield sat back. "Some men are poets, some are dreamers, but most are just men. I know girls think there should be pretty words and lovely music, but life is much more basic than that."

Curious, Anna studied her. Her mother, she knew from experience, had never been much of a philosopher. "Did you want pretty words?"

"Of course." With a smile, Mrs. Whitfield thought of her past. "Your father is a good man, a very good man, but most of his words come out of law books. I think Mr. MacGregor's a good man."

"He is. I don't want to lose him, but I can't marry him."

"Anna—"

"I'm going to live with him."

Mrs. Whitfield opened her mouth, shut it again and swallowed. "I think I'd like a drink."

Rising, Anna walked to the liquor cabinet. "Sherry?"

"Scotch. A double."

Tension dissolved in amusement as Anna poured. "Daniel had a very similar reaction." She handed her mother the glass and watched her gulp it down. "I've never hidden anything from you."

The Scotch burned through her system. "No, no, you've always been painfully honest."

"I care very much for Daniel." Honest, Anna reminded herself and let out a long breath. "I'm in love with him. That isn't something I chose, so now I feel as though I have to take back some control. If I marry him, I'll lose everything I've been working for."

Mrs. Whitfield set down the empty glass. "Your degree."

"I know you don't understand that, either. No one seems to." She ran her hands through her hair. It fell loose to her shoulders and made her remember that her combs still lay where they had fallen in the grass. The combs didn't matter, they could be replaced. Other things had been lost on that cliff top that couldn't. "What I know, in my heart, is that if I marry Daniel now I'll never finish. And if I don't, I'll never forgive myself or him. Mother, I've tried to explain to you before that being a doctor isn't simply what I want to do, it's what I have to do."

"Sometimes we have to weigh one important thing against another, Anna, and choose."

"And sometimes we don't." Desperate for reassurance, she knelt at her mother's feet. "I know it's selfish to want it all, but I've thought it through over and over. I have to be a doctor, and I don't want to live without Daniel."

"And Daniel?"

"He wants marriage. He can't see beyond that, but he will."

"Always so sure of yourself, Anna." She recognized the

look in her daughter's eyes: calm, clear and filled with ruthless determination. She nearly sighed. "You would never ask for anything, and I was fooled into thinking you were absolutely content. Then, all at once, you would demand everything."

"I didn't choose to be a doctor any more than I chose to fall in love with Daniel. Both things just are."

"Anna, a step like this can bring you a lot of pain, a lot of unhappiness. If you love Daniel, then marriage—"

"It isn't time, and I can't be sure it ever will be." Frustrated, she rose and paced the room. "I'm terrified to make that kind of mistake—for him, as well as for myself. All I know is that now, right now, I don't want to be without him. Maybe it's wrong, but would it be better, would it be right if we continued to be lovers in secret? Can you tell me it would be more acceptable if we stole a few hours here and there, a night, an afternoon?"

"I could never tell you anything," her mother murmured.

"Oh, please." More frightened than she wanted to admit, Anna went to her mother again. "Now more than ever I want your understanding. It's not just desire, though that's certainly part of it. It's a need to be with him, to share some of his dreams, because I'm not sure I'll be able to share them all. To love him in secret would be hypocrisy. He means too much for that. I won't hide what I feel. I won't hide what I am."

Mrs. Whitfield looked at her only child, at her dark, earnest eyes, her soft, sculpted mouth. She wished she had the answers. "You know what you'll be up against? What people will say?"

"That doesn't matter to me."

"It never has," her mother muttered. "I know how impossible it is to talk you out of anything once your mind's made up, and you're too old for me to forbid anything, but, Anna, you can't ask me to approve."

"I know." For a moment, she laid her head in her mother's lap. "But if somewhere inside you, if in some little part you could understand, it would be enough."

Sighing, she touched her daughter's hand. "I haven't forgotten what it is to be in love. Maybe I do understand, and maybe that's why I'm afraid for you. Anna, you've never been anything but a good daughter, but..."

She had to smile, just a little. "But?"

"You've also always been a puzzle. I know I've never actually told you I was proud of you, but I am."

Anna felt a little quiver of relief work through her. "I know I never actually told you I needed you to be proud, but I do."

"I have to admit that I always hoped that you'd forget about medicine and settle down into a marriage where I could see you happy, and yet another part of me has watched you and cheered."

Her fingers curled around her mother's. "I don't know how to tell you how much that means to me."

"I think I know. Now your father..." She closed her eyes, unable to even imagine his reaction.

"He'll be upset, I know. I'm sorry."

"I'll handle him." The words came out on impulse, but she discovered they were true. Mrs. Whitfield straightened her shoulders.

With a smile, Anna lifted her head. For a moment, for the first time, she and her mother looked at each other woman to woman. "I love you, Mother."

"And I love you." She drew her up on the sofa. "I don't have to understand you for that."

With a sigh, Anna laid her head on her mother's shoulder. "Is it too much to ask for you to wish me luck?"

"As a mother, yes." She found herself smiling. "But not as a woman."

Chapter 8

As the days passed, Anna began to fear that she'd lost. There were no phone calls, no irate visits. No white roses were delivered to the door. The ones still cluttering her room and her mother's parlor were a testimony to what might have been. And they were wilting.

More and more often she caught herself looking out the window at the sound of a car passing, dashing to the phone on the first ring. Each time she did so, she swore at herself and promised not to do it again. But, of course, she did.

She never left the hospital without scanning the lot for the blue convertible. Each time she stepped out of the wide white building she expected to see a big, broad-shouldered, red-bearded man waiting impatiently by the curb. He was never there, but she never stopped looking.

It was disconcerting to learn that she'd come to depend on him, but it was even more disconcerting to discover what she'd come to depend on him for. Happiness. She could be content without him. She could certainly be satisfied with her life and her career. But Anna was no longer sure she could be happy unless Daniel was a part of her day-to-day life.

One day, as she read aloud to a young patient with a broken leg, her mind wandered. To her annoyance she had caught herself daydreaming several times during working hours since Daniel had driven away from her house. Lecturing herself, she brought her attention back to the patient and the story. Like sand, her thoughts scattered again.

The happy-ever-after tale she spun to the sleepy little girl wasn't reality. Certainly the last thing Anna wanted was to sit quietly by and wait for a prince to fit her with a glass slipper. And of course she was too practical to believe in castles in the clouds or magic until midnight. It was nice perhaps, in a story, to dream about white chargers and heroes, but a woman wanted more in real life. In real life, a woman wanted—well, a partner, Anna supposed, not a knight or a prince who would always have to be looked up to and admired. A real woman wanted a real man, and a smart one wasn't going to sit around in a tower and wait for one to come along. She was going to live her own life and make her own choices.

Anna had always been a firm believer in the making of one's own destiny, of fighting—with logic and patience— for one's needs. So why was she waiting around? she asked herself abruptly. If she was as independent as she professed and as she intended to behave, then why was she mooning around and waiting for the phone to ring? Anyone who sat placidly by until someone else called the shots was a fool and a loser. She didn't intend to be either.

Her mind made up, Anna continued to read until the little girl's eyes closed. Shutting the book, she strode out into the hall. On the way down, she passed a frazzled, heavy-eyed intern and nearly smiled. At the moment she was certain he wouldn't understand her twinge of envy. Perhaps no one would but another med student. Still, in a few months she wouldn't be able to leave the hospital on her own whim. It wouldn't hurt to take advantage of the time she had left.

Outside, the weather was nasty. It was gray and stormy and so hot that the rain seemed to steam the moment it hit the concrete. By the time she made it to her car, she was humming and soaked to the skin. She drove across town with the radio turned up as high as her spirits.

The building that housed Old Line Savings and Loan was dignified, staid and trustworthy. As she raced across the little patch of lawn, Anna wondered if Daniel had made any changes. Inside, there was fresh paint and new carpeting but business was still transacted in hushed whispers. Anna ran a hand through her hair, scattering water, then headed for the nearest clerk. She crossed her fingers behind her back.

Upstairs, Daniel looked over the ads that would run in the paper the following week. His manager had cringed when he'd brought in the files, but the young assistant Daniel had hired had been enthusiastic. Some decisions were meant to be made on instinct. Instinct told Daniel that the ads would increase both his business and his reputation. And one was every bit as important as the other. He was not only going to put Old Line back on its feet, he would have a branch in Salem within two years.

Even as the idea germinated, his thoughts drifted away from business. He remembered a windy cliff top and a woman with sable hair and dark eyes. The thrill that rippled through him was as fresh as it had been when his arms had been around her. Her taste was a lingering sensation nothing else had been able to replace. Even here, in the privacy of his office he could smell her, quiet and sweet.

With an impatient mutter, he pushed the papers aside and strode to the window. He should be seeing other women. Hadn't he sworn he would when he'd driven away from Anna? He'd meant to, even started to. But each and every time he tried to so much as think of another woman, Anna was there. She was so firmly planted in his mind that there wasn't room for anyone else. He wasn't going to get over her.

Daniel stared out at the steadily driving rain. From the window, the Boston he looked at seemed gray and depressed. It suited his mood. After he was finished with his stacks of paperwork and meetings, he'd take a walk along the river, fair weather or foul. He needed to be alone, away from servants, employees. But not away from Anna. He could follow the Charles from end to end and never escape Anna. How could you escape what was in your blood, in your bone? And Anna was there. No matter how he tried to pretend he had a choice, Anna was there.

He wanted to marry her. Daniel whirled away from the window to pace the room with his hands thrust in his pockets and his brows lowered. He'd chosen anger over despair and fury over fear. Damn the woman, he thought yet again. He wanted to marry her. He wanted to wake up in the morning and know she was there. He wanted to come home at night and be able to reach for her. He wanted to see his child grow inside her. And he wanted these things with a desperation as foreign to him as failure.

Failure? The word alone had him clenching his teeth. He was far from ready to admit failure. The hell with other women, Daniel decided abruptly. There was only one. He was going after her.

When the phone on his desk rang he was halfway to the door. Cursing all the way he went back to yank it up. "MacGregor."

"Mr. MacGregor, this is Mary Miles, head cashier. I apologize for interrupting you but there's a young woman down in the lobby who insists on seeing you."

"Have her make an appointment with my secretary."

"Yes, sir, I suggested that, but she insists on seeing you now. She says she'll wait."

"I don't have time to see everyone who walks in off the street, Mrs. Miles." Daniel checked his watch. Anna would be out of the hospital. He'd have to catch her at home.

"Yes, sir." The cashier felt herself being squeezed between two ungiving forces. "I explained that to her, but she's very insistent. She's very polite, Mr. MacGregor, but I don't think she's going to budge."

Losing patience, Daniel swore again. "Tell her…" His voice trailed off as the cashier's words formed a picture in his mind. "What's her name?"

"Whitfield. Anna Whitfield."

"What have you got her waiting in the lobby for?" he demanded. "Send her up."

The cashier rolled her eyes and reminded herself of the raise Mr. MacGregor had given across the board when he'd bought the bank. "Yes, sir. Right away."

She'd changed her mind. Victory didn't settle over him. He soared with it. His patience, though it had cost him dearly, had paid off. She was ready to be sensible. True, he hadn't imagined discussing marriage in his office, but he was willing to make some concessions. The plain truth was he was willing to make a great many concessions. But she was coming to him. He would have everything he wanted, including his pride.

The knock on his door was brisk and businesslike before his secretary pushed it open. "Miss Whitfield to see you, sir."

He briefly nodded a dismissal before his gaze and every thought in his head focused on Anna. She stood on the thick gray carpet he'd recently had installed, dripping from head to foot. The rain had washed her face clean and left her hair dark and shiny and curling to her shoulders. She quite simply took his breath away.

"You're wet." His words came out sounding more like an accusation than a statement of concern. She met it with a smile.

"It's raining." Good God, it was good to see him. For a moment she could only smile foolishly and take him in. His tie was off, his collar open. His hair showed evidence of being combed impatiently with his fingers. She wanted to open her arms and take him to her, where she was beginning to understand he belonged. Instead, she continued to smile and drip quietly on his elegant carpet. While she smiled, he stared. For several humming seconds, neither of them spoke.

Catching himself, Daniel cleared his throat and scowled at her. "Seems to me anybody studying medicine should know better than to run around soaking wet." He pulled open the door to a cabinet and took out a bottle of brandy. "You'll find yourself spending more time in that hospital of yours than you'd like."

"I don't think a little summer shower should do me much harm." For the first time it occurred to her how she must look, with her hair dripping and tangled, her clothes splattered with rain and her shoes damp. She kept her chin up. Wet or not, she had her dignity.

"Drink this, anyway." He thrust a snifter into her hand. "Sit."

"No, I'll ruin—"

"Sit," he repeated in one terse bark.

Lifting a brow, she walked to a chair. "Very well."

She sat, but he didn't. The sweet taste of victory had already faded. He knew just by looking at her that she hadn't changed her mind. Not Anna. The truth was he never would have fallen so helplessly in love with a woman whose mind could be swayed. She hadn't come to accept his offer of marriage, and he was far from ready to accept her alternative.

His lips curved a bit. His eyes took on a light that those accustomed to doing business with him would have recognized—and been wary of. Stand off, Daniel told himself. But there was no way he would let Miss Anna Whitfield know she had him on edge. He let his gaze run down her once more as she sat ruining the upholstery of his chair.

"Interested in a loan, Anna?"

She sipped and let the brandy calm her sudden nervousness. The easy tone and slight smile didn't fool her for an instant. So, he was still angry. What else should she have expected? Would she have fallen in love with a man who could be too easily cajoled? No, she'd fallen in love with Daniel because he was precisely what he was.

"Not at the moment." To give herself time, she studied the room. "Your office is very nice, Daniel. Dignified but not stuffy." There was a bold abstract on the wall done in different tones and shades of blue. Though it seemed to be no more than random shapes and lines, the sense of sexuality was throbbingly clear. She shifted her gaze from it to his. "Definitely not stuffy."

He'd seen her study the abstract and knew she understood it. He'd paid a stiff price for the Picasso because it had appealed to him and because his instincts had told him the value would skyrocket within a generation. "You're a hard woman to shock, Anna."

"That's true." And because it was, she found herself relaxing. "I've always felt life was too important to go through it pretending to be offended by it. I've missed the roses."

He leaned a hip against the corner of his massive desk. "I thought you didn't like me sending them to you."

"I didn't. Until you stopped." She left it at that, deciding that even she was entitled to some quirks. "I hadn't heard from you in several days and I wondered if I'd shocked you."

"Shocked me?" A few moments before he'd wavered between tension and boredom. With Anna here, everything seemed settled into place again. "I'm not one to shock easily, either."

"Offended then," she suggested, "because I'd choose to live with you rather than marry you."

He nearly smiled. Had he once said he liked a woman to speak her mind—to a point? It didn't seem odd at all that his opinion on that had already changed radically. "Annoyed," he corrected. "We might even go to infuriated."

She remembered his reaction. "Yes, I think we might. You're still angry."

"Aye. You're still set in your mind?"

"Yes."

Thoughtfully he drew out a cigar, running his fingers over it once before lighting it. In business, he knew how to handle an opponent. Force him to make the pitch. It kept a man in the driver's seat when the other player had to do the explaining. Smoke wreathed over his head as he watched her and waited. "Why did you come here, Anna?"

So, he didn't intend to give an inch. She took another slow sip of brandy. All right then, neither would she. "Because I realized I didn't want to go another day without seeing you." She set the brandy aside as the haze of his smoke billowed then cleared. "Do you mind?"

He let out an impatient huff of breath. Business and personal matters didn't always have the same rules. Still, the aim was to win. "It's hard for a man to mind the woman he intends to marry wanting to be with him."

"Good." She rose then and made a vain attempt to tidy her damp skirts. "Then you'll have dinner with me tonight."

His eyes narrowed. "A man usually likes to do the asking."

She sighed and gave a little shake of her head as she walked to him. "You're forgetting what century you're in again. I'll pick you up at seven."

"You'll—"

"Pick you up at seven," she finished then rose to her toes. When she found his lips with hers, it was soft and easy and completely right. "Thanks for the brandy, Daniel. I won't keep you any longer."

He found his voice by the time she'd walked to the door. "Anna."

She turned, a half smile on her lips. "Yes?"

He saw in the smile that she expected, even anticipated an argument. Change tactics and confuse, Daniel thought, and easily drew on his cigar. "It'll have to be seven-thirty. I have a late meeting."

He had the satisfaction of seeing a quick flicker of doubt cross her face before she nodded. "Fine."

When she shut the door at her back, she let out a long pent-up breath.

By his desk, Daniel grinned, chuckled and ultimately roared with laughter. Though he wasn't sure who'd gotten the best of whom, he discovered it didn't matter. He'd always been one to try a new game, new rules. He'd give Anna the cards and the deal. But, by God, he'd still win.

The rain had slowed to a drizzle by the time Anna arrived home. She found the house empty, but the scent of her mother's perfume still lingered in the hallway. Pleased to find herself alone, she went upstairs to indulge in a long hot bath. It was a good feeling, she discovered, to have taken the initiative. Once again she was in control, though her foundation was a bit shakier than it could have been.

Daniel MacGregor was not a man who could be manipulated. She'd learned that right from the beginning. But she did believe he was a man who would respond to negotiation. Her main problem would be to keep him from seeing just how much she'd give.

Everything. She closed her eyes as she squeezed the sponge and dripped hot water over her throat and breasts. If he discovered that, if pressed into a corner, she'd give him anything he wanted, he'd press her there without hesitation. A man like Daniel hadn't made it to the top by being a pushover. But she intended to make it to the top in her own profession, as well. So she had to be equally strong, equally determined.

After she picked him up, they'd have a quiet dinner, easy conversation. Over coffee they'd discuss—rationally—their situation. Before it was over, he would understand her feelings and her position. Anna sank down in the waters with a sigh. Who was she trying to fool? That didn't sound like dinner with Daniel MacGregor for a minute.

They'd spar with each other, argue, disagree and probably laugh a great deal. He'd very likely shout. It was entirely possible she'd shout, as well. When it was over, she doubted he'd understand anything, except that he wanted her to marry him.

Something fluttered inside her at the thought. He did want her. She might have gone through her entire life without anyone looking at her in just the way Daniel did. She might have gone through her life without anyone opening those sturdy locks she'd kept on her passion. What would her life have been like then?

Bland. She smiled at the word that sprang to mind. She certainly wouldn't settle for that now. She wanted Daniel MacGregor. And she was going to have him.

Keeping her self-confidence at a peak was half the battle, she realized as she stepped from the tub. It was so easy for it to slip away degree by degree while he looked at her. She wouldn't allow it to happen tonight. With a towel wrapped around her hair, she bundled into a robe. *She* was taking *him* to dinner. Whatever slight edge that gave her, she wouldn't lose it.

Opening her closet, she frowned. Usually she knew precisely what best suited an evening she had planned. Tonight, everything she pulled out seemed too fussy, too plain or simply too ordinary. Calling herself a fool, she grabbed a sea-foam-green silk and laid it on her bed. Perhaps it was almost severely simple, but that was very possibly the best idea for the evening. If she wanted something dashing, she mused, she should have raided Myra's closet. As the thought came and went, she heard the doorbell chime.

She found herself grumbling at the interruption, something so out of character that she lectured herself all the way downstairs. As she opened the door, Myra dashed inside and grabbed both her hands.

"Oh, Anna, I'm so glad you're home."

"Myra, I was just thinking about you." By the time the words were out, she noticed the death grip on her fingers. "What's wrong?"

"I have to talk to you." For perhaps the first time in her life Myra found herself almost beyond words. "Alone. Are your parents in?"

"No."

"Good. I need a drink first. Offer me a brandy."

"All right." Amused, Anna began to lead her to the parlor. "Terrific hat."

"Is it?" Myra lifted a worried hand to the off-white cap and veil. "It's not too fussy?"

"Too fussy?" Anna poured her a double brandy. "Let me get this straight. You're asking me if something you're wearing is too fussy?"

"Don't be cute, Anna." Turning to a mirror, Myra toyed with the veil. "Maybe I should pull out the feather."

Anna glanced at the saucy little feather curling over Myra's ear. "Now I know something's wrong."

"How about the dress?" Myra slipped out of a vivid red raincoat to reveal a trim silk suit with lace at the collar and cuffs.

"It's exquisite. Is it new?"

"It's twenty minutes old."

Anna sat on the arm of a chair while her friend gulped down brandy. "You didn't have to dress up for me."

Myra let out a quick breath and straightened her shoulders before she set the empty snifter down. "This is no time for jokes."

"I can see that." But she smiled anyway. "What is it time for?"

"How soon can you toss on something wonderful and pack an overnight bag?"

"Pack?" She watched as Myra fingered the lace at her throat. "Myra, what's going on?"

"I'm getting married." She said it in a rush, then let out a small explosion of breath. Because her legs were unsteady she dropped onto the sofa.

"Getting married?" Stunned Anna sat exactly where she was. "Myra, I know you work fast and I haven't seen much of you in a couple of weeks, but *married*?"

"It wouldn't hurt to say it a few times so I'd stop losing my breath every time I hear the word. I've already babbled to the clerk in the dress shop and I don't want to do that again. If there's one thing I refuse to do, it's make a fool of myself."

"Married," Anna repeated for both of them. "To whom?" As Myra fastened and unfastened the top button of her jacket, Anna groped for a candidate. "Peter?"

"Who? No, no, of course not."

"Of course not," Anna murmured. "I know, Jack Holmes."

"Don't be ridiculous."

"Steven Marlowe."

Myra fiddled with the hem of her skirt. "Anna, really, I hardly know the man."

"Hardly know him? Why six months ago you—"

"That was six months ago," Myra interrupted, blushing for the first time since Anna had known her. "And I'd appreciate it if you'd forget anything I'd ever written you about him. Better yet, burn those letters."

"Darling, they self-destructed the moment I read them. You should have used fire-proof paper."

Despite herself, Myra grinned. "You're speaking to an engaged woman. I've put all that behind me. Look." Breathy with excitement, Myra held out her left hand.

"Oh." She was usually very casual about jewelry herself, but the simple square-cut diamond on Myra's finger seemed impossibly beautiful. "It's exquisite, really exquisite, Myra. I'm so happy for you." She was up and gathering Myra close for a hug before she laughed. "How do I know I'm happy for you? I don't know who you're going to marry."

"Herbert Ditmeyer." Myra waited for the look of astonishment and wasn't disappointed. "I know, I was pretty damn surprised myself."

"But I didn't think you even…that is, you always said he was…" Catching herself, Anna cleared her throat.

"Stuffy," Myra finished and smiled beautifully. "And he is. He's stuffy and rather sober and frustratingly proper. He's also the sweetest man I've ever known. These past couple of weeks…" She sat back, a little dreamy, a little stunned. "I never knew what it could be like to have a man treat you as though you were special. Really special. I went out with him the first time, because he'd had such a hard time asking me and I felt sorry for him. And flattered," she admitted. "I went out with him the second time because I'd had such a good time. Herbert can be so funny. It kind of sneaks up on you."

Touched, Anna watched love bloom in Myra's eyes. "I know."

"You were always such a good friend to him. I'm lucky he didn't fall in love with you. The thing is, he's been in love with me for years." With a little shake of her head, she pulled a cigarette from her purse. "We'd been going out for a couple of weeks when he told me. I was so stunned I could hardly speak. Then I tried to ease myself out gently. After all, he was very sweet and I didn't want to hurt him."

Anna lifted the ringed hand again. "It doesn't appear you eased yourself out."

"No." Still dazed, Myra stared at the diamond winking up at her. "It occurred to me all at once that I didn't want to ease myself out, that I was crazy about him. Isn't that wild?"

"I think it's wonderful."

"Me, too." She stubbed out the cigarette without having taken the first puff. "And tonight. Tonight he put this ring on my finger, told me we were flying to Maryland at eight and getting married."

"Tonight." Anna took Myra's hand again. "Tonight. It's so quick, Myra."

"Why wait?"

Why wait, indeed? She could think of hundreds of reasons, but none of them would have gotten past that dreamy look in Myra's eyes. "Are you sure?"

"I'm more sure about this than I've ever been about anything in my life. Be happy for me, Anna."

"I am." Tears swam in her eyes as she held Myra again. "You know I am."

"Then get dressed." Half laughing, half crying, Myra pushed her away. "You're my maid of honor."

"You want me to fly to Maryland tonight?"

"We agreed to elope because it was simpler than dealing with his mother. She doesn't like me and probably never will."

"Oh, Myra—"

"It doesn't matter. Herbert and I love each other. Anyway, I don't want a big fancy wedding. It takes too long. But I don't want to be married without my best friend there. I really need you, Anna. I want this more than anything in the world, and I'm scared to death."

Any objections she might have had disappeared. "I can be dressed and packed in twenty minutes."

Grinning, Myra gave her a last hug. "Because it's you I believe it."

"Just let me leave a note for my parents." She already had the pen in her hand.

"Ah, Anna…" Myra ran her tongue over her teeth. "I know your sense of honesty won't let you lie—exactly. Could you just not mention what you're going away for? Herbert and I really want to keep this quiet until we tell his mother."

Anna thought a moment, then began to write. *Taking a short trip with Myra. May do some antique shopping—which I may,* she added half to herself. *I'll be home in a day or two.* She signed it and glanced up, showing it to Myra. "Vague enough?"

"Perfectly. Thanks."

"Come on, give me a hand." As she dashed into the hall, she remembered. "Oh, I have to call Daniel and cancel dinner."

"Daniel MacGregor?" Myra's brows arched as only they could.

"That's right." Ignoring the look, Anna headed for the phone. "I'll have to let him know I can't make it tonight."

"You can have dinner with him in Maryland." Myra took the receiver from her and replaced it. "Herbert's asking him to be best man."

"I see." Anna brushed a hand casually down her robe. "Well, that's handy, isn't it?"

"Very." With a grin, Myra pulled her upstairs.

Chapter 9

She'd never flown before. At twenty, Anna had sailed to Europe in luxury and comfort. She'd traveled hundreds of miles on trains, lulled by the swaying motion and watching the landscape whiz by. But she'd never been in the air. If anyone had told her she'd be climbing into a small private plane that looked as though it could land safely in her backyard, she'd have thought them mad.

Love, she thought as she set her teeth and took the last step inside. If she didn't love Myra, she'd turn around and run for her life. She was certain the tin can with propellers could get off the ground. She wished she felt as confident about how it would get down again.

"Quite a machine, isn't it?" Daniel watched Anna take her seat before he settled in his own.

"Quite," she muttered and wondered if it came with parachutes.

"First flight?"

She started to give him a stiff and dignified yes, then saw he wasn't laughing at her. "Yeah." The word came out on a little breath.

"Try to think of it as an adventure," he suggested.

She glanced at the ground outside the window and wished she were still standing on it. "I'm trying not to think of it at all."

"You've more guts than that, Anna. I should know." Then he grinned at her. "It should be an adventure the first time. After a while flying becomes routine, and you really don't think much about it."

She told herself to relax and used the old trick of starting at her toes and working up. She never got past her knees. "I guess you're used to it. Is this the sort of plane you fly to New York in?"

With a chuckle he fastened her seat belt, then his own. "This is the plane I fly to New York in. I own it."

"Oh." As his words sank in she found that the fact that it was Daniel's plane somehow made flying in it all right. She glanced over to where Myra and Herbert were seated and strapped in, heads together. An adventure, she decided. She'd enjoy one. "So when do we start?"

"There's a lass," he murmured and signaled to the pilot. The engine started with a roar and they were off.

Though her anxiety had passed, there was an air of both celebration and tension all through the flight. Anna saw the tension in Myra as her friend twisted a lace handkerchief into knots as she laughed and talked. Herbert sat, a little pale, a little stiff, and spoke only when prodded. For herself, Anna heard the voices around her, watched the landscape beneath her with a sense of unreality. It was all happening so fast. If it hadn't been for Daniel's easy jokes and constant banter, the celebratory part of the flight might have dissolved into mild hysteria. He was, Anna noted as he flirted outrageously with Myra, enjoying himself. And while he was about it, he was keeping the bride-to-be from climbing the walls of the cabin. He wasn't just an interesting man, she realized. He was a good friend. Pulling herself out of her thoughts, Anna made an effort to be as good.

"You have excellent taste, Herbert."

"What?" He swallowed and straightened his tie. "Oh, yes. Thank you." Then he looked at Myra with his heart in his eyes. "She's wonderful, isn't she?"

"The best. I don't know what I'd have done without her. Life certainly would have been a great deal duller."

"We serious-minded people need someone with a little sparkle in our lives, don't we?" He gave Anna a nervous smile. "Otherwise, we'd just crawl into our careers and forget there was anything else out there."

Serious-minded? She let the phrase play in her head. Yes, she supposed she was. In addition, she was coming to understand that Herbert was right. "And people with— sparkle," she murmured with a glance at Myra and Daniel, "need a serious-minded person in their lives to keep them from running off cliffs."

"I'm going to make her happy."

Because his words sounded more like a question than a statement, Anna took his hands. "Oh, yes. You're going to make her very happy."

The small private plane touched down in a rural airport in Maryland. The lingering drizzle had been left behind. Here, the late-evening sky was as clear as glass and crowded with stars. The sliver of moon was like a smile. It might have been a wedding night chosen on impulse, but it was perfect. Taking Myra by the arm, Herbert led the way to the little terminal.

"The justice of the peace who was recommended to me is only about twenty miles from here. I'll check about getting a cab or a car."

"That won't be necessary." When they entered the terminal Daniel quickly scanned it then signaled to a tall uniformed chauffeur.

"Mr. MacGregor?"

"Aye. Give him the directions," he told Herbert. "I took the liberty of arranging for transportation."

Without fuss, the chauffeur gathered the suitcases and led the way outside. At the curb was a pearl-gray stretch limo.

"You didn't give a body much time to come up with a wedding present," Daniel explained. "This was the best I could do."

"It's perfect." With a laugh, Myra swung her arms around him. "Absolutely perfect."

Daniel winked at Herbert over her head. "The best man's supposed to handle the details."

Anna waited until Herbert had helped Myra inside. "This was very sweet of you."

"I'm a sweet man," he told her.

She laughed and accepted his hand. "Maybe. I wouldn't depend on it."

Inside, Myra already had her arm linked through Herbert's. "Two bottles of champagne?"

"One for before." Daniel lifted one from its bucket of ice. "One for after." He let out a cork with a hiss and a pop then poured four glasses. "To happiness."

Four glasses clinked solemnly together, but when Daniel drank, he looked at Anna. As the champagne exploded in her mouth, she realized the adventure was far from over.

By the time they arrived at the little white house, all the

champagne and the lingering tension had been drained. With her usual aplomb, Myra tidied her hair and makeup in a powder room off the hall while Anna stood by and held her hat. She took her time, but Anna noted that her hands were steady.

"How do I look?" Myra demanded, and managed a quick turn in the cramped room.

"Beautiful."

"I've always been a couple of degrees away from beautiful, but tonight I think I've nearly managed stunning."

Hands firm, Anna turned her toward the mirror again. "Tonight you're beautiful. Take a good look."

Looking at their reflections together, Myra grinned. "He really loves me, Anna."

"I know." She slipped her arm around Myra's shoulder. "You're going to make quite a team."

"Yes, we are." As her chin tilted up, her grin softened into a smile. "I don't think he realizes just how much of a team yet, but he will." On a quick breath she turned and took Anna by the shoulders. "I don't like to get sentimental, but since I only intend to get married once, this seems to be the time. You're my best friend and I love you. I want you to be as happy as I am this minute."

"I'm working on it."

Satisfied, Myra nodded. "Okay then, let's go. And listen—" she put her hand on the knob and paused "—if I stutter, don't tell anyone—especially Catherine Donahue."

Solemn eyed, Anna put a hand over her heart. "I won't tell a soul."

In a parlor with a tiny marble fireplace and summer flowers in glass vases, Anna watched her closest friend promise to love, honor and cherish. When her eyes misted, she felt foolish and tried to blink them clear. It was silly to cry over two adults making a legal contract with each other. Marriage was, after all, a contract. That was why it had to be approached so cautiously, so practically. But the first tear escaped and ran slowly down her cheek. She felt Daniel press his handkerchief into her hand as he'd done once before. Even as she sniffed into it, the ceremony was over and she found herself hugging a dazed Myra.

"I did it," Myra murmured, then laughed and gave Anna a rib-crushing squeeze.

"And without one single stutter."

"I did it," she repeated and held out her hand. Snuggled next to the diamond was a slim gold band. "Engaged and married within five hours."

Daniel took the hand she was admiring and kissed it formally. "Mrs. Ditmeyer."

Chuckling, Myra curled her fingers around his. "Be sure to call me that several times this evening so I'll learn to answer to it. Oh, Anna, I'm going to cry and destroy my mascara."

"It's all right." Anna handed her Daniel's already crumpled handkerchief. "Herbert's stuck with you now." Anna wound her arms around him and held tight.

He laughed and gave Anna a long, hard squeeze. "And she's stuck with me."

"She'll complicate your life."

"I know."

"Isn't it wonderful?" Anna kissed him hard. "I don't know about you, but I'm starving. The wedding supper is on me."

Through the recommendation of the justice of the peace and the help of the chauffeur, they found a country inn at the peak of a wooded hill. It was, as they'd been told, small, quaint and possibly closed. With a little persuasion, and the exchange of a few bills, they persuaded the owner to open the restaurant and wake up the cook. While the others were led into the dining room, Anna made an excuse about freshening up and slipped aside. Moments later, she waylaid the owner again.

"Mr. Portersfield, I can't thank you enough for accommodating us."

Though he was always glad to receive paying guests, the lateness of the hour had put him a bit out of sorts. He found it difficult, however, to resist the smile Anna sent him. "My doors are always open," he told her. "Unfortunately the kitchen closes at nine, so the meal may not quite live up to our reputation."

"I'm sure everything will be wonderful. As a matter of fact, I can almost promise that my friends will tell you it's the best meal they've ever eaten. You see—" linking her arm through his, she strolled a little farther away from the others "—they were just married a half hour ago. That's why you and I have to arrange a few things."

"Newlyweds." Mr. Portersfield wasn't a man completely without romance. "We're always pleased to have newlyweds at the inn. If we'd had just a bit of notice—"

"Oh, I'm sure the few things we need won't be too much bother. Did I mention that Mr. Ditmeyer is the district attorney in Boston? I'm sure when he gets back from his honeymoon with his new bride, he's going to praise your inn to all his friends. And Mr. MacGregor—" she lowered her voice "—well, I don't have to tell you who he is."

He didn't have the vaguest idea, but implied importance was enough. "No, of course not."

"A man in his position doesn't often find a quiet place like this to relax. Home cooking, country air. I can assure you he's very impressed by your establishment. Tell me, Mr. Portersfield, do you have a record player?"

"A record player? I have one in my room, but—"

"Perfect." Anna patted his hand and tried the smile again. "I knew you'd be able to help me."

Fifteen minutes later, she was back in the dining room. At the table was a loaf of crusty bread, a pot of butter and little else.

"Where'd you disappear to?" Daniel asked as she took her seat.

"Details. To the bride and groom," she said and lifted her water glass.

As they toasted, Myra laughed. "And I was just about to say to Herbert that he can look forward to many meals just like this—" she indicated the bread and water "—until we get a cook."

He took her hand and brought it to his lips. "I didn't marry you for your culinary prowess."

"A good thing," Anna said, then added, "she hasn't any."

A sleepy boy of about fifteen came into the room with a vase of wildflowers. A look at the dew on the petals told Anna they'd just been picked. It looked as if Mr. Portersfield was going to come through.

"Oh, how pretty." Myra reached to pluck one out as the boy wandered away and began to pull tables across the floor. Loudly. Mr. Portersfield shuffled into the room, lugging a phonograph. Within moments, there was music.

"The first dance for the Herbert Ditmeyers," Anna stated, and gestured to the space the boy had cleared on the floor. When they were alone at the table, Daniel buttered a chunk of bread and handed it to her. "You accomplished quite a lot in a short time."

Hungry, Anna bit into the bread. "Just the beginning, Mr. MacGregor."

"You know, when you asked me to dinner tonight, I had no idea we'd be having it in a country inn in Maryland."

Anna broke off another hunk of bread, buttered it and handed it to him. "I'd intended to keep things a bit closer to home myself."

"They look happy."

She glanced over to see Myra and Herbert smiling at each other as they moved around the tiny cleared space. "Yes, they do. Funny, I never pictured them together. Now that I see them, it seems so perfect."

"Contrasts." He took his palm and pressed it against hers. His was wide and hard, hers narrow and soft. "They make life more interesting."

"I've come to believe it." She linked fingers with him. "Lately."

With a smile that spread from ear to ear, Mr. Portersfield brought over a tray of salad. "You'll enjoy this," he told them as he served. "Everything straight from our own garden. The dressing is an old family recipe." After setting down the salad bowls, he fussed briefly with the flowers and then was off again.

"He certainly looks more cheerful," Daniel commented.

"And so he should," Anna murmured thinking just how much she'd paid to put a smile on his face. "Daniel…" Thoughtfully, she stabbed her fork into the salad. "About that loan you mentioned this afternoon." She took her first bite of the salad and found it as good as advertised. "I might want to take you up on it—just until we get back to Boston."

Daniel glanced over in time to see Portersfield heading into the kitchen, then looked back to see Anna's eyes dark with humor. He'd never needed anyone to add two and two for him. On a roar of laughter, he took her face in his hands and kissed her. "Interest free for you, love."

There was champagne—the only two bottles to be had at the inn. There was pot roast that melted on the fork and a scratchy Billie Holiday record. When Daniel took Myra to the impromptu dance floor, she didn't waste time beating around the bush.

"You're in love with Anna."

Because he saw no reason to deny it, he ignored her bluntness. "Aye."

"What do you intend to do about it?"

He looked down. In the comfort of his beard, his lips twitched. "I could say that was none of your business."

"You could," Myra agreed. "But I intend to find out, anyway."

After a moment's thought he decided it was best to have her on his side. "I'd have married her tonight, but she's too damn stubborn."

"Or smart." Myra smiled when she saw the heat flash in his eyes. "Oh, I like you, Daniel. I did right away. But I know a steamroller when I see one."

"Like recognizes like."

"Exactly." Pleased rather than insulted, Myra matched her steps to his. "Anna's going to be a doctor, probably the best surgeon in the country."

He scowled down at her. "What would you know about doctors?"

"I know about Anna," she said easily. "And I think I know enough about men to guess that that doesn't suit you very well."

"I want a wife," he muttered, "not a knife wielder."

"I imagine you'd have more respect for a surgeon if you needed your appendix out."

"I wouldn't want my wife to do the cutting."

"If you want Anna, you'd better be prepared to take her career. Have you asked her to marry you?"

"You're nosy."

"Of course. Have you?"

American women, he thought. Would he ever acclimatize? "I did."

"And?"

"She says she won't marry me, but she'll live with me."

"That sounds sensible."

Daniel drew her hand down so they both could see the ring gleam on Myra's finger.

"Oh, that's entirely different. I love Herbert very much, but I wouldn't have married him unless I was certain he accepted me for what I am."

"Which is?"

"Nosy, meddling, flamboyant and ambitious." Her gaze drifted toward the table. "I'm going to make him a hell of a wife."

Daniel looked down at her. Her eyes might have been dewy with love, but her chin was set. "I believe you will."

Daniel had just pulled back Myra's chair when Portersfield wheeled up a cart with a small layer cake with frothy white icing and pink rosebuds. With considerable charm, he handed Myra a silver flat-edged knife.

"With the compliments of the inn," he told her, knowing he could afford to be generous. "Our best wishes to both of you for a long and happy marriage."

"Thank you." Finding herself near tears, Myra waited until Herbert wrapped his fingers around hers on the handle.

Anna waited until the champagne was empty and the cake little more than crumbs. "One more thing." She took a key from her purse and gave it to Herbert. "The bridal suite."

He slipped it into his pocket with a grin. "I didn't think a little place like this would have one."

"It didn't until a couple of hours ago." She accepted the hugs then watched the newlyweds walk away together.

"I like your style, Anna Whitfield."

"Do you?" Buoyed by success and champagne, she smiled at him. With her eyes on his she reached in her purse again. "I have another key."

Daniel glanced down to the single key in her palm. "You tend to take matters in your own hands."

Lifting a brow, she rose. "If it doesn't suit you, you can wake Portersfield up again. I'm sure he can find you another room."

He stood, took her wrist and plucked the key from her hand. "This'll do."

With her hand in his, they left the remains of the wedding supper behind.

They didn't speak as they climbed the stairs, which creaked slightly under their weight. There was a light at the top to guide them, shielded in beveled glass and dim. All the doors they passed were closed. The inn, so recently disturbed for a celebration, was quiet. When Daniel unlocked the door to their room, he smelled the spicy mix of potpourri. It made him think of his grandmother, of Scotland, of all he'd left behind. When Anna closed the door behind them, he thought of nothing but her. Still they didn't speak.

She turned the key on a little globed lamp by the door. Subtle light spilled into the room and pooled at their feet. The windows were open to let in the warm summer air. Thin curtains stirred with it. And just barely audible, from the woods beyond came the melancholy song of a night bird.

She waited. Once, on a cliff top, she'd gone to him. Now she needed him to turn to her. Her heart was already his, though she feared to tell him. Her body would never belong to another. But she waited, touched by lamplight, surrounded by summer air.

He thought she'd never looked more lovely, though he already had dozens of memories of her locked in his mind. Dozens of fantasies. Passion, needs, love, dreams—she was all of them. His heart took the first step, and he followed.

His hands cupped her face gently, so gently that she could barely feel the pressure of his fingers on her skin. Still, the touch rippled through her. His eyes never left hers as he lowered his mouth. The kiss was soft, a bare meeting of lips, a mingling of breath. Eyes open, bodies close, they explored the sensations evoked by the teasing and brushing of mouth against mouth, the tangling and retreating of tongues.

He touched only her face; she touched him not at all, and yet in seconds two hearts were pounding.

How long they stood like that she couldn't be sure. It might have been hours or only seconds while their needs built and twisted together into a desire that bordered on pain. With a moan of delight, she let her head fall back. Her arms came around him. For an instant, the kiss deepened toward delirium. She felt her bones liquefy from her toes up until her body was a fluid mass of sensation. Reveling in it, she went limp in his arms in unqualified surrender.

It nearly drove him mad. To have Anna, strong and eager, made his blood heat and his passion soar. But to have Anna, soft and pliant, was devastatingly arousing. It made him weak. It made him strong. She seemed to seep into him degree by degree until there was no room for anything but her.

He drew back, shaken by the intensity, wary of the merging. But she stood as she was, head thrown back, arms twined around him. It was more than need he saw in her eyes, more even than knowledge. It was acceptance. He waited, his body pulsing, until his mind was nearly clear again. Then he undressed her.

The thin, almost transparent jacket she wore over her dress slid away like an illusion. He let his hands roam up her arms, over her shoulders and back again so that he could feel the skin, the muscles, the texture. And as he lingered, bewitched by the thrill of his flesh against hers, she loosened his tie then tossed it aside. Slowly, while her own blood heated to his touch, she drew his jacket from his shoulders.

He was losing himself in her again but now it didn't seem to matter. While the summer breeze sighed through the windows behind them, he pulled down the zipper of her dress. Like the breeze, it drifted to the floor.

She heard him catch his breath and felt a wild, almost wanton pride in her own body. While she stood, he seemed to drink in the sight of her, inch by inch. Her skin hummed as though his hands had stroked it. The cameo he had given her nestled in the hollow of her throat. He could trace it with his finger and feel her profile come to life. The lacy fantasy she wore was caught snug at her breast and draped lazily at her thighs. The lamplight threw her silhouette into relief and made him hunger for what he already had.

Her fingers weren't steady as she unbuttoned his shirt, but her eyes never left his. More from desire than confidence, her palms stroked over him as his shirt joined her dress on the floor.

Somewhere in the inn a clock rang out the hour, but

they'd long since forgotten such things as time and place. In unspoken agreement, they lowered themselves to the bed.

Under their weight, the old mattress creaked softly. Feather pillows yielded. He braced himself above her, needing to see her, all of her. He might have stayed like that for hours, but she reached for him.

Mouth against mouth, heated, impatient. Flesh to flesh, trembling, sensitive. The lamplight cast their shadows on the wall. The breeze carried off their sighs. The night bird still sang plaintively in the woods. They no longer heard. The world they both knew so much of, the world they both were so determined to discover had been whittled down to one room. Ambitions faded and died in the face of more desperate desires. To give, to take and to experience. To possess and to be possessed.

He buried his face against her skin and no longer noticed the scent of spices and dried flowers that wafted through the room. There was no fragrance but Anna, no taste but Anna, no voice but Anna's. Slowly, but not so gently, he took his mouth on a searing journey down her throat, over the lace and silk clinging to her breasts. Need thundered in his blood as she strained against him. With their hands caught tightly together, he let his tongue lap at the subtle curve just above the lace. With their legs tangled, he let his teeth scrape lightly over her flesh. When she called out his name, he vowed to bring her the thrill and the glory of madness.

Through the silk, his lips pulled and tugged on her nipple until it was hard and hot in his mouth and her body was as taut as a bowstring. He heard her breath tremble when he paused, then heard it catch in her throat as he turned all his skill to her other breast.

Just as slowly, just as ruthlessly, just as devastatingly,

he worked his way over her body, touching off fires she
hadn't known were there to be kindled. With his tongue
and wide-palmed hands he took her again and again to the
edge of release. She'd never known torture could be so glorious or pleasure so painful. Her skin was damp when he
pulled the last barrier away from it.

She was caught in a haze of delights—dark, secret, desperate delights. The air was heavy and tasted of him as she
drew in labored breaths. Everywhere he touched, flames
burned. His beard brushed over the soft skin of her belly
and set off an inferno of sensation. Her hands found his
hair and stroked it as the lamplight turned even this to fire.

Her mind spinning, she locked her arms around his
waist. Still riding a crest of sensation she rolled with him,
her hands seeking, reaching, finding. She felt him quiver
and pressed her mouth to his skin, tasting desire. Before
he could anticipate, before he could prepare, she slid down
and took him into her.

Sounds burst in her head. Perhaps it was her name on
Daniel's lips. Chills coursed along her flesh. They might
have been his strong fingers caressing her. As she threw
her head back, abandoned, delighted, she saw his eyes on
hers. The deep brilliant blue held its own fire, hotter, stronger than any other. Love. Clinging to it, she took them both
beyond reason.

Sated and breathless, she still held tight, and with her
eyes closed, locked everything into her: the scent of him,
the feel of his skin warmed from hers, the sound of his
breathing, fast and harsh in her ear, the look of his hand
closed tight around hers.

It was here she wanted to stay. And if the rest of the
world and all other needs could be ignored, she would. If

he were to ask now, if he were even to demand now, she was afraid she would give him all.

A hand moved down her back in one long stroke. Possession. She trembled a bit and knew she could do little to prevent it. Whatever else she wanted, whatever else she was, she belonged to him.

Her body was so small that it seemed almost weightless as she lay on him. He could feel the slight trembles, the aftershocks of passion. He couldn't live without her. He could wheel and deal and blithely slit the throat of a competitor, but he couldn't function any longer without the small serious woman whose hand was still locked in his.

Your way then, damn it. Even as he cursed her, he hooked an arm around her.

"You'll move in with me tomorrow." Grabbing a handful of hair, he drew her head back. Her way, but he wasn't giving in. "You'll pack what you have when we get back to Boston. I won't spend another night without you."

Unable to speak, she stared at him. There were dregs of desire in his eyes mixed with the fury just breaking. How did she handle a man like Daniel? Anna had a feeling it would take more than a few weeks to learn. "Tomorrow?"

"That's right. You move into my house tomorrow. Do you have anything to say about it?"

She thought a moment, then smiled. "You'd better make room in your closet."

Chapter 10

Anna had her first tour of her new home under the guidance of a stiff-backed, tight-lipped McGee. She wondered which of them was more uncomfortable. Her bags had barely been carried upstairs when Daniel had been called to the bank on urgent business. He'd left, annoyed, with a quick kiss of reassurance for her and an absentminded order to McGee to show her around. So she was there alone with a politely indignant butler and a cook who had yet to poke her head out of the kitchen.

Her first reaction was to think of an excuse and go to the hospital where she belonged. Taking the afternoon off hadn't been anything she could afford to do any more than Daniel could. Now he was gone, and she was here. Something about the straight, unyielding back of the man who led her up the stairs had her holding her ground. For Anna, pride went hand in hand with dignity. She'd made her decision, and if a butler happened to be the first to disapprove, she'd accept it. More, she was going to learn to live with it. Starting now.

"We have several guest rooms on this floor," McGee told her in his low, rolling brogue. "Mr. MacGregor also keeps his office on this level, as he finds it convenient."

"I see."

McGee tested a small tilt-top table for dust as they went. Anna had a moment to reflect that it was fortunate for whoever was in charge of the dust department that McGee didn't find any. "Mr. MacGregor entertains out-of-town business associates from time to time. We keep two guest rooms prepared. This is the master bedroom." So saying he opened a thick, hand-tooled door.

The room was large, as Daniel seemed to prefer, but sparsely decorated, as though he spent little time there. She imagined his office would be cluttered with furniture and piled with papers, more revealing of the inner man than his bedroom, which should have been the more personal room. There were no photographs, no mementos. The paint was new and the curtains stiff with starch. She wondered if he'd ever pushed them aside to look at the view. The bed was big enough for four and of lovingly carved oak. Her bags sat neatly at the foot.

She'd expected to feel odd, walking into this intimate room for the first time. She felt little but a sense of vague curiosity. There was more of Daniel MacGregor on a cliff above the sea than there was in the room where he spent his nights. But this wasn't the time to try to dissect a puzzle where she hadn't expected to find one. Her chin was lifted just a tad higher than usual when she turned back to McGee.

"Mr. MacGregor wasn't clear on the housekeeping arrangements. Is that your responsibility?"

If McGee could have stiffened his already ramrod-straight back, he would have. "A day maid comes in three times a week. Otherwise, I oversee the housekeeping. However, Mr. MacGregor informed both myself and the cook that you may wish changes."

If Daniel had walked in the door at that moment, Anna would cheerfully have strangled him. Instead, she took another deliberate study of the room. "I hardly think that will be necessary, McGee. You seem to be not only a man who knows his job, but his own worth."

Her coolly delivered compliment didn't soften him a whit, nor was it intended to. "Thank you, miss. Would you care to see the rest of the second floor?"

"Not at the moment. I think I'll unpack." And be alone, she thought desperately.

"Very well, miss." With a bow he walked to the door. "If you need anything you've only to ring."

"Thank you, McGee. I won't."

The moment he shut the door, she sank down on the enormous bed. What had she done? Every doubt she'd been able to hide, thrust aside or bury until that point came rushing out. She'd moved out of her childhood home, not into her own pretty little apartment, but into a big, rambling house where she was a stranger. A usurper. And to the stiff-lipped McGee, obviously a Jezebel. If she hadn't had her own nerves to deal with, that one point might have amused.

She'd left a nervous mother and a stunned father and had come to a huge half-empty room. She wasn't at the hospital, where the hurdles she had to navigate were at least familiar, if difficult. Nothing here belonged to her but what was in the bags at the foot of the bed.

Slowly she ran her hand over the thick white bed cover. Now, night after night, she thought, she'd be sharing this bed with Daniel. Sleeping with him, waking with him. There'd be no more simple good-nights and a retreat into privacy. He'd be there, within reach. And so would she.

What had she done? Panic rose. Gamely, Anna swallowed it. Her hand still stroked the cover. In a mirror on the far wall she saw herself—small, pale and wide-eyed on the too-big bed. She saw, too, the reflection of an oak chest of drawers, clean lined and masculine. Her legs were a little shaky as she rose to walk to it. Her fingers seemed a bit numb as she slipped the lid from a bottle of cologne. Then she smelled him—brash, vivid and very male. Her world seemed to steady. When she replaced the lid, her hands were firm and competent again.

What had she done? she asked herself for the last time. Exactly what she'd wanted to do. With a little laugh of relief, she began to unpack.

It didn't take long to distribute her things throughout the room. She'd taken little more than clothes and a few favorite pictures from her room. Still, after her things were tidied away, she felt more at ease, and somehow more at home. Of course, they would have to see about getting a dresser to match the nineteenth-century oak furniture Daniel had chosen for the room. The curtains would have to go in favor of something softer and more friendly.

Pleased, she glanced around again. It had never occurred to her that she would get such a charge out of making a few basic domestic decisions. Perhaps it wasn't anything like deciding whether to operate or treat internally, but it did bring a sense of satisfaction. Perhaps she could indeed have everything. At the moment, she thought, she was going to start by cornering McGee and going in search of a couple of comfortable chairs for the master bedroom. And a good reading lamp, she thought as she walked into the hall. If possible, she'd add a small desk for herself. The room was certainly big enough. Surely in a house this size they could find a few things that would suit. If they couldn't, she'd simply do a bit of shopping after her shift at the hospital the next day.

Once on the first floor, she was tempted to poke into the parlor or library and do some shifting herself. She held herself back for the simple reason that she understood pride. If she were to take on the project herself, it would surely damage McGee's. She would find a way to tactfully change what she wanted changed without damaging his butlerly ego. McGee was part of Daniel's life. If she were to make a success out of her decision, she would have to see that he was a part of hers.

Because she could think of no other logical place to find him, she headed for the kitchen. A few steps away from the door, she heard the voices and paused.

"If the lass is good enough for the MacGregor, she's good enough for me." It was a feminine voice but as musically Scottish as the butler's. "I see no reason for your griping, McGee."

"I don't gripe." Even through the wood, Anna detected the cool indignation. "The girl has no business here without a marriage license."

"Pish posh."

With that chuckled exclamation, Anna decided she could like the cook very well.

"Since when are you judge and confessor, I'd like to know. The MacGregor knows his mind, and so, I'd wager, does the lass, or wouldn't give her the time of day. It's what she looks like that I want to know. Is she pretty?"

"Pretty enough," McGee muttered. "At least she has the good sense not to flaunt herself."

"Flaunt herself," the cook repeated even as Anna indignantly mouthed the phrase. "A woman makes herself up for a man and she's flaunting herself. She doesn't and she has good sense. I don't know which is more of the insult. Now go on about your business and I'll be about mine, or I'll be too busy to have a look at her before dinner."

Anna was trying to decide whether to retreat or brazen it out when a cry of pain made her rush into the room. McGee was already bending over a plump white-haired woman. On the floor between them was a long-handled knife smeared with blood. Even as Anna dashed toward them, more blood was pooling at their feet.

"Let me see."

"Miss Whitfield—"

"Move!" Abandoning propriety, she shoved the butler aside. It only took a glance to show her that a slip of the knife had gashed the cook's wrist and knicked an artery. In an instant she pressed her fingers over it and stopped the pump of blood.

"It's nothing, miss." But tears were coursing down the woman's face. "I'll make a mess of you."

"Hush." Anna plucked up a dry dishcloth and tossed it at McGee. "Tear this into strips then go bring my car around."

Used to responding to authority, he began to rip. Still holding the cook's wrist, Anna led her to a chair. "Just be calm," she soothed.

"Blood," the cook managed, and went parchment white.

"We're going to take care of it." Anna continued to talk calmly, knowing how difficult it would be to manage the big woman if she keeled over. "McGee, tie a strip on her arm, just here." She indicated where he should fasten the tourniquet while she continued to close the artery with her fingers. "All right now, what's your name?"

"Sally, miss."

"All right, Sally, I want you just to close your eyes and relax. Not too tight," she cautioned McGee. "Bring the car around quickly. I'll want you to drive."

"Yes, miss." At twice his normal gait and none of his usual dignity, he scurried from the room.

"Now, Sally, can you walk?"

"I'll try. I feel light-headed."

"Of course you do," Anna murmured. "Lean on me. We're going right out the kitchen door to the car. We'll be at the hospital in five minutes."

"To the hospital." Beneath Anna's hand the woman's arm began to shake. "I don't like hospitals."

"There's nothing to worry about. I'll stay with you. I work there. Some of the doctors are very handsome." As she spoke, she eased the cook up and began to help her to the door. "So handsome you'll ask yourself why you didn't cut yourself before." By the time they got through the door, McGee was there to take most of the woman's weight.

"A fine job of emergency first aid, Miss Whitfield." Dr. Liederman rinsed his hands in a basin as he spoke to Anna. "Without it, I'd wager that woman would have bled to death before she made it to the hospital."

Anna had gotten a good look at the wound and estimated the need for ten stitches once the artery had been sealed. "A bad place for the knife to slip."

"We get suicides that don't do that good a job. A lucky thing for her you didn't panic."

Anna lifted a brow, wondering if he considered that a compliment. "If blood made me panic, I'd make a poor surgeon."

"Surgery, is it?" She hadn't chosen an easy road. He

glanced over his shoulder as he finished scrubbing the cook's blood from his hands. "It takes more than skill to use a scalpel, you know. It takes confidence."

"I thought it was arrogance," she said with a small smile.

It took him several seconds before he returned the smile. "A more accurate term. Now as to our patient, she'll be weak for a day or two and probably favor that hand for two or three weeks."

"You want the dressing changed every day?"

"Yes and kept dry. I'll want her back in a couple of weeks to take the stitches out." He turned then, drying his hands. "Though I don't imagine you'd have any trouble doing that for her."

She smiled again. "I wouldn't think of it—for another few months."

"You know, Miss Whitfield, you have a good reputation in this hospital."

That surprised her, but she reserved the pleasure. "Do I?"

"Yes, you do. And that's from the horse's mouth." He tossed the towel aside when she only stared. "The nurses."

The pleasure came now. "I appreciate that."

"You're going into your last year of medical school. I've seen enough to judge your...confidence. How are your grades?"

Pride lifted her chin. "Excellent."

With a little laugh, he studied her. "I appreciate that. Where do you want to intern?"

"Here."

He held out a hand. "Look me up."

Anna accepted it. "I'll do that."

So where in hell was everybody? Daniel had come home to find the house empty. Impatient to be with Anna, he'd

taken the steps two at a time and burst into the master bedroom. He'd had to look at the closet to assure himself she'd
actually been there. Though he'd found himself pleased to
see her clothes hanging neatly beside his, it wasn't quite
the welcome he'd had in mind. After a quick check of the
second floor, he'd started down again.

"McGee!" Cursing all servants, he came to a halt on the
landing and scowled. Bad enough his woman wasn't home,
but now his butler had disappeared. "McGee!"

Opening and slamming doors as he went, he worked
his way down the hall. He hadn't expected a brass band,
but he'd thought someone might have found the time to be
around when he got home. By the time he had entered the
kitchen door, his temper was peaking.

"Where the devil is everyone?"

"Will you stop shouting?" Her voice pitched low, Anna
stepped into the room. "I've just this minute gotten her
into bed."

"A man ought to be able to shout in his own home," Daniel began, then his temper cleared enough for him to see
the blood splattered over Anna's blouse and skirt. "Sweet
God!" He closed the distance between them in two steps
then swept her against him. "What have you done to yourself? Where are you hurt? I'll get you to the hospital."

"I've just been there." But she wasn't quick enough to
stop him from taking her up in his arms. "Daniel, it's not
my blood. I'm not hurt. Daniel!" He was nearly out the
kitchen door before she could stop him. "Sally had an accident, not me."

"Sally?"

"Your cook," she began.

"I know who Sally is," he snapped at her, then gathered her close as relief shuddered through him. "You're not hurt?"

"No." Her tone softened. He was trembling. Who would have expected it? "I'm fine," she managed to tell him just before his mouth closed over hers. Passion soared, and through it she felt his relief, which was nearly as wild. Moved, she let him take whatever comfort he wanted. "Daniel, I didn't mean to frighten you."

"Well, you did." He kissed her again, hard, and was steadier. "What happened to Sally?"

"Apparently her hands were wet and she wasn't paying as close attention to her chopping as she might have been. The knife slipped and slashed her at the wrist. She hit an artery. That's why there's so much blood. It's a serious cut, but McGee and I got her to the hospital. She's resting now. She'll need a couple of days off."

For the first time he noticed the chopping knife and the blood on the floor by the sink. With an oath, he tightened his grip on Anna. "I'll go in to her."

"No, please." From her position in his arms, she managed to stop him. "She's sleeping. It would really be better to wait until morning."

His cook, like his butler, like every one of his employees, was his responsibility. He glanced at the knife again and swore. "You're sure she's all right."

"I'm sure. She lost a good bit of blood, but I was right outside the door when it happened. Then once McGee realized I knew what I was doing, he couldn't have been more helpful."

"And where is he?"

"Parking my car. Here he is now," Anna corrected herself as the butler came through the kitchen door.

"Mr. MacGregor—" a bit pale, but as proper as ever,

McGee stopped just inside the door "—I'll have this mess cleaned up right away. I'm afraid dinner will be delayed."

"So I'm told. Miss Whitfield said you were very helpful, McGee."

Something—it might have been an emotion—flickered across his face. "I'm afraid I did very little, sir. Miss Whitfield was very efficient, and if I may say so, sir, plucky."

Anna had to swallow a chuckle. "Thank you, McGee."

"Don't worry about dinner. We'll see to ourselves."

"Very good, sir. Good night, miss."

"Good night, McGee." The kitchen door swung shut behind them. "Daniel, you can put me down now."

"No." Easily he started up the stairs. "This isn't the welcome I'd wanted for you."

She hadn't realized how good it could feel to be carried as though you were something precious. "I hadn't planned it this way myself."

He paused on the stairs to nuzzle her neck. "I'm sorry."

"It wasn't anyone's fault."

God, she tasted so good. Every hunger he had could be sated with her alone. "You've ruined your blouse."

"Now you sound like Sally. She muttered about that all the way to the hospital."

"I'll buy you a new one."

"Thank goodness," she said and laughed at him. "Daniel, don't we have anything more important to do than worry about my blouse?"

"Do you know what I was thinking of the entire time I sat through that damned meeting?"

"No. What?"

"Making love to you. In my bed. Our bed."

"I see." As he pushed open the door, she linked her hands behind his head. Her pulse was already beginning to race.

Anticipation. Imagination. "Do you know what I thought about as I was unpacking my things?"

"No. What?"

"Making love to you. In your bed. Our bed."

Hearing her say that made the room he rarely noticed seem special. "Then we should do something about it."

With her hands still linked behind his head, he tumbled with her onto the thick white cover.

It was easier to live with Daniel, to wake with him, to sleep with him, than Anna could have imagined. It seemed to her that the part of her life she had lived without him had been no more than anticipation. Yet their first weeks together weren't without adjustments. Though she had lived most of her life with her parents and the rest in the regimentation of college, Anna had always managed to move at her own pace and protect her privacy.

It was an entirely different matter to wake up with someone beside her. Especially when that someone was a man who viewed the hours spent in sleep as a waste of vital time. Daniel MacGregor wasn't one to loiter in bed or to linger over coffee. Mornings were for business, and morning started the moment his eyes opened.

Because her system was on a different time clock, she usually found herself wandering down for her first cup of coffee when Daniel was finishing his second and last cup. Goodbyes were brief and hurried and anything but romantic. Daniel and his briefcase were out the door before her mind was completely ready to function. Not exactly a honeymoon, she'd thought more than once when she settled down to a solitary breakfast, but it was a routine she could live with.

By the time she drove to the hospital, Daniel was already wheeling and dealing. While she folded linens and read to patients, he played the stock market and planned mergers and takeovers. In living with him, Anna had a better view of just how powerful Daniel was and how potentially powerful he could become. She herself had taken a call from a senator and relayed a message from the governor of New York.

Politics, she began to realize, was an aspect of his career she had never considered. He also had contacts and interests in the entertainment field. A telegram from a well-known producer or a fledgling playwright wasn't uncommon. Though he rarely attended the ballet or the opera, she learned that he made enormous contributions to the arts. It would have pleased her more if she hadn't understood they were made for business purposes.

Culture, politics, stock-market ventures or housing projects—it was all business to Daniel. And though she learned that business consumed his time and his life, he passed off her inquiries into it with the equivalent of a pat on the head. Each time he did, she tried to ignore the little twinge of frustration. In time, she told herself, he'd share. In time, he'd give her both his trust and respect.

Her life and her time were consumed by the hospital, her studies and her preparation for her final year of medical school. Daniel rarely asked her about her hours involving medicine. When and if he did, Anna took it as no more than polite interest and said little.

They spent their evenings lingering over a meal or over coffee in the parlor. Neither of them spoke of ambitions, of what drove them or of professional needs. While they were content just being with each other, it seemed to both as though a shade had been drawn over a part of their lives. Neither of them wanted to be the first to lift it.

They became misers with their social time, spending most of it alone at home. When they did socialize, it was with the newlywed Ditmeyers. Now and again there was a film, and they could sit in a darkened theater holding hands, forgetting about the pressures of the day or the uncertainty of the future. They learned of each other, of habits, whims and annoyances. Love, soothed and left to itself, deepened. But even as it did, they both fretted about what was missing from their relationship. Daniel wanted marriage. Anna wanted partnership. They hadn't yet discovered how to combine the two.

Summer heat soared in August. It boiled in the streets and hung mistily in the air. Those who could escaped to the shore. On the weekends Daniel and Anna took drives out of the city, with the top down. Twice they picnicked on Daniel's lot in Hyannis Port. They could make love there as freely and unrestrainedly as they had the first time. They could laugh or simply doze in the grass. And it was there, unexpectedly, that Daniel began to pressure her again.

"They'll be breaking ground here next week," Daniel told her one day as they shared the last of a bottle of Chablis.

"Next week?" Surprised, Anna glanced over to see him staring at the empty plot where his house would be. He could see it, she knew, as though there were already stone and mortar standing sturdy in the sun. "I didn't realize it would be so soon." He hadn't told her, she thought. He hadn't shown her, though she'd asked, any of the plans on blueprints for the house that was so important to him.

He merely moved his shoulders. "It would have been sooner, but I had some other things to tidy up first."

"I see." And he hadn't considered the other things worth mentioning, either. Anna bit back a sigh and tried to accept it. "I know the house is important to you, and it'll be beautiful, but I'll miss this." When he looked at her, she smiled and reached out to touch his face. "It's so peaceful here, so isolated—just water and rock and grass."

"It'll be all of those things after the house is up. After we're living in it." Because he felt her slight withdrawal, he took her hand. "It won't be quick—the best things aren't. It may be two years before the house is ready for us. But our children will grow up here."

"Daniel—"

"They will." His fingers tightened on hers as he cut her off. "And whenever we make love in that house, I'll remember our first time here. Fifty years from now I'll still remember our first time here."

It was all but impossible to resist him when he was like this. He was more dangerous when he spoke quietly, when his voice flowed over her. For a moment she almost believed him. Then she thought about how very far they had to go. "You're asking for promises, Daniel."

"Aye. I expect promises."

"Don't."

"And why not? You're the woman I want, the woman who wants me. It's time for promises between us." Keeping a firm hold on her hand, he reached into his pocket and drew out a small velvet box. "I want you to wear this, Anna." With a flick of his thumb, he opened the box to reveal a fiery pear-shaped diamond.

Something caught in her throat. Part of it was astonishment at the sheer beauty of the ring. The rest was fear of what the symbol meant: promises, vows, commitments. She wanted, she yearned, she feared.

"I can't."

"Of course, you can." When he started to pluck the ring from the box, she put both hands over his.

"No, I can't. I'm not ready for this, Daniel. I've tried to explain to you."

"And I've tried to understand." But his patience was wearing thin. Every day he lived with her he had to accept half of what he needed. "You don't want marriage—at least, not yet. But a ring's not marriage, just a promise."

"A promise I can't give you." But she wanted to. With each day that passed she wanted to more. "If I took the ring, I'd be giving you a promise that might be broken. I can't do that with you. You're too important."

"You don't make sense." He'd expected to feel frustration. Even when he'd bought the ring he'd known she wouldn't wear it. In some odd way, he'd even known she'd be right. But that knowledge didn't soothe the hurt. "I'm important to you, but you won't accept a ring from me."

"Oh, Daniel, I know you." Regrets washed over her as she took his face in her hands. "If I took this ring, you'd be pressuring me to accept a wedding ring in a month's time. Sometimes, I think you look at the two of us like a merger."

"Maybe I do." Anger flared in his eyes but he controlled it. He'd discovered he could when it was Anna he was angry with. "Maybe it's the only way I know."

"Maybe it is," she agreed quietly. "And maybe I'm trying to understand that."

"You look at it as a trial." He said it flatly. When she looked up, stunned, he continued in the same tone. "I'm not sure whether I'm on trial, Anna, or you are."

"It's not like that. You make it sound so cold and calculated."

"No more calculated than a merger."

"I'm not looking at what's between us as a business, Daniel."

Was he? He realized uncomfortably that he had been, but he wasn't so sure any longer. "Maybe it's time you told me just how you're looking at it."

"You frighten me." Her words came out so fast and strong that both of them sat in silence for several moments.

"Anna—" because her statement was the last response he'd expected from her, his voice was low and tentative "—I'd never do anything to hurt you."

"I know." She thought of the ring in the box, of the image of the house at their backs and rose with her nerves jumping. "If you could, I believe you'd treat me like glass, like something to be protected, cared for and admired. Somehow, it's easier for me when you lose sight of that and shout at me."

He couldn't pretend to understand her. But he rose and stood behind her. "Then I'll shout more often."

"I'm sure you will," she murmured, "when I frustrate you or disagree. But what happens when I give you everything you want?" She turned then, and her eyes were glowing with emotion. "What happens when I say all right, I give up?"

He grabbed her hands for fear she'd turn away again. "I don't know what you're talking about."

"I think you do, deep down. I think you know that part of me wants just what you want. But do either of us know if I want it for myself or just to please you? If I said yes and married you tomorrow, I'd have to toss away everything else."

"I'm not asking for that. I wouldn't."

"Wouldn't you?" She closed her eyes a moment and struggled for composure. "Can you tell me, can you be sure that you'll accept, care for, Dr. Anna Whitfield the same way you do for me now?"

He started to speak quickly, but her eyes were too dark, too vulnerable. There could be nothing with Anna but the truth. "I don't know."

She let out a quick, quiet sigh. Would he have lied if he'd known how much she'd wanted to hear it? And if he had lied, would she have taken the ring and given the promise? "Then give us both the time to be sure." Because he'd released her hands, her arms were free to go around him. "If I accept your ring, it'll be with my whole heart, with everything I am, and it'll be forever. Once it's there, Daniel, it's there to stay. That I can promise you. We both have to be sure it belongs there."

"It'll keep." The ring was back in his pocket. Anna was in his arms. They were alone, and the air was swirling with summer. When she lifted her face, he crushed his mouth to hers. "This won't," he murmured and drew her down with him.

Chapter 11

Anna took the news that they would be entertaining the governor calmly enough. Both her parents and her grandparents had entertained dignitaries from time to time. She'd been trained how to prepare a properly impressive menu, what wines to order and what brandy to serve. It really wasn't doing it that bothered her. It was the fact that Daniel had simply assumed she would.

She could have told him no. Anna lectured herself on this as she drove home from the hospital. She could have reminded him that she put in a full day between the hospital and her studies and didn't have the time or inclination to plan whether to serve oysters Rockefeller or coquilles St. Jacques as an appetizer. She could have and would have gained a brief moment of self-satisfaction. Then she would have spent the rest of her time feeling guilty for being petty and mean.

It would, after all, be their first dinner party as a couple. And it was so important to him. He wanted, she knew, to show her off as much as he wanted to give the governor a memorable meal. It should have infuriated her. Somehow she found it endearing. With a shake of her head, Anna admitted that loving Daniel could do strange things to common sense. So he could show her off; she wouldn't disappoint him. The time it took to plan the evening would be as much fun as work.

To be honest, she had to admit that preparing for a dinner party came as naturally to her as reciting the names of bones in the hand. Which reminded her, she wanted to look at Sally's the moment she got home.

Home. It made her smile. Only three weeks had passed since she'd unpacked in what had been Daniel's bedroom. It was their bedroom now. She might have her doubts about tomorrow, next week, next year, but she had none about today. She was happy. Living with Daniel had added a dimension to her life she had never expected. Because that was true, how could she explain that going on just as they were seemed the best way? The thought of marriage still sent a chill of unease down her back. And of distrust, she admitted. But whom did she distrust, Daniel or herself? She hadn't forgotten that he'd accused her of putting them both on trial. Perhaps she was, but only because she feared hurting him as much as she feared being hurt.

There were moments when it all seemed so clear to her. She'd marry him, bear his children, share his life. She'd be a doctor and develop her skill to the very height of its potential. He would be every bit as proud of her accomplishments as she was of his. She would have everything any woman could ever want, and so much more. It could happen. It would happen.

Then she would remember how carelessly uninterested he was in her work at the hospital. She would remember how he closeted himself in his office with business he never discussed with her. And how he never asked about the medical books that now littered the bedroom. Not once had he mentioned the fact that she was due back in Connecticut in a matter of weeks—or if he planned to be with her.

Could two people share a life, share a love and not share what was most vital to them? If she had the answer to that one question, she could stop asking herself any other.

With a shake of her head, Anna pulled into the driveway. She refused to be gloomy now. She was home, and that was enough.

As she walked in the kitchen door, Sally was bending over to pop something into the oven. "You're supposed to rest that hand."

"It's had all the rest it needs." Without turning around, Sally reached for a cup. "You're a bit late today."

"There was a car accident. Lots of bumps and scratches in Emergency. I stayed to hold some hands."

Sally poured coffee and set the cup on the table. "You'd rather have been cutting and sewing."

On a little sigh, Anna sat down with the coffee. "Yes. It's so hard not being allowed to do even the little things I could do. I'm not even allowed to take a blood pressure."

"It won't be long until you'll be doing a great deal more than that."

"I keep telling myself, one more year, just one more. But I'm so impatient, Sally."

"You and the MacGregor have that in common." Knowing she'd be welcome, Sally brought over a cup of her own. "He called to say he'd be late himself and for you to eat your supper if you didn't want to wait—but I could tell he was hoping you'd hold off till he got here."

"I can wait. Are you having any pain in that hand?"

"It's a bit stiff when I wake up, but there's barely a twinge even when I use it heavily." She held it out, admiring the scar that ran down the wrist. "There's a nice neat seam. Don't think I could do better myself." Then with a grin, she lowered her hand. "I don't suppose sewing up flesh is much like mending a tablecloth."

"The technique's pretty close." Anna gave the injured hand a pat. "Since Daniel's going to be late, this might be a good time for us to go over the guest list and menu for next week. I have some ideas, but if you've a specialty you'd rather—" She broke off and sniffed the air. "Sally, what have you got in the oven?"

"Peach pie." She preened. "My grandma's recipe."

"Oh." Anna closed her eyes and let the aroma flow through her. Warm peach pie on a summer's evening. "How late was Daniel going to be?"

"Eight, he said."

Anna glanced at her watch. "You know, I have a feeling that working on this menu is going to take a lot out of me." She smiled as she rose to fetch a pad and pencil. "I'll probably need a bit of something to tide me over."

"A piece of peach pie, perhaps?"

"That should do it."

When Daniel came in, Anna was still in the kitchen. Recipe cards, lists and scraps of paper littered the table where she and Sally sat. Between them was half of a peach pie and the remains of a bottle of white wine.

"I don't care how much we want to impress the governor," Anna said with her head close to Sally's. "We're not serving haggis. I know for a fact I'd turn green if I had to eat anything with entrails."

"A fine surgeon you'll make if you're squeamish."

"I'm not squeamish about what I have to look at or what I have to get my hands in. What goes in my stomach is a different matter. I vote for the coq au vin."

"Good evening, ladies."

Anna's head came up, and the smile that was already on her face grew when she saw him. "Daniel." She was up and taking both his hands. "Sally and I have been planning the dinner party. I'm afraid I may have offended her about the haggis, but I think our guests might be more comfortable with coq au vin."

"I'll leave that to the two of you," he said, and leaned down for a kiss. "Things took longer than I'd thought. I'm glad you didn't wait supper for me."

"Supper?" She still held his hands, as much now for support as anything else. Until she'd stood, she hadn't realized how fuzzy her mind was. "Sally and I were just testing out her peach pie. Would you like some?"

"Later. Though I could use a glass of that wine if you've left any." His eyes were burning from reading pages of fine print.

"Oh." She looked blankly at the bottle, wondering how it had come to be nearly empty.

"I'll have a shower first."

"I'll go up with you." Anna rummaged through the piles of paper until she found the one she wanted. "I'd like to read you this guest list so you can add anyone I've forgotten before we send the invitations out."

"Fine. Go on to bed, Sally. I'll help myself to the pie when I'm ready."

"Yes, sir. Thank you."

"You look tired, Daniel. Was it a difficult day?"

"No more than most." He slipped his arm around her as

they started up the stairs. "A few problems with the fine points of a deal I'm working on. I think we ironed them out."

"Can you talk about it?"

"I don't bring my troubles home." He gave her a little squeeze. "I spent the afternoon with your father."

"You did?" She felt a little skip of emotion but kept her voice level. "How is he?"

"Well, and keeping business and personal matters well apart."

"Yes." Her smile was a bit tight when they reached the top landing. "I suppose that's for the best."

"He asked about you." His voice was gentle now because he'd come to know her.

"He did?"

"Aye."

She entered first when Daniel pushed open the door to the bedroom. Because she felt so warm, she walked to the window to lean out. "Maybe if I hired him, he'd stop avoiding me."

"He's just worried about his daughter."

"There's nothing to worry about."

"He'll see that for himself at dinner next week."

Anna looked over, the guest list still clutched in her hand. "He'll come?"

"He'll come."

She let out a quick breath before she smiled again. "I suppose I have you to thank for that."

"Some, but I think your mother had more to do with it." He tossed his jacket and tie on one of the chairs Anna had arranged in front of the fireplace. As he unbuttoned his shirt, he could smell the summery scent of sweet peas that brimmed out of a bowl on a table by the window. Small

things. Enormous things. Daniel stopped undressing to fold
her tight in his arms.

She sensed the abrupt flurry of intense emotion that had
taken hold of him. Anna circled his waist with her arms
and let the feeling rush through her. Daniel kissed the top
of her head before he drew her away.

"What was that for?"

"For being here," he told her. "For being you." He slid
off his shoes with a little sigh of relief. "I won't be long.
Why don't you just call out the names on that list to me."
With economy of movement, Daniel stripped off the rest
of his clothes, then walked into the bath.

With only a small frown, Anna looked at the pile of
clothes on the floor. She wondered if she'd ever get used
to his carelessness about such things. Ignoring the obvious
alternative, she stepped over them. A woman who picked
up after a grown man was asking for trouble.

"There's the governor and his wife, of course," she called
out. "And Councilman and Mrs. Steers."

Daniel answered with a crude and accurate description
of the councilman. Anna cleared her throat and made a note
on the list to seat that particular couple at the opposite end
of the table from their host.

"Myra and Herbert. The Maloneys and the Cooks." She
lifted her voice over the sound of water. Still feeling warm, she
unfastened the first three buttons of her blouse. "The Donahues, with John Fitzsimmons to balance out Cathleen." Anna
peered at the list, blinking because her vision seemed blurred.

"John who?"

"Fitzspimmons—simmons. Fitzsimmons," she repeated
when she managed to get her tongue around it. "And Carl
Benson and Judith Mann. Myra told me they're about to
be engaged."

"She's built like a—" Daniel caught himself. "Very attractive woman," he amended. "Who else?"

Anna walked into the bathroom with her eyes narrowed. "Built like what?"

Behind the curtain Daniel merely grinned. "I beg your pardon?" To his surprise, Anna drew the curtain back. "Woman, is nothing sacred?"

"Just what is Judith Mann built like?"

"Now how would I know?" For safety's sake, he stuck his head under the spray. "You'd better pull the curtain to. You'll get wet."

"And how *would* you know?" she demanded and stepped, fully dressed, into the shower.

"Anna!" Laughing, he watched the water plaster her blouse against her. "What in hell are you doing?"

"Trying to get a straight answer." She waved the now soaking list at him. "Just what do you know about Judith Mann's anatomy?"

"Only what a man with good eyesight can see." He caught her chin in his hand and took a good look. "Now that I think about it I see something else."

She put a hand to his soapy chest for balance. "And what's that?"

"You're drunk, Anna Whitfield."

Dignity streamed from her as thick as the water. "I beg your pardon?"

Her haughtily delivered reply delighted him. Daniel brushed wet hair out of her eyes. "You're drunk," he repeated.

"Don't be ridiculous."

"It's drunk you are. Drunk as an Irish roof thatcher and twice as pretty. I'll be damned."

"You may well be, but I've never been drunk a day in my life. You're just trying to avoid the question."

"What's the question?"

She opened her mouth, shut it again, then grinned. "I don't remember. Have I ever told you what a magnificent body you have, Daniel?"

"No." He drew her against it before he began the task of peeling off her clothes. "Why don't you?"

"Such well-developed pectoral muscles."

Her blouse fell with a muffled splash. "And where might they be?"

"Just here," she murmured and ran a hand over his chest. "The deltoids are very firm. And of course the biceps are impressive, not obviously bulging, just hard." Her fingers slid over his shoulders and down as he tugged off her skirt. "It shows not simply strength but discipline—like the abdomen—very flat and tight." His breath caught as she explored there.

"Tell me, Anna—" he lowered his mouth to her ear and began to trace it with his tongue "—just how many muscles are there?"

Her head fell back, and the water sluiced over her. Naked, wet, pliant, she smiled up at him. "There are over six hundred muscles in the body, all attached to the two hundred and six bones that make up the skeleton."

"Fascinating. I'm wondering how many of mine you might point out."

"We could start with the muscles of the lower limbs. I admire your walk."

"Do you?"

"Yes, it's very firm and arrogant, but not quite a swagger. This, naturally, has something to do with your personality, but you also need your antigravity muscles, such as the soleus..." She bent down just enough to run a finger up his calf. Water poured over her hair. "The vasti," she continued, running a finger up his thigh, "and…" With a sound of approval, she slid her hands around to his bottom.

He grinned and let himself enjoy. He'd never had a woman give him quite so interesting a lesson. "I thought that muscle had more to do with sitting. The things you learn in anatomy class."

He switched off the water then reached for a towel to cover both of them.

"The gluteus maximus—" with an approving murmur, she ran her hands over him again "—has to stretch sufficiently or else you'd have a tendency to jackknife forward as you walk."

"Can't have that," he murmured as he gathered her up in his arms. "Especially when you're carrying precious cargo."

"And this is one of your most attractive muscles."

"Thank you." Flinging the towel aside, he lay with her on the bed. Warm night air played over damp skin.

"Now the adductors, the muscles on the inside of the thighs…"

"Show me."

"Just here." Her fingers reached down and skimmed over him just as his mouth closed over hers.

With her eyes half shut, she sighed and nuzzled into him. "I don't think you're paying attention."

"Oh, but I am. The adductors. Just here." Strong fingers pressed into firm thighs. "Just here," he repeated, "where your skin's like silk and already warm for me. And here." His hand journeyed up to tease the sensitive area where hip and thigh joined. "What are these muscles here?"

"They're—" But she could only moan and arch against him.

He caught the lobe of her ear in his teeth. "Have you forgotten?"

"Just touch me," she whispered. "It doesn't matter where."

With a sound of triumph, he took his hands over her, skimming, caressing, kneading, arousing. Like putty, she seemed willing to be molded. Like fire, she tempted and dared. Like a woman, she softened and tensed and gave. Her hands were as eager as his, her lips as hungry. Their skin dried in the warm summer air, then became damp again with excitement.

Each time, she thought hazily, each time they made love, it was more thrilling, more beautiful. The first time, the hundredth time, the edge of desire was never dulled. In a field of grass, on feather pillows it was just as volatile. In the bright light of day, in the dark secret night it was just as frenzied. She'd never stop wanting him. Of all the questions she'd asked herself, she was sure of that answer. Need for him would never fade.

They rolled over the big bed, frantic for each other, lost in each other. Trapped in pleasure, she rose up, back arched, eyes closed, her hair a wild, wet tangle. The sliver of light from the next room shot a nimbus around her that seemed to shiver with her ecstasy. Half-mad he came to her, so that kneeling on the bed they could pour pleasures over each other. Weak, vibrating, they tumbled down again and took the last step into passion.

Her limbs were wrapped around him. Her face was buried against his throat as her breath heaved in and out. Her fingers dug into his back and felt hard flesh and sweat. And as he moved into her, moved with her, she rode on the carousel, flew on the roller coaster and lost herself in the maze.

"You're stunning." Daniel stared at her as she studied herself in the mirror. "Absolutely stunning."

It pleased her to hear it, though she'd never thought much

of compliments. The dress left her shoulders bare and fell in a loose sweeping line to just above her ankles. Pearls crusted the bodice and danced along the skirt. Myra had talked her into it, though she'd needed little persuasion. True, it had taken a healthy chunk out of the money she'd put aside for board during the fall, but she was confident she'd find a way to balance her books. The look on Daniel's face, and the satisfaction she felt seeing her own reflection, made it worthwhile.

"You like it?"

How could he explain that, though he knew every intimate inch of her, just looking at her could still take his breath away? She'd been right when she'd thought he wanted to show her off. When a man had something exquisite, he needed to share it. No, he couldn't explain. "I like it so well I'm wishing the evening was already over."

She gave a last swirl, as much for herself as for him. "You look wonderful in a dinner jacket. Elegantly barbarian."

His brow lifted. "Barbarian?"

"Never change that." She held out both hands and took his. "No matter what else has to change, don't change that."

He brought her hands to his lips, kissed one, then the other. "I doubt I could, any more than you could change being a lady—even after too much wine and peach pie."

She tried to look stern but laughed. "You'll never let me forget that."

"God, no. It was one of the most fascinating evenings of my life. I'm crazy about you, Anna."

"So you've said." She lifted their joined hands to her cheek. "That's something else I don't want you to change."

"I won't. I like seeing you wear the cameo." He brushed a finger over it as was his habit.

"It means a great deal to me."

"You wouldn't take my ring."

"Daniel—"

"You wouldn't take my ring," he continued, "but you took the cameo. I'd like you to take this." Drawing a box out of his pocket, he waited.

Anna folded her hands together. "Daniel, you don't have to buy me presents."

"I think I've figured that out." But he'd yet to figure out how to accept that fact. "It might be why I want to. Humor me," he said, and made her smile.

"You've said that before." Because he smiled back, she accepted the box. "Thank you." Then she opened the box and found she could say nothing.

"Is something wrong with them?"

She managed to shake her head. Pearls and diamonds, pure in simplicity, arrogant in beauty, the earrings lay against black velvet and nearly breathed with life. From the simple orbs of milky white pearls dripped the tear-shaped glamour of diamonds. One gleamed, the other flashed and together they made a stunning unit.

"Daniel, they're…" She shook her head and looked back up at him. "They're absolutely beautiful. I don't know what to say."

"You just said it." Relieved, he took the box and removed the earrings. "I suppose you'll have to thank Myra. I asked her advice. She said something about class and flash making the best team."

"Did she?" Anna murmured as Daniel fastened the earrings on her himself.

"There now." Pleased, he stepped back to inspect. "Yes, they'll do nicely. Now maybe they'll draw the attention and keep men's eyes off all that beautiful skin you've exposed."

Laughing again, Anna lifted a hand to her ear. "Ah, an ulterior motive."

"It's hard not to worry that you'll take a good look around and see someone who appeals to you more."

"Don't be silly." Taking it as a joke, she linked arms with him. "I suppose we'd better go down or the guests will be arriving. Then McGee will scowl at us for being late and unpardonably rude."

"Ha." As they walked through the door, Daniel found her hand with his. "As if you hadn't twisted him around your finger already."

Anna gave him an innocent look as they started downstairs. "I don't know what you mean."

"Fixes scones for you in the middle of the week. Never did that for me."

"Ah, there's the door now." She paused on the bottom landing. "Promise not to glare—even at Councilman Steers."

"I never glare," he lied easily, and led her down the hall to greet the first guests.

In less than twenty minutes the big parlor was crowded with bodies and buzzing with conversation. Though Anna was perfectly aware that she and Daniel were often the topic of the moment, she made her way calmly from group to group. She hadn't needed her mother's warning to know that her decision would alienate her from some. But her choices were never made with other people's opinions in mind.

Louise Ditmeyer's greeting was a bit stiff, but Anna ignored it and, chatting, steered her to a group of friends. More than once she caught someone aiming a speculative look in her direction. It was easy enough to meet this calmly. That was her way. Anna had no idea that her cool confidence and natural graciousness did more to squelch gossip than Daniel's power or her own family name.

If there was a shadow on the evening, it came from the governor's careless request for her opinion on Daniel's projected textile factory. How could she have an opinion or even an intelligent comment? Daniel had never mentioned it to her, and she was faced with the governor's glowing praise of a project that would bring employment to hundreds and fat revenues to the state. Training kept her smile in place and brought easy answers. There was no time for anger as she introduced the governor and his wife to another couple. There was time for only a moment's envy that the governor's wife appeared to be deeply involved in his work. Pressed by her duties as hostess, Anna pushed personal disappointment to the back of her mind.

Not until her parents arrived did she feel any real tension. Holding her breath, she approached her father.

"I'm so glad you came." She rose on her toes to kiss his cheek, though she was far from sure of her reception.

"You look well." He didn't speak coldly, but she felt his reserve.

"So do you. Hello, Mother." She pressed her cheek against her mother's and smiled at the encouraging squeeze.

"You look beautiful, Anna." She shot her husband a quick look. "Happy."

"I am happy. Let me get you both a drink."

"Now don't fuss with us," her mother told her. "You have all these guests. There's Pat Donahue, I see. Just run along. We'll be fine."

"All right, then." As she started to turn away, her father caught her hand.

"Anna…" As he hesitated, he felt her hand tighten on his. "It's good to see you."

It was enough. She wrapped her arms around his neck and held for just a moment. "If I came by your office one day, would you play hooky and go for a ride with me?"

"You going to let me drive your car?"

She smiled brilliantly. "Maybe."

He winked and patted her head as he'd always done. "See to your guests."

When she turned it was to see Daniel a few feet away, smiling at her. She walked to him with her heart in her eyes. "Now you look even more beautiful," he murmured to her.

"What's all this?" Myra came up to stand between them. "The host and hostess aren't even supposed to have time to speak to each other at an affair like this. Daniel, I really believe you should go rescue the governor from our esteemed councilman before he loses his appetite. The governor, that is." When Daniel muttered something rude, she merely nodded. "Just so. Now, Anna, why don't we walk over to where Cathleen is boring the daylights out of the Maloneys. I'm dying to see her gag over your earrings."

"Subtle, Myra," Anna warned as they maneuvered through the groups. "Remember the beauty of subtlety."

"Darling, of course. But I'd really appreciate it if you'd be sure to toss your head just a little now and then. Why, Cathleen, what a nice dress."

Cathleen stopped her dissertation on her summer schedule to study Myra. Anna wasn't sure, but she thought the Maloneys sighed in unison. "Thank you, Myra. I suppose congratulations and best wishes are in order. I haven't seen you since you and Herbert ran away."

"No, you haven't." Myra sipped her drink and ignored the less than complimentary description of her marriage. Envy was the simplest of things to ignore when you were happy.

"I suppose there's something to be said for elopements, though for myself, I'd find it a rather cut-and-dried way of marrying."

"To each his own," Myra returned, and tried to remember it was Anna's dinner party.

"Oh, indeed." Cathleen gave a little nod. "But what a shame you and Herbert have decided to be hermits even after cheating us all out of a big wedding."

"I'm afraid Herbert and I haven't entertained on a grand scale yet. We want to finish our redecorating before we have more than our most intimate friends over. You understand."

Seeing the need to intervene, Anna stepped a bit closer. "I'm sure you've had a busy summer, Cathleen."

"Oh, quite busy." She gave Anna a cool smile. "Though others seem to get more accomplished in a shorter time. I took a little trip to the shore, and when I got back to Boston I learned Myra and Herbert had run off and you'd changed addresses. Are congratulations of a different sort in order?"

Anna laid a hand on Myra's arm to silence her. "Not at all. You've brought back a beautiful tan. I'm sorry I missed getting to the beach. I didn't seem to find the time."

"I'm sure you didn't." Lifting her drink, Cathleen took a long, slow sip. It wasn't easy to accept that two of the women she'd debuted with had snagged two of the most influential men in the city—particularly when she'd all but decided to set her sights on Daniel. "Tell me, Anna, just how do I introduce you and Daniel if the occasion comes up? I'm afraid I'm naive about these things."

Even Anna's patience only lasted so long. "Why should it matter?"

"Oh, it does. As a matter of fact, I'm thinking of giving a little dinner party myself. I haven't a clue how to write your invitation."

"I wouldn't worry about it."

"Oh, but I do." Her eyes widened and rounded. "I'd hate to make a faux pas."

"What a pity."

If Cathleen couldn't get a rise one way, she'd get one another. "Well, after all, one doesn't know how to politely address a man's mistress." Then she let out a gasp and squeal as Myra's drink ran down her bodice.

"Oh, how dreadfully clumsy of me." Rocking back on her heels, Myra surveyed the damage to Cathleen's pink crepe de chine. It was almost enough to satisfy Myra. "I feel like such a mule," she said lightly. "Come, I'll go up with you, Cathleen. I'll be more than happy to sponge you off."

"I can take care of myself," she said between gritted teeth. "Just keep away from me."

Myra lit a cigarette and blew smoke at the ceiling. "Whatever you say."

Feeling obligated, Anna started to take her arm. "Here, let me take you up."

"Keep your hands off me," she hissed. "You and your imbecile friend." Skirts swirling, she was pushing herself through the crowd.

"Subtlety," Anna sighed. "Didn't we speak of subtlety?"

"I didn't toss it in her face," Myra said. "And to tell the truth, I've been wanting to do that for so long. This was the first time I could and feel absolutely justified." She gave Anna a wide grin. "Do I have time for another drink before dinner?"

Chapter 12

Perhaps if Daniel hadn't overheard the incident with Cathleen Donahue he would have handled things differently. But he had. Perhaps if his anger at the insult hadn't eaten away at him, their relationship could have continued smoothly enough. But it didn't. Throughout the rest of the evening, he managed to remain the congenial host. Guests left his home well fed and content. He could barely wait to close the door behind the last of them.

"We need to talk," he told Anna before she could take her first sigh of relief.

Though she was wilting a bit around the edges, she nodded. Others might have been fooled by Daniel's easy conversation and careless generosity through the evening, but she had sensed both strain and anger. In tacit agreement, they walked upstairs to the privacy of the bedroom.

"Something has upset you," she began, and sat on the arm of chair, though she longed to take off her clothes and fall mindlessly into bed. "I know you had business with the governor. Did something go wrong?"

"My business is fine." He paced to the window and pulled out a cigar. "It's my personal life that's the problem."

She folded her hands in her lap, a sure sign of annoyance or nerves. "I see."

"No, you don't." He turned to her then, ready to snipe or charge. "If you understood, there'd be no argument about marriage. It would simply be a fact."

"Simply a fact," she repeated and struggled to remember how unproductive anger was. "Daniel, our biggest problem seems to stem from our diverse outlooks on marriage. I don't see it as simply a fact, but as the biggest step one person can take with another. I can't take that step with you until I'm ready."

"If you ever are," he shot back.

She moistened her lips. Behind her growing temper were regrets. "If I ever am."

The anger he'd held in all evening gnawed at him. "So, you'll give me no promises, Anna. Nothing."

"I told you before I wouldn't give a promise I may have to break. I'll give you everything I can, Daniel."

"It's not enough." He drew on the cigar then watched her through a haze of smoke.

"I'm sorry. If I could, I'd give you more."

"If you could?" Fury whipped through him, blinding him to reason. "*If* you could? Nothing's stopping you but your own stubbornness."

"If that were true, I'd be a fool." She rose because it was time to face him. Time, in fact, to face herself. "And perhaps I am, because I expect you to give my needs and ambitions as much respect as you give your own."

"What in hell does that have to do with marriage?"

"Everything. In nine months I'll have my degree."

"A piece of paper," he shot back.

Everything about her turned cold: her skin, her voice, her eyes. "A piece of paper? I wonder if you would call your deeds and stocks and contracts pieces of paper—pieces of paper too lofty, too important to ever be discussed with me. Or perhaps, as with the textile factory the governor asked me about tonight, you don't consider me intelligent enough to understand your work."

"I've never doubted your intelligence," he shot back. "What do deeds and stock have to do with us?"

"They're part of you, just as my degree will be part of me. I've devoted years of my life to earning it. I would think you could understand that."

"I'll tell you what I understand." Rigid with anger, he crushed out his cigar. "I understand I'm tired of coming in second place to this precious degree."

"Damn you, Daniel, no one can tell you anything." Fighting for control, she leaned both hands on her dresser. "It isn't a matter of places; it isn't a competition."

"What is it then? Just what in hell is it?"

"A matter of respect," she said more calmly, and turned to him again. "It's a matter of respect."

"And what about love?"

He spoke of love so seldom that his question nearly broke her. Tears swam in her eyes and smothered her voice. "Love is an empty word without respect. I'd rather not have it from a man who can't accept me for what I am. I'd rather not give it to a man who won't share his problems with me as well as his successes."

His pride was as strong as hers. Even as he felt her slip away from him, he gripped his pride as though it were all he had left. "Then perhaps you'd prefer it if I stopped loving you. I'll do my best." With that, he turned on his heel. Moments later, Anna heard the front door slam.

She could have fallen on the bed and given in to tears. She wanted to—maybe too much. Because she couldn't, there seemed to be only one thing left to do. Mechanically she began to pack.

The drive to Connecticut was a long and lonely one. Weeks later, Anna could remember it vividly. She drove through the night until her eyes were gritty and the sun was up. Exhausted, she checked into a motel and slept until dusk. When she woke, she tried to forget what she'd left behind. The first few days were spent finding a small apartment near the campus. She needed privacy, and indulged herself by having her own place. Her days were full with planning, preparing. Anna thought it a pity that her nights couldn't be full as well.

Anna could block Daniel out of her mind for long stretches during the day, but at night she would lie in her bed and remember what it had been like to curl up against him. She would eat alone at her little table in her little kitchen and remember how she and Daniel had lingered over coffee in the dining room simply because it was so comfortable just to talk.

She deliberately refused to install a phone. It would have made it too easy to call him. When classes began, she fell into them with an almost desperate relief.

Her fellow students noticed a change in her. The usually friendly, if slightly reserved Miss Whitfield was now completely withdrawn. She rarely spoke unless it was to ask or answer a question in class. Those who happened to drive by her apartment in the evening or late on a Saturday night invariably saw a light burning in her window. Incessant study brought shadows to eyes that even her professors began to note. She blocked any comment or question with polite but firm withdrawal.

The days blurred together as she wanted them to. If she studied hard enough, long enough, she could fall into oblivion for six hours a night and not think at all.

Connecticut in mid-September was brisk and beautiful, but Anna had taken little time to notice the foliage. The strong colors and rich scents of fall were bypassed in favor of medical journals and anatomy classes. In previous years, she'd managed to enjoy her surroundings while devoting herself to her studies. Now, if she stopped for a moment to admire the wild riot of leaves, she would think only of a cliff top and the roar of water on rock. And she would wonder, in that moment before she pulled herself away, if Daniel was building his house.

In defense, she had even avoided contacting Myra, though her friend sent her long, annoyed letters. When the telegram arrived, Anna realized she couldn't hide forever. It read simply: IF YOU DON'T WANT ME ON YOUR DOORSTEP IN TWENTY-FOUR HOURS CALL STOP MYRA STOP.

With the telegram mixed in with her notes on the circulatory system, Anna stopped between classes at a pay phone in the student lounge. Armed with change, she put the call through and waited.

"Hello."

"Myra, if you arrived on my doorstep you'd have to sleep there. I don't have an extra bed."

"Anna! Good God, I was beginning to think you'd slid into the Atlantic." Anna heard the quick snap of a lighter and an indrawn breath. "That was easier to believe than that you'd been too rude to answer my letters."

"I'm sorry. I've been busy."

"You've been hiding," Myra corrected. "And I'll tolerate that as long as it's not from me. I've been worried about you."

"Don't be. I'm fine."

"Of course."

"No, I'm not fine," she admitted because it was Myra. "But I am busy, up to my ears in books and notes."

"You haven't called Daniel?"

"No, I can't." She closed her eyes and rested her forehead against the cool metal of the phone. "How is he? Have you seen him?"

"Seen him?" Anna could almost see Myra roll her eyes. "He went crazy the night you left. Woke Herbert and I up after two a.m., demanding if you were here. Herbert calmed him down. The man's positively amazing—Herbert that is. We haven't seen a great deal of Daniel since, but I hear he's spending a lot of time in Hyannis Port supervising the building of his house."

"Yes, he would." And she could see him there, watching the machines dig and the men laying stone.

"Anna, did you know that Daniel overheard that little incident with Cathleen the night of the dinner party?"

She caught herself wallowing in self-pity and shook her head. "No. No, he didn't tell me. Oh..." She remembered the underlying fury she'd sensed in him—the same fury he'd turned on her. It explained a great deal.

"I heard him tell Herbert he'd like to wring her skinny neck. Though I approved, Herbert talked him out of it. It did seem though that the entire business had thrown him off. The man has the idea that you should be protected from any kind of insult. It's sweet really, though we can certainly take care of ourselves."

"I can't marry Daniel in order not to be insulted," she murmured.

"No. And though I'm sure he deserves a kick in the behind, darling, I'd swear his heart's in the right place. He loves you, Anna."

"Only part of me." She closed her eyes and willed herself to be strong. "I'm sorry we involved you."

"Oh, please, you know I thrive on being involved. Anna, do you want to talk about it? Would you like me to come?"

"No, really. At least not yet." Though she rubbed at her temple, Anna laughed. "I'm glad I didn't answer your letters. Talking to you has done me more good than anything else."

"Then give me your number. There's no reason why we can't talk instead of writing."

"I don't have a phone."

"No phone?" There was a shocked and pregnant pause. "Anna, darling, how do you survive?"

She stopped rubbing at her temple and really laughed. "I'm very primitive here. You'd be shocked if you saw my apartment." And she wondered if even Myra would understand the enthusiasm she'd felt while spending the best part of the afternoon with a dozen other students and a cadaver. Some things were best left unsaid. "Look, I promise, I'll sit down and write you a long letter tonight. I'll even call again next week."

"All right, then. But one word of advice before you go. Daniel's a man, so he starts with one strike against him. Just try to remember that."

"Thanks. Give my love to Herbert."

"I will. I'm counting on that letter."

"Tonight," she promised again. "Bye, Myra."

When Anna hung up, she felt truly steady for the first

time in weeks. True, she'd taken charge of her own life when she'd left Boston. She'd leased her own apartment, registered for classes. She set her own study time and was responsible for her own success, her own failure. But she hadn't been happy. She was responsible for that, as well, she reminded herself as she walked back down the hall. It was time to face the fact that she'd made her choice. If she had to live as it seemed she did—alone—then she had to make the best of it.

A glance at her watch showed her she had ten minutes before her next class. This time she'd step outside and enjoy the autumn weather instead of hurrying to the next building and burying her face in a book.

Outside, she saw the symphony of color she had almost deliberately ignored for weeks. She saw other students hurrying to class or stretched on the grass reading by sunlight. She saw the slight slope and the old red brick of the hospital. And she saw the blue convertible at the curb.

For an instant, she couldn't move. Weeks peeled away and she was coming out of the hospital in Boston to find Daniel waiting for her. Her fingers tightened on the books she carried. But it wasn't Boston, she thought more calmly. And Daniel's wasn't the only blue convertible on the east coast. It was simply a mean twist of fate that had made her walk out and see it. Pulling herself together, she started to walk away. Seconds later, she was going back to the car for a closer look.

"Want a ride?"

At the sound of his voice, she felt her heart roll over in her chest. When she turned, her face was touched with both wariness and pleasure. "Daniel, what are you doing here?" And what did she care? It was enough just to look at him.

"It appears I'm waiting for you." He wanted to touch

her, but if he touched, he'd grab. Deliberately he kept his hands in his pockets. "What time is your last class over?"

"Last class?" She'd forgotten what day it was. "Ah, an hour or so. I only have one more today."

"All right, then, I'll be back."

Be back? Dazed, she watched him walk around the hood and open the driver's door. Before she realized she intended to do it, Anna pulled open the passenger's.

"What are you doing?"

"I'm going with you," she blurted out.

He gave her a long, cool stare. "What about your class?"

She gave a desperate look around the campus before she climbed in the car. "I'll borrow someone's notes. I can make it up." But she couldn't make up another hour away from him.

"You're not the type to skip classes."

"No, I'm not." Giddy, she set her books in her lap. "My apartment isn't far. We can have some coffee. Just turn left past the hospital then—"

"I know where it is," he interrupted, but didn't add he'd known almost before the ink had dried on the lease.

The five-minute drive went quickly as dozens of thoughts ran through her head. How should she treat him? Politely? Was he still angry? For the first time since she'd known him, Anna couldn't gauge his mood. Her nerves were jumping by the time he stopped the car again. He seemed perfectly calm.

"I wasn't expecting anyone," she began as they walked up the steps to her apartment on the second floor.

"A person might be able to call if you had a phone."

"I hadn't given it much thought," she told him, then unlocked the door. "Come in," she invited.

The moment he stepped inside she realized how impossibly small the apartment was. In the living area, Daniel could all but touch the walls if he were to spread out his arms. She had a divan, a coffee table and a lamp, and hadn't seen the necessity for anything else.

"Sit down," she offered, discovering she desperately needed a moment to herself. "I'll make coffee."

Without waiting for his answer, she fled to the kitchen. When he was alone, Daniel unclenched his hands. He didn't see simply a small room, but the touches of charm. She had colorful pillows tossed on the couch and a bowl of shells on the coffee table. More than that, the tiny sun-washed room carried her scent—the same scent that had faded from their bedroom. He couldn't sit, and he couldn't stand alone. Clenching his hands again, he followed her into the kitchen.

He couldn't tell how much cooking she did in the cramped space, but she obviously worked here. On the table by the window was a portable typewriter and stacks of notes and books. Pencils worn down to nubs and freshly sharpened ones were held in a china cup. He was out of his element. He felt it. He fought it.

"Coffee will just be a minute," she said to fill the silence. He was there again, and she hadn't had enough time. She couldn't know that he was feeling precisely the same. "I don't have anything else to offer you. I haven't shopped this week."

She was nervous, he realized, hearing the jumps in her usually smooth voice. Curious, he watched and saw her hands tremble lightly as she reached for cups. He felt the knots in his stomach loosen just a little. How did he approach her? Daniel pulled up a chair and sat.

"You're looking pale, Anna."

"I haven't been getting much sun. The schedule's always frantic the first few weeks."

"And weekends?"

"There's the hospital."

"Mmm. If you were a doctor, you might diagnose over-work."

"I'm not a doctor yet." She set the coffee down, then hesitated. After a moment, she sat across from him. It was so much like their time together before. Yet it was nothing like it at all. "I happened to talk to Myra today. She said that you've started the house in Hyannis Port."

"That's right." He'd watched them break the ground, seen the foundation rise. And it had meant nothing. Nothing at all. "If we stay on schedule, the main part will be livable by next summer."

"You must be pleased." Her coffee tasted like mud, and she pushed it aside.

"I have the blueprints in the car. You might like to see them."

Her chest was tight as she lifted her head. He saw the surprise in her eyes and cursed himself for a fool. "Of course, I would."

For a moment he scowled down at his own hands. He was a gambler, wasn't he? It was time to take another chance. "I'm thinking of buying an office building down-town. Small businesses and low rent, but I think the prop-erty value should double in five to seven years." He added a lump of sugar to his coffee but didn't stir it. "I've run into some problems with the textile factory. Your father's work-ing on the kinks so we can be in production by spring."

She kept her gaze steady on his. "Why are you telling me?"

He took a minute. Confessions didn't come easily to him. But her eyes were so dark, so patient. Hard as it was, he'd realized he needed her as much as his own pride. "A man doesn't like to admit he was wrong, Anna. But more than that, he doesn't like to face that his woman turned away from him because he couldn't admit it."

He could have said nothing that could have made her love him more. "I didn't turn away from you, Daniel."

"Ran away."

She swallowed. "All right, I ran away. From both of us. Do you realize you've offered me more of yourself in the last five minutes than you did the entire time we lived together?"

"It never occurred to me that you'd want to know about factories and interest rates." He started to rise, then changed his mind when he saw the impatience in her eyes. "You'd better say what's on your mind."

"The first time I walked into the bedroom, I saw how little of yourself was there. After a while, I figured out why. You were so determined to go forward. Daniel, as much as you spoke of the home and family you wanted, you've had it in your head to do it yourself. I was to be swept along."

"There'd be no family without you, Anna."

"But you wanted to give, not to share. You never offered to show me the blueprints of the home you said you wanted for both of us. You never asked for an opinion or a suggestion."

"No. And as I watched them build the foundation, I realized I was going to have the house I wanted, but not the home I needed." He set down his spoon with a snap. "I never thought it really mattered to you."

"I didn't know how to show you." She smiled a little. "Stupid." Because she needed just a bit of distance, she rose to stand at the window. Strange, she realized, she worked here every evening and hadn't noticed the big red maple that spread in the yard. It was beautiful. How much beauty was she cutting out of her life? "Part of me wanted to share that home with you. More than anything."

"But only part."

"I guess it's the part you can't accept that held me back. That held us both back. Do you know, you never asked about my work at the hospital, about the books or about why I want to be a surgeon."

He rose, too. He'd already faced himself. Now he had to face her. "A man doesn't ask the woman he loves about her other lover."

Torn between anger and confusion, she turned. "Daniel—"

"Don't ask me to be reasonable," he interrupted. "I'm damn near ready to crawl if I have to, but don't ask me to be reasonable."

On a huff of breath, she shook her head. "All right, I won't. Let's just say then that some women can have two lovers and be happy spending their lives trying to give each what they need."

"It's a hard life."

"Not if the woman has two lovers that are willing to give her back what she needs."

There was no room to pace in the little kitchen. Instead, Daniel rocked back on his heels, his hands still clenched in his pockets. "You know, I did a lot of thinking about your doctoring these last few weeks. More, I guess, than I've wanted to do since I first saw you. There were times, Anna, when I could see you were meant for something more, but I managed to block it out. When you left and I spent my nights alone, I didn't have any choice but to think. I remembered the way you'd been with Mrs. Higgs. And the way you'd look when you'd walk out of the hospital in the evening. I remembered how you'd stood in the kitchen with blood on your blouse and explained, very calmly, how you'd dealt with Sally's wrist. She told me the doctor said you'd saved her life. Something you'd learned in one of these," he said, indicating the stack of books. "Not so hard to learn, maybe, but I wouldn't think so easy to do." He picked up a book and held it as he faced her. "No, I haven't asked you before why you want to be a surgeon. I'm asking now."

She hesitated, afraid he might make some cutting, or worse, patronizing remark. He'd come to her—a gamble. She could gamble as well. "I have a dream," she told him quietly. "I want to make a difference."

He studied her in silence, his eyes narrowed, the irises a deep, intense blue. "I have a dream," he said at length then set the book down again. For the first time, he stepped toward her. "It's a small apartment, Anna. But I think there's room enough for two."

He heard her long broken breath before she wrapped her arms around him. "We'll need a bigger bed."

"There's a lass." On a laugh, he picked her up off the floor and gave himself the pleasure of her mouth. Relief poured through him like wine until he was drunk with it. "I've missed you, Anna. I can't do without you again."

"No." With her face buried against his throat, she drew in his scent and filled herself with it. "Not again. Daniel, I've only been half-alive here without you. I tried to crowd the day with studies, to work harder, longer at the hospital, but it just didn't mean anything. I want you with me, need you with me."

"You'll have me. A bigger bed and three phones should do it."

With a laugh, she found his lips with hers. He could have his phones as long as she had him. "I love you."

"You never told me that." Unsteady, he drew her away. "You never once told me that before."

"I was afraid to. I thought if you knew how much I loved you, you might use it to make me give up the rest."

He started to deny it, then swore at himself because it was true. "And now?"

"The rest doesn't mean much if you're not with me."

He drew farther away. "Once I told you I'd thought of you looking around and seeing someone who appealed to you more. I wasn't joking."

She gave him a little shake. "You should have been."

Didn't she realize how lovely she was, how regal? Didn't she know how clumsy she could make a man feel with just a smile? "Don't believe I've taken you for granted or ever will. I may act like it, but it won't be true. You're my answer, Anna, and I want to be yours."

She rested her cheek on his shoulder a moment. It had never occurred to her that his confidence would ever waver. She loved him more knowing it could. "You are, Daniel. I haven't been sure I could give you what you seemed to want."

"I wanted a wife, a woman who'd be there at night when I came home. One who'd keep flowers in the vases and lace at the windows. One who'd be content with whatever I could give her."

She looked at the books stacked on the table, then at the man standing in front of her. "And now?"

"I'm beginning to think a woman like that would bore me within a week."

She pressed her fingers to her eyes to hold back the tears. "I'd like to think so."

"I'm not backing down." His voice was suddenly rough as he dragged her back against him. "You're going to marry me, Anna, the day after you have that degree. You'll be Dr. Whitfield for less than twenty-four hours."

Her fingers curled into his shirt. "Daniel, I—"

"Then it's Dr. MacGregor."

Her fingers froze. She took three quiet breaths before she dared to speak. "Do you mean that?"

"Aye. I always mean what I say. And you'll have to put up with me introducing my wife as the best surgeon in the country. I want to share your dream, Anna, as much as I want you to share mine."

"It won't be easy for you. While I'm an intern, the hours will be hateful."

"And in twenty years, we'll look back and wonder how we got through them. I like the long view, Anna. I wanted you to marry me because I thought you fit a slot. You didn't fit it." He took her hands in his. "Now I'm asking you to marry me because I love you exactly as you are."

She took a long time to study him. This time there would be no stepping back. "Do you still have the ring?"

"Aye." He reached in his pocket. "I got into the habit of carrying it with me."

Laughing, she lifted both hands to his face. "I'll take it now." As he started to slip it on, she closed her hand over his. "Here's a promise for you, Daniel. I'll do my best."

The ring slid on. "That's good enough."

Epilogue

Anna had slept in snatches through the night, rejecting the cot an orderly had brought her, preferring the chair beside Daniel's bed. From time to time during the night, he'd murmured in his sleep. Whenever she'd heard her name, she tried to soothe him, talking to him, reminiscing until he was restful again.

Only once did she leave him to go down and check on Shelby. The rest of the time she sat watching him sleep and listening to the all too familiar beeps and clicks of machines.

The nurses changed shifts. Someone brought her coffee before going off duty. The moon began to set. She thought of the man she loved, of the life they'd built, and sat in silence to wait.

Just before dawn, she leaned over to rest her head on the bed beside his hand. When Daniel woke, he saw her first. She was sleeping lightly.

He was disoriented for only a moment. Even though the drugs were still swimming in his system, he remembered the accident with perfect clarity. He thought briefly of his car. He was very fond of that particular toy. Then he felt the pressure in his chest, saw the tubes running from his arm.

He remembered more than the accident now. He remembered Anna leaning over him, talking, reassuring him as he was being wheeled on a gurney down the hospital corridor. He remembered the fear he'd read in her eyes, and before he slipped into unconsciousness, his one moment of blind, naked terror that he was being taken away from her.

Oddly, he thought he remembered looking down at himself from somewhere while doctors and nurses scrambled around. Then it seemed he'd been sucked back into his body, but the sensation was too vague to pinpoint. He remembered one more thing. Anna again, leaning over him, cursing at him, kissing his hand. Then he had simply dreamed.

She looked so tired, he realized. Then it came home to him how old and battered his own body felt. Furious at his weakness, he struggled to sit up and couldn't. Because the effort it cost him embarrassed him, he reached out to touch Anna's cheek. She was awake in an instant.

"Daniel." Her fingers curled around his. In a matter of seconds, he saw it all on her face: terror, relief, grief, weariness and strength. Through sheer will she controlled the need to simply drop her head to his chest and weep. "Daniel—" her voice was as cool and calm as the first time he'd ever heard it "—do you know me?"

Though it cost him, he lifted a brow. "Why in hell wouldn't I know the woman I've lived with for almost forty years?"

"Why in hell not," she agreed and gave herself the pleasure of pressing her lips to his.

"You might be more comfortable if you climbed in here with me."

"Maybe later," she promised, and lifted one of his eyelids to study his pupil.

"Don't start poking and prodding at me. I want a real doctor." He managed to grin at her.

She pressed a button beside the bed. "Is your vision blurred?"

"I can see you well enough. You're as pretty as you were the first night we waltzed."

"Hallucinating," she said dryly, then looked up as a nurse came in. "Please call Dr. Feinstein. Mr. MacGregor is awake and requesting a real doctor."

"Yes, Dr. MacGregor."

"I love it when they call you that," he murmured, and shut his eyes for just a minute. "How much damage did I do, Anna?"

"You were concussed. You've broken three ribs, and—"

"Not to me," he said impatiently, "to the car."

Setting her teeth, she folded her arms. "You never change. I don't know why I bothered to worry. I'm terribly sorry I disturbed the children."

"The children." The light in his eyes wasn't as fierce as it might have been, but it was there. "You called the children?"

He'd given her precisely the reaction she'd needed for her own reassurance. Anna pretended indifference. "Yes, I must apologize to them."

"They came?"

She knew his tactics too well. "Of course."

"What were you going to do, have a wake?"

She tidied his top sheet. "We wanted to be prepared."

He scowled at her and nearly managed to gesture toward the door. "Well, send them in."

"I wouldn't have them spend the night here. They're at home."

His mouth dropped open. "Home? You mean they didn't stay here? They left their father on his deathbed and went to drink his Scotch?"

"Yes, I'm afraid they're very feckless children, Daniel. Take after their father. Here's Dr. Feinstein now." She gave his hand a quick pat before she walked to the door. "I'll leave you two alone."

"Anna."

She paused at the door and smiled back at him. "Yes, Daniel?"

"Don't stay away long."

She saw him then as he'd been so many years before: indomitable, arrogant and strong enough to need. "Do I ever?"

She walked straight out of Intensive Care to her own office. Locking the door, she gave herself the luxury of a twenty-minute weeping spell. She'd cried there before, after losing a patient. This time she wept from a relief too great to measure and a love too strong to soothe. After rinsing her face several times in cold water, she went to the phone.

"Hello."

"Caine."

"Mom, we were just about to call. Is he—"

"Your father wants to see you," she said easily. "He's afraid you've been drinking his Scotch."

He swore, and she heard his momentary struggle for control. "Tell him we didn't put much of a dent in it. Are you okay?"

"I'm terrific. Ask Rena to bring me a change of clothes when you come."

"We'll be there in a half hour."

* * *

"It's a shame when a man has to all but die to get his children to visit him." Propped on pillows, swathed in bandages, Daniel held court.

"A couple of broken ribs," Serena said lightly and tweaked his toe from her position at the foot of the bed. She'd lain wakeful through the night in Justin's arms.

"Ha! Tell that to the doctor who put this tube in my chest. And you didn't even bring my grandson." He glared briefly at Serena before turning to Caine. "Or my granddaughter. They'll be in college before I see them again. Won't even know who I am."

"We show Laura your picture once a week," Caine offered. He continued to hold Diana's hand, wondering if he would have made it through the past twenty-four hours without her quiet, unflagging strength. "Don't we, love?"

"Every Sunday," Diana agreed.

With a grumpy mutter he turned to Grant and Gennie. "I suppose your sister has an excuse for not coming up," he said to Grant. "And it's only right Alan's with her, though he's my firstborn. After all, she's due to give me another grandchild in a couple of weeks."

"Any excuse," Grant said smoothly as Caine grinned and examined his nails.

"You're looking well, lass," he told Gennie. "A woman just blooms when she's carrying a child."

"And spreads," Gennie returned, touching a hand to her rounded stomach. "Another couple of months and I won't be able to reach my easel."

"See that you use a stool," he ordered. "A pregnant woman shouldn't be on her feet all day."

"And see that you're out of this place and on your own feet by spring," Grant told him as he slipped an arm around his wife. "You'll have to come to Maine to be the baby's godfather."

"Godfather." He preened. "It's a sad thing for a MacGregor to be godfather to a Campbell." He ignored Grant's grin, though it made his lips twitch, and looked at Gennie. "But I'll do it for you. Are you getting enough rest?"

Anna slipped a hand to his wrist to unobtrusively monitor his pulse. "He forgets that I was pregnant with Alan the last three months I interned. Never felt better in my life."

"I felt wonderful during pregnancy myself," Serena commented. "I suppose that's why I'm doing it again."

It only took Daniel a minute. "Again?"

Serena rose on her toes to kiss Justin before she smiled at her father. "Again. Seven months to go."

"Well now—"

"No Scotch, Daniel," Anna said, anticipating him. "At least not until you're out of Intensive Care."

He scowled, muttered, then opened his arms as best he could. "Come here then, little girl."

Serena leaned over the bed and held him as hard as she dared. "Don't you ever scare me like this again," she whispered fiercely.

"Now, now, don't scold," he murmured and stroked her hair. "Bad as your mother. You take good care of her," he ordered Justin. "I don't want my next grandchild born in front of a slot machine."

"Eight to five this one's a girl," Justin answered.

"You're on." Grinning, he turned to Diana. "You have to catch up."

"Don't be greedy," she told him and took his hand.

"A man's entitled to greed when he reaches a certain age, isn't that right, Anna?"

"A woman's entitled to make her own decisions—at any age."

"Ha!" Enormously pleased with himself, he surveyed the room. "I never mentioned that your mother picketed for equal rights before it was stylish, did I? Living with her's been nothing but a trial. And stop taking my pulse, woman. No better medicine for a man than family."

"Then maybe we should give you a bit more." Anna nodded to the nurse outside the door. With a sigh, she leaned against the bed. They were breaking all manner of hospital rules already. What was one more? She felt Daniel's fingers tighten on hers as Alan wheeled Shelby into the room.

"What's this?" he demanded and would have attempted to sit up if Anna hadn't eased him back.

"This," Shelby began, uncovering the bundle in her arms, "is Daniel Campbell MacGregor. He's eight hours and twenty minutes old and wanted to see his grandpa."

Alan took his son to set him in his father's arms. He'd spent the night praying he'd be able to do just that.

"What a sight," Daniel murmured, not bothering to blink the tears from his eyes. "A grandson, Anna. He has my nose. Look, he smiled at me." As Anna leaned down, he laughed. "And don't give me that hogwash about gas. Doctors. I know a smile when I see one." Looking up, he grinned at his son. "Fine job, Alan."

"Thanks." Still awed by his son, Alan sat on the edge of the bed. With one hand he covered his father's over the baby's. For a moment, three generations of MacGregor males were content.

"Campbell," Daniel said abruptly. "Did you say, Campbell?" His gaze locked on Shelby.

"I most certainly did." Her hand slipped into Alan's as she rose. She might be less than nine hours out of the delivery room, but she felt as strong as a bull. Certainly as strong as a MacGregor. "You'd better accept the fact that he's half Campbell, MacGregor." At her brother's chuckle, her chin lifted higher. "Very possibly the best half."

His eyes flashed. Anna took note of his color and approved. He opened his mouth, then laughed until he was weak from it. "What a tongue the girl has. At least you had the good sense to name him Daniel."

"I named him after someone I love and admire."

"Flattery." He signaled, reluctantly, for Alan to take the baby. Taking Shelby's hand, he held it between both of his. "You look beautiful."

She smiled, a bit stunned by the tears that swam in her eyes. "I feel beautiful."

"You should have heard her swear at the doctor." Delighted with her, Alan pressed a kiss to her temple. "She threatened to get up and go home to have the baby without his interference. She would have, too, if young Daniel hadn't had different ideas."

"Good for you," Daniel decided, and thought his name suited his grandson very well. "Nothing worse than having a doctor fussing around when you just want to get on with your business." After sending Anna a bland smile, he turned back to Shelby. "Now, I want you to get back in bed where you belong. I don't want to worry about you. You've given us all a gift."

She leaned down to kiss his cheek. "You gave me one. Alan. I love you, you old badger."

"Just like a Campbell. Go to bed."

"I'm afraid you're all going to have to run along before the hospital board calls me on the carpet."

"Now, Anna."

"If your father gets enough rest—" she turned to give

him a telling look "—he'll be moved out of ICU in the morning."

It wasn't quick, and it wasn't quiet, but Anna finally managed to clear the room. She pretended not to hear Daniel's muttered request to Justin for a game of poker later or his demand to Caine for the cigars Daniel had hidden in his office. If he hadn't made the demands, she'd have worried. No matter how Daniel had protested, she knew visits were as much a strain as a blessing. Until she was satisfied with his condition, she'd keep the future ones short. The trick would be making him think it was his idea. She'd had years of practice.

"Now—" she walked back to the bed and smoothed the hair from his brow "—I've a dozen things to see to that I let go while I was fussing unnecessarily over you. I want you to sleep."

He could be weaker now, now that it was only her. "I don't want you to go yet, Anna. I know you're tired, but I need you to stay just a little longer."

"All right." Dropping the bed guard again, she sat beside him. "Just rest."

"We did a good job, didn't we?"

She smiled, knowing he spoke of the children. "Yes, we did a very good job."

"No regrets?"

Puzzled, she shook her head. "What a foolish question."

"No." He took her hand in his. "Last night I dreamed. I dreamed of you. It started on the night we met, that first waltz."

"The summer ball," she murmured. She had only to smile to see the moonlight, smell the flowers. Odd, it had been in her dreams as well. "It was a beautiful night."

"You were beautiful," he corrected. "And I wanted you more than I'd ever wanted anything in my life."

"You were arrogant," she remembered, smiling. "And desperately attractive." Leaning over, she kissed him softly, lingeringly. The same passion that they'd felt in the beginning hovered over them. "You still are, Daniel."

"I'm old, Anna."

"We're both old."

He pressed her hand to his lips. The ring he'd given her so many years before was cool against his skin. "And I still want you more than I've ever wanted anything in my life."

Ignoring rules and procedure, Anna lay next to him and rested her head on his shoulder. "I'll lose my reputation for this." She closed her eyes. "It's worth it."

"A fine one you are to talk of reputations." He brushed his lips over her hair. The scent was the same after all the years. "It's a funny thing, Anna. I keep having this fierce craving for peach pie."

She lay still a minute, drifting, then her eyes opened on a laugh. They were young and wicked as she tilted her head toward his. "The minute you have a private room."

* * * * *

THE WINNING HAND

To the Vegas Queens, with thanks.

Chapter 1

When her car sputtered and died a mile outside of Las Vegas, Darcy Wallace seriously considered staying where she was and baking to death under the brutal desert sun. She had $9.37 left in her pocket and a long stretch of road behind her that led to nowhere.

She was lucky to have even that pitiful amount of cash on her, as her purse had been stolen outside a diner in Utah the night before. The rubbery chicken sandwich was the last meal she'd had, and she figured the stray ten she'd found in her pocket was the last miracle she could expect.

Both her job and her home in Kansas were gone. She had no family and no one to go back to. She felt she'd had every reason for tossing her clothes into a suitcase and driving away from what had been, and what would have been, had she remained.

She'd driven west simply because her car had been pointing in that direction and she'd taken it as a sign. She'd promised herself an adventure, a personal odyssey and a new, improved life.

Reading about plucky young women who braved the world, carved a path, took risks and blithely accepted challenges was no longer enough. Or so she'd told herself as the miles had clicked away on the odometer of her ancient and sickly sedan. It was time to take something for herself, or at least to try.

If she had stayed, she would have fallen in line. Again. Done what she was told. Again. And spent her life haunted by dreams and regrets.

But now, one long week after sneaking out of town in the middle of the night like a thief, she wondered if she was destined for the ordinary. Perhaps she'd been born to follow all the rules. Maybe she should have been content with what life offered and kept her eyes cast down, instead of constantly trying to peek around the next corner.

Gerald would have given her a good life, a life she knew many women would envy. With him, she could have had a lovely home tidily kept by a loyal staff, closets bursting with conventionally stylish wife-of-the-executive clothes, a summer place in Bar Harbor, winter getaways to tropical climes. She would never be hungry, never do without.

All it required was for her to do exactly as she was told, exactly when she was told. All it required was for her to keep buried every dream, every longing, every private wish.

It shouldn't have been hard. She'd been doing it all of her life.

But it was.

Closing her eyes, she rested her forehead on the steering wheel. Why did Gerald want her so much? she wondered. There was nothing special about her. She had a good mind and an average face. Her own mother had described her just that way often enough. She didn't believe it was so much a physical attraction on Gerald's side, though she suspected he liked the fact she was a small woman of slight build. Easily dominated.

God, he frightened her.

She remembered how furious he'd been when she'd cut off her shoulder-length hair, snipping away until it was as short as a boy's.

Well, she liked it, she thought with a little spurt of defiance. And it was her hair, damn it, she added, pushing her fingers through choppily cut, toffee-colored locks.

They weren't married yet, thank the Lord. He had no right to tell her how to look, how to dress, how to behave. And now, if she could just hold on, he never would have that right.

She should never have agreed to marry him in the first place. She'd just been so tired, so afraid, so confused. Even though the regrets and the doubts had set in almost immediately, even though she'd given him back the ring and apologized, she might have gone through with it rather than stand up under his anger and live through the gossip of a broken engagement. But she'd discovered he'd manipulated her, that he was responsible for her losing her job, for the threat of eviction from her apartment.

He'd wanted her to buckle. And she'd nearly obliged him, she thought now as she wiped sweat from her face with the back of her hand.

The hell with it, she decided and pushed herself out of the car. So she had less than ten dollars, no transportation and a mile hike ahead of her. She was out from under Gerald's thumb. She was finally, at twenty-three, on her own.

Leaving her suitcase in the trunk, she grabbed the

weighty tote that contained all that really mattered to her, then headed off on foot. She'd burned her bridges. Now it was time to see what was around that next corner.

It took her an hour to reach her destination. She couldn't have explained why she kept walking along Route 15, away from the scatter of motels, gas stations, and toward that shimmering Oz-like skyline of Vegas in the distance. She only knew she wanted to be there, inside that globe of exotic buildings and shapes where lights were twinkling like a carnival.

The sun was tipping down below the western peaks of the red mountains that ringed that glittering oasis. Her hunger had gone from grinding distress to a dull ache. She considered stopping for food, to rest, to drink, but there was something therapeutic about simply putting one foot in front of the other, her eyes on the tall, spectacular hotels glimmering in the distance.

What were they like inside? she wondered. Would everything be glossy and polished, colorful to the point of gaudy? She imagined an atmosphere of sex and gambling, desperation and triumph, with an underlying snicker of naughtiness. There would be men with hard eyes, women with wild laughs. She'd get a job in one of those opulent dens of indulgence and have a front row seat for every show.

Oh, how she wanted to live and see and experience.

She wanted the crowds and the noise, the hot blood and the cold nerves. Everything, everything that was the opposite of what she'd had before. Most of all she wanted to feel—strong, ripping emotions, towering joys, vivid excitement. And she would write about it all, she determined, shifting the tote which, filled with her notebooks and manuscript pages, weighed like stone. She would write, tucked in some little room looking out at it all.

Stumbling with exhaustion, she tripped on a curb, then righted herself. The streets were crowded, everyone seemed to have somewhere to go. Even at dusk, the lights of the city winked and gleamed and beckoned: *Come in, take a chance, roll the dice.*

She saw families of tourists—fathers in shorts with legs pink from the unforgiving sun, children with wide eyes, mothers with the frantic look of sensory overload.

Her own eyes were wide, the golden brown glazed with fatigue. The man-made volcano erupted in the distance, drawing screams and cheers from the crowd who'd gathered to watch and making Darcy gape with glassy-eyed wonder. The noise smothered the odd buzzing in her ears as she was jostled by the crowd.

Dazed and dazzled, she wandered aimlessly, gawking at the huge Roman statues, blinking at the neon, passing by the spurting fountains that gushed with shifting colors. It was a wonderland, loud and gaudy and unapologetically adult, and she was as lost and as fascinated as Alice.

She found herself standing in front of twin towers as white as the moon and joined together by a wide, curved bridge with hundreds of windows. Surrounding the building were seas of flowers, both wild and exotic, and pools of mirror-bright water fed by the rush of a terraced waterfall that tumbled from the topmost spear of a mountain.

Guarding the entrance to the bridge was an enormous—five times larger than life—Native chief astride a gold stallion. His face and bare chest were gleaming copper. His headdress flowed with winking stones of rich reds and blues and greens. In his hand he carried a lance with a diamond-bright tip that winked fire.

He's so beautiful, was all she could think, so proud and defiant.

She would have sworn the statue's dark eyes were alive, fixed on hers. Daring her to come closer, to go inside, to take her chances.

Darcy stepped into The Comanche on watery legs and swayed against the sudden rush of cool air.

The lobby was immense, the tile floors a bold geometric pattern of emerald and sapphire that made her head spin. Cacti and palms grew regally out of copper or pottery urns. Brilliant floral displays graced huge tables, the scent of the lilies so sweet it brought tears to her eyes.

She walked on, amazed by the waterfall that rushed down a stone wall into a pond filled with bright fish, the sparkling light that shimmered from huge crystal-and-gold chandeliers. The place was a maze of color and flash, brighter and more brilliant than any reality she'd known or any dream she'd imagined.

There were shops, the offerings in the windows as glittery as the chandeliers. She watched an elegant blonde debate between two diamond necklaces the way another might consider her choice of tomatoes.

A laugh bubbled up in Darcy's throat, forcing her to press a hand to her mouth to hold it in. It wasn't the time or place to be noticed, she warned herself. She didn't belong in such glamorous surroundings.

She turned the corner and felt her head reel at the sudden brassy sound of the casino. Bells and voices, the metallic rat-a-tat of coins falling on coins. Whirls and buzzes and hoots. The wave of energy pouring out brought a rush to her blood.

Machines were everywhere, shoulder to shoulder with their faces spinning with colors and shapes. People crowded around them, standing, sitting on stools, pulling coins from white plastic buckets and feeding the busy machines. She watched a woman press a red button, wait for the spin to end, then scream with delight as triple black bars lined up in the center. Money poured out into a silver bowl in a musical rush.

It made Darcy grin.

Here was fun, reckless and impulsive. Here were possibilities both grand and small. And life, loud, messy and hot.

She'd never gambled in her life, not with money. Money was something to be earned, saved and carefully watched. But her fingers slipped into her pocket where the last of her crumpled bills seemed to pulse with heat against her skin.

If not now, when? she asked herself with another bubbling giggle she could no longer quite control. What good was $9.37? It would buy her a meal, she told herself, gnawing on her lip. But then what?

Light-headed, her ears ringing oddly, she roamed the aisles, blinking owlishly at people and machines. They were willing to take a chance, she thought. That's why they were here.

Wasn't that why she was here?

Then she saw it. It stood alone, big and bright and fascinating. It stood taller than she, its wide face made up of stylized stars and moons. The handle was nearly as thick as her arm and topped with a shiny red ball.

It called itself Comanche Magic.

JACKPOT! it proclaimed in diamond-white lights that flashed on and off and made her dizzy. Ruby red dots flowed along a black strip. She stared, fascinated at the number showing within the blinking lights.

1,800,079.37

What an odd amount. Nine dollars and thirty-seven cents, she thought again, fingering the money in her pocket. Maybe it was a sign.

How much did it cost? she wondered. She stepped closer, blinked to clear her wavering vision and struggled to read the rules. It was a progressive machine, so the numbers would change and grow as players pumped in their money.

She could play for a dollar, she read, but that wouldn't get the jackpot even if she lined up the stars and moons on all three lines. To really play, she'd have to put in one dollar times three. Nearly all the money she had left in the world.

Take a chance, a voice seemed to whisper slyly in her ear.

Don't be foolish. This voice was prim, disapproving, and all too familiar. *You can't throw your money away.*

Live a little. There was excitement in the whisper, and seduction. *What are you waiting for?*

"I don't know," she muttered. "And I'm tired of waiting."

Slowly, her eyes on the challenging face of the machine, Darcy dug into her pocket.

With his gaze scanning the tables, Robert MacGregor Blade scrawled his initials on a chit. The man in chair three on the hundred-dollar table wasn't taking his losses in stride, he noted. Mac lifted a brow as the man held on fifteen with the dealer showing a king. If you're going to play for a hundred a hand, he mused as the dealer turned up a seven, you ought to know how to play.

In a casual gesture, Mac lifted a hand to call over one of the tuxedoed security men. "Keep an eye on him," Mac murmured. "He's thinking about making trouble."

"Yes, sir."

Spotting trouble and dealing with it was second nature for Mac. He was a third-generation gambler, and his instincts were well honed. His grandfather, Daniel MacGregor, had made a fortune taking chances. Real estate was Daniel's first love, and he continued to buy and sell property, to develop and preserve, to wheel and deal, though he was into his nineties.

Mac's parents had met in a casino aboard ship. His mother had been dealing blackjack, and his father had always been a player. They'd clashed and they'd clicked, both initially unaware that Daniel had maneuvered their meeting with marriage and the continuation of the MacGregor line in mind.

Justin Blade had already owned The Comanche in Vegas, and another in Atlantic City. Serena MacGregor had become his partner, then his wife.

Their eldest son had been born knowing how to roll the dice.

Now, just shy of his thirtieth birthday, Comanche Vegas was his baby. His parents trusted him enough to leave it in his hands, and he made very certain they wouldn't regret it.

It ran smoothly because he made certain it ran smoothly. It ran honest because it always had. It ran profitably because it was a Blade-MacGregor enterprise.

He believed, absolutely, in winning—and always in winning clean.

His lips twitched as a woman at one of the five-dollar tables hit twenty-one and applauded herself. Some would walk away winners, Mac mused, most wouldn't. Life was a gamble, and the house always had the edge.

A tall man, he moved through the tables easily, in a beautifully tailored dark suit that draped elegance over tough and ready muscle. The legacy from his Comanche heritage showed in the gold-dust skin pulled tight over his cheekbones, in the rich black hair that framed a lean, watchful face and flowed to the collar of his formal jacket.

But his eyes were Scot blue, deep as a loch and just as unfathomable.

His smile was quick and charming when a regular hailed

him. But he kept moving, barely pausing. He had work waiting in his office high above the action.

"Mr. Blade?"

He glanced over, stopping now as one of the roving cocktail waitress moved to him. "Yes?"

"I just came over from the slots." The waitress shifted her tray and tried not to sigh as Mac gave her the full benefit of those dark blue eyes. "There's a woman over at the big progressive. She's a mess, Mr. Blade. Not too clean, pretty shaky. She might be on something. She's just staring at it, you know? Muttering to herself. I thought maybe I should call security."

"I'll take a look."

"She's, well, she's kind of pathetic. Not a working girl," the waitress added. "But she's either sick or stoned."

"Thanks, I'll take care of it."

Mac shifted directions, moving into the forest of slots rather than his private elevator. Security could handle any trouble that threatened the smooth operation of the casino. But it was his place, and he handled his own.

A few feet away, Darcy fed her last three dollars into the slot. *You're insane,* she told herself, carefully babying the last bill when the machine spit it back at her. *You've lost your mind,* her pounding heart seemed to scream even as she smoothed the bill and slid it back in. But God, it felt so good to do something outrageous.

She closed her eyes a moment, breathing deeply three times, then opening them again, grabbed the shiny red ball of the arm with a trembling hand.

And pulled.

Stars and moons revolved in front of her eyes, colors blurred, a calliope tune began to jingle. She found herself smiling at the absurdity of it, almost dreaming as the shapes spun and spun and spun.

That was her life right now, she thought absently. Spinning and spinning. Where will it stop? Where will it go?

Her smile only broadened as stars and moons began to click into place. They were so pretty. It had been worth the price just to watch, to know at least she'd pulled the handle.

Click, click, click, shining stars, glowing moons. When they blurred, she blinked furiously. She wanted to see every movement, to hear every sound. Wasn't it pretty how neatly they all lined up? she thought and braced a hand against the machine when she felt herself begin to tip.

And as she touched it, as her hand made contact with the cool metal, the movement stopped. The world exploded.

Sirens shrieked, making her stagger back in shock. Colored lights went into a mad dance atop the machine, and a drum began to beat. Whistles shrilled, bells clanged. All around her people began to shout and shove.

What had she done? Oh, God, what had she done?

"Holy cow, you hit the big one!" Someone grabbed her, danced with her. She couldn't breathe, flailed weakly to try to escape.

Everyone was pushing, pulling at her, shouting words she couldn't understand. Faces swam in front of hers, bodies pressed until she was trapped against the machine.

An ocean was roaring in her head, a jackhammer pounded in her chest.

Mac moved through the celebratory crowd, nudging well-wishers aside. He saw her, a slip of a woman who looked barely old enough to be inside the casino. Her dark blond hair was short and messily cut, bangs flopping down into enormous fawn-colored eyes. Her face was angular as a pixie's and pale as wax.

Her cotton shirt and slacks looked as though she'd slept in them, and as if she'd spent her sleeping hours curled up in the desert.

Not stoned, he decided when he took her arm and felt the tremble. Terrified.

Darcy cringed, shifted her gaze to his. She saw the chief, the power and the challenge and the romance of him. He'd either save her, she thought dizzily, or finish her.

"I didn't mean—I only...what did I do?"

Mac angled his head, smiled a little. A dim bulb, perhaps, he mused, but harmless. "You hit the jackpot," he told her.

"Oh, well, then."

She fainted.

There was something wonderfully smooth under her cheek. Silk, satin, Darcy thought dimly. She'd always loved the feel of silk. Once she'd spent nearly her entire paycheck on a silk blouse, creamy white with tiny gold buttons, heart-shaped buttons. She'd had to skip lunch for two weeks, but it had been worth it every time she slipped that silk over her skin.

She sighed, remembering it.

"Come on, all the way out."

"What?" She blinked her eyes open, focused on a slant of light from a jeweled lamp.

"Here, try this." Mac slipped a hand under her head, lifted it and put a glass of water to her lips.

"What?"

"You're repeating yourself. Drink some water."

"Okay." She sipped obediently, studying the tanned, long-fingered hand that held the glass. She was on a bed, she realized now, a huge bed with a silky cover. There was a mirrored ceiling over her head. "Oh, my." Warily she shifted her gaze until she saw his face. "I thought you were the chief."

"Close." He set the glass aside, then sat on the edge of the bed, noting with amusement that she scooted over slightly to keep more distance between them. "Mac Blade. I run the place."

"Darcy. I'm Darcy Wallace. Why am I here?"

"It seemed better than leaving you sprawled on the floor of the casino. You fainted."

"I did?" Mortified, she closed her eyes again. "Yes, I guess I did. I'm sorry."

"It's not an atypical reaction to winning close to two million dollars."

Her eyes popped open, her hand grabbed at her throat. "I'm sorry, I'm still a little confused. Did you say I won almost two million dollars?"

"You put the money in, you pulled the lever, you hit." There wasn't an ounce of color in her cheeks, he noted, and thought she looked like a bruised fairy. "We'll deal with the paperwork when you're feeling a little steadier. Do you want to see a doctor?"

"No, I'm just… I'm okay. I can't think. My head's spinning."

"Take your time." Instinctively he plumped up the pillows behind her and eased her back. "Is there someone I can call to help you out?"

"No! Don't call anyone."

His brow lifted at her quick and violent refusal, but he only nodded. "All right."

"There isn't anyone," she said more calmly. "I'm traveling. I—my purse was stolen yesterday in Utah. My car broke down a mile or so out of town. I think it's the fuel pump this time."

"Could be," he murmured, tongue in cheek. "How did you get here?"

"I walked in. I just got here." Or she thought she had. It was hard to remember how long she'd walked around, goggling at everything. "I had nine dollars and thirty-seven cents."

"I see." He wasn't sure if she was a lunatic or a first-class gambler. "Well, now you have approximately one million, eight hundred thousand, eighty-nine dollars and thirty-seven cents."

"Oh…oh." Shattered, she put her hands over her face and burst into tears.

There were too many women in his life for Mac to be uncomfortable with female tears. He sat where he was, let her sob it out.

An odd little package, he thought. When she'd slid unconscious into his arms she'd been limp as water and had weighed no more than a child. Now she'd told him she'd hiked over a mile in the stunning late spring heat, then risked what little money she'd had on a yank of a slot.

That required either steel or insanity.

Whichever it was, she'd beaten the odds. And now she was rich—and for a while at least, his responsibility.

"I'm sorry." She wiped at her somehow charmingly dirty face with her hands. "I'm not like this. Really. I can't take it in." She accepted the handkerchief he offered and blew her nose. "I don't know what to do."

"Let's start with the basics. When's the last time you ate?"

"Last night—well, I bought a candy bar this morning, but it melted before I could finish it. So it doesn't really count."

"I'll order you some food." He rose, looking down at her. "I'll have them set it up down in the parlor. Why don't you take a hot bath, try to relax, get your bearings."

She gnawed her lip. "I don't have any clothes. I left my suitcase in my car. Oh! My bag. I had my bag."

"I have it." Because she'd gone pale again, he reached down beside the bed and lifted the plain brown tote. "This one?"

"Yes. Yes, thank you." Relief had her closing her eyes and struggling to calm herself again. "I thought I'd lost it. It's not clothes," she added, letting out a long sigh. "It's my work."

"It's safe, and there's a robe in the closet."

She cleared her throat. However kind he was being, she was still alone with him, a perfect stranger, in a very opulent and sensual bedroom. "I appreciate it. But I should get a room. If I could have a small advance on the money, I can find a hotel."

"Something wrong with this one?"

"This what?"

"This hotel," he said with what he considered admirable patience. "This room."

"No, nothing. It's beautiful."

"Then make yourself comfortable. Your room's comped for the duration of your stay—"

"What? Excuse me?" She sat up a little straighter. "I can have this room? I can just…stay here?"

"It's the usual procedure for high rollers." He smiled again, making her heart bump. "You qualify."

"I do?"

"The management hopes you'll put some of those winnings back into the pot. At the tables, the shops. Your room and meals, your bar bills, are on us."

She eased off the bed. "I get all this for free, because I won money from you?"

This time his grin was quick, and just a little wolfish. "I want the chance to win some of it back."

Lord, he was beautiful. Like the hero in a novel. That thought rolled around in her jumbled brain. "That seems only fair. Thank you so much, Mr. McBlade."

"Not McBlade," he corrected, taking the hand she offered. "Mac. Mac Blade."

"Oh. I'm afraid I haven't been very coherent."

"You'll feel better after you've eaten, gotten some rest."

"I'm sure you're right."

"Why don't we talk in the morning, say ten o'clock. My office."

"Yes, in the morning."

"Welcome to Las Vegas, Ms. Wallace," he said, and turned toward a sweep of open stairs that led to the living area.

"Thank you." She ordered her shaky legs to carry her to the rail, then lost her breath when she looked down at the sprawling space done in sapphires and emeralds, accented with ebony wood and lush arrangements of tropical flowers. She watched him cross an ocean of Oriental carpet. "Mr. Blade?"

"Yes?" He turned, glanced up, and thought she looked about twelve years old and as lost as a lamb.

"What will I do with all that money?"

He flashed that grin again. "You'll think of something. I'd make book on it." Then pressing a button, he stepped through the brass doors that slid open, into what surely was a private elevator.

When the doors closed again, Darcy gave in to her buckling knees and sat on the floor. She hugged herself hard, rocked. If this was some dream, some hallucination brought on by stress or sunstroke, she hoped it never cleared away.

She hadn't just escaped, she realized. She'd been liberated.

Chapter 2

The bubble didn't burst in the morning. She shot awake at six o'clock and stared, startled, at her reflection in the mirror overhead. Testing, she lifted a hand, watched herself touch her cheek. She felt her fingers, saw them slide up over her forehead and down the other side of her face.

However odd, it had to be real. She'd never seen herself horizontal before. She looked so…different, she decided, sprawled in the huge, rumpled bed surrounded by a mountain of pillows. She felt so different. How many years had she awakened each morning in the practical twin bed that had been her nesting place since childhood?

She never had to go back to that.

Somehow that single thought, the simple fact that she would never again have to adjust her body to the stingy mattress of the ancient bed sent a rush of joy through her so wild, so bright she burst into giddy laughter, unable to stop until she was gasping for air.

She rolled from one end of the bed to the other, kicked her feet in the air, hugged pillows, and when that wasn't enough, leaped up to dance on the mattress.

When she was thoroughly winded, she dropped down again and wrapped her arms tight around her knees. She was wearing a silk sleep shirt in candy pink—one of several articles of basic wardrobe that had arrived just after her dinner. Everything had been from the boutique downstairs and had been presented to her courtesy of The Comanche.

She wasn't even going to worry about the fact that the gorgeous Mac Blade had bought her underwear. Not when it was such fabulous underwear.

She jumped up, wanting to explore the suite again. The night before, she'd been so punchy she'd just wandered around gawking. Now it was time to play.

She snatched up a remote and began punching buttons. The shimmering blue drapes over the floor-to-ceiling windows opened and closed, making her grin like a fool. Opening them again, she saw she had a wide window on the world that was Vegas.

It was all muted grays and blues now, she noted, with a soft desert dawn breaking. She wondered how many floors up she was. Twenty? Thirty? It hardly mattered. She was on top of a brave and very new world.

Choosing another button, she opened a wall panel that revealed a big-screen television screen, a VCR and a complicated-looking stereo system. She fiddled until she filled the room with music, then raced downstairs.

She opened all the drapes, smelled the flowers, sat on every cushion of the two sofas and six chairs. She marveled at the arched fireplace, at the grand piano of showy white. And because there was no one to tell her not to touch, she sat down and played the first thing that came into her mind.

The celebratory, arrogant notes of "Everything's Coming Up Roses" made her laugh like a loon.

Behind a glossy black wet bar she found a small refrigerator, then giggled like a girl when she saw it contained two bottles of champagne. With the music blaring, she waltzed into the bath off the living area and grinned at the bidet, the phone, the wall-mounted TV and all the pretty toiletries arranged in a china basket.

Humming to herself, she climbed the curving chrome steps back to the bedroom. The master bath was a symphony of pure sensory indulgence from the lake-sized motorized tub in sensuous black to the acre of counter under a wall-sized lighted mirror. The room was bigger than her entire apartment back home.

Tuck in a bed, she thought, and she could live happily right here. Lush green plants lined the tiled shelf beside the tub. A separate rippled glass shower stall offered crisscrossing sprays. Lovely clear jars were arranged on glass shelves and held bath salts, oils, creams with scents so lush she moaned in pleasure at every sniff.

The adjoining dressing room boasted a walk-in closet that contained a robe and a pair of brushed cotton slippers with The Comanche logo, a triple-glass, full-length mirror, two elegant chairs and a table where fragrant flowers spilled out of a crystal vase.

It was the kind of indulgence she'd only read about or seen in movies. Plush, sleek, shimmering with wealth. Now that her initial rush of adrenaline was leveling, she began to wonder if there hadn't been some mistake.

How could this have happened? The time and circumstances after she'd begun her long hike into town were all blurry around the edges in her mind now. Snatches of it came clear, the whirling lights on the machine, her own thumping heart, Mac Blade's impossibly handsome face.

"Don't question it," she whispered. "Don't ruin it. Even if it all goes away in an hour, you have it now."

Biting her lip, she picked up the phone and punched in the button for room service.

"Room service. Good morning, Ms. Wallace."

"Oh." She blinked, looking guiltily over her shoulder as if someone had sneaked up behind her. "I was wondering if I could order some coffee."

"Of course. And breakfast?"

"Well." She didn't want to take advantage. "Perhaps a muffin."

"Will that be all?"

"Yes, that would be fine."

"We'll have that up to you within fifteen minutes. Thank you, Ms. Wallace."

"You're welcome, um, thank you."

After she hung up, Darcy hurried into the bedroom to turn off the stereo, switch the TV on and check the news to see if there were any reports of mass hallucinations.

In his office above the carnival world of the casino, Mac flicked his gaze over the security screens where people played the slots, bet on red or waited for their dealer to bust. There were more than a few diehards who'd started the night before and were still going at it. Slinky evening dresses sat hip to hip with jeans.

Ten o'clock at night, ten in the morning, it made no difference. There was no real time in Vegas, no dress code and, for some, no reality beyond the next spin of the wheel. Mac ignored the whine of an incoming fax, sipped his coffee and paced the room as he spoke to his father on the phone.

He imagined his father was doing virtually the same thing in the office in Reno.

"I'm going to talk to her in a few minutes," Mac continued. "I wanted to let her smooth out a little."

"Tell me about her," Justin requested, knowing his son's instincts for people would give him a clear picture.

"I don't know a lot yet. She's young." He kept moving as he talked, watching the screens, checking on the placement of his security people, the attitude of the dealers. "Skittish," he added. "Looked like a woman on the move to me. Trouble somewhere. She's out of her element here."

He cast his mind back, bringing the image of Darcy into focus, letting himself hear her voice again. "Small-town, Midwest, I'd say. Makes me think of a kindergarten teacher—the kind the kids would love and take merciless advantage of. She was broke and running on fumes when she hit."

"Sounds like it was her lucky day. If someone's going to hit, it might as well be a broke, small-town kindergarten teacher."

Mac grinned. "She apologizes all over herself. Nervous as a mouse at a feline convention. She's cute," he said finally, thinking of those big, dark gold eyes. "And I'd have to guess naive. The wolves are going to tear off pieces of her in short order if she doesn't have some protection."

There was a short pause. "You planning on standing between her and the wolves, Mac?"

"Just steering her in the right direction," Mac muttered, rolling his shoulders. His reputation in the family for siding with the underdog was inescapable. "The press is already hammering at the door. The kid needs a lawyer, and some straight talk, because the vultures circle right after the wolves."

He imagined the barrage of requests and demands that would come, begging for contributions, offering investments. A smattering of them would be genuine, and the rest would be playing one of the oldest games. Get the money and run.

"Keep me up to date."

"I will. How's Mom?"

"She's good. Hosting some big charity fashion show here today. And she's making noises about dropping in on you before we head back East. A quick visit," Justin added. "She misses the baby."

"Uh-huh." Mac had to grin. He knew very well his father would crawl over broken glass for a chance to visit his grandchild in Boston. "So how is little Anna?"

"Great. Just great. She's teething. Gwen and Bran aren't getting a lot of sleep right now."

"The price you pay for parenthood."

"I had plenty of all-nighters with you, pal."

"Like I said…" Mac's grin widened. "You pay your money, you make your choice." He glanced up at the quiet knock on his door. "That must be the nervous fairy now."

"Who?"

"Our newest millionaire. Come in," he called out, then curled a finger when Darcy hesitated on the threshold. "I'll keep you posted. Tell Mom I said hi."

"I've got a feeling you can tell her face-to-face in a few days."

"Good. Talk to you later."

The minute he hung up, Darcy launched into an apology. "I'm sorry. I didn't realize you were on the phone. Your assistant, secretary, whatever, came to bring me up, and she said I should just come in. But I can come back. If you're busy… I can come back."

Patient, Mac waited until she'd run down. It gave him the opportunity to see what a meal and a good night's sleep had done for her. She looked a little less fragile, incredibly… tidy, he decided, in the simple blouse and slacks he'd had the boutique send to her suite. And no less nervous than the evening before.

"Why don't you sit down?"

"All right." She linked her fingers together, twisted them, then stepped to a high-backed deep-cushioned chair in hunter green leather. "I was wondering—thinking…has there been a mistake?"

The chair dwarfed her, and made him think of fairies again, perched on colorful toadstools. "Hmm? About what?"

"About me, the money. I realized this morning, when I could think a bit more clearly, that things like this just don't happen."

"They do here." Hoping to put her at ease, he leaned a hip on the corner of his desk. "You are twenty-one, aren't you?"

"Twenty-three. I'll be twenty-four in September. Oh, I forgot to thank you for the clothes." She ordered herself not to think about the underwear, not to so much as consider that *he* was thinking of it. But color rose into her cheeks. "It was very kind of you."

"Everything fit all right?"

"Yes." Her color deepened. The bra was a lovely champagne color with edgings of lace, and was precisely her size. She didn't want to speculate how he could have been quite so accurate. "Perfectly."

"How'd you sleep?"

"Like someone put me under a spell." She smiled a little now. "I suppose I haven't been sleeping well lately. I'm not used to traveling."

There was a dusting of freckles over her pert little nose, he noted, a paler gold than her extraordinary eyes. She smelled lightly of vanilla. "Where are you from?"

"A little town, Trader's Corners, in Kansas."

Midwest, Mac thought. Hit number one.

"What do you do in Trader's Corners, Kansas?"

"I'm—I was a librarian."

Close enough for hit number two, he decided. "Really? Why'd you leave?"

"I ran away." She blurted it out before thinking. He had such a beautiful smile, and he'd been looking at her as if he were really interested. Somehow he had lulled her into the admission.

He pushed away from the desk, then sat on the arm of the chair beside hers so that their faces were closer, their eyes more level. He spoke gently, as he might to a cornered puppy. "What kind of trouble are you in, Darcy?"

"I'm not, I would have been if I'd stayed, but..." Then her eyes widened. "Oh, I didn't do anything. I mean I'm not running away from the police."

Because she was so obviously distressed, he smothered the laugh and didn't tell her he couldn't imagine her getting so much as a parking ticket. "I didn't think that, but people generally have a reason for running away from home. Does your family know where you are?"

"I don't have any family. I lost my parents about a year ago."

"I'm sorry."

"It was an accident. A house fire. At night." She lifted her hands, dropped them into her lap again. "They didn't wake up."

"That's a lot to deal with."

"There was nothing anyone could do. They were gone, the house was gone. Everything. I wasn't home. I'd just moved into my own apartment a few weeks before. Just a few weeks. I…" She pushed absently at her fringe of bangs. "Well."

"So you decided to get away?"

She started to agree, to make it simple. But it wasn't the truth, and she was such a poor and guilty liar. "No. Not exactly. I suppose that's part of it. I lost my job a few weeks ago." It still stung, the humiliation of it. "I was going to lose my apartment. Money was a problem. My parents didn't have much insurance, and the house had a mortgage. And the bills." She moved her shoulders. "In any case, without a paycheck, I wasn't going to be able to pay the rent. I didn't have that much saved myself, after college. And sometimes I… I'm not very good with budgets, I suppose."

"Money's not going to be a problem now," he reminded her, wanting to make her smile again.

"I don't see how you can just give me almost two million dollars."

"You *won* almost two million dollars. Look." He took her hand, nudging her around until she could see the screens. "People step up to the tables, every hour, every day. Some win, some lose. Some of them play for entertainment, for fun. Others play hoping to make the big score. Just once. Some play the odds, some play a hunch."

She watched, fascinated. Everything moved in silence. Cards were dealt, chips were stacked, raked in or slipped away. "What do you do?"

"Oh, I play the odds. And the occasional hunch."

"It looks like theater," she murmured.

"That's what it is. With no intermission. Do you have a lawyer?"

"A lawyer?" The amused interest that had come into her eyes vanished. "Do I need a lawyer?"

"I'd recommend it. You're about to come into a large amount of money. The government's going to want their share. And after that, you're going to discover you have friends you've never heard of, and people who want to offer you a terrific opportunity to invest. The minute your story hits the press, they'll crawl out of the woodwork."

"Press? Newspapers, television? No, I can't have that. I can't have that," she repeated, springing up. "I'm not going to talk to reporters."

He bit back a sigh. Yes indeed, he thought, this one would need a hand to hold on the walk through the forest. "Young, orphaned, financially strapped librarian from Kansas walks into Comanche Vegas and drops her last dollar—"

"It wasn't my last," she insisted.

"Close enough. Her last dollar in the slot and wins a million-eight. Darling, the press is going to do handsprings with a lead like that."

He was right, of course. She could see it herself. It was a wonderful story, just the kind she wanted to write herself. "I don't want it to get out. They have televisions and newspapers in Trader's Corners."

"Hometown girl makes good," he agreed, watching her. Suddenly he realized something else was putting panic into her eyes. "They'll probably name a street after you," he said casually.

"I don't want this to get back there. I didn't tell you everything." Because she had no choice but to hope he could help, she sat again. "I didn't tell you the main reason I left the way I did. There's a man. Gerald Peterson. His family's very prominent in Kansas. They own quite a bit of land and many businesses. Gerald, for some reason, he wanted me to marry him. He insisted."

"Women are still free to say 'no, thank you' in Kansas, aren't they?"

"Yes, of course." It seemed so simple when he said it, she mused. He would think she was an idiot. "But Gerald's very determined. He always finds a way to get what he wants."

"And he wants you," Mac prompted.

"Well, yes. At least he seems to think he does. My parents were very pleased that he was interested in me. I mean, who would think I'd catch the eye of a man like him?"

"Are you joking?"

She blinked. "What?"

"Never mind." He waved it away. "So Gerald wanted to marry you, and I take it you didn't want to marry him. What then?"

"A few months ago, I said I would. It seemed like the only reasonable thing to do. And he just assumed I would, anyway." Ashamed, she stared down at her linked fingers. "Gerald assumes very firmly. He doesn't hear the word no. It's like a genetic thing." She sighed. "Agreeing to marry him was weak, and stupid, and I regretted it immediately. I knew I couldn't go through with it, but he wouldn't listen when I tried to tell him. There was the whole ring thing, too," she added with a frown.

Fascinated and entertained, Mac cocked his head. "Ring thing."

"Well, it was silly, really. I didn't want a diamond engagement ring. I wanted something different, just…different. But he didn't hear that, either. I got a two-carat diamond, which was properly appraised and insured. He explained all about the investment value." She shut her eyes. "I didn't want to hear about the investment value."

"No," Mac murmured. "I don't imagine you did."

"I wasn't expecting romance. Well, no, yes, I was, but I knew it wasn't going to happen. I thought I could settle." She looked past him, past the screens. "I should have been able to settle."

"Why?"

"Because everyone said how lucky I was. But I didn't feel lucky. I felt smothered, trapped. He was very angry when I gave him back the ring. He barely said a word, but he was furious. Then he wasn't. He was very calm and told me he had no doubt I'd come to my senses shortly. Once I did, we'd forget it had ever happened. Two weeks later, I lost my job."

She made herself look back at Mac. He was listening, she realized with some surprise. Really listening. Hardly anyone really listened. "They talked about budget cutbacks, my performance evaluation," she continued. "I was so shocked that it took me a little while to realize he'd arranged it. The Petersons endow the library. And they own my apartment building. He had to have known I'd come crawling back."

"Sounds to me like you gave him a good kick in the ass. Not as much as he deserved, but a solid shot."

"He'll be humiliated, and very, very angry. I don't want him to know where I am. I'm afraid of him."

Something new and icy flickered into Mac's eyes. "Did he hurt you?"

"No. Gerald doesn't have to use physical force when intimidation works so well. I just want to disappear for a while. He only wants me now because he can't tolerate being refused. He doesn't love me. I simply suit his needs in a wife. Neat, quiet, well educated and behaved."

"You'd feel better if you stood up to him."

"Yes." She lowered her gaze. "But I'm afraid I won't."

Mac considered a moment. "We'll do what we can to keep your name out of it. The press should run with the mystery woman angle happily enough for a while. But it won't last, Darcy."

"The longer the better."

"Okay, let's deal with the basics. I can't distribute the money yet. You don't have any identification for one thing, and that makes it sticky. You'll need to get some. Your birth certificate, driver's license, that sort of thing. So we're back to a lawyer."

"I don't know any. Just the firm back home who handled things for my parents, and I wouldn't want to use them."

"No, they wouldn't do, not for a woman who wants to start a new life from scratch."

Her smile bloomed slowly, drawing his attention to the shape of her mouth, the full bottom lip, the deep dip centered in the top one. "I guess that's what I'm doing. I want to write books," she confessed.

"Really? What sort?"

"Love stories, adventures." She laughed and leaned back in the cushions of the chair. "Wonderful stories about people who do amazing things for love. I suppose that sounds crazy."

"It sounds rational to me. You were a librarian, so you must love books. Why not write them?"

She goggled first, then her eyes went bright and beautiful. "You're the first person I've ever told who's said that. Gerald was appalled at the very notion that I'd consider writing at all, much less romance novels."

"Gerald's an idiot," Mac said dismissively. "We've already established that. I guess you'd better buy yourself a laptop and get to work."

Staring again, she pressed a hand to her throat. "I could, couldn't I?" When her eyes began to fill, she shook her head quickly. "No, I'm not going to start that again. It's just that a life can change so completely and so quickly. The best and the worst. In a blink."

"You're handling this very well. You'll handle the rest." He rose and missed the startled look she shot him. No one had ever expressed such casual confidence in her before. "I'm not sure it's ethical, but I can contact my uncle. He's a lawyer. You can trust him."

"I'd appreciate it. Mr. Blade, I'm so grateful for—"

"Mac," he interrupted. "Whenever I give a woman almost two million dollars, I insist on a first-name basis."

Her laugh burst out, then was quickly muffled by her hand. "Sorry. It's just strange hearing that out loud. Two million dollars."

"A fairly amusing number," he said dryly, and her laughter stopped instantly.

"I never thought—I mean about your part. What it means to you, this place. You don't have to pay me all at once," she said in a rush. "It can be in installments or something."

On impulse he reached down, cupped her chin in his hand and studied her face. "You're incredibly sweet, aren't you, Darcy from Kansas?"

Her mind washed clean. His voice was so warm, his eyes so blue, his hand so firm. Her heart did one long, slow twist in her chest and seemed to sigh. "What did you say? I'm sorry?"

He skimmed his thumb over her jawline. Fairy bones, he thought absently, and catching himself wondering about

her, he dropped his hand. *Don't go there, Mac,* he warned himself, and stepped back.

"The Comanche never makes a bet it can't afford to lose. And my grandfather doesn't really need that operation."

"Oh, God."

"I'm joking." More delighted with her than ever, he roared with laughter. "You're easy. Much too easy." They'll eat her alive, he thought. "Do yourself a favor, keep a low profile until my uncle starts the ball rolling. I'll advance you some cash."

He moved behind the desk and unlocked a drawer where he kept the petty cash. "A couple thousand should hold you. We've arranged for credit at the shops here for you. I imagine you'll want to make arrangements to have your car towed in." Expertly he counted out hundreds, then fifties.

"I'm having a little trouble breathing," Darcy said weakly. "Excuse me."

Mac glanced up, watched in some alarm as she lowered her head between her knees.

"I'll be all right in a minute," she told him when she felt his hand on the back of her head. "I'm sorry. I'm being an awful lot of trouble."

"No, but I'd definitely prefer it if you didn't faint again."

"I won't. I was just a little light-headed for a second." When the phone rang, she jolted, then sat straight up. "I'm taking too much of your time."

"Sit." He pointed, then snatched up the phone. "Deb, tell whoever it is I'll get back to them." He hung up again, narrowed his eyes and felt a genuine wave of relief that her color was back. "Better?"

"Much. I'm sorry."

"Stop apologizing. It's a very annoying habit."

"I'm—" She pressed her lips together, cleared her throat.

"Good." He picked up the stack of bills and handed it to her. "Go shopping," he suggested. "Go play. Get a massage or a facial, sit by the pool. Enjoy yourself. Have dinner with me tonight." He hadn't meant to say that, hadn't a clue where it had come from.

"Oh." He was frowning at her now, which was only more confusing. "Yes, I'd like that." Feeling awkward, she rose and pushed the bills into her pocket. She hadn't brought the lovely little shoulder bag the boutique had sent her, because she'd had nothing to put in it. "I don't know what to do first."

"It doesn't matter. Just do it all."

"That's a wonderful way of thinking." Unable to help herself, she beamed at him. "Just do it all. I'll try that. I'll let you get back to work." She started for the door, but he went to it with her and opened it. She looked up again, groping for the right words. "You saved my life. I know that sounds dramatic, but it's the way I feel."

"You saved it yourself. Now take care of it."

"I'm going to." She offered her hand, and because it was irresistible, he lifted it to his lips.

"See you later."

"Yes. Later." She turned and walked away without her feet touching the ground.

Mac shut the door, then dipping his hands into his pockets, stood staring at it. Darcy the Kansas librarian, he mused. Not his type. As far from his type as they came. The little pull he felt, he assured himself, was just concerned interest. Almost brotherly.

Almost.

It was the eyes that were doing it, he supposed. How was a man supposed to resist those big, wounded fawn eyes? Then there was the shy little hesitation in her voice followed by those quick bursts of enthusiasm. And the genuine sweetness of her. Nothing saccharine or cloying, just innocence, he supposed.

Which circled right back to the point. Not his type. Women were safer when they knew how to play the game. Darcy Wallace didn't have a clue.

Well, he couldn't very well hand her the money then toss her into the fray without a shield, could he?

Just steer her in the right direction, he promised himself, then wave goodbye.

With this in mind, he went back to his desk and picked up the phone. "Deb, get me Caine MacGregor's office in Boston."

Chapter 3

It was a different world. Perhaps even a different planet. And she, Darcy thought as she stepped cautiously into the sparkling boutique, was now a different woman.

The Darcy Wallace who so often had her nose pressed against the window of such pretty places was now inside. And she could have whatever she wanted. That gorgeous beaded jacket there, she thought—not daring to touch it— or that fluid column of ivory silk.

She could have them, both of them, all of them. Because the world had turned upside down and somehow had shaken her out and dumped her right on top.

She stepped in a little farther, peeked into a long glass display cabinet. Beautiful, sparkly things. Foolishly wonderful decoration for ears and wrists and fingers. She'd always wanted to wear something that sparkled.

Odd, she'd never felt that special thrill she'd expected when she'd worn Gerald's ring on her finger. His ring, she realized now. Of course, that was it. It hadn't really been hers at all.

"May I help you?"

Startled, she looked up and nearly backed guiltily away from the display. "I don't know."

The woman behind the counter smiled indulgently. "Are you looking for anything special?"

"Everything seems special."

The indulgent smile warmed. "I'm glad you think so. We're very proud of our selection. I'd be happy to help you if I can, or you can feel free to browse."

"Actually I have a dinner tonight, and nothing to wear."

"That's always the way, isn't it?"

"Literally nothing." When the clerk didn't appear especially shocked by this confession, Darcy drummed up the courage to go on. "I suppose I need a dress."

"Formal or casual?"

"I have no idea." Realizing the quandary, Darcy scanned the gowns and cocktail suits on display. "He didn't say."

"Dinner for two?"

"Yes. Oh." She turned back. "It's not a date. Exactly."

Willing to play, the clerk angled her head. "Business?"

"In a way. I suppose." She pushed at the hair that was tickling her ear. "Yes, that must be it."

"Is he attractive?"

Darcy rolled her eyes. "That doesn't begin to describe him."

"Interested?"

"You'd have to be dead ten years not to be. But it's not that sort of…thing."

"Maybe it could be. Let's see." Lips pursed, the clerk studied Darcy through narrowed eyes. "Feminine but not fussy, sexy but not obvious. I think I have a few things you might like."

* * *

The clerk's name was Myra Proctor. She'd worked at the Dusk to Dawn Boutique for five years since she and her husband had moved to Vegas from Los Angeles. He was in banking, and she had worked in retail most of her adult life. She had two children, a boy and a girl. The girl had just turned thirteen and would surely make her mother's hair gray. Though, at the moment, Myra's hair was a sleek auburn.

Darcy learned all this because she asked. And asking helped put her at ease while Myra approved or rejected outfits.

One cocktail dress, beaded jacket, evening purse and sparkly earrings later, Myra gave her a gentle nudge toward the salon.

"You ask for Charles," Myra advised. "Tell him I sent you. He's an absolute genius."

"What," Charles demanded when Darcy sat in the cushioned silver salon chair, "happened to your hair? An industrial accident? A near-terminal illness perhaps? Mice?"

Wincing, Darcy cowered under the stark white cape that had been draped around her. "I'm afraid I cut it myself."

"Would you remove your own appendix?"

She could only hunch her shoulders as he glowered down at her with searing green eyes under dark, beetled brows. "No. No, I wouldn't."

"Your hair is a part of your body and requires a professional."

"I know. You're right. Absolutely." The back of her throat began to tickle and she swallowed gamely. It wasn't the time to laugh, however nervously, she reminded herself. Instead she tried an apologetic smile. "It was an impulse, a rebellion actually."

"Against what?" His fingers dove into her hair and began to knead and tug. "Being well-groomed?"

"No. Well…there was this man, and he kept telling me how I should wear it, and how it should be, and it made me mad, so I whacked it off."

"Was this man your hairdresser?"

"Oh, no. He's a businessman."

"Ha. Then he has no business telling you how you should wear your hair. Cutting it off was brave. Foolish, but brave. The next time you want to rebel, go to a professional."

"I will." She took a deep breath. "Can you do anything with it?"

"My dear child, I've worked miracles with much worse." He snapped his fingers. "Shampoo," he ordered.

She'd never felt more pampered in her life. It was so beautifully indulgent to lie back, to have her hair washed, her scalp massaged, to listen to the birdlike murmurs of the shampoo girl. Even when she was back in Charles's chair, she felt none of the stomach-quivering anxiety that often rode hand in glove with a haircut.

"You need a manicure," Charles ordered, snipping away. "Sheila, squeeze in a manicure and pedicure for—what was your name, dear?"

"Darcy. A pedicure?" The thought of having her toes painted was so…exotic.

"Hmm. And you'll stop biting your nails immediately."

Chastised, Darcy tucked her hands under the cape. "It's a terrible habit."

"Very unattractive. You're fortunate, though. You have thick, healthy hair. A nice color. We'll leave that alone." He brought a section of hair up between two fingers, snipped. "What do you use on your face?"

"I have some moisturizer, but I lost it." Self-consciously she rubbed at her nose.

"The freckles are charming. You'll leave them alone, too."

"But I'd rather—"

"Are you picking up the scalpel?" he asked, arching one of his thick, black brows, then nodding, satisfied, when she shook her head. "I'm going to do your face myself. If you don't like the look, you don't pay. If you do like it, you not only pay, you buy the products."

Another gamble, Darcy thought. Maybe she was on a roll. "Deal."

"That's the spirit. Now…" He angled her head, snipped again. "Tell me about your love life."

"I don't have one."

"You will." He wiggled those eyebrows. "My work never fails."

By three, Darcy walked back into her suite. She was loaded down with purchases, and still floating. On impulse, she dumped everything on the sofa and dashed to the mirror. Myra had been right. Charles was a genius. Her hair looked pert, she decided with a chuckle. Almost sophisticated. Though it was even shorter than she had dared cut it, it was sleek and just a little sassy.

Her bangs didn't flop now, but spiked down over her forehead. And her face… Wasn't it amazing what could be done with those tubes and brushes and powders? They couldn't make her a raving beauty, but she thought—she hoped—she'd stepped up to the threshold of pretty.

"I'm almost pretty," she said to her reflection, and smiled. "I really am. Oh, the earrings!" She whirled and dashed toward the bags, thinking the glitter against her face might just take her that final step.

Then she saw the red message light blinking on her phone.

No one knew where she was. How could anyone call her when no one knew? The press? Had the news gotten out already? No, no, she thought, clutching her hands together. Mac had promised not to give out her name. He'd promised.

Still her pulse hammered in her throat as she picked up the phone and pushed the message button. She was informed she had two new voice mail messages. The first was from Mac's assistant and had her releasing the breath she'd been holding. Mr. Blade would pick her up for dinner at seven-thirty. If that wasn't suitable, she had only to call back and reschedule.

"Seven-thirty is fine," she whispered. "Seven-thirty is wonderful."

The last message was from Caine MacGregor, who identified himself as Mac's uncle and invited her to call him back at her convenience.

She hesitated over that. She found she didn't want to face the practical business of it all. Somehow it seemed much more romantic when it all remained dreamlike and impossible. But she'd been raised to return phone calls promptly, so she pulled out the chair at the desk, sat, and dutifully made the long-distance call to Boston.

When Darcy opened her door and found Mac holding a single white rose, she considered it another miracle. He was something out of one of the stories she'd secretly scribbled in notebooks for years. Tall, dark, elegantly masculine, heart-stoppingly handsome with just an edge of danger to keep it all from being too smooth.

The miracle was that he was there, holding out a long-stemmed rosebud the color of a summer cloud, and smiling at her.

But what popped out of her mouth was the single thought that had revolved in her muddled brain since her call to Boston.

"Caine MacGregor is your uncle."

"Yes, he is."

"He was attorney general of the United States."

"Yes." Gently Mac lifted Darcy's hand and placed the rose stem in it. "He was."

"Alan MacGregor was president."

"You know, I heard that somewhere. Are you going to let me in?"

"Oh. Yes. But your uncle, he was *president,*" she said again, slowly, as if she'd been misunderstood. "For eight years."

"You pass the history quiz." Mac closed the door behind him and took a good long study of her. A warm hum of approval moved through his blood. "You look fabulous."

"I—really?" Distracted not only by the compliment, but the delivery, she glanced down. "I would never have chosen this," she began, running a hand over the copper-hued skirt of a dress that was shorter, snugger and certainly more daring than anything in her previous wardrobe. "Myra at the boutique, the evening wear boutique downstairs, picked it out. She said I belonged in jewel colors."

"Myra has an excellent eye." And likely deserved a raise, he thought, making a circling motion with his finger. "Turn around."

"Turn—" Her laugh was both pleased and self-conscious as she executed a slow twirl.

A big raise, Mac decided as the flippy little skirt danced around surprisingly delightful legs. "They're not there."

"What?" Her hand fluttered to the dipping bodice, checking. "What isn't there?"

"Wings. I expected to see little fairy wings."

Flustered, she laughed again. "The way this day has gone, I wouldn't be surprised to see them myself."

"Why don't we have a drink before we go to dinner, and you can tell me how the day's gone?"

He walked to the bar to take a bottle of champagne out of the minifridge. She loved to watch him move. It was the animal grace she'd only read about, sleek and confident. And again, slightly dangerous. But to see it…she let out a little sigh. It was so much better than just imagining.

"Charles cut my hair," she began, thrilling to the celebratory sound of the cork popping.

"Charles?"

"In your salon?"

"Ah, that Charles." Mac selected two flutes from the glass shelves and poured. "The customers tremble, but always go back to Charles."

"I thought he was going to boot me out when he saw what I'd done." She gave her short locks a tug. "But he took pity on me. Charles has definite opinions."

Mac skimmed his gaze over her hair, then down until his eyes met hers. "I'd say in your case he saw the wings."

"I'm only to pick up scissors to cut paper from now on." Her eyes danced as she accepted the glass Mac offered. "Or pay the consequences. And, if I bite my nails, I'll be punished. I was afraid to ask him how. Oh, this is wonderful," she murmured after a sip. Closing her eyes, she sipped again. "Why would anyone drink anything else?"

The pure sensual pleasure on her face had the hum in his blood quickening. A babe in the woods, he reminded himself. It seemed wiser all around to keep the bar between them. "What else did you do?"

"Oh, the salon took forever. Charles kept finding other things he said were absolutely essential. I had a pedicure."

Humor danced into her eyes again. "I had no idea how wonderful it is to have your feet rubbed. Sheila put paraffin on my feet. Can you imagine? My hands, too. Feel."

He took the hand she held out, in all innocence. It was small and narrow, the skin as smooth as a child's. He had to check the urge to nibble. "Very nice."

"Isn't it?" Delighted with herself, Darcy smiled and stroked a finger over the back of her hand. "Charles said I have to have a full body loofah and some sort of mud bath, and… I can't even remember. He wrote it all down and sent me to Alice at the spa. She makes the appointments. I have to be there at ten—after I work out in the health club, because he believes I've been neglecting my inner body, too. Charles is very strict. May I have some more?"

"Sure." A little war between amusement and baffled desire waged inside him as he poured more champagne.

"This is a wonderful place. It has everything. Wonderful surprises around every corner. It's like living in a castle." Her eyes closed with pleasure as she drank. "I always wanted to. I'd be the princess under a spell. And the prince would scale the walls, tame the dragon—I always hated when they killed the dragon. They're so magical and magnificent. Anyway, once the prince came, the spell would be broken, and everything in the castle would come to life. The colors and the sounds. There'd be music and dancing. And everyone would be so happy. Ever after."

She stopped, laughed at herself. "The champagne's going to my head. This isn't at all what I wanted to talk to you about. Your uncle—"

"We'll talk about it over dinner." He slipped the flute from her hand and set it aside. He spotted the glittery little evening bag on a table and handed it to her.

She slanted him a look as he led her to the elevator. "Can I have more champagne at dinner?"

Now he had to laugh. "Darling, you can have whatever you want."

"Imagine that." With a blissful sigh, she leaned against the smoked glass wall.

He pushed the button for the circular restaurant on the top floor. She'd bought perfume, he thought, something woodsy and perfect for her. He decided the best place for his hands was in his pockets. "Did you try out the casino?"

"No. There was so much else to do. I looked around a little, but I didn't know where to begin."

"I think you began pretty well already."

She beamed up at him as the doors opened. "I did, didn't I?"

He led her through a small palm-decked foyer and into a candlelit dining room ringed by windows where silver gleamed against white linen.

"Good evening, Mr. Blade. Madam." The maître d' made a slight bow and, with his shoe-black hair and round body, reminded Darcy of Tweedledee of Alice fame.

Another rabbit hole, she thought as they were led to a curved banquette by the window. She never wanted to find her way out.

"The lady enjoys champagne, Steven."

"Of course. Right away."

"It must be so exciting living here. It's like a world to itself. You like it, don't you?"

"Very much. I was born with a pair of dice in one hand, and a deck of cards in the other. My mother and father met over a blackjack table. She was working as a dealer on a cruise ship, and he wanted her the minute he saw her."

"A shipboard romance." It made her sigh. "She was beautiful."

"Yes, she is beautiful."

"And he would have been dark and handsome, and maybe a little dangerous."

"More than a little. My mother likes to gamble."

"And they both won." Her lips tipped up, deepening the dip in the center. "You have a big family."

"Unwieldy."

"Only children are always jealous of big, unwieldy families. You're never lonely, I bet."

"No." She had been, he thought. There was no doubt of it. "Loneliness isn't an option." He nodded approval to the label as the sommelier offered the bottle of champagne.

Thrilled by the ritual, Darcy studied every step, the elegant spin of the white cloth, the subtle movement of the sommelier's hands, the muffled pop of cork. At Mac's signal, a small amount was poured into Darcy's glass for tasting.

"It's wonderful. Like drinking gold."

That earned her a pleased smile from the sommelier, who finished pouring with a flourish before nestling the bottle in a silver bucket of ice.

"Now." Mac tapped his glass lightly against hers. "You talked with my uncle."

"Yes. I didn't realize, not until I'd made the call. Then I did—Caine MacGregor, Boston. I know I started to stutter." She winced. "He was very patient with me." A laugh bubbled up and was partially swallowed. "The former attorney general of the United States is my lawyer. It's so odd. He said he would take care of things—my birth certificate, the red tape. He didn't seem to think it would take very long."

"MacGregors have a way of moving things along."

"I've read so much about your family." Darcy accepted the leather-bound menu absently. "Your grandfather's a legend."

"He loves hearing that. What he is, is a character. You'd like him."

"Really? What kind of a character?"

How did one describe Daniel MacGregor? Mac wondered. "An outrageous one. Big, loud, bold. A Scotsman who built an empire on grit and sweat and shrewdness. He sneaks cigars—or my grandmother lets him believe he's sneaking them. He'll skin you at poker. Nobody bluffs better. He has an amazing heart, strong and soft. For him, family comes first and last and always."

"You love him."

"Very much." Because he thought she'd enjoy it, he told her of how a young, brash Daniel had come to Boston looking for a wife, had set his eyes on Anna Whitfield and, tumbling into love, had wooed and won her.

"She must have been terribly brave, becoming a doctor. There were so many obstacles for a woman."

"She's amazing."

"And you have brothers? Sisters?"

"One brother, two sisters, assorted cousins, nephews, nieces. When we get together it's...an asylum," he decided, making her laugh.

"And you wouldn't change it for the world."

"No, I wouldn't."

She opened her menu. "I always wondered what it would be like to—oh, my. Look at all this. How does anyone decide what to order?"

"What do you like?"

She looked up, gold eyes sparkling. "Everything."

She sampled all she could manage. Tureen of duck, wild greens, little salmon puffs topped with caviar. Unable to resist, Mac scooped up some of his own stuffed lobster and held the fork to her lips. Her eyes closed, a quiet moan rippled in her throat, her lips rubbed gently together. And his blood flashed hot.

He'd never known a woman so open to sensual pleasure, or so obviously new to it. She'd be a treasure in bed, absorbing, lingering over every touch, every taste, every movement.

He could imagine it clearly—much too clearly—the little sighs and murmurs, the awakenings.

She gave one of those little sighs now as her long lids opened slowly over dreamy eyes. "It's wonderful. Everything's wonderful."

It was all flowing through her, mind and body, soft lights, strong flavors, the froth of wine and the look of him. She found herself leaning forward. "You're so attractive. You have such a strong face. I love looking at it."

From another woman it would have been an invitation. From her, Mac reminded himself, it was a combination of wine and naiveté. "Where do you come from?"

"Kansas." She smiled. "That's not what you meant, is it? I have no finesse," she confessed. "And when I relax, I tend to say things that pop into my head. I'm usually nervous around men. I never know what to say."

He arched a brow. "Obviously I don't make you nervous. That's my ego you hear thudding at your feet."

She chuckled, shaking her head. "Women are always going to fantasize about men like you. But you don't make me nervous, because I know you don't think of me that way."

"Don't I?"

"Men don't." She gestured with her glass before sipping. "Men aren't quickly attracted to women who aren't particularly physically appealing. Willowy blondes," she continued, eyeing his plate and wondering how to ask for another bite. "Sultry brunettes, glamorous redheads. Attention focuses on them, it's only natural. And strongly attractive men are drawn to strongly attractive women. At least initially."

"You've given this a lot of thought."

"I like to watch people, and how they circle toward each other."

"Maybe you haven't looked closely enough. I find you very appealing, physically." He watched her blink in surprise as he slid a little closer. "Fresh," he murmured, giving in to the urge to cup a hand at the back of her slender neck. "And lovely."

He saw her gaze flit down to his mouth and return, startled, to his eyes. He heard the little rush of breath shudder through her lips. It was tempting, very tempting to close the slight distance, to complete the circle she'd spoken of. But she trembled under his hand, a trapped bird not entirely sure of her wings.

"There," he said quietly. "That shut you up. Nervous now?"

She could only move her head in short, rapid nods. She could all but feel his mouth on hers. It would be firm, and hot and so clever. The fingers at the back of her neck had stroked some wild nerve to life. She could feel it career through her, bumping her pulse to light speed.

The dawning awareness in her eyes, the flicker of panic behind it had his fingers tightening briefly on her nape. "You shouldn't dare a gambler, Darcy." He gave her neck what he hoped was a friendly squeeze before easing back. "Dessert?"

"Dessert?"

"Would you like some?"

"I don't think I could." Not with her stomach muscles in knots and her fingers too unsteady to hold a fork.

He smiled slowly. "Want to try your luck?" When she swallowed, he added, "At the tables."

"Oh. Yes. I think I would."

"What should I play?" she asked him when they walked into the noise and lights of the casino.

"Lady's choice."

"Well." She bit her lip, tried to keep her mind off the fact that he had his hand at the small of her back. It did no good to tell herself she had no business thinking of him that way. "Maybe blackjack. It's just adding up numbers, really."

He ran his tongue around his teeth. "That's part of it. Five-dollar table," he decided. "Until you get your rhythm." He led her toward a vacant chair in front of a dealer he knew to be both patient and personable with novices. "How much do you want to start with."

"Twenty?"

"Twenty thousand's a little steep for a beginner."

Her mouth dropped open, then curved on a laugh. "I meant dollars. Twenty dollars."

"Dollars," Mac said weakly. "Fine—if you think you can stand the excitement."

When he reached for his wallet, she shook her head. "No, I have it." She pulled a twenty out of her bag. "It feels more like mine this way."

"It is yours," he reminded her. "And at twenty, not a hell of a lot's going to be mine again."

"I might win." She slid onto a stool beside a portly man in a checked jacket. "Are you winning?" she asked him.

He tipped a beer to his lips and winked at her. "I'm up about fifty, but this guy." He gestured toward the dealer. "He's tough."

"You keep coming back to my table, Mr. Renoke," the dealer said cheerfully. "Must be my good looks."

Renoke snorted, then tapped his cards. "Give me a little one, pal."

The dealer turned up a four. "Your wish, my command."

"There you go." Renoke waved a finger over the cards to indicate he'd hold with nineteen. When the dealer held on eighteen, Renoke patted Darcy's shoulder. "Looks like you brought me some fresh luck."

"I hope so. I'd like to play," she added.

"Changing twenty," the dealer announced and shoved the bill into a slot with a clear plastic box. Darcy neatly stacked her four five-dollar chips. "Bets?"

"Put a chip on the outline there," Mac instructed.

The cards moved quickly, slipping out of the shoe and snapping lightly on felt. She was dealt a six and an eight, with the dealer showing ten.

"What do I do now?"

"Take a hit."

She tilted her head, looked up at Mac. "But I'm beating him, and a ten would put me over, wouldn't it?"

"Odds are his down card is over two. Play the odds."

"Oh. I'll take a hit." She pulled a ten, then frowned. "I lost."

"But you lost correctly," the dealer told her with a grin.

She lost correctly twice more and, with brows knit in concentration, slid her last chip into place. And hit black-jack. "I didn't even have to do anything." She wiggled more comfortably on the stool and sent Mac an apologetic look. "I think I'll play incorrectly for a while, just to see what happens."

"It's your game."

With some surprise, he watched her play against all logic

and build her little stack of chips up to ten, dwindle them down to three, then build them back up again. She chatted with Renoke, learned about his two sons in college and neatly stacked her chips.

A twenty-dollar stake, he mused, and she was up to two hundred. The woman was a marvel.

He caught the eye of a dealer at another table, a subtle signal of trouble on the brew. "I'll be right back," he murmured to Darcy, giving her shoulder a light squeeze.

It wasn't hard to spot where the trouble was centered. The man in the first chair was down to three hundred-dollar chips. Mac judged him to be roughly forty, a little worse for liquor and a poor loser.

"Look, you can't deal cleaner than that, you ought to be fired." The man jabbed a finger at the dealer while other players eased out of their chairs and looked for calmer water. "I can't win more than one hand out of ten. And that little bitch who was dealer before you's no better. I want some damn action here." He thumped his fist on the table.

"Problem?" Mac stepped up to the table.

"Back off. This is none of your damn business."

"It's my business." A subtle signal had his floor man, already moving toward the table, stopping. "I'm Blade, and this is my place."

"Yeah?" The man lifted his glass, gulped. "Well, your place is lousy. Your dealers think they're slick, but I can spot them." He slammed his glass down. "Bled me for three grand already. I know when I'm being taken."

Mac's voice remained low, his eyes cool. "If you want to lodge a complaint, you're welcome to do so. In my office."

"I don't have to go to your stinking office." In one violent gesture, he knocked his glass from the table. "I want some satisfaction here."

Mac held up a hand to hold off the two security guards who were moving rapidly in his direction. "You're not going to get it. I suggest you cash in and take your business elsewhere."

"You're kicking me out?" The man shoved away from the table. On his feet he wasn't steady, but he was big, burly and his fists were clenched. "You can't kick me out."

Ready violence flashed into Mac's eyes in a quick, icy flare. "Want to bet?"

Rage had the man trembling, visibly. But drunk or not, he recognized the cold fury staring him down. "The hell with it." He snatched up his chips, sneered. "I should've known better than to trust some Indian dive."

Mac's hand shot out like a lightning bolt, grabbed the man by the shirtfront and hauled his bulk onto his toes. "Stay out of my place." His voice was dangerously quiet, his eyes flat as ice. "I see you in here again, and you won't leave standing. Escort this…gentleman to the cashier," Mac instructed his security team. "Then show him the door."

"Yes, sir."

"Half-breed son of a bitch," the man shouted as he was led away.

Mac's head jerked around when a hand touched his arm. Instinctively Darcy backed away from the frigid fury on his face. The muscles beneath her fingers were like iron and she quickly dropped her hand. "I'm sorry. I'm so sorry. He was dreadful."

"Plenty more where he came from."

All she could think was if anyone ever looked at her with eyes that icy, that powerfully cold, she would shatter into tiny shards. "There shouldn't be." She bent down, started to pick up the glass the man had knocked to the floor, but Mac snagged her hand and tugged her up again.

"What are you doing?"

"I was going to clean up the—"

"Stop." His temper was still on the end of a straining leash, and the order snapped out. "You don't belong here," he muttered, and began to pull her away from the tables and the still-gawking crowd. "It isn't all fun and games. It isn't a damn castle. There are people like that in every corner."

"Yes, but—" He was striding so quickly through the breezeway to the hotel area that she had to trot to keep up.

"You ought to be back in Kansas, tucked away in your library."

"I don't want to go back to Kansas."

He pulled her into the elevator and jammed in his master card for her suite. "They'll gobble you up in one tasty bite. I damn near did it myself."

"I don't know what you're talking about."

"Exactly." He rounded on her, frustration, fury, self-disgust punching inside his gut. Her eyes were as big as saucers, that delectably curved top lip just beginning to tremble. "Exactly," he said again, struggling for calm. "I have to go down and take care of this. Stay up here."

"But—"

"Stay up here," he repeated, pausing between each word, then giving her a nudge out of the elevator and into her suite before he did something insane. Like clamping his mouth on hers. "You worry me," he muttered as she stared at him. "You're really starting to worry me."

They continued to stare at each other until the doors shut.

Chapter 4

Darcy kept her spa appointments the next morning because she thought it would be rude not to. But her heart wasn't in it. Even being scrubbed with exotic sea salts, massaged with oils that made her think of some Egyptian handmaiden and having her face packed with thick cool goo the color of ripe pomegranates didn't lift her mood.

He wanted her to leave, and she really had nowhere to go.

It didn't seem to matter that as soon as the documents came through she'd be able to travel to all the dazzling places she'd read and dreamed about. She wanted to stay here, in this wonderful, exciting place, with all the lights and the sounds and the crowds and the seamy edges.

She wanted to gamble again, to drink champagne, to buy more sparkling earrings. She wanted just a little more time in a world where men with faces that should be sculpted in copper paid attention to her as if she were worthy of their interest.

She wanted, more than anything, a few more magical days with Mac before her coach turned into a pumpkin and the glass slipper no longer fit.

She wanted him to smile at her again in the way that transformed his face into one glorious piece of art.

He was so lovely, not just to look at, she thought, but to be with. He had a way of turning those wonderful blue eyes on her and making her think he really cared about what she thought, how she felt, what she had to say.

She'd never been able to talk to another man the way she could talk to him. Without feeling inadequate and foolish. Or simple, she supposed.

But she'd taken up too much of his time, gotten in the way. She'd always been better off fading into a corner and watching other people live. Once you stepped out too far, into those lights, you ended up doing something silly or foolish that made those who knew...*things* wish you'd slip away again.

The money wasn't going to change who she was. A pretty dress, a new haircut—it was only gloss. Under it, she was still awkward and average.

"You're going to love this."

Shaking off the blue mood, Darcy looked over at the technician. She'd already forgotten the woman's name, which was, in Darcy's opinion, as rude as not keeping the appointment in the first place. Flat on her back on the padded table, she focused on the nameplate pinned to the breast of the soft pink uniform.

"Am I, Angie?"

"Absolutely."

To Darcy's shock, Angie tugged down the thin blanket and began to paint warm brown mud on her breasts. "Oh!"

"Too warm?"

"No, no." She would not blush, she would not blush, she would *not* blush. "What's this for?"

"To make your skin irresistible."

"Nobody's going to see it where you're putting it on," Darcy said dryly, and Angie laughed.

"Hey, this is Vegas. Your luck could change any time."

"Maybe you're right." Giving up, Darcy closed her eyes.

She and her new, irresistible skin had barely stepped back into her suite when the buzzer sounded. Her tongue tied itself into knots the minute she opened the door and saw Mac.

"Got a minute?" he asked, then stepped inside when she only nodded. "I don't have much time, but I wanted to let you know the press has the bit between their teeth. The mystery woman angle has them fired up. They'll play that for a few more days, but it won't stop there. There's bound to be a leak sooner rather than later. You'll need to be prepared for that."

"I'm not going back to Kansas." It came out in a burst, fueled by an anger that surprised them both.

Mac raised his eyebrows. "So you said."

"I'm not going back," she repeated. "I have enough of the cash you advanced me to get a hotel room."

"And you'd do that because…"

"You said I shouldn't be here."

"I don't believe I did." But he remembered his temper of the night before, and thought he might have said something along those lines. "It's certainly not what I meant." Annoyed with himself, he dragged a hand through his hair. "Darcy—"

"I know I've been taking up a lot of your time. You feel responsible for me, but you don't have to. I'm perfectly content to keep out of the way. I can just stay up here and write. That's what I did last night after…well, after."

He held up a hand, guessing correctly it would stop the flood of words. "I'm sorry. I was out of line. I let that idiot last night get to me, and I took it out on you." He dipped his hands into his pockets. "But it did make me realize that you shouldn't have been there, and that you certainly shouldn't be wandering around a casino alone."

She'd been on the point of yielding when his final statement put her back up again. "You think I'm stupid and naive."

"I don't think you're stupid."

Her eyes flashed, fascinating him with the sudden and unexpected fire of gold. "Just naive, then. Probably a bit incompetent and certainly too…" Her mind went on a fumbling search for the word. "Too midwestern to take care of myself in the big, bad city."

His eyebrow arched in a way she found both charming and infuriating. "You are the one who walked into town with less than ten dollars, no purse and nothing but the clothes on her back, aren't you?"

"So what! It got me here, didn't it?"

"Point taken," he murmured.

"And last night wasn't the first time I've seen an evil-minded drunk, either. I'm from Kansas, not Dogpatch. We've got plenty of drunks in Kansas."

"I stand corrected." And struggling mightily not to grin.

"And you needn't feel obligated to look after me as if I were some stray puppy who might run out into traffic. There's absolutely no reason for you to worry about me."

"I didn't say I was worried about you. I said you worried me."

"It's the same thing."

"It's entirely different."

"How?"

He studied her. Color was warm in her face, her eyes were dark and shining. It wasn't just anger she was feeling, he realized, but bruised pride as well. And that was undeniably his fault. He sighed. "You're really leaving me no choice. You worry me," he repeated, and laid his hands on her shoulders. "Because..." Slid them down her arms, around her waist. Watched her lips part in surprise just before he covered them with his.

The world tilted. Every coherent thought in her mind tumbled out and scattered. Hopelessly lost. His mouth was just as she'd imagined it would be. Hot and firm and clever. But now it was on hers, luring her into some exciting airless space where everything shimmered and shook. Colors brightened, blurring around the edges before they melted together and turned as liquid as her bones.

His tongue swept over hers, teasing, inviting, mixing his dark, intimate taste with her own. Smooth, so smooth, that glide of tongue, that slide of lips, that she seemed to coast bonelessly down the long chute of sensation toward a spreading pool of liquid heat.

Her hands had come up to clutch at his arms for balance. He could feel the pressure of her short nails through his jacket, a contrasting signal of anxiety even as her lips opened and gave. Nerves and surrender, a dangerous mix, punctuated by the helpless little whimpers of pleasure that sounded in her throat, combined to take him deeper than he'd intended, to make him want more, much more than he'd expected.

What he'd begun churned through him and demanded he finish—his way. Then and there, and thoroughly. She was aroused. So was he. However innocent, she wasn't a child. And he wanted her. God, he wanted her.

Her eyes remained closed as he drew her away. He watched the tip of her tongue trace her curvy, unpainted lips before she pressed those lips together, like a woman lingering over a particularly lush taste. Even as her lashes fluttered, a hot fist of need balled in his gut.

Her eyes were dark and clouded, fixed now on his. A flush glowed on her cheeks. A swallow rippled her throat.

Damn, he wanted, desperately wanted to take her in one greedy gulp until nothing was left but the sighs.

"Why…" Her breath was coming too fast for the words to be steady. "Why did you do that?"

Be careful with her, he reminded himself. *Very careful.* "Because I wanted to. Is that a problem?"

She stared at him for a long moment. "No," she answered with such weighty seriousness he nearly smiled. "I don't think so."

"Good. Because I'm not finished yet."

"Oh." His arms were tightening, easing her close again. Bodies met again. "Well…" Her eyes drifted shut. "Take your time."

Her innocence was as bright as a beacon, and outrageously arousing. No, not a child, he thought again, but the odds were weighted heavily against her. And he had no right to use that as leverage. Grappling for control, he rested his forehead on hers. *Slow down,* he ordered himself. *Better yet, stop.*

"Darcy, you're a dangerous woman."

Her eyes flew open. "Me?"

The shock in her voice did nothing to relieve the tension centered in his gut. The tension was a bad sign, he decided, a signal not just of desire, but of desire for her. Very specific, very exact and completely inappropriate. "Lethal," he murmured, then stepped back.

But he kept his hands on her shoulders, not quite able to break all contact. She was searching his face now, her big gold eyes still blurred from the first kiss, her mouth pursed in anticipation of the next. He could have lapped her up like cream.

"Have you ever had a lover?"

She blinked, then her gaze lowered to stare at the buttons of his shirt. The shirt was black and silky. It had felt warm and smooth under her hands. She wanted to touch it again. To touch him. "Not exactly."

His brow lifted again. "Despite its infinite and entertaining varieties, sex remains a fairly exact pastime."

She had the distinct impression he didn't intend to kiss her again, after all. Sexual frustration was a new, and not entirely pleasant, sensation. Vaguely insulted, she frowned up at him. "I know what sex is."

No, he thought, she didn't. She didn't have a clue what he wanted to do with her, to her. If she did, he imagined she'd run as far and as fast as her pretty fairy legs would carry her. "You don't know me, Darcy. You don't know the rules around here, or the pitfalls."

"I know how to learn," she said testily. "I'm not a moron."

"Some things you're better off not learning." He gave her shoulders a light squeeze when the phone began to ring. "Answer the phone."

She turned on her heel, stalked over to the desk and snatched up the receiver. "Yes? Hello?"

"And who might this be?"

The abrupt demand in a thick burr was so commanding she answered immediately. "This is Darcy Wallace."

"Wallace? Wallace, is it? And would you spring from William Wallace, the great hero of Scotland?"

"Actually..." Confusion had her pushing a hand through her hair. "He's an ancestor on my father's side."

"Good blood. Strong stock. You can be proud of your heritage, lass. Darcy, is it? And are you a married woman, Darcy Wallace?"

"No, I'm not. I—" She snapped back and her brows drew together. "Excuse me, who is this?"

"This is Daniel MacGregor, and I'm pleased to make your acquaintance."

She managed to close her mouth, take a breath. "How do you do, Mr. MacGregor?"

"I do fine, fine and dandy, Darcy Wallace. I'm told my grandson is paying a call on you."

"Yes, he's here." Weren't her lips still tingling from his? "Um. Would you like to speak to him?"

"That I would. You have a fine, clear voice. How old might you be?"

"I'm twenty-three."

"I wager you're a healthy girl, too."

Totally at sea, she nodded her head. "Yes, I'm healthy." She only blinked at Mac when he cursed under his breath and grabbed the phone away from her.

"Shall I check her teeth for you, Grandpa?"

"There you are." Pleasure, and no remorse, rang in Daniel's voice. "Your secretary transferred me. Of course, I wouldn't have to be transferred all over hell and back to have a word with my oldest grandchild if you ever bothered to call your grandmother. She's feeling neglected."

It was an old ploy, and made Mac sigh. "I called you and Grandma less than a week ago."

"At our age, boy, a week's a lifetime."

"Bull." He couldn't stop the smile. "You'll both live forever."

"That's the plan. So, I hear from your mother—who bothers to call home from time to time—that you lost yourself a million-eight and change."

Mac ran his tongue around his teeth, glancing over as Darcy wandered to the window. "You win some, you lose some."

"True enough. And was the lass I was just speaking to the one who robbed you?"

"Yes."

"A Wallace. Good, clear voice, good manners. Is she pretty?"

Mac eased a hip on the desk. He knew his grandfather well. "Not bad, if you overlook the hunchback and the crossed eyes." Idly he flipped open the notebook on the desk as Daniel's hearty laughter rang in his ear.

"She's pretty then. Got your eye on her, do you?"

Mac lifted his gaze from the pages crowded with margin-to-margin writing, and studied the way Darcy stood facing the window. The sun was a halo over her hair. Her hands were linked together in front of her. She looked as delicate as a wildflower in the unforgiving heat of the desert.

"No." He said it definitely, finally, wanting to mean it. "I don't."

"And why not? Are you going to stay single all your life? A man your age needs a wife. You should be starting a family."

As Daniel blustered on about responsibility, duty, the family name, Mac cocked his head and read a page. It was about a woman sitting alone in the dark, watching the lights of the city outside her window. The sense of solitude, of separation, was wrenching.

Thoughtfully he closed the book again, laying a hand over it as he watched Darcy watch the city. "But I'm having such fun, Grandpa," he said, when Daniel finally paused for breath, "working my way through all the showgirls."

There was a moment's pause, then a roar of laughter. "You always had a mouth on you. I miss you, Robbie."

Daniel was the only one who ever called Mac by his childhood name—and then he used it rarely. Love, Mac thought, was inescapable. "I miss you, too. All of you."

"Well, if you'd tear yourself away from those showgirls, you could come visit your poor old granny."

Obviously Anna MacGregor wasn't within hearing distance. Mac could imagine the punishment she would mete out if she heard her husband call her "poor," "old" or "granny." "Give her my love."

"I will, though she'd prefer you give it to her yourself. Put the lass back on the phone."

"No."

"No respect," Daniel muttered. "I should have taken a strap to you when you were a boy."

"Too late now." Mac grinned. "Behave yourself, Grandpa. I'll talk to you soon."

"See that you do."

Mac stayed where he was after he replaced the receiver. "I'll apologize for The MacGregor's interrogation."

"It's all right." She kept her back to him, stared out at the sun shining on towering buildings. "He sounds formidable."

"Hard shell, soft center."

"Mmm." She hadn't meant to eavesdrop, but how could she have helped hearing Mac's part of the conversation?

The love and exasperation in his voice had touched her. And his words had cleared up her confusion.

Showgirls. Of course he would be attracted to the long legs, the beautiful bodies, the exotic faces. He'd only been curious, she supposed. That's why he'd kissed her. But damn him, damn him for stirring up all this need that she'd managed to live very contentedly without until now.

"I seem to have gotten distracted from the point of coming to see you." He waited for her to turn and face him. At a casual glance she appeared perfectly composed. But he couldn't seem to glance at her casually. He was compelled to search, and a search of those eyes revealed bruises and storms. "Now you're angry."

"No, I'm irritated, but I'm not angry. What was the point," she began, then paused significantly, "of your coming to see me?"

That flair for sarcasm surprised him. The edge of it pricked at him enough to have him pushing off the desk and shoving his hands into his pockets. "The point was the press. I know you're concerned about your name getting out. We're being deluged with calls for the full story. I can hold them off, but it's bound to leak, Darcy. The hotel employs hundreds, and several people already know your name. Sooner rather than later, one of them is going to talk to a reporter."

"I'm sure you're right." She supposed she should be grateful he'd given her something else to worry about. "I'm sure you think I'm a coward, not wanting Gerald to know where I am."

"I think that's your business."

"I am a coward." She said it defiantly, tossing up her chin in a challenging gesture that contrasted with her words. "I'd rather agree than quarrel, rather run that fight. But that's why I'm here, isn't it? Here with you, about to become wealthy. Cowardice works for me."

"He can't hurt you, Darcy."

"Of course he can." Lifting her hands, she gave a weary sigh. "Words hurt. They bruise the heart and scar the soul. I'd rather be slapped than battered with words." Then she shook her head. "Well, whatever happens, happens. How much time do you think I have before my name gets out?"

"A day or two."

"Then I should make the most of it. I appreciate you letting me know. You must be busy. I don't want to keep you."

"Kicking me out?"

She managed a small smile. "We both know you have other things to do. I don't need you to baby-sit."

"All right." He started for the door, then stopped and turned with his hand on the knob. "I wanted to kiss you again." He watched her gaze flick warily to his face. "A little too much for your own good, and maybe for my own."

Her heart stuttered. "Maybe I'm tired of my own good, and willing to gamble."

Something flashed into his eyes that made her shudder. "High stakes, bad odds. Too risky for a novice, Darcy from Kansas. First rule is never bet what you can't afford to lose."

When he closed the door quietly behind him, she let out the breath she'd been holding. "Why do I have to lose?"

She kept to herself the rest of the day, writing furiously in her notebook. The garage that had towed in her car called to tell her it was repaired. On impulse she asked the mechanic if he knew anyone who would buy it. She was finished with it, after all, and with everything else—save her notebooks— that she'd brought with her from Trader's Corners.

When the mechanic offered her a thousand dollars, she

snapped it up without bargaining, and hurried out to sign over the paperwork.

There was a slick little laptop computer sitting on her desk when she returned, with a note telling her that it was hers to use during her stay, courtesy of The Comanche. Thrilled, Darcy stroked it, examined it, experimented with it, then settled down to transcribe her notes onto the screen.

She worked straight through dinner and into the evening until her eyes blurred and her fingers went numb. Hunger rumbled in her stomach. It was tempting to reach for the phone, to order something to be brought to the room. To stay hidden.

Instead she picked up her purse, squared her shoulders. She was going out, she decided. She'd have a meal, some wine if she wanted. Then, by God, she was going to gamble.

The tables were crowded and the air stung with smoke and perfume when she entered the casino. She wanted to watch, to study. Figure the odds, Mac had said. Learn the rules. She intended to do just that. She liked the world here, the hard-edged brightness of it, the thrill of risk.

She wandered through, loitering by a blackjack table long enough to see a man in shirtsleeves with a thin black cigar clamped between his teeth lose five thousand dollars without flinching.

Amazing.

She studied the spin of the wheel, the teasing bounce of the little silver ball at roulette. Saw stacks of chips come and go. Odd or even. Black or red.

Fascinating.

Behind it all was the never-ending beeps and whistles and clinks of the slots. Lights beckoned. Jackpot. She studied the technique of an elderly woman who leaned on a walker and mumbled to the spinning face of a machine. And gave a cheerleader's shout when quarters cascaded into the metal dish.

"Fifty bucks," the woman said, shooting Darcy a steely smile. "About time this sucker paid off."

"Congratulations. It's poker, isn't it?"

"That's right. Been nickel-and-diming me for two hours. But it's heating up now." She gave the machine a friendly thump with her walker, then stabbed the red button again. "Let's go, sweetheart."

It looked like fun, Darcy decided. Simple, uncomplicated, and an excellent place to start. She walked down the line until she came to an unoccupied machine, then slid onto the stool. After reading the instructions, she put a twenty in the slot and watched her credits light. She pushed the button, grinning as her hand was dealt.

In his office, Mac watched her on-screen. He could only shake his head. In the first place, she was playing like a chump, one credit at a time. If she wanted to hit, she needed to play four, a buck a hand. Now she was holding two kings instead of going for the straight flush.

It was pitifully obvious she'd never played poker before in her life.

Well, he'd keep an eye on her, make certain she didn't lose more than a few hundred.

He glanced over at the door when a knock sounded, then his smile spread with delight when his mother poked her head in. "Hello, handsome."

"Hello, gorgeous." He caught her around the waist in a fierce hug and pressed his lips to her soft, burnished gold hair. "I didn't expect you for another day or two."

"We finished up early." She cupped his face in her hands and smiled at him. "And I wanted to see my boy."

"Where's Dad?"

"He'll be right along. He got waylaid in the lobby so I deserted him."

Mac laughed and kissed her again. She was so beautiful, with soft skin, exotic eyes a unique shade of lavender, and strong facial bones that guaranteed grace and beauty for a lifetime. "Serves him right. Come sit down. Let me get you a drink."

"I would love a glass of wine. It's been a long day." With a sigh Serena sat in one of the leather chairs, stretched out long legs that rustled with silk. "I talked to Caine this morning. He tells me he's getting the paperwork finished up for this woman who hit the big machine here. The press is full of Madam X," she added.

With a short laugh, Mac poured a glass of his mother's favorite white wine. "I can't think of a title that suits her less."

"Really. What's she like?"

"See for yourself." He gestured to the screen. "The little blonde in the blue blouse at the poker slot."

Serena shifted, sipping her wine as she studied the monitor. She lifted a brow as Darcy held a pair of eights and tossed away the best part of a flush. "Not much of a player, is she?"

"Green as they come."

Serena's gambler's heart warmed when Darcy pulled another two eights. "Lucky little thing, though. And pretty. Is it true she was dead broke when she walked in here?"

"Just about down to her last dollar."

"Well, good for her." Serena lifted her glass to toast the screen. "I'm looking forward to meeting her. Oh, good, someone's going to give her a little help."

"What?" Alerted, Mac looked back at the screen and saw

a man slip onto the stool beside her. He saw the quick, flirtatious grin, the easy brush of a hand on Darcy's shoulder. And Darcy's wide-eyed, attentive smile. "Son of a bitch."

Mac was halfway out the door before Serena could leap to her feet. "Mac?"

"I've got to get down there."

"But why—"

As her son dashed off, Serena decided there was only one way to find out why. She set her wine aside and hurried after him.

Chapter 5

People were so nice, so friendly, Darcy thought. And so helpful, she decided as she smiled at the attractive man in the Stetson who'd settled down beside her at the slots.

His name was Jake, and he was from Dallas, which, as he said, practically made them neighbors.

"I'm really new at this," she told him confidentially, and his sunshine blue eyes laughed into hers.

"Why, I could spot that right off, sugar. Now like I said first off, you want to plug in the maximum credits for each hand, otherwise you don't get yourself a full payoff when you hit."

"Right." Dutifully Darcy pressed the credit button, then punched for the deal. She studied her hand thoughtfully. "I've got two threes, so I hold them."

"Well now, you could." Jake laid a hand over hers before she could press to hold the cards. "But you see, you're after that royal straight flush, right? That's the jackpot. You got yourself the ace, queen and the jack of hearts there. Couple treys aren't going to get you anything. Even a triple's just keeping you in the game."

She nibbled her lip. "I should throw away the threes?"

"If you're going to gamble—" he winked at her "—you should gamble."

"Right." She furrowed her brow and let the threes go. She plucked an ace and a five. "Oh, well, that's no good." Still she remembered what the blackjack dealer had said, and turned to Jake with a smile. "But I lost correctly."

"There you go." She was cute as a brass button, he thought, sweet as a daisy and looked to be just as easy to pick. Charmed, he leaned in a little closer. "Why don't I buy you a drink, and we'll talk poker strategy."

"The lady's unavailable." Mac dropped a proprietary, and none too gentle hand on Darcy's shoulder.

Her head whipped up, her shoulders tensed. "Mac." He had that frigid look in his eyes again, she noted. Not that he spared her a glance. The ice was all for her new friend from Dallas. "Ah, this is Jake. He was showing me how to play the poker machine."

"So I see. The lady's with me."

Jake ran his tongue around his teeth and, after a brief internal debate, decided he wanted to keep those teeth just where they were. "Sorry, pal. Didn't know I was poaching." He rose, tipped his hat to Darcy. "You hold out for that royal straight flush now."

"Thank you." She held out her hand, confused when Jake's eyes shifted to Mac's before he accepted.

"My pleasure." After a short and silent male exchange, Jake swaggered off.

"I'd been doing it wrong," Darcy began. And that was as far as she got.

"Didn't I tell you not to come down here at night alone?" The fact that he was speaking softly didn't lessen the power and fury behind the words. It only added to them.

"That's ridiculous." She wanted badly to cringe, and had to force herself not to. "You can't expect me to sit in my room all night. I was only—"

"This is exactly why. Ten minutes at a machine and you're getting hit on."

"He wasn't hitting on me. He was helping me."

Mac's opinion of that was short and pithy and put some steel back in Darcy's spine.

"Don't swear at me."

"I was swearing in general." He put a hand under her elbow and hauled her to her feet. "The cowboy wasn't going to buy you a drink to be helpful. He was just priming the pump, and believe me, yours is easily primed."

She started to shake, and realized it was just as much from anger as fear. "Well, if he was, and it is, it's my business."

"My place. My business."

She hissed in a breath, tried to jerk free and failed. "Let go of me. I don't have to stay here. If I'd wanted some overbearing male ordering me around, I'd still be in Kansas."

His smile was as thin and sharp as his name. "You're not in Kansas anymore."

"That's both obvious and unoriginal. Now let go of me. I'm leaving. There are plenty of other places where I can gamble and socialize without being harassed by the management."

"You want to gamble?" To her shock and—God help her—excitement, he backed her up against the machine with something close to murder in his eyes. "You want to socialize?"

"Mac?" Deciding she'd seen quite enough, Serena stepped up, a bright, friendly smile in place. "Aren't you going to introduce me?"

He turned his head and stared. He'd completely, totally forgotten about his mother. He saw easily beyond the smile to the command in her eyes. And felt twelve years old again.

"Of course." With a smoothness that blanketed both his straining temper and embarrassment, he shifted his grip on Darcy's arm. "Serena MacGregor Blade, Darcy Wallace. Darcy, my mother."

"Oh." Not nearly as skilled as Mac, Darcy didn't come close to hiding both her distress and mortification. "Mrs. Blade. How do you do?"

"I'm so happy to meet you. I just got into town and was about to ask Mac about you." Still smiling, she slid an arm around Darcy's shoulders. "Now I can ask you in person. Let's go get a drink. Mac," she added, casting a smug look over her shoulder as she led Darcy away, "we'll be in the Silver Lounge. Tell your father where I am, will you?"

"Oh sure," Mac muttered. "Fine." He resisted, barely, giving the slot a swift kick, and instead dutifully cashed Darcy out.

In a relatively quiet corner of a cocktail lounge gleaming with silver tables and rich black cushions, Darcy ran her fingers up and down the stem of a glass of white wine. She'd taken one sip, to clear her dry throat, but was afraid to take more.

Mac was probably right about one thing, she'd decided. She didn't hold her liquor very well.

"Mrs. Blade, I'm so terribly sorry."

"Really?" Serena relaxed against the cushions and took stock of the young woman facing her. Prettier still up close, she mused, in a delicate, almost ethereal, way. Big innocent eyes, a doll's mouth, nervous hands.

Not the type her son usually looked at twice, she reflected. She knew very well his taste generally ran to the long, lean and, in her opinion, somewhat brittle sort of woman. She also knew him well enough to be sure he rarely, very rarely lost his temper over one.

"Mac did ask me not to come down to the casino alone at night."

Serena arched a brow. "I can't see that he'd have any right to do that."

"No, but…he's been so kind to me."

"I'm glad to hear that."

"What I mean is, he really only asked me that one thing. It's understandable he'd be angry I didn't listen."

"It's understandable he'd be angry because he's used to getting his way." Serena studied Darcy over the rim of her glass. "That's not your problem."

"He feels responsible for me."

It was said in such a miserably depressed tone that Serena had to swallow a chuckle. She had an inkling her son felt a bit more than responsibility. "He's always taken his responsibilities seriously. Again, not your problem. Now, tell me everything." She leaned forward, inviting confidences. "I've gotten it all second hand—either from what Mac told my husband or the papers. I want the whole story, straight from the source."

"I don't know where to start."

"Oh, at the beginning."

"Well." Darcy contemplated her wine, then risked another sip. "It was all because I didn't want to marry Gerald."

"Really?" Delighted, Serena inched closer. "And who is Gerald?"

* * *

An hour later, Serena was fascinated, charmed and feeling sentimentally maternal toward Darcy. She'd already decided to extend her quick trip to several days when she covered Darcy's hand with hers. "I think you've been incredibly brave."

"I don't feel brave. No one's ever been as kind to me as Mac has, and I've made him so angry. Mrs. Blade—"

"I hope you'll call me Serena," she interrupted. "Especially since I'm going to offer you some unsolicited advice."

"I'd appreciate some advice."

"Don't change anything." Now Serena squeezed Darcy's hand. "Mac will deal with it, I promise you. You be exactly what you are, and you enjoy it."

"I'm attracted to him." Darcy winced then scowled down at her empty glass. "I shouldn't have had the wine. I shouldn't have said that. You're his mother."

"Yes, I am, and as such I'd be insulted if you weren't attracted to him. I happen to think he's a very attractive young man."

"Of course. I mean…" She trailed off, her eyes shifting up, then going wide. "Oh." She barely breathed as she stared at the man who stepped up to the table. "You *are* the chief."

Justin Blade flashed a grin at her, then slid into the booth beside his wife. "You must be Darcy."

"He looks so much like you. I'm sorry. I don't mean to stare."

"The day I mind being stared at by a pretty young woman is the day life stops being worth living."

Justin draped an arm around his wife's shoulders. He was a tall, lean man with black hair streaked with silver as bright as the table and his eyes were green, sharp and deep in a tanned and weathered face. They skimmed over Darcy with both approval and interest.

"Now I know what Mac meant about the fairy wings. Congratulations on your luck, Darcy."

"Thank you. It doesn't seem real yet." She glanced around the glittery lounge. "None of it does."

"Any plans for your new fortune? Other than giving us the chance to win some of it back."

She smiled now, fully. "Oh, he is like you. Actually, I seem to win a little every time I play." She tried to make it sound apologetic, but spoiled it with a chuckle. "But I have put some back—into the shops and salons."

"A woman after my own heart," Serena declared. "We do have wonderful shops here."

"And they genuflect when they see you coming." Justin's fingers drifted up into his wife's hair and began toying with the strands.

It made Darcy realize she'd never seen her parents touch like that, so casually, so intimately. Not in public or private. And realizing it made her unbearably sad.

"Another round, ladies?" Even as he asked, Justin was signaling for a waitress.

"Not for me. Thank you. I should go up. I thought I'd look for a new car tomorrow."

"Want company?"

Darcy fumbled with her purse as she rose, and smiled hesitantly at Serena. "Yes, if you'd like."

"I'd love it. Just call my room when you decide what time you want to go. Someone will find me."

"All right. It was nice meeting both of you. Good night."

Justin waited until Darcy was out of earshot before lifting an eyebrow at his wife. "What's going on in your head, Serena?"

"All sorts of interesting thoughts." She turned her head so that her lips brushed his.

"Such as?"

"Our firstborn nearly punched a cowboy for having a mild flirtation with our Kansas pixie."

"Another wine for my wife, Carol, and a draft for me," he said to the waitress before shifting to face Serena. "You must be exaggerating. Duncan's the one who likes to trade punches over pretty women, not Mac."

"I'm not exaggerating in the least. Fangs were bared, Blade," she murmured. "And murder was in the air. I believe he's seriously smitten."

"Smitten?" The word made him laugh, then his laughter faded into unexpected anxiety. "Define 'seriously.'"

"Justin." She patted his cheek. "He's nearly thirty. It has to happen sometime."

"She's not his type."

"Exactly." She felt her eyes sting and sniffled. "She's nothing like his type. She's perfect for him." Resolutely she blinked back the tears. "Or I'll find out if she's perfect before long."

"Serena, you sound uncomfortably like your father."

"Don't be absurd." Sentimental tears dried up with the insult. "I have no intention of manipulating or scheming or plotting." She tossed her head. "I'm simply going to…"

"Meddle."

"Discreetly," she finished, and beamed at him. "You are very attractive." She skimmed her fingers through the silver wings of his hair, lingered there. "Why don't we take these drinks upstairs, up to bed."

"You're trying to distract me."

"Of course I am." Her smile was slow, seductive and sure. "Is it working?"

He took her hand to pull her to her feet. "It always has." He kissed her fingers. "Always will."

Habitually, Mac slept from about three in the morning to nine, straddling shifts and ending his day after peak hours. Barring trouble, he could safely leave the full responsibility of the casino for that stretch of time to his shift and pit bosses and floor men. Morning hours routinely were dedicated to the massive paperwork the casino demanded—the banking, accounting, staff meetings, the hirings and firings.

He'd taken over as casino manager of Comanche Vegas when he'd been twenty-four, and had set the tone. The surface was friendly, noisy, full of movement and action. But underneath, it was ruthlessly organized and the bottom line was profit.

As he was one himself, he could spot a card counter across the blackjack pit after a five-minute study. He knew when to let them ride, or when to move them along. Employees were expected to be personable and honest. Those who met his standards were rewarded. Those who didn't were fired.

There were no second chances.

His father had built The Comanche out of guts and grit, and had turned it into a polished, sharp-edged jewel in the desert. Mac's responsibility was to keep the sheen high and he took his responsibilities seriously.

"The first half of the year looks good." Justin leaned back in his chair, removed the reading glasses he privately despised, then handed Mac back the computer-generated spreadsheet. "Up about five percent from last year."

"Six," Mac said with a flash of grin. "And a quarter."

"You've got your mother's head for math."

"I live for numbers. Where is Mom? I thought she'd want to sit in on this meeting."

"She's off with Darcy."

Mac set down the personnel file he'd just picked up. "With Darcy."

"Shopping. Refreshing young woman." Justin's face was as bland as it would have been if he'd held three aces. "Makes it hard to regret handing her seven figures."

"Yeah." Mac caught himself drumming his fingers on the file and stopped. "The press is pushing for a name. I've got half a dozen assistants fielding calls."

"Even without her name, the publicity's humming. It can't hurt business."

"The hotel manager reports an upswing in reservations in the last two days. Play on the machine she hit on is up thirty percent."

"When her story gets out—and that pretty face is splashed over the national news—they'll flood in here."

"I'm putting on three extra floor men, and I'd like to promote Janice Hawber to pit boss."

"You know your staff." Justin took out a slim cigar. "We'll likely get the ripple effect at other locations." When Mac opened the file, Justin waved the cigar, spiraling smoke. "Let's take a break here. Whatever happened to that long-legged brunette who liked baccarat and Brandy Alexanders?"

"Pamela." His father didn't miss a trick, Mac thought. "I believe she's playing baccarat and drinking Brandy Alexanders over at the Mirage these days."

"Too bad. She added a nice...shine to the tables."

"She was looking for a rich husband. I decided to fold before things got sticky."

"Hmm. Seeing anyone else?" At Mac's lifted brow, Justin grinned. "Just trying to keep up with the tour, pal. Duncan changes dancing partners so often I just give them numbers."

"Duncan juggles women like apples," Mac said, thinking of his brother. "I find one at a time's less complicated. And no, I'm not dancing at the moment. You can report back to Grandpa that his oldest grandchild continues to be lax in his duty to continue the line."

Justin chuckled and puffed on his cigar. "You'd think four great-grandchildren would satisfy him for a while."

"Nothing will satisfy The MacGregor until every last one of us is married and clucking around a brood of kids." Mac moved his shoulders restlessly. "At least he could nag one of the others for a bit. Pick on D.C."

"He does pick on D.C." Justin grinned. "Alan tells me he picks at the boy until D.C. holes up in his garret, paints and swears he'll die a bachelor just to spite Daniel. So then Daniel goes to work on Ian, who just smiles charmingly, agrees with everything Daniel says, and cheerfully ignores him."

"Maybe I'll slip one of their names into our next conversation—strictly in the spirit of self-preservation—and shift his focus for a while."

The door burst open. "Speak of the devil," Mac murmured as he got to his feet.

The MacGregor stood in the doorway, grinning widely. His white hair flowed back from a broad and deeply seamed face offset by eyes that twinkled bright blue and a wild, snowy beard. His shoulders were as broad as the grill of a truck. And the hand that slapped Justin enthusiastically on the back was as big as a ham.

"Give me one of those pitiful excuses for a cigar," Daniel boomed, then caught Mac in a bear hug that could have toppled a rabid grizzly. "Pour me a Scotch, boy. Flying cross-country puts a thirst in a man."

"You had a Scotch on the plane." Caine MacGregor strode into the room. "Charmed the flight attendant out of one when I wasn't looking. If Mom finds out, she'll kill me."

"What she doesn't know won't hurt you." Daniel plopped his bulk into a chair, sighed lustily and looked around with great pleasure. "Well now, how about that cigar?"

Knowing the rules—and Anna MacGregor's wrath—Justin turned to his brother-in-law. "Anna dump him on you?"

"Ha!" Daniel thumped the cane he used as much for looks as for convenience.

"He wouldn't stay home. She sends her love and her sympathy. Good to see you." Caine gave both Justin and Mac a hard hug. "Where's Rena?"

"Shopping," Justin told him. "She should be back shortly."

"Give me a damn cigar." Daniel glowered and thumped his cane again. "And where's the lassie who skinned you for over a million? I want to meet her."

Mac turned to study his grandfather. Formidable, Darcy had said. It appeared she was going to find out firsthand just how formidable.

Dazed and flushed, Darcy carted bags and boxes into her suite. Similarly burdened, Serena was right behind her.

"Oh, that was fun." With a sigh, Serena dumped everything on the floor and dropped into a chair. "My feet are killing me. Always a good sign of shopping success."

"I don't even remember what I bought. I don't know what came over me."

"I'm a terrible influence."

"You were wonderful." It had been one of the most monumental days in Darcy's life. Being propelled from store to store, having blouses and dresses tossed at her, modeling them in front of Serena's assessing eyes. "You know everything about clothes."

"A lifetime love affair. Darcy, run up and put on that yellow sundress. I'm dying to see it on you again. Try it with the white sandals and the little gold hoop earrings." She rose to nudge Darcy toward the stairs. "Indulge me, won't you, honey? I'll order us up a well-deserved cold drink."

"All right." Halfway up, she turned and looked back. "I had the best time. I don't think I'll be able to bring myself to buy that sports car, though. It's so impractical."

"We'll worry about that later." Humming to herself, Serena walked away to order some lemonade.

The child was starved for attention, she thought. It was so easy to see, and so easy to read between the lines when Darcy spoke of her childhood. She doubted anyone had ever taken her on a whirlwind shopping spree, or giggled with her over foolish lingerie, or told her how pretty she looked in a yellow dress.

It made Serena's heart ache to remember how stunned Darcy had looked when she'd laughed and hugged her as they'd debated over earrings. And the wistful glance she'd sent the bright blue sports car before she'd given her attention to the sober and practical sedan she said was more suitable.

As far as Serena could tell there had been far too much suitable in Darcy's young life, and not nearly enough fun.

That, she determined, was going to change.

When the phone rang, Darcy called from upstairs. "Oh, can you—I'm not—"

"I'll get it." Serena picked up the phone. "Ms. Wallace's suite." Her eyes gleamed, her smile spread as she listened to the voice. "Yes, indeed, we're back."

Her mind calculated at a speed and in a direction that would have made Daniel puff out with pride. "Why don't we do that here? I'm sure she'd be more comfortable. Yes, now's fine. See you in a minute."

Humming again, Serena strolled to the base of the stairs. "Need any help?"

"No. There are so many boxes. I just found the dress."

"Take your time. That was Justin on the phone. You don't mind if we do a little business, do you?"

"No."

"Good. I'll order up more drinks." Champagne, she decided, considering.

Ten minutes later, Darcy took the first turn on the steps just as the elevator opened. She froze where she was, staggered by the rich mix of male voices, the sudden rush of energy that poured out of the elevator along with them.

Then she could only see Mac.

Serena watched the way her son's eyes locked on Darcy's, the way they darkened, held. And she was sure.

"There's my girl." Daniel grabbed his daughter in a fierce hug. "You don't call your mother enough," he scolded her. "She pines."

"I've been spending a lot of time nagging my children." She kissed him lavishly on both cheeks, then turned to embrace her brother. "How are you? How's Diana? How're the kids?"

"Everyone's fine. Diana's tying up a case and couldn't get away. She'll be sorry she missed you."

"Well now." Daniel leaned on his cane and studied the woman who'd frozen like a statue on the stairs. "You're just a wee lass, aren't you? Come on down, and let's have a better look at you."

"He rarely bites." Mac crossed to the base of the steps, held out a hand.

Her legs were wobbly, and she knew her fingers weren't steady so she pretended not to see his hand. But he took hers anyway, giving it a reassuring squeeze that clutched at her heart.

"Darcy Wallace, The MacGregor."

She was afraid she wouldn't find her voice. He looked so big, and so fierce with white brows knitted together over sharp blue eyes. "I'm happy to meet you, Mr. MacGregor."

The scowl stayed in place another moment, then transformed into a smile so wide and so bright she blinked. "Pretty as a sunbeam." He gave her cheek a gentle pat with his huge hand. "Tiny as an elf."

Her lips curved up in response. "It's only that you're so big. If William of Scotland had had more like you, he would have won."

Daniel let out his bark of a laugh, and winked at her. "Now, there's a lass. Come sit and talk to me."

"You can interrogate her later. I'm Caine MacGregor."

She shifted her gaze to the tall man with silver and gold hair and strong blue eyes. "Yes, I know. I'm so nervous." She clutched her hands together. How many legends could one person meet in one day? "I studied about you in school. Everyone thought you'd run for president."

"I leave the politics to Alan. I'm just a lawyer. Your lawyer," he added, taking her arm and leading her to a chair at the glossy conference table. "Want me to clear this rabble out while we consult?"

"Oh, no, please." She scanned the faces around her, lingered on Mac's. "Everyone here has a part in this."

"All right. It's straightforward enough." He sat and opened his briefcase. "I've got your birth certificate, your social security card, a copy of the police report from the purse snatching last week. You're unlikely to recover anything from that."

She stared down at the papers he handed her. "It doesn't matter. You got all of this so quickly."

"Connections," he said with a wolfish grin. "I have copies of your last two years' tax returns. There are some forms for you to fill out and sign. A number of them."

"All right." She tried not to gape at the stack he began to produce. "Where do I start?"

"I'll explain them as we go along." He glanced up, wiggling his brows at his family. "Haven't you all got something better to do?"

"No." Daniel took a chair for himself. "Can't a man get a drink around here while all this legal mumbo jumbo's going on?"

"I ordered drinks." To distract him, Serena sat on the arm of his chair and began to tell him about her grandchild's latest accomplishments.

Listening carefully, Darcy filled out each form. She hesitated over the address, then wrote in the name of the hotel. When Caine didn't correct her, she relaxed a little and continued to note down the required information.

"Your identification's in order," Caine told her. "You'll be able to reapply for a driver's license, credit cards, that sort of thing. You didn't indicate a bank."

"A bank?"

"The transfer of funds will be done electronically, from account to account. The oversize check Mac will present you with is just for publicity. Photo op, and positive publicity for The Comanche. The actual business is accomplished quickly and efficiently by transferring the amount of your winnings from The Comanche's account to yours. Do you want the money sent to your bank in Kansas?"

"No." She refused swiftly, then fell into silence.

"Where do you want it sent, Darcy?" Caine asked gently.

"I don't know. Maybe it could just stay in the same bank. Here?"

"That's not a problem. You're aware that the IRS gets the first bite."

She nodded, signing her name to the last form. Under her lashes, she watched Mac go to the door to let in the room-service waiter.

Mac wore black trousers and a white shirt. Both looked soft, almost fluid, and she wondered about the texture, wished she could run her fingertips over them. Over him.

"You're going to need financial advice."

"What?" Flushing, berating herself for not paying attention, she looked over at Caine. "I'm sorry."

"Tomorrow morning, you're going to have a great deal of money. You'll need a financial advisor."

"You can't do that?"

"I can give you some basic and initial guidance. After that, you're going to want someone who specializes. I can give you some names."

"I'd appreciate it."

"That's pretty much it." He leaned back. "We'll open you an account, the money will be transferred. And you're set."

"Just like that?"

"Just like that."

"Oh." She pressed a hand to her suddenly jittery stomach. "God." Once again she searched out Mac's face, hoping he'd tell her what to do, what to say. But he only watched her, his eyes steady and unreadable.

With an impatient huff for her son, Serena rose. "I'd say this calls for a celebration. Mac, darling, open the champagne. Darcy, you get the first glass."

"It's so nice of you, all of you, but—" She jolted when the cork popped.

"I've never lost a million to anyone more appealing." Justin took the glass from his son and carried it to Darcy. "Enjoy it." He leaned down to kiss her cheek.

Warmth spread in her stomach, pressure weighed on her chest. "Thank you."

"Congratulations." Caine took her hand, covered it with both of his.

Then everyone was lifting glasses, and talking. She was hugged, kissed by everyone, with the notable exception of Mac. He only lifted a hand to her cheek, skimmed a finger down it.

There was laughing, and arguments over the time and place for a family dinner, which, she realized with shock, included her. Serena draped an arm casually around her shoulder while telling Caine he was an idiot if he thought she'd settle for pizza for such an occasion.

Emotions were clawing at her, rising up to squeeze her heart, to close her throat and burn her eyes. She heard her own breath begin to hitch and clamped down hard.

"Excuse me." She managed to mumble it before turning quickly for the stairs. Horribly aware the laughter had stopped, she rushed up, closed herself in the bathroom. She held on, carefully turning the water on full in the sink so the sound would cover her sobs.

She sat on the floor, curled up into herself and wept like a baby.

Chapter 6

The suite was quiet when Darcy came out again. She didn't know whether to be relieved or mortified to realize they'd left her alone. She would have to fumble her way through apologies and explanations, she told herself. But for now she could settle her nerves and emotions.

She glanced around the bedroom, scanning the shopping bags, the boxes. The right thing to do, she told herself, was to put everything away, to tidy up, to put at least this part of her life in order.

She was just unwrapping a new blouse when she heard footsteps on the stairs. Clutching the blouse, she stared at Mac as he stopped at the top of the suite.

"Are you all right?"

"Yes. I thought everyone had gone."

"I stayed," he said simply, then crossed to her. He glanced down at the blouse she continued to hold in white-knuckled fingers. "Nice color."

"Oh. Yes. Your mother picked it out." Feeling foolish, Darcy relaxed her fingers and turned away to hang the blouse in the closet. "I was so rude, leaving that way. I'll apologize to everyone."

"There's no need for that."

"Of course there is." She spent several seconds adjusting the shoulders of the blouse on the padded hanger as if their evenness was of monumental importance. "It's just that everything seemed to hit me all at once." She went back to unfold slacks, then repeated the procedure, lining up the edges of the hem perfectly.

"That's understandable, Darcy. It's a lot of money. It'll change your life."

"The money?" Distracted, she glanced back, then fluttered her hands. "Well, yes, I suppose the money's part of it."

He angled his head. "What else?"

She started to pick up a box, then set it back on the bed and wandered to the window. It still felt odd to stand there against the glass, with a world she'd only begun to touch spread like a banquet at her feet.

"Your family's so…beautiful. You have no idea what you have. You couldn't. They've always been yours, you see, so how could you know."

She watched the signs of the casino across the street, beckoning, daring, inviting. *Win, Win, Win.*

It wasn't so terribly hard to win, she thought. But it was much, much trickier to keep the prize.

"I'm a watcher," she told him. "I'm good at it. That's why I want to write. I want to write about things I see, or want to see. Things I'd like to feel or experience." She lifted her hands to rub her arms, then made herself turn back to him. "I watched your family."

She looked so lovely, he thought. And so lost. "And what did you see?"

"Your father playing with your mother's hair when they sat together in the lounge last night." She saw the confusion in his eyes and smiled. "You're used to seeing them touch each other—casually, affectionately, so you don't notice when it happens. Why would you?" she murmured, swamped with envy. "He put his arm around her, and she leaned into him, sort of…" Eyes half-closed, she moved her body as if yearning for another. "Settled into the curve because she knew exactly how she'd fit there."

Darcy closed her eyes, laid a hand over her own heart as she brought the scene back into focus. "And while he talked to me, he toyed with the ends of her hair. Tangled them, combed them through, wound the strands around his finger. It was lovely. She knew he was doing it, because there was a little light in her eyes. I wonder if it takes another woman to recognize that."

She opened her eyes again and smiled. "I never saw my parents touch that way. I think they loved each other, but they never touched that way, that easy and wonderful way. Some people don't. Or they can't."

She sighed and shook her head. "I'm not making sense."

He could see it himself, now that she'd painted it for him. And she was right, he realized. It was so much a part of his life, a part of his family, he didn't notice it.

"Yes, you are."

"It's more—it's all of it. Everyone piling in here a little while ago. You were part of it again, so you couldn't have really seen it. The way your grandfather hugged your mother. So strong and tight. For that instant she was the center of his world, and he of hers. And more, when she sat on the arm of his chair. He laid his hand on her knee.

Just put it there, to touch. It was so lovely," she said quietly. "The way she and your uncle argued about where to have dinner, and laughed at each other. All the little looks and pats and the shorthand of people who know each other, and like each other."

"They do like each other." He could see that her eyes were overbright again, and reached out to touch her hair. "What is it, Darcy?"

"They were so kind to me. I'm taking money from them, a lot of money, but everyone's drinking champagne and laughing and congratulating me. Your mother put her arm around my shoulders." It made her voice break, forced her to fight to steady it. "It sounds ridiculous, I know it, but if I hadn't gone up right then, I would have grabbed on to her. Just grabbed on and held. She would have thought I was crazy."

Lonely? Had he thought she was lonely? He understood now the word didn't come close. "She would have thought you wanted a hug." He slipped his arms around her, felt her tremble lightly. "Go ahead, grab on to me. It's all right."

He eased her closer, pressed his cheek to her hair. He could feel her hesitation, the battle of emotions that had her standing very still. Then her arms came around him, wrapped tight. Her breath came out on a long, broken sigh.

"We're big on grabbing in my family," he told her. "You won't shock any of us if you take hold."

It felt so good to press up against the strong wall of his chest, to hear the steady beat of his heart, to smell the warmth of his skin. Closing her eyes, she let herself absorb the comfort of his hand stroking gently over her back.

"It's just so foreign to me. All of this. All of them. You. Especially you."

Her voice was husky and low. Her hair was soft under

his cheek and fragrant as a meadow. Affection, he reminded himself as her slender little body molded to his, not lust. Friendship, not passion.

Then she turned her head as if to sniff his neck and needs stirred restlessly.

"Better now?" He started to ease away, but she clung. His lips brushed her temple, lingered. He held her, let her hold him and told himself it was only because she needed it.

"Mmm."

The dress had thin straps crossing over the smooth flesh of her back. His fingers began to trace along them, under them. She moved in a long, catlike stretch under the caress, jangling his brain.

It was the only excuse he had for the fact that his lips trailed down her face, found hers and plundered.

He forgot to be gentle. She was pressed against him in the stream of sunlight, all gold and soft and willing. The kiss demanded surrender, and she gave it, flowing into his arms like heated wine, her mouth yielding under the assault of his as if it had only been waiting. Had always been waiting.

Her mind was spinning in slow, expanding circles that spiraled up toward something desperately wanted. The strength of him, the power of those arms that wrapped possessively around her was desperately exciting. Knowing she was helpless against him made her quiver, yet she gloried in the power of him.

This was need, she thought wildly. This, finally this. A wild burst of light and energy and raw nerves. The thumping heart, the racing pulse, the explosion of heat.

Thrilled, she gave herself to it, to him.

In one strong stroke, his hands slid down her back, over the curve of her bottom, lifting her, pressing heat desperately to heat. His mouth swallowed her gasps, greedily, ravenously. He could imagine himself filling her, buried in her, taking her where they stood and driving into her until the hot ball of frustration broke free and gave him peace.

He caught himself as his hands gripped those delicate straps over her back, at the point of rending. He looked down into her eyes, wide, unseeing and still swollen from tears.

He set her aside so abruptly she staggered, scalded her with a look when she crossed her hands over her heart as if to hold it in place.

"You're too damn trusting." The words whipped out at her, but the lash was for himself. "It's a miracle you survived a day on your own."

God, my God, was all she could think. Was the blood supposed to burn like this? It was a wonder her skin didn't burst into flame. She lifted her fingers to her mouth where her lips continued to tingle and ache. "I know you won't hurt me."

He'd come close, dangerously close, to ripping off her clothes, shoving her against the wall and taking her without thought or care. Now, he thought, she was standing there, staring at him out of eyes filled with arousal and—worse, much worse—trust.

"The hell I won't." He said it roughly, hoping to save them both. "You don't know me, and you don't know the game, so I'll tell you, don't bet against the house. The house always wins in the end. Always."

She couldn't catch her breath. "I won."

His eyes flashed. "Stick around," he challenged. "I'll get it back. And more. More than you'll want to lose. So be smart."

His hand whipped out, cupped the back of her neck

firmly. He wanted her to cringe. If she did he'd be able to resist all the things he wanted to do. "Run away. Take the money and run far and fast. Buy yourself a house with a picket fence and a hatchback in the driveway and shade trees in the yard. Because my world isn't yours."

She almost shuddered at his words. But if she did, she'd prove everything he said was true. "I like it here."

His lips curved into something between a smile and a sneer. "Honey, you don't even know where you are."

"I'm with you." And that, she realized with a fresh and towering thrill, was all she really wanted.

"You think you want to play with me?" He angled his hand at the back of her neck to bring her to her toes. "Little Darcy from Kansas? First raise and you'll fold your cards and scramble."

"You don't scare me."

"Don't I?" He damn well should, he thought. And he damn well would, for her own good. "You haven't even got the guts to risk having some jerk back home find out where you are. You'd rather sneak out of your own town like a thief instead of taking a stand. Now you think you can play with the high rollers?" With another short laugh, he released her and turned to leave. "Not bloody likely."

His words were a sharp slap of shame to an exposed cheek. She winced from the blow but steadied herself. "You're right."

He stopped at the top of the stairs and turned back. She was still standing by the window with her arms wrapped tight around her body, her eyes lit with a passion that contrasted sharply with the defensive stance.

He wanted, quite desperately, to go back, gather her close again and just hold her. Not simply because she needed it, he realized with something akin to panic. Because he did. Outrageously.

Her breath came out in one explosive puff. "You're absolutely right. How do we do it?"

The images that careered through his mind had him taking careful hold of the banister. "Excuse me?"

"How do we inform the press? Do you just give out my name, or do we have to do something like a release or a press conference?"

The combination of shame and irritation he felt was lethal. He took a moment, rubbing a hand over his face as he searched for control. "Darcy, there's no point in rushing into that."

"Why wait?" She stiffened her spine. "You said that it was going to leak shortly anyway. I'd prefer to have some control. And I can hardly expect you to have any respect for me if I continue to hide this way."

"This isn't about me. It's long past time you started thinking not just *for* yourself, but thinking *of* yourself."

"I am. And it is about me." Odd, she thought, how saying that, realizing that, felt so calming. "It's about taking a stand, not being pushed around, pressured or maneuvered. I might not be a high roller, Mac, but I'm ready to play my hand."

She turned, moving quickly before she could change her mind, and picked up the bedside phone. "Do you call the press, or do I?"

He studied her another moment, waiting for her to fold. But her eyes stayed level, her jaw remained set. Saying nothing, he walked to her, took the phone out of her hand, then punched in an extension.

"This is Blade. I need you to set up a press conference. We'll use the Nevada Suite. One hour."

* * *

"I pushed her into this." Behind the service entrance of the Nevada Suite, Mac shoved his hands into his pockets and watched as Caine briefed Darcy on the press conference.

"You gave her breathing room," Serena corrected. "If you hadn't run interference, she'd have been dropped straight into the media days ago. Without time to settle and prepare." She gave her son a quick, supportive pat on the arm. "And without one of the top lawyers in the country beside her."

"She's not ready for this."

"I think you underestimate her."

"You didn't see her an hour ago."

"No." And though she wondered what had passed between Darcy and her son, she resisted prying. "But I'm seeing her now. And I say she's ready."

Serena linked an arm through her son's and studied the woman listening attentively to Caine. Darcy had topped the yellow sundress with a short white jacket. It was a smart look, Serena decided. Simple and sunny.

The girl was a little pale, she mused, but she was holding her own.

"She's going to surprise herself," Serena murmured. *And you,* she added silently. "Caine's going to be right there with her—and all of us are here, backing her up."

Justin slipped through the heavy door, nodded to his son, laid a hand lightly on his wife's shoulder. "We're set. The audience is a bit restless. Do you want me to make the announcement?"

"I'll do it." He watched the way his mother's hand lifted to lie over his father's, the way their bodies brushed. The unit they made. It was something so natural to both of them, he realized he wouldn't have noticed, or would have taken it for granted. Until Darcy.

"I haven't appreciated you enough." He covered their joined hands with his. "Not nearly enough."

Justin frowned thoughtfully as Mac walked to Darcy. "Now, what was that about?"

"I'm not sure." Serena smiled, a bit mistily. "But I like it. Let's go keep The MacGregor distracted so Darcy can get through this smoothly."

Darcy was terrified. Everything Caine had told her was already jumbled into mush in her head. Pride kept her rooted to the spot even when her imagination conjured a picture of herself running like a rabbit.

Her heart drummed hard staccato beats in her head as Mac came toward her.

"Ready?"

Time to stop running, she told herself. "Yes."

"I'm going to go in, give them a brief rundown, then you'll come in and field some questions. That's all there is to it."

He might as well have told her she was to perform a tap dance while juggling swords. But she nodded. "Your uncle's explained how it works."

"The girl's not a moron," Daniel barked. "She knows how to speak for herself. Don't you, lass?"

The bright blue eyes demanded confidence. "We're about to find out." She squared her shoulders and walked to the side door to peek out. "So many." Her stomach did a painful lurch as she scanned the dozens of faces in the ballroom. "Well." She stepped back. "One or a hundred it's the same thing."

"Don't answer anything you're not comfortable with," Mac said briefly, then stepped out.

The noise level rose with rustling movements and speculative murmurs as he climbed the short stairs to a long platform.

Confidence, Darcy reflected, watching the way he moved, the easy way he stood behind the dais and spoke into the microphone. His voice was clear, his smile easy. When laughter broke out among the gathered reporters, she blinked.

She hadn't heard the words, just the tone. She understood he was setting a casual and friendly one.

It was so easy for him, she thought. Facing strangers, thinking on his feet, being in control. The sea of faces didn't have his nerves jangling, the shouted questions didn't shake his poise in the least.

"Okay?" Caine put a hand to the small of her back.

She drew in a breath, held it, let it out. "Okay."

Attention shifted in a wave when she stepped out. Cameras whirled as photographers jockeyed for a better angle. Television crews zoomed in. A barrage of questions was hurled at her the minute she stepped up to the mike. She jolted a little when Mac reached down to adjust it for her.

"I—" Her voice boomed back at her, making her want to giggle nervously. "I'm Darcy Wallace. I, ah…" She cleared her throat and struggled to dredge something coherent out of the jumble of thoughts in her mind. "I hit the jackpot."

There was laughter, some appreciative applause. And the questions shot out too fast to separate one from the other.

"Where are you from?"

"How do you feel?"

"What are you doing in Vegas?"

"What happened when…"

Why? How? Where?

"I'm sorry." Her voice frayed around the edges, but when

Mac moved closer, she shook her head fiercely. She would do this, she promised herself. And she would do it without making a fool of herself. "I'm sorry," she repeated. "I've never talked to reporters before, so I don't really know how. Maybe it would be better if I just told you what happened."

It was easier that way, like telling a story. As she spoke, her voice steadied, and the fingers that had gripped the edges of the dais like a lifeline relaxed.

"What was the first thing you did when you realized you'd won?"

"After I fainted?" There was such quick laughter at her answer that her lips curved up in a smile. "Mr. Blade gave me a room—a suite. They have beautiful rooms here, like something out of a book. There's a fireplace, and a piano and gorgeous flowers. I don't think it all even started to sink in until the next day. Then the first thing I did was buy a new dress."

"Lass has a way with her," Daniel announced.

"She's caught them." Serena beamed approval. "She has no idea how charming she is."

"Our boy's taken with her." Daniel wiggled his eyebrows when his daughter sent him an arched look. "See how he hovers over her, like he's ready to scoop her up and cart her off if anyone gets too close. He's smitten."

She wasn't quite ready to give him the satisfaction of agreeing. "They've only known each other a few days."

Daniel merely snorted, then leaned in close to whisper in her ear. "And how long did it take you to catch this one's eye?" He jerked a shoulder toward Justin.

"Slightly less time than it took me to realize you'd maneuvered us together in the first place."

"Married thirty years now, aren't you?" Unrepentant, Daniel grinned. "No, don't thank me," he continued, patting her cheek. "A man's got to look after his family, after all. They'll make pretty babies together, don't you think, Rena?"

She only sighed. "At least try to be subtle about it."

"Subtle's my middle name," Daniel said with a wink.

"Good job." Caine gave Darcy a congratulatory embrace the minute the door closed behind them.

"It wasn't as hard as I thought it would be." Relief flooded through her. "And now it's over."

"It's just beginning," Caine corrected, sorry to put that doe-on-alert look back in her eyes. "Mac will keep them busy for now," he said, nodding as his nephew went out to bat cleanup for the press.

"But I told them everything."

"They're always going to want more. And you can expect dozens of calls requesting personal interviews, photos. Offers for your life story."

"My life story." That, at least, made her laugh. "I barely had a life before a few days ago."

"The contrast is only going to add fuel. The tabloids are going to play with this, so be prepared for speculation that you were directed to Vegas by psychic aliens."

When she laughed, he guided her at a quick pace toward the service elevator. He didn't want to frighten her, or dull that bloom of success, but knew she needed to be prepared.

"The calls to offer you tremendous investment opportunities are going to start, too. Financial advisors, legitimate and not, are going to camp on your doorstep. The stepsister of the cousin of the kid who sat behind you in first grade is going to try to hit you up for a loan."

"That would be Patty Anderson," Darcy improvised with a weak smile. "I never liked her anyway."

"Good girl. Do yourself a favor. Don't answer the phone for a couple of days. Better yet, we can arrange for Mac to have the desk take your calls until things cool off a bit."

"That's like running again, isn't it?"

"No. It's protecting yourself, and it's staying in control. If you want to do interviews, you can set them up. When you've figured out what it is you want to do, you contact a financial advisor. Whatever you do, you do at your pace."

"I'm in charge," Darcy said when they stopped at the door of her suite.

"Exactly. If you have any questions or concerns, you can call me. I'll be around through tomorrow. After that, you can reach me in Boston."

"I don't know how to begin to thank you."

"Enjoy yourself." He gave the hand she offered a squeeze. "And don't forget how much fun it was to buy a new dress."

"Keep it simple," she murmured, understanding.

"Atta girl." He bent to kiss her cheek. "I'll see you later."

Alone, Darcy stepped into the suite. Keeping it simple wasn't as easy as it sounded. She was a rich woman with her fifteen minutes of fame in its initial seconds. The message light on her phone was blinking, and the phone itself began to ring. Taking Caine's advice, she ignored it, waiting until it stopped, then taking the receiver off the hook.

Problem solved, she thought, for now.

But she had much deeper, much more complex problems that sudden wealth had nothing to do with.

She was in love and knew there was no point in questioning it, debating it or denying it. Her heart was the one thing she'd always been sure of.

Often she'd imagined what it would be like to lose it, the thrill and the anxiety of the fall. She'd always wondered who it would be who would make everything inside her yearn. How they would be together—for in her dreams he'd loved her as well.

But this wasn't a dream or imagination. Loving Mac was simply and brutally real, with the physical needs so much sharper and more vital than she'd believed herself capable of.

She wanted him, to touch him, to taste, to fulfill the promise of that frantic kiss. She wanted to tremble with the knowledge she was desirable, and oh, she wanted to know what it was to lose herself in sensations.

Just as much, she wanted to curl up against him and know she was welcome there. Even expected there. She wanted to exchange those quiet looks that people who were truly intimate could use as effectively as words.

To be loved in return.

That wasn't a simple matter.

But something about her stirred him, and that in itself was a miracle. If he could want her, perhaps there was a chance for more. It wasn't any more impossible, she supposed, than winning more than a million dollars on the single pull of a lever.

Comforted by that, she snuggled into the corner of the sofa, rested her head on the big, soft pillow tucked there and let herself imagine.

She dreamed of showgirls, dozens of them with endless legs and bountiful breasts showcased in brief, glittering costumes and colorful, floating feathers.

She stood among them, miles too short, wearing layers too plain to be noticed. A wren among exotic birds.

Their long legs flashed, their lush bodies turned and twirled while she stumbled through the complex routine.

She couldn't keep up, couldn't compete. No matter how hard she tried, she was always a step behind.

Mac stood watching, a small, amused smile on his face. Beautiful women with long, curvy bodies spun gracefully, seductively around him. Take your pick, they seemed to say.

His gaze flicked down to her face when she stopped in front of him. *Where did you come from? You don't belong here.*

But I want to stay.

He only patted her cheek, then gently nudged her along. *This isn't the place for you, Darcy from Kansas. You don't even know where you are.*

I do know. I do. And it could be the place for me. I want it to be.

And there was Gerald, taking her hand, tugging her away. He had that impatient frown on his face, that irritated scowl in his eyes.

It's time to stop this foolishness. If you insist on pretending to be what you're not, you're only going to embarrass yourself. I'm tired of waiting for you to come to your senses. We're going home.

"I'm not going back." She murmured it as she broke through the surface of the dream. "I'm not going back," she said more definitely, opening her eyes to find the room had become dark while she'd slept.

She lay there another moment, ordering both the dream and the depression that accompanied it to fade.

"I'm staying here." She wrapped her arms around the pillow. "No matter what."

Chapter 7

Darcy had been at The Comanche nearly a week and was amazed at how much of the hotel she'd yet to explore.

She'd managed to catch the stunning display of horsemanship presented in the auditorium twice a day, where beautiful fast horses and daring riders in authentic Comanche costumes teamed up for a spectacular performance.

She'd wandered around the lavish outdoor pool with its sparkling water contained in bright tile cannily shaped in a wide *C,* and dipped her fingers into the smaller lagoon, secluded by palms and fed by a musical waterfall.

She'd indulged herself in the spa and treatment center, had roamed nearly half the wide array of shops, but had yet to slip inside any of the three theaters or walk through the many ballrooms and conference rooms, or find an excuse to visit the business center.

The longer she was a guest of The Comanche, she thought, the more it seemed to grow.

When the elevator let her out on the roof, she stepped into a lush oasis of palms and tangling flowered vines. The morning sun showered onto the rich blue waters of the pool, shooting diamonds of light onto the surface.

Chaises and chairs in the hotel's colors of sapphire and emerald were arranged to offer ease to sun worshipers or those who preferred the shade.

Seated at one of the glass tables under the jewel tone stripes of a slanted umbrella was Daniel MacGregor.

He got to his feet when he saw her, and Darcy was again struck by the raw power of the man who had lived nearly a century, had built empires, raised a president, stood at the head of a fascinating family.

"Thanks so much for agreeing to see me like this, Mr. MacGregor."

He winked and gallantly pulled out a chair for her. "A pretty woman calls and asks to see me alone, I'd be a fool to say no." He took his seat across from her. Instantly a waiter appeared with a pot of coffee. "Do you want breakfast, lass?"

"No." She smiled weakly. "I'm too nervous to eat."

"Food's just what you need then. Bring the girl some bacon and eggs—you need some meat on you," he said to Darcy. "Scramble the eggs, and don't be stingy with the hash browns. And bring me the same."

"Right away, Mr. MacGregor."

And that, Darcy mused as the waiter scurried away, was likely the typical response of those who came into Daniel MacGregor's orbit. Right away, Mr. MacGregor, and off they rushed to follow orders.

"Now." He picked up his cup. "You'll eat and see if you don't feel steadier. A lot's happened to you in a short time. Anybody'd be a bit rocky. My grandson's taking good care of you?"

"Yes. He's been wonderful. All of you have been wonderful."

"But the ground seems a bit boggy under your feet."

"Yes." Her breath came out in a whoosh of relief that he understood. "It's all so…foreign. Exciting," she added, scanning the lush rooftop garden. "I feel as if I've dropped down into the middle of a book, and I'm vague on the first chapters and don't have any idea how it's going to end."

"Nothing wrong with enjoying the page you're on."

"No, and I have been." Self-consciously she lifted a hand to finger the silver-and-gold twists that dangled from her ear. "But I have to think about what's going to happen when I turn that page. I can't keep buying new clothes and earrings, and living in the moment. Money's a responsibility, isn't it?"

He leaned back, lips pursed as he studied her. Delicate she might look, he mused, but there was nothing delicate about her brain. He had a feeling it was both strong and flexible. All the better, he decided. The wife of his grandson should possess a nimble mind and not a shallow one.

"That it is," he said, and smiled at her.

The smile confused her. It was so…canny. And there were secrets dancing in those bright blue eyes. A little flustered, she picked up her coffee, forgetting to add her customary cream. "There were dozens of calls on my voice mail when I checked it this morning."

"That's to be expected."

"Yes, I know. Mac told me it would happen, but I didn't imagine there would be so many. Reporters…" She laughed a little. "People from magazines I've read, television shows I've watched suddenly want to talk to me. I haven't done anything. I haven't saved a life or found the cure for the common cold or given birth to quintuplets."

His brows shot up. "Do multiple births run in your family?"

"No."

"Pity," he murmured. He'd have enjoyed twin babies. Still, he brushed that aside as Darcy stared at him in confusion. "You've lived a common fantasy. Instant wealth. And you're young, pretty, you come from a small town in the Midwest and you were down to your last dollar. It's a good story. People who read it or hear it can root for you, and imagine it could happen to them."

"Yes, I suppose that's true. It's only fair I talk to some of them." She paused as the waiter returned with two heaping plates. Daunted, Darcy stared down at hers while Daniel dug into his with gusto.

"Eat up, girl. You need some fuel."

She picked up her fork. "I didn't know they served meals up here."

Daniel grinned. "They don't. Just drinks and such as a rule. But it's a fine thing to break the rules now and then. You wanted to be private," he reminded her. "And not many come up here so early in the day. The restaurants inside will likely be packed with people wanting the special buffet and the like."

"There are six restaurants," she told him. "I read about them in the hotel guide. Six. And four swimming pools."

"People have to eat, and some like to be seen around the pool when they're not gambling."

"I can't get over how…huge this place is. Theaters and lounges, the open-air auditorium. It's a maze."

"And all roads lead back to the casino. It's not a casual design," he added with a wink. "Whatever else there is to do in a hotel of this nature, gambling's the hub."

"It's beautiful and exciting. Then you come up here, and

you can look beyond it all and see the desert. I love looking at the desert."

"One of the reasons there aren't any windows in the casino. Wouldn't want any distraction." He shot her a warrior's grin. "You should eat a good breakfast, then when it's settled, take yourself a nice swim. I swim most every day. Keeps me young."

It was more than that, Darcy thought. It was the energy, the avid interest in life, the delight in the challenge of it that kept him vital. She was counting on that interest and that delight. "Um... Mr. MacGregor, Caine—gave me a list of names. Financial advisors, brokers, that sort of thing."

Daniel grunted and, since no one was around to stop him, dashed salt on his potatoes. "You need to protect your capital."

"I understand that, particularly since a large percentage of the calls on my voice mail were from people wanting to discuss my finances. One offered to fly me into Los Angeles, put me up at the Beverly Wilshire so that I could take a meeting."

Frowning, she buttered a piece of toast. "Most of them sounded very interested in discussing portfolios and investments, but none of them were on the list your son gave me."

"That doesn't surprise me."

"I wrote them down. I have both lists. I wondered if you would mind looking at them? I know your son prefers giving me a range of choices, but I think I'd do better if I was pointed in a specific direction."

"Let's have a look." Daniel pulled his glasses out of his pocket, perched them on his nose as Darcy took her lists from her purse. "Ha! Vultures, fly-by-nights. Grifters." With barely a glance he slapped the first list facedown. "You'll want to stay away from these, lass."

She nodded. "That's what I thought. That's the list of the ones who called. This is the one your son gave me."

He tapped his fingers on the table as he read the second list. "The boy learned, didn't he?" Pleased with the names Caine had offered, Daniel scratched his chin through his beard. "Any one of these would do well for you. The best thing is for you to interview the top man at each firm, get a feel for it. Let them woo you, then trust your gut."

She was already trusting her gut but wasn't quite ready to tell him what she wanted. "I've never had any money, never had more to worry about—and over—than what I could juggle in my checking account month to month. Last night, I tried to imagine what a million dollars would look like. I couldn't. And now, even after taxes, I have a bit more than what I can't even imagine."

Daniel poured himself a second cup of coffee. Anna would hate it, he thought with delight, if she knew he was slurping up that much caffeine. "Tell me what you want from your money."

From it, she thought. Not what she wanted to do with it, but what she wanted from it. "Time," she said immediately. "Time enough so that I can do what I've always wanted to do. I've always wanted to write, and always had to steal the time to do it. I want that first, the time to finish my new book, then time to start the next," she said with a smile. "Because I want to be a writer, and the only way to be one is to write."

"Are you any good at it?"

"Yes, I am. It's the only thing I've ever really been good at, really felt confident about. I just need another few weeks to finish the one I'm working on."

"The money'll buy you more than a few weeks."

"I know. I intend to have fun with it, too." Her eyes

glinted as she leaned forward. "I'm starting to realize that fun wasn't a big part of my life. I'm going to correct that. Whoever said money couldn't buy happiness must have been happy to begin with. Because if it can't, at least it can buy the opportunity to explore being happy." She laughed and settled back. "I'm going to explore being happy, Mr. MacGregor."

"That's a sensible thing."

"Yes, I think it is. Being happy isn't something I'm going to take for granted," she said quietly, "or something I intend to waste."

He laid his big hand over hers. "Have you been so unhappy?"

"I suppose in some ways I have been." She moved her shoulders restlessly. "But I have a chance now to make choices, for myself. It makes all the difference in the world. So I want to make good choices."

"I think you will." He gave her hand a squeeze and a pat. "You've already started to."

"I want to use the money well. And I want to give some back."

"To my grandson?"

"Oh." She laughed again and propped her elbows on the table. "In the casino. Yes, indeed. That's part of the fun, isn't it? But I meant to give some of that money, that time and that opportunity to explore happiness back. I want to make a donation, to literacy, I think. It fits, doesn't it?"

"Aye." He reached out to pat her cheek. "It fits, and you wear it well."

"I don't know how it's done, though. I thought you would."

"I'd be happy to help you with it." When the waiter came to remove their plates, Daniel waved a hand. "Leave hers," he ordered. "She hasn't eaten enough. Now," he continued as Darcy and the waiter exchanged resigned glances, "you'll have your time, your opportunity, and you'll have given something back. Unless you intend to toss around money like confetti, and you don't strike me as an idiot, you'll have quite a bit left over. What do you want from that?"

She bit her lip, easing forward. "More," she said, then blinked when he threw back his head and roared with laughter.

"Now there's a lass with a head on her shoulders. I knew it."

"It sounds greedy, but—"

"It sounds sane," he corrected. "Why should you want less? More is better, after all. You want your money to work for you. I'd call you a fool if you wanted otherwise."

"Mr. MacGregor." She took a deep breath and rolled the dice. "I want you to take my money and make it work for me."

The blue eyes narrowed. "Do you now? And why is that?"

"Because it seems to me I'd be a fool to settle for less than the best."

His eyes remained narrowed, fixed on her face so intensely she felt heat rising to her cheeks. Certain she'd gone too far, she started to babble an apology.

Then the mouth surrounded by that white beard began to curve. "Neither of us are fools, are we, lass?"

"No, sir."

"Well then." Grinning, his eyes sparkling with challenge, he twisted the gold knob on his cane. When it hinged back, he slipped out a thick cigar. With the lighter he took out of his pocket, he touched tip of flame reverently to tip of cigar, his bright eyes closing in pleasure as he took the first puffs.

"I know it's a lot to ask, Mr. MacGregor, but—"

"Daniel," he said, and grinned fiercely. "We're partners,

aren't we? Eat," he ordered when Darcy only stared at him. "I've a couple ideas for how to get you that 'more' you'd like. Are you a gambler, little girl?"

With her head light and her heart soaring, Darcy bit into a piece of bacon. "It looks like I am."

Mac had a lot on his mind. The media was executing a full-court press, scrambling for access to Darcy. Reporters were wild for interviews and personal data. The morning editions, both local and national, had played variations on the theme.

Little Darcy From Kansas Hits Yellow Brick Road
From Kansas To Oz On Three-Dollar Bet
Over The Rainbow With A Million For Kansas Librarian

Normally he would have been amused, and certainly pleased at the positive publicity the story generated for Comanche Vegas. Reservations in the hotel were soaring, and he had no doubt that the casino would be three deep at the slots and tables as long as the story was hot.

He could handle the demands on his time, the incessant requests for interviews and photos. He could add staff to each shift, and intended to work the floor himself during peak periods. In fact, his parents had already agreed to extend their stay a few days and pitch in. And he preferred, just now, to have his plate overfull.

God knows he needed the distraction to keep his mind off his libido. It was suddenly and insistently on edge due to one small, big-eyed woman with a shy smile.

He wasn't inclined toward a serious relationship and certainly didn't intend to become involved with an innocent, naive woman who didn't know the difference between a straight and a flush.

He considered himself a disciplined man who knew

how to control his baser instincts and resist temptations. He didn't play at love like his brother, Duncan. Nor did he consider it a pesky fly to be swatted aside like his sister Amelia. And he certainly had no intention of settling down and raising a family at this stage of his life as his sister Gwen was doing.

For Mac love was something to be dealt with eventually, when there was time, when the odds were favorable and when there was a good chance of raking in all the chips.

He wanted what his parents had. Perhaps he hadn't realized that quite so clearly until Darcy had pointed out just what they did have together. But he could admit he had always used them as his yardstick where relationships were concerned.

It was undoubtedly the reason he'd avoided any long-term or serious ones up to this point.

He enjoyed women, but involvement beyond a certain level led to complications, and complications invariably led to hurt on one side or the other. He'd been very careful not to hurt any of the women who had brushed in and out of his life.

He had no intention of breaking that particular rule now.

As far as Darcy Wallace was concerned, he'd decided it was a bad bet all around. She was too inexperienced, too vulnerable.

He was setting her firmly off-limits. Friendship, he ordered himself. A steadying hand until she had her feet firmly under her, and nothing more.

Then he stepped onto the rooftop garden and saw her. She was sitting at one of the tables, her big, elfin eyes wide and intent on his grandfather's face. Their heads were close together, like conspirators, he thought, and wondered what the hell was going on between them.

She looked so…fragile, he decided, so slimly built with those pretty, ringless hands clasped together like a schoolgirl's. She'd worked a foot out of one strappy sandal, and was waving the shoe by a single strap hooked around toes painted a soft shell pink.

The image that flashed through his mind of nibbling on those pretty toes and working his way up those slender legs had him muttering a curse.

Lust, something he normally accepted and enjoyed, was currently driving him mad.

Irritation still simmered in his eyes as he stepped through the palms and up to the table. Daniel leaned back, beamed and wiggled his eyebrows. "Well, there's a likely lad. Want some coffee, boy?"

"I could do with a cup." Because he knew Daniel well, Mac didn't trust him a whit. He scraped back a chair, straddled it and met his grandfather's cheerful gaze. "What's going on here?"

"Why, I'm having breakfast with this pretty young thing, which you'd be doing yourself if you weren't slow-witted."

"I've got a casino to run," Mac said shortly, and turned his sharp eyes to Darcy. "Did you get some rest?"

"Yes, plenty, thank you." She jolted when Daniel thumped his fist on the table.

"God Almighty, boy, is that any way to greet a woman in the morning? Why aren't you telling her how pretty she looks, or asking her if she'll take a drive with you this evening?"

"I'm working this evening," Mac said mildly.

"The day a MacGregor can't find time for a sweet-eyed woman is a sorry day. A sorry day, indeed. You'd like a drive, wouldn't you, lass, up into the hills in the moonlight?"

"I—yes, but—"

"There." Daniel thumped his fist again. "Are you going to do something about this, boy, or do I have to hang my head in shame?"

Considering, Mac picked up the cigar smoldering in the ashtray. He studied it thoughtfully, turned it in his hand. "And what's this?" Lifting his brow, Mac smiled thinly at his grandfather. "This wouldn't be yours, would it, Grandpa?"

Daniel's gaze slid away. He studied his own fingernails intently. "I don't know what you're talking about. Now—"

"Grandma would be very displeased if she thought you were sneaking cigars behind her back again." Idly Mac tapped the ash. "Very displeased."

"It's mine," Darcy blurted out, and both men turned to stare at her.

"Yours?" Mac said in a voice that dripped like honey.

"Yes." She jerked her shoulder in what she hoped was an arrogant shrug. "So what?"

"So…" Mac's teeth flashed in a grin. "Enjoy," he suggested, and handed her the cigar.

The challenge in his eyes left her little choice. Defiantly she took a puff. Her head spun, her throat closed, but she managed to muffle most of the cough. "It's very smooth." She wheezed as she choked on smoke.

Her eyes teared as she gamefully puffed again. Mac had to resist an urge to tug her into his lap and nuzzle her. "I can see that. Want a brandy to go with it?"

"Not before lunch." She coughed again, felt her stomach pitch. "Your grandfather—" She coughed, blinked away tears. "Your grandfather and I were discussing business."

"Don't let me stop you. Done with this?" He picked up a slice of her bacon. He bit in neatly then grinned. She was turning a very interesting shade of green. "Put that down, darling, before you pass out."

"I'm perfectly fine."

"You're a rare one, Darcy." Adoring her, Daniel rose. He tipped up her chin, kissed her full on the mouth. "I'll get started on that business we were speaking of." He sent his grandson a glowering look. "Don't shame me, Robbie."

"Who's Robbie?" Darcy asked dizzily when Daniel strode off.

"I am, to him, occasionally."

"Oh." She smiled. "That's sweet."

"You're going to make yourself sick," Mac muttered, and took the cigar from her fingers. "I didn't think you'd do it."

She let her reeling head fall back. "I don't know what you're talking about."

With a sigh, Mac picked up her water glass and held it to her lips. "Did you really think I'd rat on him? Come on, sip a little. The smoke's made you punchy."

"It's not so bad. I kind of like it." She turned her head to smile at him. "You wouldn't have told? About the cigar?"

"It wouldn't have mattered. My grandmother knows he sneaks them every chance he gets."

"I wish he were my grandfather. I think he's the most wonderful man in the world."

"He likes you, too. Steady now?"

"I'm fine." She studied what was left of the cigar as it smoked in the ashtray. "I may just take it up." But she drank the water again to cool her throat. "He shouldn't have teased you that way, about taking me for a drive."

With a few deliberate taps, Mac put out the cigar. "He's decided you suit me."

"Oh." The idea wound through her mind, then warmed her heart. "Really?"

"The MacGregor's fondest wish is to see all of his grand-children married and producing babies. And the more he has to do with it, the better. He actually arranged for my sister, and two of my cousins, to meet men he'd specifically picked out for them."

"What happened?"

"In those cases, it worked, which only makes him more difficult to control. He's on a streak. And just now…" He angled his head, skimmed his gaze over her face. "He's decided you'll do for me."

"I see." She supposed the quick thrill and sense of glee was inappropriate. But it was very hard to control the curve of her lips. "I'm flattered."

"So you should be. I am, after all, the oldest grand-child—and he's a fussy man when it comes to family."

"But it irritates you."

"Mildly," he admitted. "As much as I love him, I've no intention of going along with his grand schemes. I apologize if he got you out here this morning to put ideas in your head, but I'm not looking for marriage."

Her eyes went wide and dark. "Excuse me?"

"I suspected, when I was told the two of you were to-gether up here, that he'd been planting seeds."

The warmth that had settled inside her iced over and went rock hard. "And, of course, someone like me would be fertile ground for such seeds."

Her tone was so quiet, so pleasant, he missed the flash. "He can't help it. And your name being Wallace put a cap on it. Strong Scot blood," he said with a grin and a burr. "He'd consider you tailor-made to bear my children."

"And since you're not in the market for a wife or chil-dren, you thought it only fair to nip in the bud any ideas he might have planted in my vulnerable mind in that area."

He caught the underlying frost in the tone now. "More or less," he agreed, cautiously. "Darcy—"

"You arrogant, self-important, *insulting* son of a bitch." She sprang to her feet so abruptly the table jerked. The water glass toppled over and crashed on the tiles as she stood vibrating with temper, her fists clenched and eyes blazing. "I'm not the empty-headed, dim-witted, *needy* fool you seem to think I am."

"That's not what I meant." More than a little wary, he got to his feet. "That's not at all what I meant."

"Don't stand there and tell me what you didn't mean. I know perfectly well when I'm being considered a corn-for-brains moron. You're not the first who's made that mistake, but I swear to God, you're going to be the last. I'm perfectly aware that you don't want me."

"I never said—"

"Do you think I don't know I'm not your type?" Furious, she shoved the chair into the table, and sent another glass crashing. "You prefer big-busted showgirls with eight feet of leg and yards of hair."

"What? Where the hell did that come from?"

Straight out of her dream the night before, but she'd be damned if she'd tell him. "I don't have any delusions about you. Just because I would have slept with you doesn't mean I expected you to sweep me off to the altar. If all I wanted was marriage, I could have stayed exactly where I was."

She still looked like a fairy, he noted, one who could—and would—spitefully turn an incautious man into a braying jackass. "Before you break any more glassware, let me apologize." He put a restraining hand on the back of the chair before she could jam it into the table again. "I didn't want my grandfather to put you in an uncomfortable position."

"You've accomplished that all on your own." Mortification mixed with temper to send her color high. "It may surprise you to know that I asked Daniel to meet me here this morning, and—though it may crush your outrageous ego—it had nothing whatsoever to do with you. It was a business meeting," she said rather grandly.

"Business?" He squinted against the sun. "What sort of business?"

"I don't believe that's any of your concern," she told him coldly. "But since you'll undoubtedly harass Daniel over it, I'll tell you. Daniel has agreed to be my financial advisor."

Intrigued, Mac slipped his hands into his pockets and rocked on his heels. "You asked him to handle your money?"

"Is there any reason I shouldn't?"

"No." Hoping to cool her off a bit, he smiled and inclined his head. "You couldn't do better."

"Precisely."

And he, Mac thought, couldn't have done any worse. "Darcy—"

"I don't want your apology." Her voice glittered with ice. "I don't want your excuses or your pitiful reasons. I believe we both understand perfectly well the status of our relationship." She snatched up her purse. "You can bill me for the cost of the glasses."

He couldn't stop the wince as she stormed off, slapping her way though the palms. He had both feet up to the knees in his mouth, he decided, grimacing at the sparkle of shattered glass on the tiles.

Getting them out would be the first problem, he thought.

The second problem would be a great deal more complex.

Just how was he going to deal with the fact that the woman who had just ripped the skin off his hide utterly fascinated him?

Chapter 8

For the next two days Darcy concentrated on her writing. For the first time in her life, she decided, she was going to do what she wanted, when she wanted. If she wanted to work until three in the morning and sleep until noon, there was no one to criticize her habits. Dinner at midnight? Why not?

It was her life now, and sometime during those first furious hours, she realized she was finally living it.

She was going to miss Daniel, she thought. He'd returned East the day before, with a promise to keep in close contact on the investments he was making for her. He'd issued an open invitation for her to visit his home in Hyannis Port.

Darcy intended to take him up on it. She'd grown very fond of the MacGregors. They were warm, generous and delightful people—even if one particular member of the clan was arrogant, insulting and infuriating.

He actually thought sending her flowers was going to

make up for it. She sniffed as she glanced over at the lush arrangement of three dozen silvery white roses she'd instructed the bellman to place on the conference table. They were the most beautiful flowers she'd ever seen—which he undoubtedly knew, she thought, hardening her heart as she sat at the desk.

She hadn't acknowledged them, or the sweet basket of button-eyed daisies that stood perkily on her bathroom counter, or the vase of stunning tropical blooms that graced the bureau in the bedroom.

The roses had come first, she remembered, tapping her fingers on the desk. Barely an hour after she'd stormed back into her room after the conversation with Mac, the bellman had knocked on her door. The note with them had been a smooth apology she'd easily ignored.

It was no one's business but hers that she'd tucked the card away in her lingerie drawer.

The daisies had come the next day, with a request that she call him when she had a moment. She'd tucked that card away, too, and had ignored the request—just as she'd ignored his insistent knocking at her door the previous evening.

This morning it was birds-of-paradise and hibiscus with a much pithier request.

Damn it, Darcy. Open the door.

With a short, humorless laugh, she turned on her laptop. She would *not* open the door, not to him. Not the literal door of her room, or the metaphorical door to her heart. It wasn't simply mortifying that she'd allowed herself to fall in love with him, it was…typical, she thought and clenched her teeth.

Pitiful, lonely woman meets sophisticated, handsome man and tumbles face-first at his feet.

Well, she'd picked herself up now, hadn't she? He could send her an acre of flowers, a ream of notes, but it wasn't going to change a thing.

She had her direction now. As soon as she completed the draft of her book, she was going to a Realtor. She intended to buy a house—something big and sand colored that faced the open mystery of the desert and the majestic ring of mountains.

Something with a pool, she decided, and skylights. She'd always wanted skylights.

Settling here had nothing to do with Mac, she told herself. She liked it here. She liked the hot winds, the sprawling desert, the pulse of life and promise that beat in the air. Las Vegas was the fastest growing city in the U.S., wasn't it, and reported to be one of the most livable?

It said so in the glossy hotel guide on her coffee table.

Why shouldn't she live here?

When the phone rang she merely scowled at it. If it was Mac thinking she was the least bit interested in speaking to him, he could think again. She ignored the call, rolled her shoulders once, then dove back into the story.

Mac prowled his office restlessly while his mother scanned the printout of bookings for the next six months. "You've got a wonderful lineup here."

"Mmm." He couldn't concentrate, and it infuriated him.

He'd only wanted to warn her about his grandfather's tendency for plots and schemes. For her own good, he thought, moving from window to window as if to improve his view. And he'd apologized repeatedly. She didn't even have the courtesy to acknowledge it.

He'd come close, far too close, to using his passkey and circumventing the control on her private elevator. And that, he reminded himself would have been an unforgivable invasion of her privacy and a breach of his responsibilities to The Comanche.

But what the hell was she doing in that suite? She hadn't had a meal outside of it since that breakfast on the roof. She hadn't stepped foot in the casino, or any of the lounges.

Sulking. It was so unattractive, he decided, and sulked a bit himself.

"It serves me right for trying to look after her," he muttered.

"What?" Serena glanced over, then shook her head. She knew very well she'd had only the stingiest slice of her son's attention for the past hour. "Mac, what's wrong?"

"Nothing's wrong. Do you want to see the entertainment schedule?"

She lifted her eyebrows and waved the printout. "I'm looking at it."

"Oh. Right." He turned to scowl out the window again.

With a sigh, Serena set the papers aside. "You might as well tell me what's bothering you. I'll just nag you until you do anyway."

"Who'd have thought she could be so stubborn?" The words exploded out of his mouth as he whirled back. "If she can be this damn perverse, how the hell did she get pushed around so much?"

Serena hummed in her throat then, crossing her legs, settled back. Women rarely ruffled Mac, she mused, and took it as a very good sign. "I assume you're talking about Darcy."

"Of course, I'm talking about Darcy." Frustration simmered in his eyes. "I don't know what the hell she's doing, locked in that suite day and night."

"Writing."

"What do you mean writing?"

"Her book," Serena said patiently. "She's trying to fin-ish the first draft of her book. She wants to have that done before she starts querying agents."

"How do you know?"

"Because she told me. We had tea in her suite yesterday."

It took monumental control to keep his mouth from fall-ing open. "She let you in?"

"Of course, she let me in. I talked her into taking a short break from it. She's a very disciplined young woman, and very determined on this. And talented."

"Talented?"

"I persuaded her to let me read a few pages of the book she'd finished last year." Serena's lips curved up into a pleased smile. "I was impressed. And entertained. Does that surprise you?"

"No." He realized it didn't, not in the least. "So she's working."

"That's right."

"That's no excuse for being rude."

"Rude? Darcy?"

"I'm tired of the silent treatment," he muttered.

"She's not speaking to you? What did you do?"

Mac set his teeth and shot a withering look at Serena. "Why do you assume I did anything?"

"Darling." She rose, crossing over to lay a hand on his cheek. "As much as I love you, you're a man. Now, what did you do to upset her?"

"I was simply trying to explain The MacGregor to her. I came across them with their heads together, and Grandpa started in on why didn't I take this pretty young girl for a drive in the moonlight. You know the routine."

"Yes, I do." Daniel "Subtle" MacGregor, she thought

with a windy sigh. "Exactly how were you trying to explain him to her?"

"I told her he wanted his grandchildren married, settled and producing more little MacGregors, that it appeared he'd picked her out for me. I apologized for him, and explained that I wasn't looking for marriage, and she shouldn't take him too seriously."

Serena stepped back, the better to stare at her firstborn. "And you used to be such a bright child."

"I was only thinking of her," he retorted. "I thought he was setting her up. How was I supposed to know she'd asked him to meet her on business? I admit I put my foot in it." He jammed his hands into his pockets. "I apologized, several times. I sent her flowers, I've called—not that she'll answer the damn phone. What the devil am I supposed to do? Grovel?"

"It might be good for you," Serena murmured, then laughed as he hissed at her. "Mac." Gently she cupped her hands on his face. "Why are you so worried about it? Do you have feelings for her?"

"I care what happens to her. She stumbled in here like a refugee, for God's sake. She needs someone to look out for her."

She kept her eyes level on his. "So your feelings for her are...brotherly."

He hesitated just a moment too long. "They should be."

"Are they?"

"I don't know."

Loving him, she skimmed her fingers back into his hair. "Maybe you should find out."

"How? She won't talk to me."

"A man who has both MacGregor and Blade blood in his

veins wouldn't let something like a locked door stop him for long." She smiled, kissed him firmly. "My money's on you."

Darcy's eyes were closed as she tried to visualize the scene before letting the words come. Now, finally, though danger shadowed every corner, her two main characters would come together. No longer would they resist this vital and primitive pull, no longer would needs that swam in the blood and slammed in the heart be denied. It was now. Had to be now.

The room was cold and smelled of damp the blazing fire had yet to conquer. The blue haze of a winter moon slipped through the windows.

He would touch her. How would he touch her? A brush of knuckles on her cheek? Her breath would catch, strangle in her throat, shudder through her lips. Would she feel the heat of his body as he drew her close? What would be the last thing running through her mind in those seconds just before his mouth lowered, took possession of hers?

Insanity, Darcy thought. And she would welcome it.

Keeping her eyes closed, Darcy let the words run through her mind and onto the page. The sudden shrill of the phone was so abrupt and out of place in her chilly cabin in the mountains, she snatched it up without thinking.

"Yes, yes, hello?"

"Darcy." The voice was grave, undeniably irritated, and all too familiar.

"Gerald." The passion and promise of the scene vanished, replaced by nerves. "Ah, how are you?"

"How would you expect me to be? You've caused me a great deal of trouble."

"I'm sorry." The apology was automatic, making her wince the moment it was out of her mouth.

"I can't imagine what you were thinking of. We'll discuss it. Give me your room number."

"My room number?" Nerves shot directly to panic. "Where are you?"

"I'm in the lobby of this ridiculous place you chose to land in. It's beyond inappropriate—which I should have expected given your recent behavior. But we'll straighten it out shortly. Your room number, Darcy?"

Her room? Her haven. No, no, she couldn't let him invade her sanctuary. "I—I'll come down," she said quickly. "There's a seating area near the waterfall. It's on the left of the reception desk in the main lobby. Do you see it?"

"I could hardly miss it, could I? Don't dawdle."

"No, I'll be right down."

She hung up, pushed away from the desk. Despair closed in and was resolutely fought back. He couldn't make her do anything she didn't want to do, she reminded herself. He had no power here, no control. He had nothing that she didn't give him.

But the hand that picked up her purse wasn't completely steady. Her legs wanted badly to shake as she walked to the elevator. She concentrated on keeping her knees from knocking together all the way down.

The lobby was crowded with people, families of tourists who wandered through to toss coins into the pool at the base of the waterfall or to see the live-action show in the open-air amphitheater. Guests checked in, checked out. Others were lured by the ching of slots and headed for the casino.

Gerald sat in one of the curved-back chairs near the bubbling pool. His dark suit was without a wrinkle, his hard, handsome face without a smile as he scanned the activity around him with a glint of derision in his dark eyes.

He looked successful, Darcy thought. Removed from

the chaotic whirl around him. Cold, she decided. It was his cold nature that had always frightened her.

His head turned as she approached. Even as his eyes skimmed over her, registering both surprise and disapproval of her choice of pale green shorts and a peach blouse, he got to his feet.

Manners, she thought. He'd always had excellent manners.

"I assume you have an explanation for all of this." He gestured to a chair.

The gesture, she mused, was just one of the ways he took control. *Sit, Darcy.* And she'd always quietly obeyed.

This time she stood.

"I decided to relocate."

"Don't be absurd." He dismissed this with a wave of his hand before taking her arm and pulling her firmly into a chair. "Do you have any idea what embarrassment you've caused me? Sneaking out of town in the middle of the night—"

"I didn't sneak." Of course she had, she thought.

He merely arched a brow, adult to child. "You left without a word to anyone. You've been irresponsible, which again, I should have expected. Taking a trip like this without any planning. What did you expect to accomplish?"

Escape, she thought. Adventure. Life. She linked her fingers together, laid them in her lap and tried to speak calmly. "I wasn't taking a trip. I was leaving. There's nothing for me in Trader's Corners."

"It's your home."

"Not anymore."

"Don't be more foolish than necessary. Do you have any idea what sort of position you've put me in? I find my fiancée gone—"

"I'm not your fiancée, Gerald. I broke our engagement some time ago."

His gaze never wavered. "And I've been more than patient, giving you time to come to your senses and calm your nerves. This is how you behave. Las Vegas, for pity's sake."

He placed his hands neatly on his knees and leaned forward. "People are gossiping about you now. And that reflects poorly on me. You've been splashed all over the national news—some sort of three-day wonder."

"I won nearly two million dollars. That's news."

"Gambling." He sneered on the word, then leaned back again. "I'll handle the press, of course. The interest will die down soon enough, and it's a simple matter to put a positive spin on the incident, to play down the sordid."

"Sordid? I put money into a slot machine. I hit the jackpot. What's sordid about it?"

He spared her a weary glance. "I wouldn't expect you to understand the underlying thrust of this, Darcy. Your innocence, at least, does you credit. We'll arrange for the money to be transferred—"

"No." Her heart was beginning to pound in her throat.

"You can hardly leave it in Nevada. My broker will invest it properly. We'll see that you get a nice allowance from the interest."

An allowance, she thought, through the dull buzzing in her head. As if she were a child who could be indulged with carefully controlled spending money. "It's already being invested. Mr. MacGregor, Daniel MacGregor is handling it."

Shock reflected in his eyes as his hand shot out to grip hers. "My God, Darcy, you're not telling me you've given over a million dollars to a stranger?"

"He's not a stranger. And actually, he has slightly under

a million for now. There are taxes and living expenses to consider."

"How could you be so stupid?" His voice rose, making her cringe back from it, and the disgusted fury in his eyes. "Put it together—a simpleton could see it. MacGregor has a financial interest in this hotel. And now he has the money you took from this hotel."

"I'm not stupid," Darcy said in a quiet voice. "And Daniel MacGregor isn't a thief."

"My lawyer will draw up the necessary papers to transfer the funds—what there are left of them. We'll have to work quickly." He glanced at his watch. "I'll have to call him at home. Inconvenient, but it can't be helped. Go up and pack while I deal with this latest mess you've made. The sooner I get home, the sooner this can be mended."

"Did you come for the money or for me, Gerald?" She flexed her hand in his, then let it lie passively. She would never win in a physical altercation so she concentrated her efforts, and her anger, into the verbal. "It occurs to me that your pattern would have been to call and order me home once you knew where I was. You wouldn't have bothered to rearrange your busy schedule and come in person. You wouldn't have felt the need. You'd have been so sure I'd have tucked my tail between my legs and come back when you snapped your fingers."

"I don't have time for this now, Darcy. Go pack, and change into something suitable for travel."

"I'm not going anywhere."

Fury had his fingers biting into hers as he jerked her to her feet. "Do what you're told. Now. I will not tolerate a public scene."

"Then leave, because you're about to get one."

A hand dropped lightly onto her shoulder. She knew before he spoke that it was Mac. "Is there a problem here?"

"No." She didn't look at him, couldn't. "Gerald, this is Mac Blade. He runs The Comanche. Mac, Gerald was just leaving."

"Goodbye, Gerald," Mac said in a mild tone that flashed just around the edges. "I believe the lady would like her hand back."

"Neither Darcy nor I require your interference."

Mac stepped forward until they were eye-to-eye. "I haven't begun to interfere, but I'd be happy to." His smile was lethal. "In fact, I've been looking forward to the opportunity."

"Don't." More angry than frightened now, Darcy pushed her way between them. "I'm perfectly capable of handling my own problems."

"Is this what you've been up to, Darcy?" Disgust laced Gerald's voice as he stared down at her. "Letting yourself be seduced by this...person? Deluding yourself that he would want anything more from you than to cheat you out of the money you took from him, and some cheap sex on the side?"

She felt the ripple behind her, sensed that Mac was braced to attack, and quickly swung her hands back to grip his arms. "Please, don't. Please." The muscles seemed to vibrate against her restraining fingers. "It won't help. Please."

She ignored the interested onlookers who were busy pretending not to watch. Perhaps it helped, just a little, that her back was firmly pressed against the solid wall of Mac's chest. But she knew she had to stand on her own now, or she'd never manage to do so.

"Gerald, what I do, where I do it and with whom has nothing whatever to do with you. I apologize for ever agreeing to marry you. It was a mistake I tried to rectify, but you never wanted to hear me. Other than that, I have nothing to be sorry for."

She drew a fresh, steadying breath while she watched his jaw clench. He wanted to hit her, she realized, and found she wasn't surprised. If she hadn't found the courage to run, he would have ended up using fists, as well as words. Sooner or later, intimidation wouldn't have been enough.

The certainty of that gave her the will to finish it. "You maneuvered and manipulated me, because you could. And that's why you wanted to marry me—at first anyway. After that, you insisted on it because you couldn't and wouldn't accept some little no one refusing you—and having to explain a broken engagement to the neighbors."

His face had gone stone cold. "I'm not going to stand here while you air our personal business in public."

"You're free to leave anytime. You came here because I'm suddenly some little no one with a great deal of money. That ups the stakes—and so does the press. I'm sure a few enterprising reporters have made their way to Trader's Corners, and it wouldn't take much for any of them to dig up that we'd once been engaged. Embarrassing for you, but it can't be helped.

"I'm telling you now, as clearly as I know how, that you'll never get your hands on me or my money. That I'm never coming back. I live here now, and I like it. I don't like you, and I realize I never have."

He stepped back from her abruptly. "I can see now that you're not the person I believed you to be."

"I can't tell you how happy that makes me. Cut your losses, Gerald," she said quietly. "And go home."

He angled his head, studying both her and Mac with equal disdain. "As far as I can see, the two of you are well suited to each other, and this place. If you mention my name in the media, I'll be forced to take legal action."

"Don't worry," Darcy murmured as he strode away. "I seem to have forgotten your name already."

"Well done." Unable to resist, Mac lowered his head and pressed a kiss to the top of hers.

She only closed her eyes. "However it was done, it's over. Thanks for offering to help."

"You didn't appear to need it." But she was starting to tremble now. "Let me take you upstairs."

"I know the way."

"Darcy." He turned her around, leaving his hands on her shoulders. "You wouldn't give me the satisfaction of breaking his face. You owe me."

She drummed up something that passed for a smile. "All right. I always pay my debts."

He kept an arm around her shoulders as he walked her to the elevator. Instinctively he rubbed a hand up and down her arm to ease the trembling. "Did you get my flowers?"

"Yes, they're very nice." Her voice went prim, pleasing him. "Thank you."

He used his passkey to access her floor. "My mother tells me you've been working."

"That's right."

"So...the reason you haven't answered my calls—or let me into your room is because you've been busy writing. Not because you hold a grudge."

She shifted uncomfortably. "I don't hold grudges. Usually."

"But you're making an exception for me."

"I suppose."

"Okay. You've got two choices. You can forgive me for being... I believe 'arrogant' and 'insulting' was the way you put it, or I'm going to be forced to go after Gerald and pound my frustrations out on him."

"You wouldn't do that."

"Oh, yes." He smiled darkly. "I would."

She stared at him even after the elevator doors slid open. "You would," she realized with something between shock and horrified delight. "It wouldn't solve anything."

"But I'd enjoy it so much. So are you going to invite me inside, or do I go find him?"

She jerked a shoulder and tried not to be pleased. "Come in. I'm probably too distracted to work anyway."

"Thanks." He glanced toward her desk. "How's it going?"

"Very well."

"My mother said you let her read a couple pages."

"She made it hard to say no. Would you like a drink? Some coffee?"

"Nothing right now. Are you going to let me read some of your book?"

"When it's published you can read the whole thing."

He shifted his gaze from the desk to her face. Her color was back, which relieved him. She'd looked much too pale, and much too fragile, downstairs. "I can make it hard to say no, too. It runs in the family. But you're a little shaky at the moment, so I'll wait."

"It's just a reaction." She cupped her elbows in her palms. "I was afraid when he called."

"But you went down and met him."

"It had to be done."

"You could have called me. You didn't have to do it alone."

"Yes, I did. I had to know I could. It seems foolish now to realize I'd ever been intimidated by him. He's so pathetic, really." She hadn't understood that before, she thought now. Hadn't seen the sorry man under the bully. "Still, if I hadn't been, I might not be here. I might not have met you. I have to be grateful for that."

She clasped her hands together. "I appreciate you not hitting him after he insulted you that way."

His eyes stayed on her face. "I wouldn't have hit him for me."

New emotions swam into her eyes. "I knew, when you came, it would be all right. That I would be all right. And I wasn't afraid anymore. He thought that we've been... I was glad he did, because I'd never let him touch me. And he thinks you have."

He knew it was a mistake to cross to her. The odds were weighted wrong for both of them. "He'll stew about that for a long time. It's almost as good as beating him senseless."

The warmth spreading in her chest was nearly painful. "I'm glad you were there."

"So am I. Are we friends again?"

His knuckles brushed her cheek, made her breath catch, strangle in her throat and shudder through her lips. "Is that what you want to be?"

Her eyes were wide and dark. Her lips parted, full of anticipation, invitation. And irresistible. "Not entirely," he murmured and lowered his mouth to hers.

She knew now what thoughts scrambled through the brain in those last seconds before the mating of lips. Wild and desperate images so bold and tangled they had no name. She stretched up to her toes, her body pressing into his, her hands streaking up his chest to grip his shoulders as she let herself tumble into those shockingly bright colors and shapes.

Her mouth was so eager, so soft and warm and giving.

He wanted more of it. Her body was so slight, so pliant, so ready. He wanted all of it. The need was huge, raw as a groan, and forced him to fight for control.

"Darcy—" He started to ease her away, swore that he would, but her arms wound around his neck.

"Please." Her voice was husky, a tremble of urgency. "Oh, please. Touch me."

The whispered request was as seductive as a rustle of black silk. Desire swarmed through him, roaring in his head, throbbing in his loins. "Touching won't be enough."

"You can have enough." She could drown in need, she thought frantically. Already she was going under. "Make love with me." Her voice sounded desperate and very far-away as her lips raced over his face, melted onto his. "Take me to bed."

It was as much demand as offer. Everything inside him responded to both. "I want you." He tore his mouth from hers to press it to her throat. "It's insane how much I want you."

"I don't want to be sane. I don't want you to be. Just once—be with me."

He let the wheel spin. He swept her up in his arms and watched her eyes turn gold with awareness. The fact that she weighed little more than a child terrified him. "I won't hurt you."

"I don't care."

But he did. He nuzzled a sigh from her as he carried her to the stairs and started up. "The first time I brought you up here, I wondered about you. Who is she? Where does she come from?" He laid her on the bed, stroked his fingers down the column of her throat. "What am I going to do with her? I still haven't figured it out."

"When I woke up and saw you, I thought I was dreaming." She lifted a hand to his cheek. "Part of me still does."

He turned his head to press his lips into the cup of her palm. "I'll stop if you ask me." He took her mouth again, going deep, sinking in. "For God's sake, don't ask me."

How could she? Why would she, when nerves and pleasure and needs were dancing just under her skin? The spread was slick under her back, and his hands were already stroking small, separate fires into life over her body. His mouth drew and drew and drew from hers as if she contained some life force he craved.

Craved.

No one had ever made her feel wanted like this.

His fingers trailed over her as though he found her delicate, special. And when his hand closed over her breast, molded it, her mind emptied.

She was unbearably responsive, her body arching, giving, inviting him to do as he wished. Gently, he ordered himself, go gently here. He blurred her mind, and his, with kisses as he opened her blouse and began to explore warm, smooth flesh.

Her trembles aroused him, almost brutally. Every quiver of her muscles was a miracle to be exploited, then savored. For he found he could savor, the texture of that skin curving subtly above the cup of her bra, the flavor of her throat where the pulse beat so hard and fast.

He drew her up, nibbling tortuously at her mouth as he slipped her blouse aside.

Hesitantly she reached for the buttons of his shirt. She wanted to touch him, to see. To know. A sound of dizzy delight escaped her when she saw her white hands against the dusky gold of his chest.

So strong, she thought, fascinated by the ridge of muscles under her fingertips. So hard and strong and male. Thrilled, she leaned forward to press her lips to his shoulder, to absorb the taste.

He felt something like a growl working through him and pushed down a sudden, violent need to devour. Instead he took her face in his hands, watching her, drinking her in even as his mouth took hers again. Watching still, for those flickers of surprise and pleasure in her eyes, as he slipped her bra aside, as he cupped her breasts in his hands, skimmed his thumbs over nipples that went hot and stiff.

Then he laid her back to capture one sensitized point with his mouth.

Her hand fisted in the spread, dragging at it as hot, liquid sensation flooded her system. A pulse was pounding between her legs, all but burning there. She heard her own moan, a wanton, throaty sound of pleasure as she wrapped around him, racked by edgy, questing needs.

"Easy." He wasn't certain if he were calming her or himself. But her restless movements beneath him had control nearly slipping out of his hands.

He rolled with her, tugging away the spread she'd tangled around them, sinking with her into the pool of pillows. He dragged at her shorts, drawing them down, away, then toyed with the last barrier, the little swatch of blush-colored lace.

"Oh, my." Her hips jerked and her vision blurred. "I can't—"

"You should be dancing through the woods under a full moon." He murmured it, delighting in her body, the shape of it, the glorious response of it to every touch. He traced a scatter of freckles on her quivering belly and smiled as he shaped a star. "Should've figured it."

Then he slid a finger under the lace.

Pressure slammed into her, a smothering weight of velvet

that had her fighting for one gulp of air. Heat flashed with the shock of a fireball. Her eyes went blind, the stunned cry ripped from her throat, and the pressure burst into a flare of pleasure dark as moonless midnight.

She went limp with it, the hand that had gripped his shoulder sliding bonelessly to the tangled sheets.

So hot, he thought, and his hands weren't completely steady as he drew the lace down her legs. So wet. So beautifully ready. He felt his heart slamming in his chest as her heavy eyes flickered open and that clouded gold fixed on him.

"I've never…"

"I know." He was the first, and it made him mad to have her. "Again," he murmured, and brought her close, so desperately close that her hips arched up to meet him when he came into her.

His muscles screamed, his blood seemed to snarl as he met both heat and resistance. "Hold on." He panted it, linked his hands with hers.

She felt herself reaching again, flying toward that astonishing peak. The pain was a shock, so mixed with pleasure she couldn't separate the two. Then she was opening for him, taking him into her. Mating. And there was only pleasure.

Movement and magic combined to sweep her off on some high, curving wave that crested so slowly, so gracefully that she seemed to tremble on its peak endlessly before sliding down, and down into a quiet and shimmering pool.

Resting there, with him on her, in her, she wrapped herself around him and sighed his name.

Chapter 9

She could smell the heady and exotic fragrances of the tropical bouquet on her dresser. The sun poured through the windows and beat warmly against her face.

If she kept her eyes closed she could picture herself in some lush and deserted jungle, gloriously naked and tangled around her lover.

Her lover. What a marvelous phrase that was.

She let it repeat in her mind, over and over, as she turned her head to press her lips to his throat. But when he started to shift, she tightened her grip.

"Do you have to move?"

His mind didn't seem to want to clear. She was still inside it as completely as he was still inside her. "You're so little."

"I've been working out." She wanted to keep tasting it, the hot, dusky flavor of his throat. "I'm starting to get biceps."

He had to smile. He eased back just enough to pinch her

upper arm where the tiny muscle melted like wax under his fingers. "Wow."

She laughed. "Okay. I'm *almost* getting biceps. In a few more weeks, nobody's going to call me Pencil-Arm."

"You don't have pencil arms," he murmured, distracted by the texture of her skin along her elbow. "They're slender. Smooth."

She studied his face, marveling at the concentration in his eyes as he traced his finger from her shoulder to her wrist. Did he have any idea just what that absent brush of fingers did inside her body? She didn't see how he could, or how he could possibly understand what it was like for her to look at that beautifully sculpted profile and know that for a little while he belonged to her.

Was it because she was in love with him that their lovemaking had taken on such a brilliant sheen? Was it because he was her first, her only, that she couldn't imagine being so close, so intimate with anyone else?

Whatever the reason, she would treasure what he'd given her. And she would hope she'd given him something he would remember in return.

"I have to ask." Her smile was a little apologetic. "I know it's probably pitifully typical, but...well, I need to know."

His gaze had come back to her face, and it was wary. He was afraid she would ask him how he felt, what he wanted, where this was leading. Since he was still struggling with the first part of that, he had no idea what followed.

"Was I—was it..." How did one phrase it? "Was it all right?" she asked him.

Then tension in his stomach dissolved. "Darcy." Struck by a wave of tenderness, he lowered his mouth and kissed her, long and deep. "What do you think?"

"I stopped being able to think." Her eyes opened slowly, glowed into his. "Everything got jumbled. I always imagined that I'd remember all the details, sort of step-by-step. But I couldn't pay attention. There was so much to feel."

"Sometimes…" He wanted her mouth again, and took it. "Thinking's overrated."

"Thoughts just slide out of my head when you do that." Her hands stroked down his back as she floated on the kiss. "And when you started to touch me, everything got so…hot."

He groaned against her mouth, then swallowed her gasp as he hardened inside her. "You don't have to pay attention," he told her. "Just let me have you."

Her breath came fast and thick, shattered on each long, slow stroke. She came on a moan and a shudder that ripped through him like claws. He gripped her hips, lifted them. "More. Give me more this time," he demanded, and drove deep, dragging her over the edge with him.

Later, when she was alone, she caught her reflection in the mirror over the bed. Her eyes went wide with shock at the image of herself, hair tousled, face glowing, her naked body sprawled over a tangle of sheets.

Could this be Darcy Wallace? The dutiful daughter, the conscientious librarian, the shy and pitiful doormat from Kansas?

She looked…ripe, she decided. Aware. And oh, so satisfied. Then she bit her curving lip as she wondered if she'd have the nerve to look up into the mirror the next time Mac made love with her.

The next time.

Overcome with joy, she hugged a pillow and rolled. He wanted her. She didn't care what the reasons were, it was enough that he did. There had been simmering promise in the kiss they'd shared before he'd left her. He'd asked her to have a late supper with him in his office.

He wanted her.

Was it so impossible to believe she could find a way to make him keep wanting her? And to find a way to turn that wanting into love?

Curling into the pillow, she rested her head. It would be a gamble. She would be risking what she had now in the hope for more. Because he'd been right, she admitted. What he'd said in the rooftop garden had been a bull's-eye. She did want marriage and family and permanence. She wanted children. She wanted, desperately, to be able to take this love that threatened to flood right out of her heart and give it.

And for once in her life, she wanted to feel loved in return. Not the lukewarm affection of duty, not the kindly indulgence of affection, but the hot-blooded and dangerous love that sprang from passion and lust and blind need.

The kind of love that could hurt, she thought, squeezing her eyes shut. The kind that lasted and grew and shot up and down the hills of the roller coaster and demanded screams of delight and terror.

She wanted it all. And she wanted it with Mac Blade.

How would she win his heart? She sighed a little, absently snuggling into the pillow as her limbs grew heavy. She would figure it out, she promised herself and sighed toward sleep.

After all, the only way to win was to play. And she was on a hot streak.

She wore the beaded jacket she'd fallen in love with on her first day at the hotel. Under it was a daring little excuse for a dress in lipstick red. The jacket gave her confidence, made her feel glamorous.

The dress made her feel just a bit sinful.

She wanted to try her hand at blackjack again, decided she might make it her signature game. If she was going to live in Vegas—and she was—and be involved with a man who ran a casino—which she hoped to be—she needed to be skilled in at least one form of gambling.

The slots, she decided, didn't take skill. She'd proved that herself. Roulette appeared to be a bit repetitive, and craps...well, it looked wonderfully exciting and rousing, but she just couldn't follow the action.

But the cards were self-explanatory, and they always came up in a different and intriguing order.

She wandered for a while, just enjoying the crush of people, the raucous sounds, the pulse of excitement. The tables were crowded tonight, and the cards moved, fast and sharp. She was toying with joining a game, and had talked herself into risking a hundred dollars for the night when Serena came up beside her.

"I'm glad to see you decided to get out for a while." Angling her head, Serena took in the glittery jacket. "Celebrating?"

"Um." Darcy felt color flood her face. She could hardly tell Mac's mother she was, in her way, celebrating making love to him. "I just wanted to dress up. I bought all these clothes and I've been living in slacks and shorts."

"I know just how you feel. Nothing perks up the soul like a great dress. And that's a great one."

"Thanks. You don't think it's too...red?"

"Absolutely not. So are you going to try your luck here?"

"I was thinking about it." She nibbled her lip. "I hate to join a table where everyone knows what they're doing. It must be irritating to have a novice plop down and slow the game."

"It's part of the game, and the luck of the draw. If you stick to the five- or ten-dollar tables, most people will be willing to help you out a bit."

"You were a dealer."

"Yes, I was. And a good one."

"Would you teach me?"

"To deal?"

"To play," Darcy stated. "And to win."

"Well…" Serena's smile spread slowly. "Go get us a table in the bar. I'll be along in a minute."

"Split your sevens."

Eyes sober, Darcy followed instructions, setting the two sevens she'd been dealt side by side on the silver table in the lounge. "And this is supposed to be good, right? Not stressful because now I have two hands to worry about."

Serena just grinned. "Cover your bet on the second hand." She dealt Darcy her next cards. "Three for ten on your first hand, six for thirteen on your second. Dealer has an eight showing, what do you do?"

"Okay." Darcy wiped her damp palms on her knees. "I double down on the first hand, then take a hit." Remembering the ritual she'd been taught, she counted out the bar nuts standing in the place of chips, then tapped a finger on her cards. "A three—thirteen. I have to take another one."

"Pulled a six for nineteen. Holding on nineteen?"

"Yeah. Now we do this one." She tapped her finger on the second hand and winced at the steely eyes of the king she drew. "Well, at least that was fast."

"Busted on twenty-three." Serena raked in the nuts, and cards, then turned over her down card. "Dealer has eleven, fourteen, and breaks on twenty-four."

"So I win on the first hand, but I doubled the bet so it's like winning twice. That's good."

"You're getting it. Now if you want to buck the house, you let that bet ride on the next hand."

Darcy stared down at her pile of nuts. "It's a lot—twenty nuts on one hand."

"Two thousand." Serena twinkled at her. "Didn't I mention the nuts are a hundred a pop?"

"Good God, I've eaten a dozen. Let's go for it."

"Is this game open, ladies?"

Serena tipped up her face for her husband's kiss. "You got a stake, pal, you got a chair."

He snagged a bowl of pretzels from a neighboring table. "I think I can afford a few hands."

"Thousand-dollar chips. We got us a high roller." Delighted with the game, Serena rubbed her hands together. "Place your bets."

When Mac found them a half hour later, Darcy was sitting hip to hip with his father and giggling as she piled a mix of nuts and pretzels into a sloppy mountain on the table. "You're not supposed to hit on seventeen when the dealer's showing a two," Darcy said, sniffing experimentally at the smoke from Justin's slim cigar. "Why did you?"

"He's a card counter." Mac pulled up a chair and sat between his parents, eyeing his father. "We don't like card counters around here. We ask them politely to take their money elsewhere."

"I taught you how to count cards before you could handle a two-wheeler."

"Yeah." Mac's grin flashed and spread. "That's why I can spot 'em."

"Your father's still as slick as he was when he bet me a walk on the deck of the ship on one hand of twenty-one. He hit on seventeen then, too."

"Oh." Darcy's heart sighed. "That's so romantic."

"Serena didn't think so at the time." Justin sent Serena a long, slow smile. "But I changed her mind."

"I thought you were arrogant, dangerous and cocky. I still do," Serena added, sipping at her wine. "I just learned to like it."

"Are you two going to flirt with each other or play cards?" Mac demanded.

"They can do both," Darcy told him. "I've been watching."

"Learned anything?"

It was the delivery, smooth as silk, that flustered her as much as the words. She looked at him, large eyes shuttered by dark lashes. "If you don't bet, you don't win."

"I've got a couple hours off." He spoke to the table at large, but his eyes were on Darcy's as he rose, held out a hand. "I'll see you tomorrow," he said to his parents, then drew Darcy to her feet. "Let's go out."

"Out?"

"There's more to Vegas than The Comanche."

"Good night," she called over her shoulder as Mac was already pulling her away.

Justin drew on his cigar, tapped it idly. "The boy's a goner," he decided.

The minute she stepped outside, Darcy realized she hadn't been out of the hotel after sunset since she arrived. For a moment she simply stood, between the tumbling sapphire water of a fountain and the grand gilded statue of the chief.

The lights were dazzling, the traffic edgy. Vegas was a woman, she thought, part honky-tonk, part siren, bold, brassy and seductive.

"It's so…much," she decided.

"And there's always more. The Strip's a few blocks long, a few blocks wide, but you can smell money in every foot of it. Gambling's the core, but it's not a one-factory town anymore. Headliners, circus acts, wedding bells and rides for the kids."

He glanced back at the wide and towering double arch that was The Comanche. "We added a thousand rooms five years ago. We could add a thousand more and still fill them."

"It's a huge responsibility. Running an enterprise of this size."

"I like it."

"The challenge?" she wondered. "Or the power, or the excitement?"

"All of it." He turned back, then taking her hand stepped back. He hadn't gotten beyond her face in the bar. Those eyes of hers always seemed to capture his mind first. Now he took in the glittering glamour of her jacket and the invitational red of her dress.

"I should have stolen more than a couple hours. You need to be taken out on the town."

"I'd love a couple of hours. Where should we go?"

"I can't manage a drive into the mountains in the moonlight, but I can take you for a walk through a tunnel full of fantasies."

He took her walking on Freemont, where the street was covered and full of lights. Colors circled and bled overhead, and the ever present clack of the slots added a musical, carnival feel. She could marvel at the light show, delight in the music and walked hand in hand with him on what was so suddenly and unexpectedly an innocent date.

He bought her ice cream, and made her laugh.

She rode the elevator to the top of The Stratosphere with him, thrilled at the idea that she was rising up inside of that towering needle that stood at the edge of the Strip. And though she stared then gulped at the sight of the rooftop roller coaster, the silent challenge in his eyes had her scooting into the car with him.

"I've never ridden a roller coaster in my life."

"You might as well start with a champ," he told her.

"I tried a Tilt-A-Whirl once at a carnival but…" She trailed off. "Are you sure this is safe?"

"Almost everyone who gets on gets off again. The odds are good." He laughed at the horrified look in her eyes, then took advantage—as he'd intended to—when the coaster started its climb and she gripped him in a death hold. "I want to kiss you."

"Okay, but you could have done that on the ground." She lifted her face, which she'd buried in his shoulder.

"Not yet," he murmured, but laid his hands on her cheeks. "Not quite yet."

Lulled, she smiled and her heart began to beat normally again. "It's not so bad. I didn't realize it would be so nice and slow."

Then they dipped, spinning fast into a free fall that shot her stomach hard against her ribs and burned white-hot fear into her throat.

"Now." And he took her mouth greedily as they swung over the edge of the world.

She couldn't breathe. There wasn't even breath to scream. They were flying, rocketing up, plunging down, shoved into the void then snatched back while his mouth assaulted hers with a single-minded intensity that left her stupefied.

Speed, light, screams. And that firestorm of stunning heat that refused to be stopped. Dizzy, breathless, helplessly caught in the crosshatch of arousal and fear, she clung to him.

And gave him what he'd wanted—crazed, half-terrified surrender.

Her head was still reeling after they'd jerked to a stop. Her fingers continued to grip his jacket, as if fused there. "God." The word exploded from her lips. "I've never felt anything like that before." She shuddered once. "Can we do it again?"

His grin flashed. "Oh, yeah."

She felt drunk and giddy by the time they stood on the street again. "Oh, that was wonderful. It made my head spin." She laughed as he slipped a supporting arm around her waist. "I won't be able to walk a straight line for hours."

"Then you'll have to lean on me—which was part of my plan."

Laughing again, she threw back her head to watch an explosion of fireworks. Jewel colors shot into the black sky, and fountained there. "Everything's so bright here, so bold. Nothing's too high or too big or too fast." She turned into him. "Nothing's impossible here."

Wrapping her arms around his neck, she kissed him with a passion that had waited a long time to wake. "I want to do everything. I want to do everything twice, then pick the best and do it again."

He slid his arms under her jacket and discovered to his delight that the dress left her back bare to his hands. "We've got a little time before I have to get back. What would you like to do?"

"Well…" Her eyes sparkled in the neon. "I've never seen an exotic dancer."

"And your second choice would be?"

"I just wonder what it would be like in one of those places where the women dance topless and slide around on those poles."

"No, I'm definitely not taking you to a strip joint."

"I've seen naked women before."

"No."

"All right." She moved a shoulder, began to walk casually beside him. "I'll just go by myself some other time."

He shot her a look, narrowed his eyes, but she only smiled up sunnily. He considered himself highly skilled at judging a bluff. And knew when he was up against a better hand.

"Ten minutes," he muttered. "And you don't say a word while we're inside."

"Ten minutes is fine." Delighted with the victory, she tucked her arm through his.

"The patriotic one was double-jointed, I'm sure of it." With another fascinating experience under her belt, Darcy breezed into Mac's office just ahead of him. "The one with the little flag over her—"

"I know the one you mean." Every time he thought he had her pegged, Mac thought, she flustered him. She hadn't been the least bit embarrassed or shocked. Instead she'd been fascinated.

"The way they slid around on that pole, they must practice for hours. And the muscle control, it's phenomenal."

"I can't believe I let you talk me into taking you into a place like that."

"I had no idea."

"Obviously."

"No, I mean about you." She sat on the arm of a chair. He was already behind his desk, scanning the screens.

"What about me?"

"That under that suave, sophisticated exterior, you're really a fuddy-duddy at heart."

He stared at her, unsure if he should be amused or insulted. "Anyone who uses the expression 'fuddy-duddy' in a sentence automatically assumes fuddy-duddy status."

"I never heard that."

"It's written down somewhere. Are you hungry?"

"Not really." She couldn't sit still and rose to circle the room. "I had such a wonderful time. It's been the most incredible day of my life—and I've had some incredible days lately. Everything's churning about inside me." She wrapped her arms around herself as if to hold it all in. "I don't think there's any room for food."

Her jacket caught the lights as she moved, glittering like jewel-toned stars that reminded him of the fireworks. But it was her face—it always seemed to be her face—that held his attention. "Champagne?"

She laughed, a warm delighted sound. "There's always room for champagne. Imagine me being able to say that. It's like every minute I'm here is another little miracle."

He took a bottle from the small refrigerator behind the wet bar, watching her as he opened it. She was glowing, he thought, eyes, cheeks, lips. Everything about her seemed to pulse with energy and fresh, unshadowed joy.

Seeing it, feeling it, aroused, contented and unnerved him. *Be with me,* she'd asked him. And being with her, on a walk down a crowded street, alone in a tumbled bed, over a candlelit table, was becoming uncomfortably vital.

But she was glowing. How could he take his eyes off her? "I like seeing you happy."

"Then you must be having a good night, too. I've never been so happy." She took the glass he offered, twirling around as she sipped. "Can I stay here with you awhile, watch the people?"

Did she really have no idea how she affected him? he wondered. "Stay as long as you want."

"Will you tell me what you're looking for when you watch the screens? I don't see anything but people."

"Trouble, scams, tells."

"What are tells?"

"Everybody has them. Gestures, repetitive habits that tell you what's going on in the head." He smiled at her. "You link your fingers together when you're nervous. It keeps you from biting your nails. You cock your head to the left when you're concentrating."

"Oh. Like the way you put your hands in your pockets when you're frustrated—so you don't punch someone."

He lifted a brow. "Good."

"It's easy when you're watching a handful of people, but there are so many," she added, gesturing to the screens. "How do you pick them out?"

"You get to know what to look for. This is only backup. The first line of defense against scam artists is the dealer." He walked up behind her, laid a hand on her shoulder so they could watch the screens together. "Then the floor man, the pit boss, the shift boss. And over it all is the eye in the sky."

"This?"

"No, this is a wink. We have a control room with hundreds of screens like this. The staff in there watches the casino from every angle, and they're linked to the floor men, the shift and pit bosses with radios. They'll spot a hand mucker—"

"A what?"

"Card palming. The scam artist is dealt say a six and an eight, he palms them, and switches them with a queen and ace for a blackjack. Cheating's a problem—more now than it used to be when you were dealing with loaded dice and fast hands. We're talking body computers these days."

Body computers, she thought, scam artist. Hand mucking. Wouldn't that be a fascinating backdrop for a book? "What do you do when you catch someone cheating?"

"Show them the door."

"That's it?"

"They don't walk out with our money."

The chill in his voice had Darcy glancing back at his face. "I bet they don't," she murmured.

"We run a clean room, the cameras there and in all the counting areas help keep it honest. But the house always has the edge. It's not hard to win money in The Comanche, but odds are, you won't keep it."

"Because you want to keep playing." She understood that. It was so hard to stop when there was a chance for more.

"And the longer you play, the more you'll put back."

"But it's worth it, isn't it? If you've enjoyed yourself. If it's made you happy."

"As long as you know what you're risking." He saw that she understood they were no longer talking about table games and slots.

"The danger's part of the allure." Her heart began to thud as he took the glass from her hand and set it aside. "That, and the whiff of sin. You get a taste for it."

"And why stop at a bite or two, when you can have all you want." His gaze roamed over her face, lingering on her mouth, then sliding down. "Take off your jacket."

"We're in your office."

His eyes came back to hers, and his smile was slow and dangerous. "I wanted you, here, the first day you came in. Now I'm going to have you, here. Take off your jacket."

Mesmerized, she slipped it off, let it fall in a colorful pool over the arm of the chair. When she realized she'd linked her fingers together, she pulled them apart. And made him smile again.

"I don't mind you being nervous. I like it. It's exciting to know you're a little afraid, but when I touch you, you'll give." He reached out to toy with the sassy red strap on her shoulder. The dress clung to every quiet curve. "What've you got on under there, Darcy?"

Her breath shuddered out. "Hardly anything."

His eyes flashed, a clash of swords in the sun. "I don't want to be gentle this time. Will you risk it?"

She nodded, would have spoken, but he was already dragging her against him. His mouth was bruising and hungry and tasted of such raw passion she could only marvel he felt it for her.

Then he was pulling her to the floor, and the shock of that alone had her gasping. His hands took her over, body and mind, racing over her, taking, possessing, inciting a fury of sensations.

All she could think was that it was like the roller coaster, a fast and reckless ride. Glorying in it, she yanked desperately at his jacket, tugged at his shirt while the pulse pounding in her seemed to scream hurry, hurry, hurry.

She moaned as he peeled the dress down, and the sound raged through his blood. Her breasts were small and firm and when he filled his mouth with the taste of them she fisted her hands in his hair, urging him to take more. Desperate for the taste of flesh, her flesh, he used tongue and teeth until she writhed under him, her sobbing breaths like a drumbeat to his greed.

But still it wasn't enough.

His mouth streaked down, laying a line of heat on skin that had gone hot and damp. Her muscles quivered beneath his tongue, her body shivered under his busy, relentless hands. His own breath was ragged when he gripped her restless hips and lifted them.

The fast plunge ripped a scream from her throat. The fire that shot through her was molten, shocking her system with sensations so acute she feared for a moment they would simply tear her apart. The climax rushed through her, a towering wave of hot, hard pleasure that tossed her high, sucked her deep. Helpless, she tossed an arm over her eyes and let it drag her where it would.

When she thought there could be no more, he pulled her mercilessly over the next edge.

She lay bonelessly as he yanked off the rest of his clothes. Her skin glowed under the lights, flushed and damp. Her mouth was swollen from his. When he drew her up, her head fell weakly back, leaving him no choice but to plunder her soft mouth.

"Stay with me." He murmured it as he assaulted her neck, her shoulders. He shifted, bringing her over him, brought her down until she took him into her, closed that glorious heat around him.

Her moan was long and deep and broken. He watched as flickers of fresh pleasure moved over her face and into the clouded eyes that opened and fixed on his.

"Take what you want." His hands moved up her body and covered her breasts.

She was already moving. Her body was unable to rest. There was a shock of control, of power, a nervy kind of energy that demanded movement. Tantalizing. She arched back and drove herself mad.

Everything inside her was as bright, as brilliant, as reckless and bold as the world she now lived in. A world where nothing was too big or too fast, or too much.

He was quivering beneath her, and his hands were rough as they gripped her hips. A new thrill snaked through her, the knowing that she was taking him with her.

Stay with me, he'd demanded. And she wanted nothing more than to obey.

When the climax bowed her back, when it had her melting down on him, he rolled her over, his body plunging, his heart pounding, until both body and heart emptied themselves into her.

Chapter 10

The phone woke Darcy at five past nine. She thought blear-
ily that her days of working an ordinary eight-hour day
were over. It had been nearly four in the morning when
she'd given in to exhaustion. And even then she'd been
wrapped around Mac.

Since she was alone in the big bed, she had to assume
he'd figured out a way to function on little to no sleep. If
he could learn, so could she.

She yawned widely, reached for the phone with her eyes
still hopefully shut. "Hello?" she mumbled, and buried both
her head and receiver in the pillow.

Fifteen minutes later she was sitting straight up in
bed, staring at nothing. Maybe she'd been dreaming, she
thought, and stared at the phone. Had she actually just
talked to an editor in New York? Had that editor actually
asked to see her work?

She pressed a hand to her heart. It was beating, fast but

steady. She could feel the light chill from the air-conditioning on her bare shoulders. She was wide-awake.

Not a dream, she told herself, bringing her knees up and wrapping her arms tightly around them. Not a dream at all.

Her story was all over the media—the editor had said as much. Darcy had told reporters that she was writing a book, and now the next miracle had happened. A publisher wanted to see it.

It was only because of the attention from the press, Darcy thought, resting her forehead on her knees. She was an oddity, a story in herself, and the publisher would consider her manuscript because of the public's interest in the writer, and not the work.

And that, she thought with a sigh, didn't make her a writer.

What difference did it make? She sat straight again, balling her fists. It was a foot in the door, wasn't it? A chance to see if—no, not to see, she corrected, to *prove* her work had merit.

She'd send the first book in, and the opening chapters of the second. She would let them stand or fall on their own.

Tossing the sheets aside, she scrambled out of bed, bundled into a robe and raced downstairs to turn those first two chapters into gems.

She said nothing to Mac, to anyone, afraid she would jinx herself. Superstition was another new character trait, or perhaps one she'd kept buried. She worked steadily through the day, ruthlessly cutting, lovingly polishing her words until she was forced to admit she could do no better.

While the pages printed out, she retrieved her list of agents. If she intended to be a professional, she told herself, then she would need professional representation. It was time to take the big risk. Finally take it.

They were just names to her, faceless power symbols. How would she know which one to pick, which one would see something inside her worthy of their time and attention?

The face of the slot had been only stars and moons, she remembered. She'd gambled everything once. It wasn't so hard to do it again. Following impulse, she shut her eyes, circled her finger in the air, then jabbed it onto the list.

"Let's see how lucky you are," Darcy murmured, and calculating she had fifteen minutes before offices closed on the East Coast, picked up the phone.

Twenty minutes later she had representation, or at least the promise to read the manuscript and sample of her work, and to negotiate if the publisher made an offer.

More than satisfied, Darcy typed up a cover letter, then called the desk to request an overnight bag and form before she could change her mind.

She nearly did so while the bellman waited for her to seal the envelope. She very nearly gave in to the dozens of excuses whirling in her head.

It wasn't ready. She wasn't ready. The book needed more work. She needed more time. She was sending work she'd slaved over to strangers. She should ask someone's advice before she mailed the pages. She should call the agent back and tell her she wanted to finish the second manuscript rather than submitting the first.

Coward, she berated herself and, setting her jaw, handed the bellman the envelope. "Will this go out today?"

"Yes, ma'am. It'll be in—" he glanced at the address on the form "—New York tomorrow morning."

"Tomorrow." She felt the blood drain out of her face. "Good. Thank you." She handed him some crumpled bills as a tip, then sat down the minute he was gone and dropped her head between her knees.

It was done. There was no going back now. In a matter of days she would know if she was good enough. Finally good enough. And if she wasn't...

She simply couldn't face failing at this. Not this. As long as she could remember, she'd wanted this one thing. Had set it aside time after time after time. Now there was no one to tell her to be practical, to accept her own limitations. There were no more excuses.

Steadier, she sat up, took two long breaths. She'd plugged in her stake, she told herself, and she'd pulled the lever. Now she would have to wait for the end of the spin.

When the phone rang, she stared at it, horrified. It was the editor calling back, she thought frantically, telling her there had been a mistake.

Holding her breath, she picked up the phone. "Hello," she said, with her eyes tightly shut.

"Hello yourself, little girl."

"Daniel." His name came out on something close to a sob.

"Aye. Is something wrong, lass?"

"No, no." She pressed a hand to her face and let out a quick, nervous laugh. "Everything's fine. Wonderful. How are you?"

"Right as rain." The way his voice boomed through the receiver seemed to prove it. "I thought I should let you know, I lost every penny in a leveraged buyout."

"I—I—" She blinked so rapidly the room spun in front of her eyes. "All of it?"

His laughter roared out, forcing her to pull the receiver several inches away from her ear. "Just joking with you, lass."

"Oh." She pressed a hand to her speeding heart. "Ha-ha."

"Got your blood moving, didn't it? I'm just calling to let you know we made some money already."

"Made some? Already?"

"You know, Darcy girl, you're using the same tone for the good news as you did for the bad. That's a good sign of a steady nerve."

"I don't feel steady," she admitted. "But I feel lots of nerves."

"You'll do. We made a tidy little sum on a short-term deal, an in and out sort of thing. You should go buy yourself a bauble."

She moistened her lips. "How big a bauble?"

He laughed again. "That's my girl. We pulled in a quick fifty, just getting our feet wet."

"I can get some nice earrings for fifty dollars."

"Fifty thousand."

"Thousand," she repeated though her tongue seemed to tangle on the word. "Are you joking again?"

"Buy the bauble," he told her. "Making money's a fine way to pass the time, but enjoying it's better. Now tell me when you're coming to see me. My Anna wants to meet you."

"I may be coming East—on business—in the next few weeks."

"That's fine then. You plan to come here, spend some time, meet the rest of the family, or those I can gather up. Children scatter on you. It's a crime. My wife pines for them."

"I will come. I miss you."

"You've a sweet heart, Darcy."

"Daniel...do you..." It had to be delicately put, she thought, but it had to be put. "Mac mentioned, that is, he seemed to think you might have the idea that we'd suit each other. That you were, well, planting seeds along those lines."

"Planting seeds, is it! Planting seeds. Ha! The boy needs a cuff on the ear. Did I say a word? I ask you."

"Well, not exactly, but—"

"Where do they get this idea that I'm scheming behind their backs? I didn't drop you into his lap, did I?"

"No, but—"

"Not that it doesn't take a push to get these young people to do their duty—and to see what's best for them. Dawdle around is what they do. My wife deserves babies to bounce on her knees in her twilight years, doesn't she?"

"Yes, of course. It's just that—"

"Damn right I do—she does," he corrected quickly. "Boy's going to be thirty in another month or so, and is he settling down to make a family? He is not," Daniel rolled on before Darcy could speak. "And what's so wrong with giving him a bit of a nudge, I'd like to know, if you suit him?"

"Do I?" she murmured. "Do I suit him?"

"I'm saying so, and who'd know better?" He huffed, then his voice shifted, became sly and persuasive. "He's a good-looking young man, don't you think?"

"Yes, I do."

"Strong stock, a good brain. There's a kind heart in him, too, and a fine sense of responsibility. He's a steady one, stands for his friends and his family. A woman couldn't do better than my Robbie."

"No, I don't see how she could."

"We're not talking about she," Daniel said with some impatience. "We're talking about you. You've got a spark for him now, don't you, Darcy girl?"

She thought of the fireworks exploding over the city the night before. Her spark for Mac was every bit as huge and bright and volatile. "Daniel, I'm so desperately in love with him."

"Well now."

"Please." She winced at the booming pleasure in his voice. "I'm trusting you with that because I need to tell someone."

"Why aren't you telling him?"

"Because I don't want to scare him off." There, she'd said it, she thought, biting her lip. It was no more than a plot.

"So…you're giving him some time to woo you, and come around to thinking it was his idea."

Now she winced. "It's not really that devious. It's just—"

"What the devil's wrong with devious? Devious gets the job done, doesn't it?"

"I suppose." Her lips trembled into a smile. How could she help it? "He cares for me, I know he does, but I think part of it comes from that fine sense of responsibility. I'm willing to wait until he doesn't feel responsible."

"Don't wait too long."

"I'm hoping I won't have to." She smiled. "I have some ideas."

She wasn't in the market for a bauble, but she rented a car. Buying one was going to wait until she could decide if the sports car or the sedan suited her new and developing lifestyle.

She secretly hoped it would be the sports car.

Armed with maps, she began the task of familiarizing herself with the city, the one beyond the Strip. She cruised downtown, noting the huge building cranes that loomed like giant, hovering birds. Growth was everywhere, from the spectacular hotel resorts, to the developments that sprawled into the desert.

She parked and walked the malls, the grocery store and drugstores, giving herself a chance to observe the life that pulsed here beyond the casinos.

She saw children playing in yards, houses tucked side by side in neighborhoods. She saw schools and churches, quiet streets and crowded ones. She saw sprawling homes that faced the eerie peace of the desert and the tumble of rocks that made the mountains beyond.

She saw a life she could begin to build.

Circling back, she found a library and went inside to gather more information on the place she would make her home.

It was after seven when she got back to her suite, pleasantly tired and more than eager to put her aching feet up. She was certain she'd walked twenty miles. Though she hadn't bought a bauble, she had made an appointment to view a property the following day.

She thought she might become a home owner very soon.

"There you are." Mac stepped up to the elevator the moment the doors opened. "I was getting worried."

"I'm sorry. I was out exploring." She tossed her purse aside and started to smile, but her mouth was soon busy against his.

He knew the sense of relief was out of proportion, as was the irritation he'd felt when he hadn't been able to find her anywhere in the hotel. "You shouldn't have gone out alone. You don't know your way around."

Responsibility, she thought, and wanted to sigh. "I got a map. I thought it was time I saw a little more of the city."

She started to tell him about the house she planned to see the next day, then held her tongue. The news was hers for now, she thought, just as the call from New York was hers.

"You spent some time in the sun." He ran a fingertip down her nose and made her wrinkle it.

"I'll have to remember to get a hat before I turn into one big freckle. The air's so hot and dry. It must be murder on the skin, but I really love it."

"It's easy to get dehydrated."

"Mmm. You're right." She walked over to take a bottle of water from behind the bar. "I saw people with water bottles hooked on their belts. Like hikers or explorers, and so much building going on. Men in hard hats working a hundred, two hundred feet in the air. Slot machines in the grocery store."

"You went to a grocery store."

"I wanted to see what it was like," she said, evading. "All this boom in the downtown area, then suddenly, you're in a quiet suburban neighborhood, with kids and dogs in the yard, and it all seems so cozily settled."

"I'd have taken you around if I'd known you wanted to go."

"I knew you were busy."

"I'm not busy now. My parents booted me out, with orders to take the night off."

A smile curved her lips. "I really love your parents."

"So do I. Come for a drive with me." He held out a hand. "We'll find some moonlight."

In the distance, Vegas shimmered like a mirage. The floor of the desert stretched in every direction, barely marred by the slice of road. Overhead the sky was a clear, dark sea, studded by countless stars and graced by the floating ball of a white moon.

In the distant hills a coyote called, and the plaintive

sound carried like a bell on the air that had cooled with moonrise.

He'd put the top down so that she could lay her head back and let starlight shower on her face. Wind danced lightly across the sand as they sat in silence.

"You forget this exists when you're in there." She looked toward the colors and shapes of the city. "The West, wild and dangerous and beautiful."

"A long way from Kansas." It was too easy to picture her there, away from the arid wind, the gaudy lights. "Do you miss the green? The fields?"

"No." She didn't have to think about it. "There's something so powerful in the siennas and soft reds, the baked-out greens and browns of this land. But you didn't grow up here, either." She turned her head to look at him. "You lived back East, didn't you?"

"The house is in New Jersey, just outside of Atlantic City. My parents didn't want to raise a family in hotel rooms over a casino. But we spent plenty of time there. Duncan and I used to hunker down in the security bay over the tables. Before everything was electronic, that's where they watched the room. My mother would have skinned me if she knew I'd taken him up there."

"Rightfully so. It must have been dangerous."

"Part of the appeal, right?" His grin flashed and to her secret joy he began to play absently with her hair. "There's a story about the night one of the men fell out and landed facedown on a craps table."

"Ow! Was he hurt? What happened?"

"Rumor persists that some guy bet five dollars on his ass. The game doesn't stop for much."

She chuckled and settled her head on his shoulder. "It

was exciting for you, being a part of all of that. Why did you choose to work here and not back East?"

"There's only one Vegas. No point in settling for less than the best."

Her heart gave a little jerk at the sentiment, spoken with such casual confidence. But she ignored it. "Is the rest of your family involved with the casinos?"

"Duncan's managing the riverboat. It suits him down to the ground, cruising along the Mississippi and charming the ladies."

"You're close?"

"Yeah. We are, all of us. Geography doesn't change that. Gwen's a doctor, lives in Boston—as do several assorted cousins. She had a baby a few months ago."

"Boy or girl?"

"A girl. Anna, after my grandmother. I have two or three hundred pictures," he added with a smile, "if you'd like to see her."

"I'd love to. You have another sister, the youngest?"

"Mel. She's a live wire. The eyes of an angel and the right hook of a middleweight."

"I imagine she needed both," Darcy said dryly. "You probably teased her unmercifully."

"No more than was my right and duty. Besides, I'm the one who taught her how to punch. No girlie little slaps for my baby sister."

"I bet they're all beautiful. With heart-stopping faces and killer smiles." She turned her head, let herself trace his mouth with her fingertip. "And between the looks and the breeding, they're a confident bunch. The kind who walk into a room, take one slow glance around and know exactly where they stand. I always envied that innate sense of self."

"I thought the word was *arrogance.*"

"It is, but it's not always a criticism. Did you argue all the time?"

"As often as humanly possible."

"No one argued in my house. They reasoned. At least in an argument you have a chance to win."

"I've noticed you hold your own in that area."

"Beginner's luck," she claimed. "Wait until I'm seasoned a bit. I'll be a terror." She grinned. "Then I'll learn how to punch, in case arguing doesn't work."

Her lips were still curved when his lowered to them. The easy kiss turned dark quickly, began to heat rapidly around the edges. They both shifted, moving into it, into each other.

Emotion surged through him so powerfully, so violently that fury sprang up to tangle with need. "I shouldn't want you this much." He dragged her head back to try to clear his own. But all he could see were those dark gold eyes, and what was the shadow of himself drowning in them. "It's too damn much."

She remembered his words of the night before and gave them back to him. "Take what you need."

"I've been trying to. It doesn't stop."

The words sent a wild thrill soaring through her. Recklessly she knelt on the seat beside him, watched his gaze lower and follow the movement of her fingers as she unbuttoned her blouse. "Try again," she murmured.

He should never have touched her, was all he could think, because now he couldn't seem to stop. He drove the long, straight road back to Vegas at a fast clip, with Darcy sleeping like a child beside him, her head on his shoulder.

He'd taken her in the front seat of the car like a hormone-rattled teenager. He'd driven himself into her with a blind desperation, as though his life had depended on it.

And Lord help him, he wanted to do it again.

He'd broken all the rules with her. A man who made his living with games knew the rules, and when they could and should be ignored. He'd had no right to ignore them with her.

She'd been innocent and alone, and had trusted him.

He'd let his needs, and hers, step ahead of that. Now he was so tangled up in her, in what he wanted, in what was right, that nothing was clear.

He was going to have to step back. There was no question of it. She needed room, and the chance to test those wings of hers. No one had ever given her that chance, including himself.

He could keep her, he knew it. She thought she loved him, and he could make her go on thinking it. Until eventually, he thought with an inner lurch, that glow of hers began to fade against the neon and glitter, and that light of fascinated joy dulled in her eyes.

Keeping her would ruin her, change her and eventually break her. That was one gamble he wouldn't take.

Caring for her left him only one answer. He had to back away and give her a nudge in the opposite direction. In the direction that was right for her.

He should do it quickly for her sake, and yes, for his own.

She was the only woman who'd ever slipped uninvited into his mind at odd hours of the day and night. He wanted to resent it but found that he was already afraid of the time that would come when she would fade into a memory.

And he was already furious thinking of the time when he would become little more than that to her.

She'd think of him now and then, he reflected, when she was tucked into some pretty home in a green-lawned suburbia. Children playing at her feet, a dog sleeping in the yard and a husband who wouldn't appreciate the magic of her nearly enough on his way home for dinner.

It was exactly where she belonged, exactly where she would go once he worked up the courage to cut the ties that bound her to him. Ties of gratitude, excitement and sex, he thought and despised himself for wanting to hold her with them.

He'd spoken no less than the truth when he'd told her she didn't belong in the world he lived in. He believed that absolutely. She would come to the same truth once the gloss had dulled a bit.

Virtue and sin didn't mate comfortably.

He glanced down as he drove along the Strip and watched the carnival lights from the neon splash over her face. He would have to let her go, he told himself. But not yet.

Not quite yet.

Chapter 11

The house grew up out of the sand like a little castle fashioned of soft colors and magic shapes. Darcy's first sight of it shot an arrow of love and longing into her heart.

It was tucked among palms, and desert plants were scattered near the wide sunny deck. The soft red of the tile roof accented the cool ivory and buffed browns of the exterior. The multilevels gave it a variety of charming rooflines and made her think of artistically placed building blocks.

It had a tower, a canny little spear that had her romantic heart picturing princesses and knights, even while the practical part of her nature snagged it greedily as the perfect writing space.

It was already hers, even before she stepped inside. She barely heard the Realtor's professional chatter.

Only three years old. Custom-built. The family moved back East. It's just come on the market. Bound to be a quick mover.

"Hmm." Darcy responded simply as they started up the brick walkway to the door flanked by glass etched with stars.

Stars had been lucky for her, she thought.

She stepped into the entrance onto the sand-colored tiles, let her gaze travel up to the lofty ceiling. Skylights. Perfect. It was an airy space with walls painted a cool, soft yellow. She would leave them alone, she decided, listening to her heels click on the tile as she wandered.

Another deck stretched along the back, accessed by atrium doors in a quiet blond wood. No dark colors here, she thought. Everything would be light, fresh. Her eyes gleamed with pleasure as she looked beyond the deck to the sparkling waters of the swimming pool.

She let the Realtor expound on the wonders of the kitchen, the subzero refrigerator, the custom-made cabinets, the granite counters. And was charmed by the cozy breakfast area tucked into a bay window. That was for family, she thought. For lazy Sunday mornings, and rushed school days, for quiet late nights and cups of tea.

She would enjoy cooking here, she thought, studying the range, the double ovens, the mirror black cooktop. She'd always been a plain and pedestrian cook, but she thought she would like experimenting with recipes, with herbs, sauces.

The maid's room and laundry area off the kitchen were easily as big as her entire apartment in Kansas. Darcy didn't miss the irony, or the wonder of it.

She'd put a trestle table in the dining room, she mused. That would suit the tone and go well with the small tiled fireplace for chilly desert nights. Watercolors for the walls, soft bleeding tones.

She'd learn how to entertain, have intimate, casual dinner parties as well as sparkling, sophisticated ones. Loud, bawdy, backyard barbecues. Yes, she thought she could be a good, and what was better, an interesting hostess.

She toured each of the four bedrooms, checking views, space, approving the builder's choice of random-width pine for the floors, and the bright jazz of contrast tiles scattered in amusing patterns among the neutral colors of the baths.

She knew she goggled at the master suite, and didn't care. The two-level area boasted its own private deck, fireplace, an enormous dressing area with closets large enough to live in and a bath that rivaled the one at The Comanche with a lagoon-sized motorized tub in an unexpected clay color.

The treated skylight above it cut the glare while offering a dazzling view of desert blue sky.

Ferns, she imagined, in copper and brass pots, crowded together, all lush and green. She would jumble them on the wide ledge behind the tub and every bath would be like swimming in a secluded oasis.

The tower was octagon shaped, generous with windows. The walls were cream, the floor tiles the color of stone. Her workstation would go there, she decided, facing the desert. Not a desk, but a long counter, perhaps in a sharp, deep blue for contrast. It would have dozens of drawers and cubbyholes.

She needed to go shopping for a computer system—a fax, a desktop copier. Reams of paper, she thought with a giddy burst of joy.

She would put a love seat on the other side of the room and create a small seating area, and she'd want shelves there, floor to ceiling, for books and small treasures.

She would sit there, writing hour after hour, and know she was a part of everything around her.

The Realtor had been silent for the past several minutes. She'd been in the game long enough to know when to sell, and when to step back. The potential buyer didn't have much of a poker face, she mused, already imagining the tidy commission.

"It's a lovely property," the Realtor said now. "A quiet, settled neighborhood, convenient for shopping but tucked just far away enough from the city to offer a sense of solitude." She offered Darcy a bright smile. "So, what do you think?"

Darcy pulled herself back and focused on the woman. "I'm so sorry, I've forgotten your name."

"It's Marion. Marion Baines."

"Oh, yes, Ms. Baines—"

"Marion."

"Marion. I appreciate you taking the time to show me through."

"Happy to do it." But she felt a little hitch in her stomach, a sign of a sale slipping away. "It might feel a little large for your needs. You did say you were single."

"Yes, I'm single."

"It might seem a bit overwhelming, but empty houses often do. You'd be amazed how it all comes together when it's furnished."

Darcy had already seen it come together as she could picture it furnished, perfectly, in her mind. "I'll take it."

"Oh." Marion's smile faltered, then spread. "Wonderful. I'm so pleased you want to make an offer. If you like we can use the kitchen to fill out the paperwork, and I can present your offer to the sellers this afternoon."

"I said I'd take it. I'll pay the asking price."

"You—well." Something in that fresh face and youthful eyes had her hesitating. Even as she ordered herself to keep her mouth shut and close the deal, she found herself speaking. "Ms. Wallace, Darcy... I'm contracted to represent the sellers, but I realize this is the first time you've bought property. I feel obligated to mention that it's usual to make an offer of...somewhat less than the asking price. The sellers may accept it, or counter."

"Yes, I know. But why shouldn't they get what they want?" She smiled and turned back to gaze out the window. "I'm going to."

It was so simple really, she discovered. A few forms to be filled out, papers to be signed, a check to be written. Earnest money, it was called. Darcy liked the sound of it. She was very earnest about the house.

She listened as home loans were explained to her, fixed interest rates, balloon payments, mortgage insurance. Then decided to keep it simple and pay cash.

When the settlement date was set, she breezed out to her rented car, thrilled by the knowledge that in thirty short days she would have a home.

The minute she was back in her suite, she grabbed the phone. She knew she had to call Caine, ask him to represent her interests in the settlement or recommend a local real estate lawyer. She needed to choose an insurance company and take out a home owner's policy. She wanted to shop for furniture, to pick out dishes and linens.

And oh, she'd forgotten to measure the windows for the plantation blinds she wanted.

But first she wanted to share her news and excitement.

"Is Mac—Mr. Blade available?" she asked when Mac's assistant answered the phone. "It's Darcy Wallace."

"Hello, Ms. Wallace. I'm sorry, Mr. Blade's in a meeting. May I take a message?"

"Oh...no, thank you. If you could just tell him I called."

She hung up, deflated as the image in her head of driving him out to the house and telling him it was hers faded. It would have to wait.

She buried herself in work instead, pushing herself toward the end of the book. If her luck held and the agent she'd contacted wanted to see more, she intended to be ready.

When two hours had passed and he hadn't returned her call, she resisted the urge to pick up the phone again. She made herself coffee, then spent another hour tweaking an earlier chapter.

When the phone rang, she pounced. "Hello."

"Darcy. Deb said you called earlier."

"Yes. I wondered if you could spare an hour. There's something I want to show you."

There was a hesitation, a humming kind of silence that had her shifting in her chair.

"I'm sorry. I'm tied up here." In his office Mac sat at his desk and realized the first step away was the hardest. "I'm not going to have any time for you."

"Oh. You must be busy."

"I am. If anything's wrong I can send the hotel manager or the concierge up."

"No, nothing's wrong." The cool formality of his voice made her shudder. "Nothing at all. It can wait. If you have time tomorrow…"

"I'll let you know."

"All right."

"I have to go. Talk to you later."

She stared at the phone in her hand for several seconds before replacing it slowly on the hook. He'd seemed so distant, so different. Hadn't that been mild irritation in his voice, an underlying impatience?

No, she was imagining things. Finding her hands gripped tightly together, she swore at herself and separated them.

He was just busy, she told herself. She'd interrupted his work. People hated to be interrupted. It was her own sense of disappointment—which was foolish—that was making her overreact to a very natural incident.

He'd spent the whole of last evening with her, she remembered, had made wild, almost desperate love to her under the stars. No one could need a woman so much in the night then flick her off like a pesky gnat the next day.

Of course they could, she admitted and pressed her fingers to her eyes. It was naive, even stupid to pretend it couldn't and didn't happen.

But not with Mac. He was too kind, too honest.

And she loved him far, far too much.

He was just busy, she insisted. She'd taken up huge amounts of his time over the past two weeks. Naturally he would need to catch up, to concentrate on business, to take some breathing room.

She wasn't going to sulk about it. Darcy straightened her shoulders, tucked the chair back in place. She would concentrate on work herself, and take advantage of what was going to be a long, solitary evening.

She worked for another six hours, remembering to turn on the lights only when she realized she was working in the dark. She drained the pot of coffee and found herself stunned when she came to the end of her book.

Finished. Beginning, middle and end. It was all there now, she thought giddily, all inside this clever little machine and copied onto a small slim disc.

To celebrate she opened a bottle of champagne, though it was a bit of a struggle, and drank an entire glass. With reckless abandon she poured a second and took it to the desk with her to start refining the draft.

She put in twelve hours and went through half a bottle of the wine, which she counteracted with more coffee. It was hardly a wonder that when she finally tumbled into bed she was chased by odd and jumbled dreams.

She saw herself in the tower of her new house, alone. All alone and crowded there by mountains of paper and an enormous computer. Through the window she could see dozens of scenes flip by, like a fast-forward through a movie. Parties and people, children playing, couples embracing. The noise—laughter and music—was muffled by the glass that surrounded her.

When she pounded on it, no one heard her. No one saw her. No one cared.

She was in the casino, sitting at the blackjack table. But she couldn't add up her cards, couldn't calculate the math. Didn't know what to do.

Hit or stand. Serena, elegant in a mannish tux, watched her impassively. *Hit or stand,* she repeated. *You have to make the choice, then deal with it.*

She doesn't know how to play. Mac stepped up beside her, gave her a brotherly pat on the head. *You don't know the rules, do you?*

But she did, she did. It was just that she couldn't seem to add the cards. There was so much at stake. Didn't they understand how much was at stake?

Never bet more than you can afford to lose, Mac told her with a cool smile. *The house always has the edge.*

Then she was alone again, stumbling along the arrow-straight road through the desert and the lights and colors of Vegas were trapped behind the rippling waves of heat, floating there. No matter how far she walked she couldn't get any closer.

Dust rose in a cloud as Mac drove up, his hair streaming in the wind. *You're going in the wrong direction.*

But she wasn't. She was going home.

He reached out, touched her cheek in an absent, avuncular gesture that made her cringe. *You don't belong here.*

"Yes, I do." Her own furious shout woke her. Sitting up in bed she was stunned by the raw and genuine extent of her anger. She seethed with it, forced herself to take deep, calming breaths.

The sun was bright on her face because she'd forgotten to draw the drapes the night before.

"No more bedtime champagne for you, Darcy," she muttered, rubbing her face as if to rub away the edges of the dreams.

Noting it was already nine, she gave in to impulse and grabbed the phone. Serena answered on the second ring.

"It's Darcy. I hope I'm not calling too early."

"No. Justin and I are just having our first cup of coffee."

"Are you busy today?"

"I don't have to be. What did you have in mind?"

Darcy stood back, nervously twisting her fingers as Serena walked through the first floor of the house.

"I know this might seem sudden," Darcy began. "It's the only one I looked at. But I had a picture in my head of what I wanted, and this…this was even better than that."

"It's…" Serena turned a last circle, then smiled. "Beautiful. It suits you so well. I think you've made a perfect choice."

"Really? Really?" Swamped with joy, Darcy steepled her hands at her mouth. "I was afraid you'd think I was crazy."

"There's nothing crazy about wanting a home of your own, or investing in excellent property."

"Oh, I wanted to show someone so badly. I raced back yesterday as soon as I'd signed the contract. I wanted to show Mac, but he was busy, and well…"

She moved her shoulders and stepped away before she could see Serena's troubled frown. As far as Serena knew, her son hadn't been any busier the day before than normal.

"You told him you bought a house, but he didn't have time to come out and take a look?"

"No, I just told him there was something I wanted him to see. I guess it's silly, but I wanted him to see it first. Please don't tell him about it."

"No, I won't. Darcy, why did you decide to buy a house here, in Vegas?"

"That." Her response was instant as she walked over to the doorway to gaze out at the desert. "It pulls at me. For some people it's water, for some it's mountains, or it's big, bustling cities. For me it's the desert. I had no idea until I got here, and then I knew."

Glowing with pleasure, she turned back. "And I love the Strip, the fantasy of it, the magic and the snap in the air that says anything can happen. Everything does happen. Everybody needs a place, don't you think, that makes them believe they could accomplish something there? Even if it's nothing more than being happy."

"Yes, I do think that, and I'm glad you found it." Still she crossed the room, brushed a hand over Darcy's hair. "But it has to do with Mac, too, doesn't it?" When Darcy didn't answer, Serena smiled softly. "Darling. I can see how you feel about him."

"I can't help being in love with him."

"Of course, you can't. Why should you? But is the house for him, Darcy?"

"It could be," she murmured. "But it's for me first. It has to be. I need a home. I need a place. That's what I'm doing here. I know I can't expect him to feel about me the way I do about him. But I'm willing to gamble. If I lose, at least I'll know I played the game. No more watching from behind the window," she murmured.

"My money's on you."

Darcy's grin flashed like sunlight. "I ought to tell you that I've fallen in love with Mac's family, too."

"Oh, baby." Serena wrapped her close, rubbing cheeks, and reminded herself she hadn't raised any idiots. Mac would come to his senses soon. "Show me the rest of the house."

"Yes, and I was hoping you could go with me to look at furniture."

"I thought you'd never ask."

Darcy was glad to be busy, to have so many details juggling for space in her mind. Colors, fabrics, lamps. Should she convert the smallest bedroom into a library or would the downstairs den suit that purpose best?

Did she want ficus trees flanking the doorway on the main level, or palms?

Every decision was monumentally important to her, and a giddy delight.

Though she yearned to share them all with Mac, they'd had no time alone together for two days.

He was putting all his efforts into keeping his mind occupied and off her. Time, he'd decided, and space, were what both of them needed to ease back far enough and analyze their relationship.

He missed her miserably.

Freedom was undoubtedly what she needed, he told himself. He paced his office, giving up on the idea of work. She hadn't called him again, and from the information he'd discreetly drawn from the staff, she'd been spending nearly as much time out of the hotel as in it.

Flexing those fairy wings, he imagined.

He hadn't let her do that, not really. He'd carried her along, deluding himself initially that he was helping her, then justifying the rest because he'd wanted her.

And still wanted her.

She'd come into his life lost and wounded and desperate for affection. He'd taken advantage of that. It hardly mattered what his motives were, the results were the same.

He imagined she believed herself in love with him. The idea had crossed his mind more than once to take advantage of that as well. To keep her for himself. To see that she went on believing it as long as possible.

After all, she had no experience. No man had touched her before he had touched her. She'd tumbled from a sheltered existence into a dazzling fantasy world. He could sweep her along in that world, keep her dazzled. And his.

It would be easy. And unforgivable.

He cared far too much to trap her, to clip those wings and watch the innocence tarnish. Her life was just beginning, he reminded himself. And his was already set.

Then she burst into his office, her eyes huge, her cheeks wax pale. "I'm sorry. I'm sorry, I know you're busy. I know I shouldn't disturb you, but—but—"

"What is it? Are you hurt?" He had his hands on her in one thumping heartbeat.

"No, no." She shook her head frantically, clutched at his

shirt. "I'm okay. No, I'm not okay. I don't know what I am. I sold my book. I sold my book. Sold it. Oh, God, I'm dizzy."

"Sold it? Take slow breaths, come on, slow and deep. That's it. I thought the book wasn't finished."

"The other one. The one—last year. She said the new one, too. Both of them." Giving up, she dropped her forehead to his chest. "I need a minute. I can't think straight." Then she jerked her head up again, laughing wildly. "It's like sex. Maybe I should have a cigarette."

"Have a seat instead."

"No, I can't sit down. I'd bounce right off the chair. They bought the book, no, the books. Two-book contract. Can you imagine? I beat the odds. Again."

"Who bought the book, Darcy? And how?"

"Oh, okay." She gulped in another breath. "A few days ago I got a call from an editor in New York. Eminence Publishing. She'd seen me on the news, and she asked me to send her some of my work."

"A few days ago?" The stab of disappointment was sharp and sudden. "You never mentioned it."

"I wanted to wait until I had an answer. Boy, have I got one now." She pressed her fingers to her eyes as tears swam close. "I'm not going to cry, not yet. I picked an agent off my list. I knew the publisher only wanted to see my work because of the publicity, but there was a chance they'd like it. So I hired an agent."

"Over the phone."

"Yes." The obvious disapproval in his tone made her sigh. "I know it was risky, but I didn't want to wait. The agent called this morning and said they'd made an offer, a very decent offer. Then she advised me to turn it down."

As if that part were just sinking in, Darcy pressed a hand

to her stomach. "I couldn't believe it. I had a chance like this, what I've wanted all my life, and she said to say no."

"Why?"

"That's what I asked her. She said…" Darcy closed her eyes, reliving the moment. "She said I had a strong talent, that I told a powerful story, and they were going to have to pay more for it. If they balked, she told me she would take the book to auction. She believed in me. So I took the chance. Ten minutes ago, they bought them both. Now I think I'll sit down."

She all but slid into a chair.

"I'm so happy for you, Darcy." He crouched in front of her. "So proud of you."

"All my life I wanted this. No one ever believed in me." She let the tears come now. "'Be sensible, Darcy. Keep your feet on the ground.' And I always was. I always did because I never thought I was good enough for more."

"You're good enough for anything," he murmured. "More than good enough."

She shook her head. "I always wanted to be. When I was in school, I worked so hard. Both my parents were teachers, and I knew how important it was to them. But no matter how much I put into it, I brought home B's instead of A's. They'd look at my report card, and there'd be this silent little sigh. They'd tell me I'd done well, but I could do better if I just worked harder. I couldn't do better. Just couldn't. It was the best I could do, but it was never good enough."

"They were wrong."

"They didn't mean to be so critical. They just didn't understand." Wanting the anchor, she held tight to his hands. "I used to show them the stories I'd write, just once wanting them to be impressed, enthusiastic. It just wasn't in them, so I stopped showing them. And I stopped looking for their approval, at least outwardly."

She sighed, wiped at her face with her fingers. "I never sent off the first book. Couldn't find the courage to. I suppose inside I was always hoping, waiting for someone to tell me I was good enough. Now I've done it, and someone has."

"Here." He pulled a handkerchief out of his pocket and pressed it into her hands.

"I'm not sad." She sniffled, mopped at her face. "There's just so much going on inside me. So many things have been happening. I had to tell you."

"I'm glad you did. News like this can't wait." He framed her face in his hands, and after a brief internal struggle, pressed his lips to her forehead rather than her mouth. "We'll have to celebrate." He let his hands linger on her face a moment, then dropped them and rose. "We'll get together for drinks and you can tell me your plans."

"Plans?"

"You'll want to fly into New York for a few days, I imagine. Meet your publisher, your agent."

"Yes, maybe next week."

So soon, he thought and suffered as he looked down at her tear-streaked face and made the break. "You'll be missed around here," he said lightly. "I hope you'll keep in touch, let us know where you settle."

"Settle. But… I'm coming back here."

"Here?" He lifted a brow, then smiled. "Darcy, as delighted as we've been to have you, you can't keep living in a high roller's suite." He laughed a little and sat on the edge of his desk. "A high roller, you're not. You're more than welcome to stay until you finalize your travel plans."

He was running a business, she thought frantically. She'd been taking advantage of his generosity, occupying an expensive suite for two weeks. "I hadn't thought. I'm sorry. I'll book another room when I get back until—"

"Darcy, there's no reason for you to come back here."

"Of course there is." Her heart began to flutter hard in her throat. "I live here."

"The Comanche's not your home. It's mine." He wasn't smiling now, and his eyes had gone cool and hard. It was the only way he could face the stunned hurt on her face. "It's time for you to start your own life, and you can't do that here. You've accomplished something really extraordinary. Now enjoy it."

"You don't want me anymore. You're not just kicking me out of your hotel. You're kicking me out of your life."

"No one's kicking you out of anything."

"No?" She managed a half laugh and balled the handkerchief in her fist. "How stupid do you think I am? You've been avoiding me for days. You've barely touched me since I came in the room. Now you're giving me a little pat on the head and telling me to run along and have a nice life."

"I do want you to have a nice life," he began.

"As long as it's somewhere else," she retorted. "Well, that's too bad, because I'm having my life here. I bought a house."

He'd prepared himself for a miserable scene, for tears, for recriminations. But he was stunned speechless. "What? You bought what?"

"I bought a house."

"Have you lost your mind? A house? Here? What were you thinking of?"

"Myself. It's a new concept for me and I like it."

"You don't buy a damn house the way you do a new dress."

"I'm not the bubble-brain you apparently think I am. I know how to buy a house, and I've done it."

"You have no business buying a house in Vegas."

"Oh really?" Her emotions were careering so fast she didn't know how her words could keep pace. "Do you own the entire city and its environs now? Well, I seem to have found the one little spot you don't have control over. I like it here, and I'm staying."

"Life is not an endless cruise down the Strip."

"And Vegas is not only the Strip. It's the fastest growing city in the country, and one of the most livable. It has an excellent school system, job opportunities abound and the housing is very affordable. Water's a problem, and that's an issue that's going to have to be seriously addressed in the near future. However, the crime rate is markedly low in comparison with other major cities and the area's continuing ability to reinvent itself gives it high marks for potential into the next century."

She paused, her eyes glittering when he said nothing. "I'm a writer. I was a librarian. I damn well know how to research."

"Did your research mention how many pawnshops are in Vegas per square mile? Did it touch on prostitution, corruption, money laundering, gambling addictions?"

"Actually, it did," she said evenly now. "Sin exists. It may shock you to know I was aware of it before I came here."

"You simply haven't thought this through."

"You're wrong. Absolutely wrong. I didn't buy this house blind, and I didn't buy it so I could keep falling at your feet. I bought it for me," she said fiercely. "Because I found something I always wanted and never expected to have. But don't worry, Vegas is big enough so that I won't get in your way."

"Wait a minute. Damn it," he muttered, and put a hand on her shoulder to turn her. But she spun around, lifting both hands with a look in her eye that warned him to keep his distance.

"Don't. I don't need placating, and I don't intend to cause a scene. I'm grateful to you, and I don't want to forget that. I fully intend to have a relationship with your parents, your family and don't want to put them, or you, in a position that makes that difficult. But you hurt me," she said quietly. "And you didn't have to."

She walked to the door, shut it firmly behind her.

Chapter 12

"So we agree to forgive two million of Harisuki and Tanaka's baccarat losses." Justin lounged in the wide leather chair, pretending he didn't notice his son's inattention. "That puts them into the casino for ten and twelve million respectively. We comp the rooms, the meals, the bar bills and cover their wives' spending spree in the boutique. They'll be back," he said, drawing idly on his cigar. "And they'll drop the next several million right here instead of across the street. You arranged for the limo for them tomorrow?" He waited a beat. "Mac?"

"What? Yes. It's taken care of."

"Good. Now that we've finished all that up, you can tell me what's on your mind."

"Nothing in particular. Do you want a beer?"

Justin indicated assent with a wave of his hand. "We always had to pry problems out of you. Your determination to handle everything yourself is admirable, but it's annoying." He smiled cheerfully at his son and accepted the cold brown bottle. "However, in this case, prying isn't necessary—trouble with Darcy."

"No. Yes. No," Mac repeated, and blew out a breath. "She sold her book. Actually she sold two books."

"That's wonderful. She must be thrilled. Why aren't you?"

"I am. I'm happy for her. It's what she's always wanted. I don't think I realized how much she wanted it. This will give her a whole new direction."

"Is that what's worrying you? She won't need you anymore?"

"No. The whole issue is for her to move ahead with her life. This was just some breathing space for her."

"Was it? Mac, are you in love with her?"

"That's not the point."

"It's the only point that counts."

"I'm wrong for her. This place is wrong for her." Restless, he stalked to the window, staring out at the carnival of neon and colored fountains. "Once she focuses she'll see that."

"Why are you wrong for her? It seemed to me you complemented each other very well."

"I run a casino. My peak hours are when sensible people are tucked into their beds." He jammed his hands into his pockets. "She's lived a sheltered life. More, a repressed one where she's been held back, held down. She's just starting to realize what she can do and be and have. I don't have any right to interfere with that."

"You're making this black-and-white, sinner and saint. I don't think either of you qualify. You're a businessman, and a good one. She's an interesting, refreshingly enthusiastic young woman."

"Who walked in here a few weeks ago," Mac reminded him. "A few weeks ago and at a turning point in her life. She can't possibly know what her feelings are."

"You underestimate her. But regardless, aren't your own feelings important?"

"I've already let my feelings take over more than once. She walked in here untouched." Mac turned back, his eyes swirling and dark. "I changed that. I should have kept my hands off her, but I didn't. I couldn't."

"Now you're going to punish yourself for being human," Justin concluded. "You're going to deny yourself a relationship that makes you happy, and your reasoning is she'll be better off."

"She's dazzled," Mac insisted, wondering why saying it all out loud this way made it sound so wrong and so foolish. "And only seeing what she wants to see. She bought a house, for God's sake."

"Yes, I know."

"And—you know." Mac stared at his father.

"She took your mother to see it the day after she signed the contract. I went to see it myself. It's a fine piece of property, an intriguing, attractive home."

"It's ludicrous to buy a house in a place you've only been for a few weeks, and when you've spent most of that time in a hotel casino. She's living in a fantasy land."

"No, she's not. She knows exactly what she wants, and I'm surprised you don't realize that. If you don't want her, that's a different matter."

"I can't stop wanting her." It was like an ache that couldn't be eased. "I was sure I could."

"Wanting's easy. The first time I saw your mother I wanted her. That was as natural as breathing. But loving her terrified me. Sometimes it still does."

Surprised, Mac lowered to a chair. "You make that part look easy, too. You always have. You're so…matched," he decided.

"Is that the problem?" Justin leaned over, put his hand over Mac's.

"No, not a problem. It's just that marriages work in our family. The odds are against it, but they work for us." He studied the gold band on his father's finger. Thirty years, he thought, and it still fit. That was a kind of miracle. "I figure they work because we're careful to find a mate—in the literal sense of the word. A match."

"You're seeing your mother and I as a set, something that came that way. It's not true. We were a half-breed ex-con who'd gotten lucky and the privileged daughter of wealthy, indulgent parents. Long odds, Mac, on a pair like that."

"But you were heading in the same direction."

Justin leaned back again, eyes sharp. "The hell we were. What we did was beat a new path, and there were plenty of bumps along the way."

"You're telling me I've made a mistake," Mac murmured. "And maybe you're right." He ran his hand over his face. "I'm not sure anymore."

"You want guarantees? There aren't any. Loving a woman's the riskiest game in town. You either put up your stake, or you back away from the table. But if you back away, you never win. Is she the woman you want?"

"Yes."

"I'll ask you again. Are you in love with her?"

"Yes." Admitting it intensified the ache. "And yes, it's terrifying."

Sympathizing, Justin smiled. "What do you want to do about it?"

"I want her back." He let out a long breath. "I've got to get her back."

"How bad have you screwed it up?"

"Pretty bad." It made him slightly ill to realize just how poorly he'd played his hand. "I all but shoved her out the door."

"It may take some fast talk to get her to open her side of that door again."

"So I'll talk fast." Misery vanished in a spurt of reckless energy. It was a new hand, he thought, fresh cards. And everything he had was going into the pot. "I'd better go down and try to work this out with her. She must be sitting in her room, miserable, when she should be out celebrating."

"I think you lose on that one," Justin murmured, studying the screens.

"There's a pair of star-shaped diamond earrings in the jewelry store downstairs." Mac checked his pocket to make certain he had his passkey for the elevator. Just in case. "She should have something special to celebrate selling her book."

He was suddenly nervous, a sensation he wasn't accustomed to. "Do you think the earrings and flowers are overkill?"

Justin ran his tongue around his teeth. "I don't think you can ever overkill in a situation like this. But...you're not going to find Darcy in her room."

"Hmm?"

"You better take a look. Screen three, second craps table from the left."

Anxious to be on his way, Mac glanced absently at the screen. Then looked again. His wounded fairy was decked out in that little killer of a red dress with spiked heels to match, and was blowing on a pair of dice.

"What the hell is she doing?"

"Going for an eight. That's her point. Five and a three," he said, and grinned when he heard his son slam the door on his way out. "The lady wins."

"Come on, baby. Come on, doll. Bring it home."

The man cheering beside Darcy was old enough to be her father, so she didn't mind the little pat he gave her butt. She took it as a good-luck wish.

She shook the dice in her hand, leaned over the long table and let them fly. Cheers roared out, and money and chips changed hands too quickly for her to follow.

"Seven! All right." She pumped a fist in the air. After raking in her pile of chips, she began recklessly distributing them again. "This on the point, and this, um, behind. Five's my point."

"Roll 'em, blondie." The man on the other side of her plunked a hundred-dollar bill on the table. "You're hot."

"Damn right I am." She sent the dice tumbling, squinting through the smoke, and howled with triumph when the ivories came up three and two.

"I don't know why I thought this game was so hard." She grinned then gulped from the fresh glass of champagne someone handed her. "Hold this, will you?" She shoved the glass at the butt-patter and picked up the dice. "Let mine ride," she told the croupier. "God, I *love* saying that!" She tossed the dice, then danced on three-inch heels.

Mac had to elbow his way through a crowd gathered four deep. His first sight of her was a tight little butt molded into clinging red. He caught her elbow just after her toss, and his words were swallowed by the roar of players and onlookers.

"What the hell do you think you're doing?"

She tossed back her head, drunk on victory. "I'm kicking your ass. Back up and give me room so I can kick it some more."

He snagged her wrist as she leaned over to scoop up the dice. "Cash in."

"The hell I will. I'm smoking."

"Come on, pal, let the lady roll."

Mac merely turned his head and iced down the eager player on the corner of the table with a look. "Cash her in," he ordered the croupier, then dragged Darcy through the bitter complaints of the crowd.

"You can't make me stop playing when I'm on a streak."

"You're wrong. This is my place, and I can make anybody stop playing anytime. The house has the edge."

"Fine." She jerked her arm free. "I'll take my business elsewhere, and I'm let them know the management at The Comanche can't hold up under a run of honest luck."

"Darcy, come upstairs. We need to talk."

"Don't tell me what I need to do." She pulled away again sharply, almost pleased when heads turned and attention zeroed in on them. "I told you I wouldn't cause a scene, but I will if you push me. You can kick me out of your casino, and you can kick me out of your hotel, but you can't tell me what I need to do."

"I'm asking you," he said with what he considered amazing patience, "to come with me so we can discuss this privately."

"And I'm telling you, I'm not interested."

"Okay, the hard way." He scooped her up and over his shoulder. He'd taken ten strides before she broke through the shock and began to struggle.

"Let go of me. You can't treat me this way."

"You made your choice," he said grimly, and ignored

the stunned looks of guests and staff as he carted her to the elevator.

"I don't want to talk to you. I'm already packed. I'm leaving in the morning. Just let me go."

"The hell I will." He keyed in her floor, then dumped her back on her feet. "You've got a stubborn streak in you, and I'm—" He broke off when her fist punched into his stomach. It didn't do much more than bounce off and cause him to lift a coolly amused brow.

"We'll have to work on that."

Conceding that she was outgunned, Darcy folded her arms. When the doors opened into her suite, she sailed out. "This may be your place, but this is my room until morning, and I don't want you in it."

"We need to straighten things out."

"Things are perfectly straight, thank you just the same."

"Darcy, you don't understand."

She shoved away the hands he'd laid on her shoulders. "That's just it, isn't it? You don't think I understand anything. You think I'm a fluff-brained idiot who doesn't know how to take care of herself."

"I don't think you're an idiot."

"But fluff-brained just the same," she countered. "Well, I'm sharp enough to know that you got tired of me and your solution was to brush me off like an irritating child."

"Tired of you?" At the end of his rope, he dragged his hands through his hair. "I know I made a mess of it. Let me explain."

"There's nothing to explain. You don't want me. Fine. I'm not going to jump off a roof over it." She jerked a shoulder and turned away. "I'm young, I'm rich, I have my career to think of. And you're not the only man in the world."

"Just a damn minute."

"You were the first." She shot a searing look over her shoulder. "That doesn't mean you have to be the last."

Which had been one of his points. Exactly one of the reasons he'd been so determined to step away. But hearing it from her, seeing that hot, female look in her eyes had a rage bubbling up in him so violently it hazed his vision.

"Watch your step, Darcy."

"I've watched it all my life, and I'm finished. I like leaping before I look. And so far I'm landing on my feet. If and when I fall it'll be my problem and no one else's."

Panic skidded up his spine because he could see she meant it. She could do it, would do it. "You know damn well you're in love with me."

Her heart toppled and cracked. "Because I slept with you? Please."

However derisive her words, her fingers had linked together and twisted. It was just enough of a tell for him to call her bluff. "You wouldn't have slept with me if you hadn't been in love with me. If I held you right now. If I put my mouth on yours, you'd tell me without saying a word."

Every defense crumbled. "You knew, and you used it."

"Maybe I did. I've had a hard time with that, and made more mistakes because I couldn't get past it."

"Are you guilty or angry, Mac?" Wearily she turned away again. "You broke my heart. I'd have given it to you on a platter. It wasn't even enough for you not to want it, you ignored it."

"I told myself I was doing it for you."

"For me." A laugh choked out. "Well, that was considerate of you."

"Darcy." He reached out, but her shoulders rounded as she cringed away. An ache sliced through him as he dropped his hands again. "I won't touch you, but at least look at me."

"What do you want from me? Do you want me to say it's all right? That I understand. I won't hold it against you. It's not all right." Her breath hitched in a sob that was brutal to control. "I don't understand, and I'm trying not to hold it against you. You weren't obligated to feel what I felt—that was my gamble. But in the end you could have been kind."

"If I'd trusted my feelings, we wouldn't be having this conversation. And I don't want to have it here." When a hunch came this sudden and strong, he knew to ride it out. "I want to see your house."

"What?"

"I'd like very much to see your house. Now."

"Now?" She passed a hand over her eyes. "It's late. I'm tired. I don't have the keys."

"What's the name of the Realtor? Do you have a card?"

"Yes, on the desk. But—"

"Good."

To her confusion he walked to the phone, dialed the number and in less than two minutes was on a first-name basis with Marion Baines and jotting down her address.

"She'll give us the keys," Mac told Darcy when he hung up. "Shouldn't take more than twenty minutes to get to her place."

"You're a powerful man," she said dryly. "What's the point of this?"

"Take a chance." He smiled in challenge. "Leap before you look. Do you want a jacket?"

She refused one, and would have refused to go with him if she hadn't wanted one scrap of pride to take with her. They didn't speak. She thought that was best. Perhaps, somehow, this quiet drive would settle the nerves and let them part—if not as friends—with some respect for each other.

He seemed to know his way. He picked up the keys without incident, then easily wove toward the outskirts where her house stood, a soft silhouette under the slowly waning moon.

"Trust you," he murmured, scanning the shape. "You found a castle, after all."

It nearly made her smile. "That's what I thought when I saw it. That's how I knew it was mine."

"Ask me in."

"You've got the keys," she noted, and opened her door.

He waited until she'd rounded the hood, then held the keys out to her. "Ask me in, Darcy."

She fought the urge to snatch the keys from him, telling herself he was trying to do what he could to make the situation less miserable. She accepted the keys and started up the walk.

"I've never been in it at night. There are floodlights in both the house and yard."

He thought about her out there, alone, at night. "Is there a security system?"

"Yes, I have the code." She unlocked the door and turned directly to a small box beside it. She disengaged the alarm, then switched on the lights.

He said nothing, but walked through much as his mother had done. But in this case, the silence unnerved her. "I've been looking at furniture, found many pieces that I like."

"It's a lot of space."

"I've discovered I like a lot of space."

She'd put plants on the decks, he imagined. Cheerful pots full of lush green and delicate blossoms she'd baby.

She'd want soft colors inside, cool and soothing, with the occasional flash to shake things up.

It amazed him how clearly he could imagine it, and how easy it was to know her after so little time.

He switched on the outside lights and watched them flood the blue water of the pool and the rippling sea of the desert beyond.

It was stunning, powerful, and in its own way calm as the night sky. Maybe he'd lost sight of this, he mused, this other side of the world from where he'd chosen to live. And because of that, had refused to accept her place there.

"This is what you want."

"Yes. This is what I want."

"The tower. You'll write there."

She ached a little, because he would know. "Yes."

"We never celebrated." He turned back. She was standing in the center of the empty room, her hands linked, her eyes shadowed. "My fault. I need you to know, Darcy, how happy I am for you, and how sorry I am I spoiled the moment."

Guilt, she thought. He was too kind a man not to feel it. "It doesn't matter."

"It matters," he corrected. "A great deal. I'd like to try to explain. I'd like you to try to see it from my viewpoint. You fell into my arms, literally, the first time I saw you. You were alone, lonely, a little desperate, completely vulnerable and impossibly appealing. I wanted you too much, too quickly. I'm good at resisting temptation, that's why I'm good at what I do. But I couldn't resist you."

"You didn't seduce me, you didn't force me. It was a mutual attraction."

"But it wasn't an even hand." He stepped toward her, relieved when she didn't back away. "I took you because I wanted you, because I could, because I needed to, knowing you'd want and need more. Deserved more. But I didn't intend to give it to you."

"It was a chance I took. You told me flat out, before we were lovers, you didn't have marriage on your mind. I didn't fall in bed with you blindly."

He paused a moment, surprised. "You gambled on me changing my mind?"

"The odds might have been long that you'd fall in love with me, but they weren't infinitesimal." The edge had come back into her voice. "Your grandfather thinks I'm perfect for you. So does your mother."

He very nearly choked. "You talked to my mother?"

"I love your mother," she said passionately. "And I have a perfect right to have someone to talk to."

"I didn't mean it that way. I'm getting off the track," he said with a sigh. "The way I saw it, you needed a little time to settle, to explore the possibilities, to have some fun and indulge yourself. So you'd gamble a little, spend some money, take a few rides. Discover sex."

"So you were what, tutoring me? How much more insulting can you possibly be?"

"I'm not trying to insult you. I'm trying to tell you what I believed, and that I was wrong."

"You haven't begun to say you were wrong yet. Maybe you should get started."

"You've got a nasty streak." He dipped his hands into his pockets. "I never noticed it before."

"I've been saving it up. So the little country mouse comes to the big city and the clever city mouse lets her taste a bit of sin, then shows her the door before she damns her soul to perdition? Is that close enough?"

"A long, wide nasty streak. You were alone and afraid and over your head."

"And you tossed me a float."

"Shut up." Patience straining, he gripped her arms. "Nobody ever gave you a choice. You said so yourself. No one gave you a chance. No one let you bloom. God, Darcy, you've done nothing but bloom since you got here, since you had that chance, that choice. How was I supposed to take that choice away from you? You've never been anywhere else. You've never been with anyone else. I wasn't going to watch you living in a hotel, wandering through a casino, locking yourself to me because you didn't know any better."

"And that's your way of giving me a choice. Funny, that's just the kind of choice people have been giving me all my life."

"I know. I'm sorry."

"So am I." She lifted her hands to his arms and pushed until he released her. "Are we finished?"

"No. Not yet."

"Oh, what's the point of this?" She strode away from him, her sassy shoes clicking on the tiles. "Why do you want a tour of the place now? Do we pretend we're pals? What are we doing here?"

"I wanted to finish this here because it's not my place. It's yours." He waited until she turned back. "The house always has the advantage."

"I don't know what you're talking about."

"My father told me something tonight I'd never considered. He said wanting is easy, but loving is terrifying." His eyes stayed locked on hers. "You terrify me, Darcy, right down to the bone." He watched as she wrapped her arms tight around her body. "When I look at you, I'm scared senseless."

"Don't do this. It's not fair."

"I tried to be fair, and all I did was hurt you, and make myself miserable. I'm playing a new hand now, and when the house has the edge, I can't afford to play fair. There's no point in backing away," he said when she did just that. "I'll only keep coming after you. You brought this on yourself. I'd have let you go."

He caught her, ran his hands from her shoulders to her wrists then back again. "You're trembling. Scared?" He touched his lips to the corner of hers. "That must mean you still love me."

Her breath was hot in her chest, tangling in her throat. "I won't have you feeling sorry for me. I don't—"

The kiss was sudden and violent. Her heart slammed once, twice, hard against her ribs then began a wild and unsteady beat.

"Is that what you think this is? This feels like pity to you?" He took her mouth again, diving deep. "Damn, this dress drives me crazy. I could have killed every man at that table tonight just for looking at you. I'll have to buy you a dozen more like it."

"You're not making sense. I don't know what you're saying."

"I love you."

This time her heart took one high, joyful leap. "You do?"

"I love everything about you." He lifted her hands, pressed them to his lips, then gently untangled her fingers. "And I'm asking you to buck the odds and give me another chance."

Her lips trembled, then curved. "I'm a big believer in another chance."

"I was counting on it." This time he kissed her gently, easing her into his arms. "But you're going to have to let me move in here."

"Here?" She was floating, drifting, close to dreaming. "You want to live here?"

"Well, I figure this is where you'll want to raise the kids."

"Kids?" Her dazzled eyes flew open again.

"You want kids, don't you?" He smiled when her head bobbed up and down. "I like big families—and coming from one, I'm a traditionalist. If we're going to make kids together, you have to marry me."

"Mac." It was all she could say, just his name. Nothing else would get through.

"Willing to risk it, Darcy?" He lifted her hands again, pressed them to his heart. "Want to take a gamble on us?"

His heart beat under her hands, and was no steadier than hers. "It so happens," she said with a brilliant smile, "I'm on a hot streak."

He laughed, scooped her off her feet in one wide, dizzying circle. "So I've heard."

* * * * *